Paint Me Fearless

Paint Me Fearless
Copyright © 2020
Hallie Lee

ISBN: 978-1-952474-27-9

Cover concept and design by Jonathan Grisham for Grisham Designs.

Published by WordCrafts Press
Cody, Wyoming 82414
www.wordcrafts.net

Paint Me Fearless

The Shady Gully Series
Book 1

HALLIE LEE

WordCrafts Press

For Mama and Daddy

Prologue

He was tall, lean, and at least ten years younger than me. His eyes were deep blue, and at this moment, full of pleasure. Exhilaration. Joy. His expression and demeanor mirrored my own. Except for the anxiety and eagerness that made my legs buckle.

Can one experience anxiety and eagerness simultaneously? Yes, I decided. One can.

He placed his hand gently on my shoulder, and I followed him. Our legs and feet were bare, creating an intimacy I hadn't expected. It was an unfamiliar emotion that made me suddenly feel unsure. Vulnerable.

"Just breathe," he said.

I obeyed. Shivered as I let myself go deeper in the water. Soon my calves were submerged, and seconds later the water was up to my waist. He was so tall that the water hadn't yet reached his upper thighs.

His presence, so large and looming, reassured me. It reminded me I wasn't alone. However unsteady my body was, and it was, his capable hands guided me deeper and deeper into the water.

He spoke softly to me now.

Distracted by the comforting embrace of the warm water, I had trouble focusing. Felt my knees buckle again.

I looked at his mouth, the sincerity in his eyes... and finally I smiled. Nodded with conviction.

No more anxiety, no more fear. Just excited now.

I said words back to him. Repeated what he said.

The tone that came from my mouth was confident. It sounded strange to me. I'd never been confident a day in my life. But on this day my words were full of something akin to... peace.

Finality.

Why had it taken me so long to get here? So many wasted years. Such a wasted life. Tears slipped from my eyes as I thought of the insecure girl, the anxious wife, the unrewarded mother. The failures, the losses, the disappointments.

But I didn't regret that. Those were simply things I experienced. What I regretted now, in this moment of clarity and grace, was that I let all that anguish define me. Shame me into hiding. I let the brokenness rob my life.

I was a slave to my fears. My insecurities.

But not anymore. Not after this.

When the young man with the blue eyes gently placed his hand along the middle of my back, I followed him willingly...

PART I

Chapter One

The Squirrel Looked Fine To Me
Robin

All day I kept hearing about this new girl. It put me in a bad mood. I didn't even know I had sixth period with her until Bubba told me.

"You gotta see her, Robin. She looks just like you. Except she's good lookin'."

Bubba's flabby belly jiggled as he and Daryl, his Cohort in Crap, high-fived like they were already in high school. Like they were foxy and cool. As if. Even if Daryl and Bubba made it out of junior high, they'd *never* be foxy and cool.

I acted like I didn't hear them and instead sat at my desk and pretended to write a note to my best friend, Claire. I didn't really like Claire, but we'd agreed to be best friends last week. Her last note to me was pretty lame, except for the neat way she'd folded it. Claire knew how to do things like that, which was why I figured it would be good to be her best friend.

When I heard the sporty guys tromping into class, I straightened my shirt over the roll around my belly. Converse shoes and flashes of blue and white everywhere, the junior high athletes liked to make an entrance. Lenny, the quarterback, headed straight for the window. Supposedly he had the talent to go varsity, whatever that meant.

He raised his arms, held up his imaginary gun, and shot a fluffy squirrel, who fluttered along the branch of an oak tree just outside the classroom window.

"*Puuhhh. Puuhhh.*" Gunshot sounds. Lenny nodded, pleased with his aim.

"Nailed him," confirmed Ricky, his best friend.

The squirrel looked fine to me. In fact, he came closer to the window, twitched his tail, and chomped on an acorn while giving Lenny the eye.

"I'ma get me a few this weekend at my camp." Mitch tugged at his blue-and-white letter jacket, winking at his friends. "Squirrels, I mean."

I rolled my eyes. Mitch was some kind of back. Halfback, fullback, hunchback, I don't know, but of all the sporty guys, I hated him the most. Number one, he wasn't even cute or foxy. Number two, he always acted like he was in on some secret that you weren't, as if you weren't good enough to even imagine all the great things going on in his world. Like stupid hunting trips at some camp in the swamp. And number three, Mitch acted like this camp in the swamp was the playboy mansion, and he himself was the old perv guy kissing all the girls.

"Yeah, right," Ricky teased. Ricky was the guy who caught the throws Lenny threw, whatever that was called. A split end or a loose end or something. He was okay, especially when he put Macho Mitch in his place.

Love's Baby Soft perfume wafted down the row of desks as Claire hurried into class and sat behind me. "It's not your camp, dork," she told Mitch. "It's your uncle's camp. And I doubt you'll be getting any action unless it's kissing yourself in the mirror."

Besides the cool note folding thing, this was another reason I liked Claire being my best friend. She said stuff, and she wasn't scared of anybody, and I wanted to be more like that. Except without so much Love's Baby Soft.

"Who dunked you in the perfume, Claire?" Mitch coughed. "Are you trying to hide some BO or something?"

5

Claire ignored him. Instead she focused on tossing me another note. It was like a beautiful pink present. How did she fold it like that? This one was shaded in pink crayon with bright-purple headlines: *NEW GIRL!!!!*

"Have you seen her?" Claire was breathless.

"No." And I didn't want to. I hated new girls and the way they twisted me up inside. The way I always got kicked down the Popular Pyramid, especially if they were pretty and—

"Coach is on his way." Dean the Brainiac made his way to his usual front-row desk. He wore glasses and was tall, like a giraffe. He was on the football team, but I didn't know what kind of end or back he was… or if he even played. Dean was kind of like that. Always around, but hard to remember.

Except today he seemed more talkative than usual. "He's got the new girl with him. She's got a weird name."

"I heard she's foxy." Macho Mitch puffed his chest out like a rooster.

"Where's she from?" Daryl asked. "I heard a big city."

"Probably," Bubba said. "Girls are better lookin' in big cities."

"Yeah," Ricky nodded. "Girls in Belle Maison are gorgeous, not like here in Shady Gully."

"Belle Maison isn't really a big city," Dean pointed out. "In fact, it's relatively small compared—"

"And Shady Gully isn't a city at all," Lenny added. "Right, Dean?"

"Nope. We're just a small-town community in the great state of Louisiana."

Claire coughed. "The shithole of the world."

Shocked, I whipped my head across the row to stare at Claire. She actually uttered a curse word, and even more daring, she did it just as Coach Calvin's shadow loomed at the entrance of the classroom door.

Claire was my idol.

Two seconds. That's all it took from the moment Coach led

the new girl through the door to the pivot of heads in my direction. And I even heard someone gasp out loud. But that could have been me.

This was worse than I'd imagined. She was worse than I'd imagined.

She stood there on full display, dwarfed by Coach Calvin's extreme bulk and height, but she seemed confident. Coach mumbled something, her name probably, where she was from, but I couldn't hear. I could only see.

If only I were blind.

If I were blind, I wouldn't have to look at her and see that she was short like me. Less than five feet tall. I wouldn't have to see that she had short dark hair just like I did. Or that her eyes were brown just like mine. Even the way she stood there smiling at the class and up again at Coach... it was just like me.

Except that it wasn't. There wasn't a roll around her belly. Her crisp white shirt was neatly tucked into her blue jeans. Her hair was shiny and soft, not coarse and bushy like mine. She wore lip gloss and mascara and... my heavens, was that blush?

Not a smudge of Clearasil dotted her face in a pathetic attempt to hide pepperoni-sized patches of acne. And another dagger to my heart—no Coke-bottle glasses sat atop her perfect nose. I hated her on sight. Again, if only I were blind.

Suddenly my heart pounded, and my vision blurred. Oh no! Now God was punishing me, and I really *was* going blind! I dropped my head and rubbed my eyes in fright. And then to my horror, a big, sloppy tear splashed right in the middle of Claire's pink note.

"Robin? Robin?" Coach's voice penetrated my panic. "Are you okay?"

I guess I still had my hearing, so that was a plus.

"I... yes. Allergies."

"I told ya, Robin," Bubba mocked. "Y'all are twins. Kinda."

I prayed that everyone would turn away from me and focus once again on the new girl. Sure enough, Dean the Brainiac in the front row wanted to know about where she was from. "What's Albuquerque like?"

"I don't even know how to spell that city," Lenny mumbled.

"Much less say it," Ricky added.

Coach Calvin offered the new girl a piece of chalk and asked her to write *Albuquerque* on the chalkboard for the class.

"It's a giant city with lots of people, and it hardly ever rains there," she said.

Oh, kill me now. Her voice even sounded like an Eagles ballad. Dean smiled up at her.

"Oh," she added, "and there's a hot-air balloon festival every year."

"Where in Mexico is this?" Mitch asked. "Sounds like an awesome road trip."

The new girl chuckled, and Coach explained, "It's in the state of New Mexico, Mitch. Not the country."

The class laughed, and Mitch's face turned apple red. For a moment I thought I could rally and claw my way out of my pit of embarrassment and enjoy Mitch's pain, but I couldn't.

"I knew that, Coach," Mitch said. "I was just messing around."

More raucous laughter. Coach nodded and gestured like he was instructing a player on the football field. "All right, all right. That's enough. We need to get on with our lesson." As the class erupted in groans I glanced at the clock. Forty more minutes left of this nightmare.

"Why don't you write your name on the board?" Coach suggested to the new girl. "That way everyone can remember to stop by after class and welcome you to Shady Gully Junior High. And to Shady Gully."

"More like condolences," Claire muttered. I realized I'd forgotten all about Claire and her pink note. The perfectly folded present. Back when life was good.

"Where'd you get your name?" Lenny asked the new girl. "It's different."

"Do you have a nickname or something?" Dean asked.

She smiled across the classroom. Literally across. Like she was accepting an award or something. "My mama loves history, and she said Désireé was the name of Napoleon's lover."

The silence was so thick that only the sound of Lenny's born-again squirrel could be heard, happily chattering his way along a wobbly branch on the oak tree.

The Albuquerque girl with the name of a lover underlined a word on the chalkboard for emphasis. She placed the chalk back into the tray and grinned at her new admirers. "People call me Desi. For short."

Obviously charmed, Dean pulled out the chair next to him for Desi. From Albuquerque. Named after a lover.

She was everything I wasn't. She was the better me.

Her desk creaked a little as she turned around and looked at me. When she smiled, I turned away and looked out the window.

But all I saw was the dang squirrel, who hopped along the ledge of the window… as he too scrambled to get a closer look at the dazzling Desi.

Chapter Two

Jennings, I Presume?
Desi

On the bus ride home, a husky high school guy wearing cowboy boots and a western belt slipped into the seat in front of me. He stretched his arm along the top of his seat and casually turned back to me. "Howdy," he offered with a lazy drawl.

"Uh... howd... hi?"

He grinned and let out a low chuckle.

His name was Adam, and he said he was going to be a country music star one day. He just thought I should know.

"Is that so?"

"Count on it," he said.

He had reddish hair. A nice smile. I believed him.

He chatted for a bit, pointing out dirt roads here and there. "Yonder direction is where the Wolfheart clan stays. You need to steer clear of Brad and his bunch. Ain't no place for a girl like you."

Interesting that Adam already had me pegged for a particular kind of girl. I resisted the flair of irritation. Instead went with a wide-eyed, earnest nod. "Thanks. Good advice."

"My pleasure." Adam tipped his imaginary cowboy hat.

Mama said to smile and make friends, so I figured I could add Adam to the list. He ought to count for more than one, seeing as how he was going to be the king of Nashville one day.

He rolled the bus window down, and the breeze felt good. It was a hot breeze, but that might be as good as it was going to get here in Shady Gully, Louisiana.

Adam hummed a song, and it wasn't half-bad. He acted real casual about it, but I could tell he was giving it his best effort. I sat back in my seat, surveying my surroundings.

Country roads indeed. No red lights, traffic jams, or five-car pileups. Just twisty blacktop paths and an occasional house set back from the road.

Here and there the bus would stop and let somebody off. I was fascinated by the wide range of dogs that rushed down the driveways. Some were big and scary and would bark right up to the point they saw their kid get off the bus. Then their tails would wag and beat a cloud of dust around them. Some dogs were little and yappy, but just like the others, they greeted their own and led them inside to what I imagined were milk and cookies and reruns of *Gilligan's Island*.

"Do you have a dog?" I asked Adam.

So consumed with his melody, it took him a moment to focus. "Huh? Well, yeah. Of course. Don't you?"

"No."

"Well, this is me." Adam rose.

I hadn't noticed before how tall he was and found it amusing the way he hunched over to avoid bumping his head on the roof of the bus.

"It was a pleasure to make your acquaintance, Désireé."

The bus slowed at a modest red brick house with a long driveway. Naturally, a German Shepherd waited at the edge. He looked older, a little scruffy, whiter around the face. He didn't bark either. Just sat there eyeing the bus like a perfect gentleman.

"That there is Waylon." Adam pointed.

"Jennings, I presume?" I enjoyed the flash of surprise on Adam's face.

"Yes, ma'am." He tipped his imaginary cowboy hat once more and stepped off the bus.

I watched him greet Waylon with an affectionate pat on the head.

"Hey, Adam." I leaned my head out the opened window. "You can call me Desi."

"Desi. I like it. It sounds almost like a song." He waved and did a little back and forth with his fingers, almost as if he were already writing the lyrics. I watched as he and Waylon moseyed down the driveway toward the house.

I definitely wanted a dog. I deserved a dog, didn't I? After all, I had to leave my daddy and all my friends and move to this strange place with Mama… all because she'd fallen in love with another man.

I leaned back in my seat, embracing the bumps and sways of the bus, thinking about names for my dog.

"Mama!" I ran up the concrete steps and pushed my way through the trailer's screen door. I couldn't wait to share my news about my future dog with my Sunny. Mostly though, I couldn't wait to see her. I'd missed her all day and was feeling a little unsettled about school and all the kids I'd met and the humidity and… everything.

"Mama!" I called again, making my way down the narrow living room of our mobile home. I snatched a few chocolates from the bowl on the kitchen table and followed the sound of the music in the extra bedroom. It was an old tune called "The Last Farewell" by a British folk singer named Roger Whitaker.

The tune seemed both grand and sad. It was full of bold instruments that masked lyrics about death and final goodbyes. Mama mostly played it when she was sad. She'd choke up a little at the end, at the part about being beautiful and loving dearly. My stomach fluttered a bit when I considered the gloomy song combined with the darkness of the trailer.

Of course, the trailer being dark wasn't unusual. Especially after Mr. Tom's lecture last week about saving electricity. He stressed the importance of turning off the lights when we left a room and not leaving the refrigerator open and most of all not messing with the thermostat.

"In here, kitten!" The sound of her voice made me smile. Sunny was in a happy mood.

"What do you think?" A portable fan oscillated around the small room, sending Sunny's blond tendrils astray while air-drying a painting on an easel.

My mama looked like sunshine. Bright-red lipstick. Summer-orange pants with a matching yellow-and-orange hippy blouse. A flaming-red scarf around her head. And today, on this glorious day, she'd drawn what she called her "smoldering-but-oh-so-subtle" beauty mark on her right cheek.

My heart fluttered at the sight of her. She, my Sunny, was the safest place in the world.

"Beautiful," I told her. "You're just beautiful."

"Not me, silly. My ship."

She tilted her head, studying her painting with a critical eye. It was indeed a ship, sailing along the ocean against the hazy light of a full moon.

"I love it. The ocean is such a pretty blue."

She looked at the ocean, and her expression changed. Maybe I should have made a bigger deal of the ship? I added quickly, "The ship looks neat as well. It must be very well built to get through those choppy waters."

She turned the music down, lit a cigarette, and gazed at her painting again. "The ocean does look quite turbulent, doesn't it?" Sunny beamed.

My heart leapt. "Yes, the captain must be very brave."

"Oh, he is, Desi. And he's handsome too." She laughed in that big, full-on way that drew everyone to her. After a beat and a long puff of her menthol Kool, she switched her attention to me. "Now, let me look at you. And I want to hear about your first day in this quaint little place. Did you do what I told you?"

"Yes. I made friends and reinvented myself." I tried not to roll my eyes. Tired suddenly, I flopped down on the lounge chair and popped a few chocolates into my mouth.

"Excellent! What did you go with? The friendly and sweet girl next door? The bold and flirty girl with pizzazz, or the smart and focused girl destined for success?"

"Well, I'm not really sure…"

"Oh wait, I want to guess. This is fun. Let's go fix a drink." When she picked up her ashtray, I followed her down the hall. "Oh, hell's bells." She stopped, doubled back, turned the light off in the painting room, and unplugged the fan. "Now, let's go."

While she poured an ice-cold Coke and set it on the table in front of me, I tried to remember which reinvented girl she'd preferred. I watched her pour vodka into a glass full of ice and tonic water, trying to read her expression as she squeezed a lemon into the concoction. She closed her eyes and took a long sip. When she opened them again, she looked at me. Expectantly.

"I guess… I'm the girl with a little bit of all of that."

Her mouth formed an O. "Excellent!"

"Yeah. I guess I'm going for a friendly, bold, and des-tined-for-success kind of girl."

"Of course you are. And most of all, you have what, Desi?"

"Pizzazz?"

"Yes, you do." Impulsively Mama reached over, held my face in her hands, and softly kissed my forehead. "You have pizzazz."

It wasn't true. I didn't have pizzazz. But I loved when she said it.

"Now, let's talk goals."

"Okay. But there's something I want to talk to you about—"

"What's going on in school? What sort of activities can my friendly, bold, and destined-for-success kitten do to propel her onward and to the top?"

"I don't know, Mama." I absently grabbed another chocolate from the bowl. "Truth is, this place is weird. Like they call teach-ers 'Coach,' and I don't think the kids really liked me much. The only person who was really nice to me was this kid on the bus. Guess what I noticed at all the houses when the bus stopped?"

"Desi. Focus." She moved the bowl of chocolates away from me. "Come on now. What is happening at school? What are the kids buzzing about?"

"Buzzing about?" I made a face. "I don't think they're buzzing about anything. They thought Albuquerque was in Mexico. The country!" I felt myself getting worked up. "Isn't that strange? They're very different from us. From me."

"But, Desi, isn't that wonderful?"

"No, it's not. It's terrible. The only girl who was a little like me hated me. I could tell."

"I doubt that. How could anyone hate you?"

"Easily. Nobody likes me except you, Mama."

"Come on, Desi. Let's think now. Parties? Anybody having any parties?"

"No. And they wouldn't invite me anyway."

"What about football games? You said there was a coach."

I could see she wasn't going to let this go, and I really wanted to talk about my new dog. "Yeah. They really like football here."

"Okay. That's a start."

"And I think there is this day tomorrow. It's like a spirit day, I guess. It's called Mix Match Day, and everyone is supposed to wear mismatching clothes."

"Now that sounds like fun! We can work with that! Yes indeed." She was happy again.

"And I heard someone say something about cheerleader tryouts, but I don't think I'd be any good—"

"Oh yes, that's perfect! You will be the most wonderful cheerleader. Now we have a goal. Don't you think?"

I didn't really think much of anything except that I had a headache and my stomach hurt and I wanted a puppy. Mama was happy though, and she had that focused, intense look on her face. There was no stopping her now.

She filled her glass with ice, set it on the table, and smiled with excitement. She whipped her red scarf off and tied it around my head.

"Oh, that's darling. And I've got a lavender-and-pink skirt. It's plaid, Desi. Isn't that atrocious? We can pair it with that baby-blue top of yours. Oh, and you can wear two different shoes!"

I had to giggle. It did sound very mismatched. "How about eyeshadow? I could wear two different colors."

"Oh, that's brilliant! I absolutely love it!" A few hours later, my Mix Match outfit was strewn across my bed, complete with clashing earrings and non-matching socks.

"Trust me, my darling girl," Sunny said. "By the end of the day, everyone is going to be talking about the girl with pizzazz! My beautiful Désireé!"

The table was set, and the soup simmered on the stove. Sunny was three drinks in when the wheels of Mr. Tom's pickup truck crackled on the gravel driveway.

"I'm just not sure about a dog, Desi." The trailer was hot, and the sides of Mama's blond hair were flattened with sweat. "Tom's here," she said anxiously. "I need to go freshen up."

I followed her to her bathroom and watched as she put on fresh lipstick and fluffed up her hair. "But why not?" I whined. "They're so cute. I could get a small one."

The sound of the screen door rat-a-tatting and Mr. Tom's big voice echoed from the living room. "I'm home! Where are my girls?"

Mama turned to me and whispered, "We'll see. You'll have to jolly him up a little. And a little oodling might help."

"There's my lovey." Mr. Tom gave Mama a kiss and an affectionate pat on the butt. "Say, what's a man gotta do to get a drink around here?"

"I'll fix you one," I offered. Mama winked at me, then turned her attention to him.

I could hear them chuckling in the bedroom as I fixed Mr.

Tom's drink. Mama was all his now. I'd had my time with her, but now she'd switched gears and the rest of the evening would revolve around him.

The ice rattled in the glass as I entered their bedroom. Mr. Tom was sitting on the bed, and Mama was in front of him, bent over facing in the opposite direction. She held his booted foot between her legs while he used his other foot to push on her rump. A little squirming and grunting, and his boot came off in her hands.

"Hey, Desi, this is how cowboys take their boots off at night," he bellowed.

"Let's do the other one." Sunny giggled. They switched positions, and sure enough she was able to pull the other boot off. More laughter.

Mr. Tom wiggled his toes and groaned with relief. I handed him his drink. "Thank ya, beautiful. How was your day today?"

My mission was clear. "It was good, but it could have been better."

"Oh?"

"I have something to ask you." I launched myself onto his lap and gave him a big kiss on the cheek. "Please. Pretty please. Please."

Mr. Tom, amused, winked at Sunny. "Oh, here it comes."

Jollying. Oodling. I'd never heard the expression until Mr. Tom came into our lives. They gave me a funny feeling in my stomach, even when it was Sunny doing all the jollying and oodling.

But I'd learned from the best, and I nuzzled Mr. Tom's neck, and ruffled his hair.

I really, really wanted a dog.

Chapter Three

Jump, Shout, Knock Myself Out
Robin

T he Charlie was killing me. Seriously choking me to death.
I gagged out loud. My mother gave me the eye via the rearview
mirror. "What on earth is wrong with you?"

Now that I had her attention, I coughed and sputtered for
greater effect. "It's that gross perfume you wear." I knew I was
being crabby today, but I couldn't seem to stop myself. My
mother was an easy target.

Every day she dropped us off at school before going to her
job at the public library. There she would work all day assisting
patrons and doing library things. After that she would come
home and fix dinner and do her best to keep my bratty brothers from killing each other. Then she would read while my dad
watched TV. And the next day, she would get up and do it all
over again.

I felt bad sometimes that she had such a crappy life. And yet I
couldn't help being mean to her. It was an urge I couldn't control.

"Your brothers don't seem to mind."

"That's because they're evil little miscreants."

"Oh," commented my mother, Mabel. "Great word. I like the
way you're expanding your vocabulary."

"It was on *Christmas Vacation*. That's how the sister described her little brother. Lucky for her, she only had one miscreant in her family."

"What about Cousin Eddie?" Mama, trying to be playful.

I scowled. I decided a while back that the reason my mother liked going to church so much was because it broke up the boringness of her life. Sunday school and Wednesday prayer night were boring, but a different kind of boring.

I sighed. Watched Ernie pick his nose and Max rub his tummy.

"I want it," Max begged.

Ernie flicked the booger at him, and since I was seated between them, it landed on me. More specifically, on my Coke-bottle glasses. I screamed and swatted my glasses.

Ernie, ten years old with the maturity of a six-year-old, moved his face up to mine. "What does it look like, Robin? Is it magnified?"

"Y'all are so gross. Did you see what they did, Mama?" The process of trying to clean my glasses spurred them on, and they clutched their bellies in fits of laughter.

"Did it look like four boogers since you have four eyes?" This from seven-year-old Max.

I gave him a mean look and pinched his arm. His squeal brought me great pleasure.

"Seriously, can't we drop them off at a shelter or something?"

My mother shushed them as we pulled into the Shady Gully Elementary parking lot. "Now, I want y'all to behave today," she told them. "Think about how y'all would want to be treated. Give me a kiss."

They jumped out of the car and ran over to embrace Mama. She kissed the tops of their heads, then said a prayer over each of them.

"Dear Lord," I mumbled, "let them fall off the monkey bars and break at least one limb today. Multiple limbs would be ideal. But I'll take what I can get. Amen."

"What's going on with you?" my mother demanded once we were on the road again. "You're impossible lately."

"No, they're impossible. I didn't even do anything. I always get in trouble when it's really—"

"Robin, you were on the warpath this morning."

I retreated into myself then. Glared out the window, made myself small. If that was possible for a fatty like me.

"I want to get contact lenses," I said impulsively. "I'm going to be in high school next year, and I'm tired of being teased about how ugly I am. I'm fat, I have a pizza face, and I…"

Mama did the discreet rearview-mirror-thing again. Waited me out. It always worked. I bit my lower lip, resisted.

"You what, Robin?"

"I'm going out for cheerleader."

"I know."

"I'm not going to make it."

"You've been practicing. You're doing fine."

"No, I'm terrible. I won't make it. And I hate my life."

Mama carefully steered into my school's parking lot but wasn't ready to let me out. She turned around in her seat. "You have a blessed life. You're healthy. You have food to eat. Jesus has given our family an abundance—"

"Stop doing that. It's not always about Jesus."

"Yes," Mama said firmly. "Everything is always about Jesus. And right now you're letting the devil win, Robin. He knows just how to zero in on all your insecurities and twist you up."

I opened the door when I saw Claire up ahead, walking toward homeroom. "There's Claire. I have to go."

"Close the door. I want to talk to you about your new best friend."

"Mama, I'm going to be late—" Something about her expression convinced me to close the door and listen to her. "What?"

"I don't like you spending so much time with her. I think she's part of the reason you're so unsettled lately. I've heard she likes to stir up trouble."

"Oh my God, Mama. Did your church ladies tell you that? Claire is fine. She's cool, and I like her."

"Her family doesn't have a good reputation. They don't belong to a church. Not even a Catholic church."

I fumed inside. Tried hard to swallow the angry words bubbling up in my throat. I watched Dorky Dean the Brainiac get out of his mom's car, gangly, shirt tucked in, hair wet down. Good lord, he even kissed his mom goodbye. Total nerd.

"I have to go. Even choirboy Dean is headed to homeroom."

"I see that. Now, he's a nice young man. Comes from a good family. You should—"

Exasperated, I opened the door with a groan, grabbed my books, and slammed the door in dramatic fashion.

"I love you, honey. Have a good day." I could hear her praying over me as I walked away. I didn't turn back or bother to tell her to have a good day. What was the point?

Her life sucked.

This was the last practice before tryouts. The sound of girls chanting and tumbling on mats echoed off the gymnasium walls. I was terrible. Everyone knew it too. Even Claire said if only I could do a cartwheel or the splits, I might have a chance.

If only.

Claire was hanging close to the girls who knew they were gonna make it. Popular girls, like Dolly with her blond hair and her buddies Kendra and Ashley. They were cheerleaders last year, so it was a given they'd make it again this year.

"Okay, team," shouted Coach Becky, the tryout coordinator. "Let's line up and do it from the beginning."

The Bouncy girls, Dolly, Ashley, Kendra—and even Claire—rushed to the front. I hung close to the safe confines and shadows of the rear, even though I had trouble seeing Coach's direction.

"Dolly, do you want to get us started?" Coach Becky asked.

"Sure!" Dolly chirped. "Y'all ready?"

The thirty or so hopefuls nodded in the affirmative and pressed their arms flat against their thighs. I, at least, could manage that. "Ready!" Dolly chanted with a slight bend to her knees. "Okay!" Everyone raised their fists to their hips in a snappy motion. I was a little late but felt sure I did okay, or that no one noticed since I was in the back.

The cheer began. "We're gonna jump! Shout!" Swirl, circle. "Knock ourselves out!" Arms up, across… or was it across and then up?

"We're gonna win!" Swish! Stomp! Oh no, I forgot to stomp!

"No doubt!" Everyone jumped, clapped, and showed off their best jerky kick. "Go Wildcats! Yay! Yay!"

I messed the whole cheer up.

"It's hard, isn't it?" A voice sounded behind me. I turned and saw the new girl from Albuquerque with the lover's name. Also known as the Superstar from Mix Match day.

Everyone was still talking about her crazy ensemble, which showed up even the Bouncy girls' outfits. I mean, who ever thought of pink lipstick on the top lip and orange lipstick on the bottom lip? It was so over the top that even the teachers were impressed. And naturally, what would have been laughable on anyone else, somehow looked "fetching" on her. That was the exact word Principal Jethro used when he presented her with the "Best" ribbon. Fetching.

And now here she was, witnessing my humiliation. Could this day get any worse?

"All right, girls, you're looking great," Coach Becky encouraged, which brought on another round of Wildcat love. "Let's try it one more time, but let's have the back come to the front, and you girls in the front head to the back."

Noooo. Please no. I glanced at the exit and calculated how quickly I could disappear through the swinging doors.

"Oh hell's bells," Ms. Mix Match muttered as she trudged to the front. For some inexplicable reason, I fell into step behind her, foregoing my chance to escape.

"Désireé," Coach Becky called. "How about you start us off this time?" When she hesitated, Coach offered encouragement, "Come on. You're doing great, and you just learned this cheer. You can do it."

As Coach's compliment evoked a swell of resentment from the back of the gym, Ms. Albuquerque's poise wavered. I positioned myself directly behind Coach's new pet, hoping her nerves would be more noticeable than mine.

"Ready!" But her command was surprisingly confident. "Okay!"

"We're gonna jump! Shout! Knock ourselves out—" Her voice was clear, her moves were sharp, and her coordination was on point. What happened to "It's hard, isn't it"?

I, on the other hand, was completely lost. Eventually I just stopped trying. Just stood there wishing I could make myself disappear.

"We're gonna win!" Swish! Stomp! "No doubt!"

A rumble of cheers echoed throughout the gym.

"Great job," Coach Becky said. "Go home and practice, everybody. Get a good night's sleep. Tomorrow is the day." More cheers.

I couldn't for the life of me figure out what there was to cheer about.

"Robin." Coach walked over. "Try to keep your arms straight on the motions. And if you mess up, just smile and keep going. Okay?"

Mortified and unable to speak, I nodded. The saving grace was that most of the girls were already running for the doors and hopefully unaware of my being singled out.

I headed to the bleachers to retrieve my backpack, hoping my dad was on time in the pickup lane for a change.

"It's Robin, right?"

It was her again. Why couldn't she just leave me alone?

"I get confused at that second part too. You know, when it goes 'knock ourselves out, we're gonna win'?"

I ignored her.

"I learned this trick to make it easier. If you want, I can show you."

I was still having trouble finding my voice. So instead I summoned up one of my meanest looks, the kind I reserved for the miscreants, and I walked away.

"The auditorium is packed," Ashley said in a breathless voice. She'd peeked through the stage curtains and reported back to the cheerleader hopefuls.

"I'm so nervous," Dolly said as she freshened her lip gloss.

I didn't think she looked all that nervous, but her pink lips sure looked good.

"Where are the football players?" Kendra wanted to know. "I want to make sure they're on my best side." She and Dolly laughed.

Even from inside the small room off stage, known as the Blue Room, we heard garbled "Go cats, go!" chants. Some of the girls were praying, others were primping, and others were still practicing their moves.

I couldn't sleep last night despite Coach Becky's instructions. Nor was I able to eat, which surprised everyone in my family.

I was starting to feel a little woozy though, and beads of sweat broke out on my forehead. I nervously pushed my glasses up my nose, trying hard to remember the first move of my cheer. But I couldn't. I was a total blank!

Suddenly my throat felt thick and watery, like I was going to puke. How was I ever going to get up on stage all by myself and jump, shout, knock myself out? I couldn't do it. I had nobody to hide behind. What had I been thinking?

Feeling my stomach suddenly tumble, I looked toward the bathroom in panic. But the door was closed. My eyes flitted anxiously around the Blue Room. Landed on Ms. Mix Match, who practiced her cheer motions with an intense look of concentration. As I watched her, I remembered a few things about the cheer.

My gaze moved to Claire, who was whispering in Dolly's ear. Claire, for a best friend, was no help at all. In fact, she was so focused on the Bouncy girls she was missing my SOS regarding a looming bathroom emergency.

"She's really good," I heard Claire say, talking about Albuquerque girl.

"Yeah," Dolly replied. "She might actually make it." Dolly didn't look happy about it.

Coach Becky came in just as the MC's voice cranked up in the auditorium. "Such an exciting time… selecting next year's Shady Gully High School Cheerleading Squad!"

Uh-oh. Now I couldn't work up enough saliva to swallow. Help!

"Okay, girls, try to breathe," Coach Becky offered. "Here's how this is going to work—"

"I'm gonna be sick," a pale girl with red hair mumbled. I eyed her position and its distance to the bathroom. If the door ever opened, I was pretty sure I could take her down.

"When the MC calls your name, I want you to enter the stage with your best cartwheel or roundoff—"

"What about Robin?" Kendra asked.

The Bouncy girls chuckled. So did Claire. Coach Becky gave them a stern look. I seriously couldn't swallow and was beginning to think trying out for cheerleader was going to kill me. How embarrassing would that be?

"Anyone who isn't comfortable with gymnastics should just jump and clap and show a lot of school spirit. We'll all be cheering for you back here, and so will the crowd."

I felt a presence next to me and was surprised to see Ms. Mix Match leaning toward me, offering a sip from her water bottle. I hesitated. No, I decided. I wasn't that desperate.

"When will we find out who makes it?" Ashley asked. "Today?"

"Possibly. Each student will get a ballot and pick their top eight. As soon as the votes are counted, we'll let you know."

The MC's voice rose. He was wrapping up. I suppressed a cough, or was that a gag? I had no choice but to take the water bottle Ms. Albuquerque offered, which was thankfully in my hands before I had to ask.

"You've all done a great job. I'm proud of you." Coach motioned for us to gather close and form a circle. "What do y'all say we raise up a little prayer?" Everyone grabbed a hand, and since Claire turned out to be a traitor, I was left with only Coach Becky's hand to hold.

And apparently Ms. Albuquerque's, because just like the water, it appeared without my asking. I wasn't thrilled, but what could I do?

"Désireé," Coach asked. "You want to lead us?"

"Ma'am? No, I… uh… that's okay."

The Blue Room got quiet.

"Go ahead now. Lead us in the Lord's Prayer," Coach Becky encouraged.

"Uh… um…" Silence.

Bowed heads popped up one by one. I noticed Dolly giving Kendra and Ashley the eye.

"I don't…" mumbled Mix Match.

Claire made a face. "Come on. It's about to start."

Ms. Albuquerque's hand trembled in mine.

"Come on. It's the Our Father," Dolly snapped. "Everybody knows it."

A lengthy and painfully awkward hush filled the room.

"Coach," Dolly said. "Just let me do it."

I didn't know what came over me. I couldn't explain it.

Was it the snotty way the Bouncy girls reveled in the new girl's pain? Or was it Mix Match's damp, shaky hand in mine?

"We'll do it together," I whispered.

I lowered my head. "Our Father, who art in heaven, hallowed be thy name. Thy Kingdom come, thy will be done, on earth as it is in heaven—"

Eventually she mumbled after me, getting the hang of following my words. "Give us this day, our daily bread, and forgive us our trespasses, as we forgive those who trespass against us. Lead us not into temptation, but deliver us from evil—"

As the prayer ended, her hand remained firm in mine. "For thine is the kingdom, the power, and the glory forever."

"Amen," everyone said.

The new girl looked at me. "Good luck, Robin."

I smiled. "Good luck, Desi." And I meant it.

Chapter Four

Sounds Like A Fairy Tale
Desi

Baby oil and iodine. Winston and Robin. But most of all Robin. Those were the ingredients to a perfect summer. Unfortunately, school started next week, so that meant everything was going to change. Again. I felt anxious and excited all at the same time. I hated change, but maybe this time, for once, it would be okay. Now that I had Robin.

Robin flipped a page of the *Tiger Beat* magazine. Pointed. "You think he's cute?"

I glanced at the oily thumbprint she'd left on the heartthrob's striking face. Shrugged.

"Well, I think he's foxy," Robin said. "I'd totally have sex with him."

"Robin!" I cracked up. "You're full of it." We were sprawled on a blanket in the grass next to my driveway, slathered in a potion that was supposed to transform us into bronze Hawaiian beauties by the end of summer. It had worked for Robin. Not so much for me. "You're really dark."

We were on our stomachs, me in my bikini and Robin in her one-piece. Winston, my adorable yellow cocker spaniel who wasn't really a puppy anymore, trotted over for a scratch. He panted in the heat.

"Yeah," she said. "It's in my genes. I just wish I had the skinny gene like you. Winston looks hot."

"I can relate. I hate this humidity." Robin could lay out all day, but not me. I sat up and opened our snack bag, pulled out a bag of Doritos and a Dr Pepper. "Want one?"

"No. I have two more pounds to lose before school starts Monday. I've already lost three since…" She trailed off, focusing instead on Winston's black button eyes. "Who's he named after again?"

"Winston Churchill. Mama named him. You know how she is about history."

"Sunny is the coolest person I've ever met. I wish I had a mom like her."

"She wants to paint a picture of us."

"Oh my God, that is so cool! Really?" Animated, she sat up, pushing her glasses—which weren't there anymore—up her nose. "When? I need to lose about twenty pounds first. Or maybe she can just paint me skinny. You think she can do that?"

"Robin, stop it. You're going to be all the talk when school starts. Your new contact lenses, being a Pepster, and—"

"Whatever." She rolled her eyes. "I know you can't understand. Sunny can though. She told me she's battled her weight all her life."

Hell's bells. When had Mama told her that? Robin idolized her, and she didn't need any encouragement when it came to her obsession with weight. I changed the subject. "So, when do the Pepsters have their first meeting? Are you excited?"

"Friday. Same as the cheerleaders and the band and the football players. I can't wait. This year is gonna be fun."

"I know. I'm nervous though."

"Why? You're co-captain." Her voice turned suddenly conspiratorial. "Okay. I can't take it anymore. I'm gonna tell you something, but you can't say anything." She went on, not waiting for a response. "There's this lady at church, Mrs. Dupree, and, well, she's Mrs. Shanna May's second cousin on her daddy's side—"

"Mrs. Shanna May that works in the office?"

"Yeah. Well, she told Mama"—Robin glanced at Winston, lowering her voice—"she told Mama you got more votes than anybody."

"What?" I tried to hide my grin. "That can't be true." I still couldn't believe I'd made cheerleader, and then been named co-captain, and now this?

"It's true, Desi. Mrs. Shanna May helped count the votes."

Oh my gosh! Sunny was going to freak out!

I tried to tone down my delight since Robin hadn't made cheerleader. The funny thing though, was once tryouts were over, Robin hadn't seemed all that disappointed. She'd joined the Pepsters, a cheer club which didn't require tryouts, and traveled to all the ball games just like the cheerleaders. That meant we could sit together on the travel bus and everything.

"My mom said I shouldn't tell you." Robin made a face. "As if, right? I found out when you were at your dad's last week." Robin absently picked up a Dorito.

"I can't believe it," I said, still reeling. "I'm glad you told me."

"How was your dad anyway? You haven't said much about your trip to Mexico." Robin reached into the bag for another chip.

"It's not Mexico—"

She laughed out loud. "I know. Just joshing ya." She held out her hand, and I handed her my Dr Pepper.

"It was okay. It's weird because at first I didn't want to go. We've been having so much fun this summer, and I didn't want to miss anything." I scratched Winston's belly. Watched his leg kick in a contented trance. "But in the end, when I had to leave him and say goodbye, it really hurt."

"What's he like? Is he like Mr. Tom?"

"No. They're total opposites." My vehemence in distinguishing their differences surprised me.

"Really? How so?"

I sipped the Dr Pepper and passed on the Doritos while I pondered her question. "In every way. My Daddy is short, not tall like Mr. Tom. He's quiet, not loud like Mr. Tom."

"Is he handsome like Mr. Tom?"

"You think Mr. Tom is handsome?" I made a face.

Robin shrugged. "For an old person, I guess."

"I don't know. My daddy has a nice smile, and he calls me pumpkin, and… he's my daddy. I always know what to expect from him. He's always steady. He never changes."

Robin nodded as she finished the chips. "I want to meet him. I bet I'd like him."

"You would. Maybe next summer you could come with me to visit him. Or maybe Thanksgiving, if Mama lets me go. We could go to Santa Fe." I laughed. "He wants me to bring Winston next time."

Robin clapped her hands. "That would be so cool!" She wadded up the empty chip bag and gave me a solemn look. "I'm not big fans of my mom and dad, but I don't know what I'd do if they got a divorce."

"It's not fun, I'll tell you that."

"Do you know what happened?"

I turned toward Winston, thinking hard on whether to tell Robin the whole story. I knew she was a solid friend, but it was kind of embarrassing, and I didn't want to ruin everything.

"You know how Sunny is." I shrugged. "I guess Daddy just wasn't exciting or romantic enough for her."

"Yeah." Robin looked thoughtful. "Sunny seems way too sophisticated for Shady Gully. It's crazy y'all ended up here."

"I know. Mr. Tom had some connections with the phone company and was able to quickly get transferred to Belle Maison. They were in a hurry to leave town and… start their new life." I grinned. "I'm glad we did though."

"Me too. I—" Robin looked stricken. "Desi! You let me eat Doritos! Crap!"

"You only ate a few." I mopped my face with the beach towel. "Come on. I can't take it anymore. Let's go see what Sunny's doing."

Robin jumped up and grabbed our specially concocted bottle

31

of baby oil and iodine while I picked up the blanket and the snack bag. We slogged toward the trailer, Winston in tow.

"I'm drained," I groaned.

"I started taking Dexatrim."

We were almost to the steps. I stopped in shock. "What? That's like a drug, isn't it?"

"It's not a drug. It's an appetite suppressant. And it works."

"How'd you get it?"

"From Brad Wolfheart. He's got all kinds of stuff." She shot me an offended look. "I can't believe you haven't noticed the three pounds I lost."

"Robin, you need to be careful with that."

"Easy for you to say. You can eat a whole bag of Doritos and not gain an ounce."

I hadn't eaten the Doritos, I thought, but kept my mouth shut.

Sunny appeared in the doorway, a kaleidoscope of bright color from her pink headband to her paint-splattered smock. She took a dramatic puff of her Kool cigarette. "There they are! My dazzling sun-kissed darlings."

Robin beamed. "Sunny!" She followed Mama through the door. "What did you paint while we were laying out?"

Winston and I trailed behind, giving Sunny plenty of room to do what she did best... mesmerize her audience with her radiant, all-encompassing personality.

I filled Winston's water bowl while Mama chatted with Robin about school. "The first day of high school is such an exciting time. And, Robin, honey, it's a perfect time to—"

"Reinvent yourself," I said.

"That sounds like fun," Robin said. "What do I have to do?"

Sunny let out a giant laugh. "Not a thing. With those gorgeous eyes of yours, all the work is already done."

When Robin blushed, I poked her. "You do have the prettiest

eyes, Robin. Mine are squinty and beady, but yours are like…
what do you always say, Mama?"

"Saucers," Sunny said. "You just need to show them off. Desi,
go run and get my makeup bag, and let's play a little. Come and
see my painting, Robin."

When I joined them in the painting room, Robin gawked at
Sunny's painting. Since I was Sunny's daughter, I recognized
the magnificent scene illustrating the Battle of Waterloo.

"Who is that little guy with his hand in his jacket?" Robin asked.

Sunny reached for the makeup bag, gently pulling Robin to
a seat beside her. "That, my dear, is Napoleon Bonaparte, also
known as the Emperor of the French."

"Oh," Robin breathed, closing her eyes as Mama began the
makeover. I watched as Mama's long, slender fingers brushed a
light shadow under Robin's brows.

"And yet he was of Italian descent, which explains his pro-
pensity for romance." She winked. We giggled. "He became
prominent during the French Revolution, and he was a brilliant
military leader." Sunny leaned back, inspecting Robin's face as
if it were a painting. "Close your eyes for me."

Robin did as she was told, barely able to contain herself.

Mama rifled through her eyeliner collection. "I say we go with
either smoky indigo or sultry black. What do you think, kitten?"

"The blue. Definitely the blue one." I handed her the eyeliner,
marveling at Robin's beauty. I felt a sudden uncontainable burst
of happiness. What could be better than playing makeup with
a happy Sunny and my best friend?

"Napoleon is considered one of the greatest commanders in
history," Sunny said as she theatrically swept eyeliner along
Robin's lids. "His campaigns are still studied at military schools
to this day."

"Hurry and get to the good stuff," I urged. Sometimes I had
to rein her in when she talked history, or she'd get bogged down
on boring details rather than the romance part.

"The good stuff, eh?" She raised her eyebrow. "Why, you wicked,

wicked girls." Sunny held the eyeliner up to avoid poking Robin, who doubled over in laughter. "Laugh with your eyes open, goose, or it will smear."

Once Robin and I had our giggling under control, Mama rouged Robin's cheeks and added a bit of concealer here and there. Finally, she sat back and admired her work, turning Robin's chin this way and that. "Stunning."

Sunny motioned me over, and I traded spots with Robin. "Don't look yet," I told Robin. "Wait for me." I closed my eyes and let Mama do her magic.

"Joseph, Napoleon's brother, had his eye on Désireé first," Sunny continued. "But Napoleon discouraged him once he got a look at her because he was smitten and wanted her for himself."

"Did they get married?" Robin asked.

"Alas, no," Sunny said dramatically. "They fell in love and were engaged, but it was a time of war and great chaos. Napoleon was transferred, and they were forced to be apart for a long time. When he came back, her feelings had cooled."

"What? That's so sad," Robin said.

"I agree," Sunny scoffed, as if personally offended. "Désireé ended up marrying General Jean-Baptiste Bernadotte. And Napoleon wrote a very gracious letter of congratulations to the couple. That's the kind of man he was."

Robin frowned. "I don't think I could be that nice if my boyfriend married someone else."

"Oh, but their love was so deep, so all-consuming, that even though he married Josephine, and Désireé had her life with Bernadotte, they were forever devoted to each other. They lived out their lives with much regret."

"Really?" Robin lamented.

"That's what I believe," Sunny said. "Years later Napoleon wrote a romantic novella, a sort of fictionalized version of their doomed romance."

I glanced at Robin. "I'll never get why she named me after a lady who had a doomed romance. I'm jinxed for sure."

"Oh, don't be silly." Mama puckered her lips so I would do the same. When she capped the lipstick, she pronounced me: "Lovely."

She picked up a mirror, holding it just within our reach. "You two are going to have the best of times. You'll meet the loves of your lives, and your children will be friends, and you'll live happily ever after."

"Sounds like a fairy tale," I said.

Mama looked suddenly melancholy. "Fairy tales can come true. Sometimes you just have to help them along."

She handed us the mirror. Robin grabbed my hand. On the count of three, we flipped it. Robin gasped. "Oh... I can't believe this is me."

"You look really pretty," I said.

She blushed a beautiful pink. "Not as pretty as you."

Sunny sat back, lit another Kool cigarette, and watched us for a minute. "How about we have a big party when school starts? A bonfire maybe?"

I glanced excitedly at Robin, who was still a bit dazed after seeing herself in the mirror. "For real, Mama? Are you serious? Would Mr. Tom let us do that?"

Sunny flicked ashes into an ashtray. "Might take a little oodling."

"Oh, I can be the best oodler! A bonfire would be fun," I squealed.

"It would," Robin said. "We could roast hot dogs and marshmallows and invite the football players. Even the stuck-up Bouncy girls."

We moved our faces together, rubbing foreheads in a fit of delight.

"Yes." Sunny nodded. "Let's do it. I want to have a look at the pickings. We'll find you both a Prince Charming."

That night, long after Mr. Tom had gone to bed, I heard Sunny coming down the hall to my bedroom. I didn't hear her, per se. I heard the clinks of the ice in her glass. Winston's tiny tail thumped under the covers beside me.

"Hey, kitten, you asleep?"

I smiled in the dark. "No, I'm too excited about the bonfire."

Mama laughed in that deep-throated way I loved. It was her really-happy-in-a-Sunny-kind-of-way laugh. "It's going to be special for you. We're going to make it a bonfire that kids will talk about for years to come."

She sat on the edge of my bed, and I reached for her hand. As always, it was there.

"I thought we could put lights in the trees, make like a little canopy," she said. "We could do blue and white lights. Would that be good?"

I sat up in the dark and leaned against my pillow. "That would be the best! I'm so excited. I'm so happy, Mama." The moonlight shone through the curtains just enough for me to see the blond curls falling around her ears.

She squeezed my hand. "Good. I want you to always be happy. You're so special, Desi. I know great things are going to happen for you."

The way she said it, with such certainty and conviction, I almost believed she could make it happen through sheer will. "I hope so."

She nuzzled my nose. "I know so. In fact…" She took a sip of her cocktail, her lips turning up in a grin. "I heard from a little birdie that you got the most votes for cheerleader."

"What?" Stunned, I sat up all the way. "Mama, what? Who told you that?" I couldn't believe Robin told her! My stomach knotted, and I couldn't figure out why. Was it because Robin got to be the one to tell her and not me? Or was it because now that she knew, we could share in the excitement together?

Sunny chuckled. "Just a little birdie. Someone who cares about you and is happy for you. Like me."

A cough, guttural and raspy, echoed through the trailer. Mr. Tom must be getting some water. For the briefest of moments, I felt Mama's hand clutch mine a little tighter.

"I better go see if he needs anything." Mama tipped her glass and finished her cocktail. When she kissed me, I could smell the sweet mixture of lemon and vodka. It made me happy. It was Sunny.

"Good night, my Desi. Sleep well."

When she reached the door, I felt anxious and didn't want her to go. "Mama?"

She turned, a little wobbly. "Yes, kitten?"

"Are you happy? I'm so happy, and I want you to be happy too."

"Yes, Desi. Sunny's just a tad-tired tonight. Oodling is hard work."

"I know. But we did good, huh, Mama?"

"You bet we did." She gently shut the door.

I felt sad for some reason.

But then I thought about the bonfire, and the sadness went away. My last thoughts before falling asleep were filled with images of blue and white tiki lights, happy birds sporting indigo eyeliner, and oodling French revolutionaries…

Chapter Five

A T-Shirt That Said Boogie
Robin

As we drove up Desi's driveway, I imagined I was a queen and my royal colors were blue and white. All the twinkling lights were celebrating me, and the huge buffet tables overflowing with food were in my honor. The heads turning eagerly to welcome me were—

"I don't know about this." An unpleasant voice in a disagreeable tone crashed my fantasy. "Some of those kids look like they've already graduated," fretted my mother. "And is that? Oh my."

Mama tapped the brakes. How embarrassing. I quickly snapped out of my fantasy as I realized that the turned heads weren't to welcome me but to stare in confusion as my mother lurched along the driveway.

Okay. Back to reality. I wasn't the queen. Desi was, but I was okay with that because that made me at the very least a princess. Or maybe top dog in the queen's royal court. The bottom line was that because of Desi, my whole life had been upgraded. Like this terrific party that was going to be amazing if only my mother would just stop talking.

"It is," she said. "Robin, I see people drinking beer. Oh Lord, I'm thankful your father isn't here to see this."

"Just let me off here. That way you don't have to see it either."

"Don't get snappy with me." She shot me a look. A stern look. I figured I'd better low key it, or this drop off could escalate. "Sorry. I just need to find Desi so we can change." Everyone had come straight from the football game, so I needed to replace my Pepster skirt with my new Chic jeans. "Mama, I'm not gonna do anything bad. It's just a party, and I'm spending the weekend with Desi. I'll be at church Sunday morning."

My mother said nothing. Just let out a long, beleaguered sigh.

I scanned the crowd, searching for a particular blue-and-white football jersey. When I saw Dorky Dean with his blue-and-white number forty-two tucked precisely into his blue jeans, I pointed. "Look, there's Dean. He wouldn't be here if there was any kind of mischief going on, now would he?" Good gracious, he couldn't even be cool and wear it out like the other players.

I grabbed my bag with my jeans and overnight clothes and glanced again at her, but there was still no change in her expression. Time to pull out the big guns.

"You like Desi, don't you?"

"Of course I do." Finally, a break in the ice. Albeit a small one, as she continued to scan the crowd as if she expected a police raid at any minute.

And then out of nowhere, an animated Desi rushed to the car. "Hey, Mrs. Mabel! Did you see the game?"

"I did. It was very exciting. And you're a very good cheerleader."

"Thanks." Desi grinned sheepishly. "I messed up on the Razzmatazz cheer. Did you see that? In the third quarter?"

"No," Mama said. "I'm sure no one noticed."

"The second I messed up, I looked into the bleachers, and there was Robin, doing the motions with her hands. So I was able to get back on track, thank goodness." She leaned into the car, reached over my mother, and high-fived me.

I started the chant. "We've got Razzmatazz!"

Desi joined in. "Pep, punch, and pizzazz!"

We finished with a raucous "Hey, you, you've been had!"

Mama chuckled. "Okay, okay. You girls have fun tonight." She looked pointedly at me. "And behave."

"Oh, yes, ma'am," Desi assured. "We will. Mama will have her home Sunday before church. Oh, and she wants to have coffee with you one day next week if you're free. She said she'd come to the library and pick you up."

Mama's eyes widened. "Well, how nice. I'll look forward to that. And, Desi, we'd love for you to come to church with us one Sunday."

"Mama." I rolled my eyes, mortified.

"I'd love to! Thanks." Desi beamed. "How about this Sunday?"

We were in Desi's room, changing into our Chic jeans. The bonfire was raging, and we could hear music and kids laughing through the window. "You don't have to go to church, Desi. Sorry you got hoodwinked into that."

"No, I want to go." As Desi slipped on her size three jeans, I tried—I really did—not to compare. But it was hard as I yanked and tugged at my size nines, and still couldn't get them zipped.

"Lay on the bed," Desi ordered.

She pushed me onto the bed, and we both giggled as she helped me pull on the zipper. We started laughing so hard, I had to push her off. "Stop," I cackled. "I can't suck in when I'm laughing so hard." And there we went again, rolling in another fit of hilarity.

Desi was the only person in the world who didn't judge me. I couldn't explain it, but it was like Desi saw me for me. She saw *me* first, before the fat me. Sometimes I felt like she didn't think I was fat at all.

"Here." She unscrewed the top off a lip gloss. "Habanero Heat. What do you think?"

"It's really red. I like it. What is haba… habo…" I puckered so she could put some on my lips.

"Oh, hell's bells, you need to come to New Mexico with me so I can school you on hot peppers. Come on—let's go."

I followed her toward the door.

"Guess what?" she turned, grinning.

"What?"

"Adam's here."

"Adam with the big belt buckle and cowboy hat?" As we walked outside, the humidity hit us like a hammer. I could feel my hair frizzing on the spot.

"Yep. He's going to be a star one day. And he's writing me a song—"

I didn't hear the rest. All at once we were swathed in the sounds of a party in full swing. While I could see Desi's lips moving, all I heard was Hank Williams Junior singing about New York City and how "A Country Boy Can Survive."

Girls and boys swayed to the music, lost in the glory of their own small-town mantra. Even Claire, who despised Shady Gully, was arm in arm with Mitch and Daryl. Claire, like me, wore a blue-and-white Pepster top. Like me, she hadn't made cheerleader. The difference was, I was Desi's best friend, and she wasn't.

"Hey, Desi! Robin!" Dolly, the bounciest of the Bouncy girls, waved at us. "Y'all come here."

Yep, suddenly I was a cool kid in great demand. A relevant part of the Shady Gully High hierarchy. As Desi headed to her fellow cheerleaders, I took a moment to ponder the wonder of it all.

I loved Desi, I really did, but something had changed this summer in the way I thought of myself. I didn't hate myself so much. Whether it was because Desi loved me back, or because I didn't feel so alone anymore, or because I had something to look forward to every day, somehow I felt more included and significant. And it made all the difference.

Even to the point I didn't need to follow Desi over to the Bouncy girls and suffer through their lame points of view. I felt fine meandering around the bonfire on my own.

I reached into an ice chest and dug around for a Coke, only a little surprised to see Mama had been right, and there was beer at the party. My hand rested on an ice-cold Miller Lite for a moment.

"Better not." A voice bellowed behind me.

I pulled out a Dr Pepper and glared at Dorky Dean with his jersey perfectly tucked into his pants. "What's it to you? What are you gonna do?"

Dean grinned. "I doubt I'd do much, but you can bet that Jesse and James over there are eagle-eyeing everything."

Jesse and James were Dolly's twin brothers. They were a couple of years ahead of us but acted like they were the elders of Shady Gully High. Their dad, Brother Wyatt, was the pastor at Shady Gully Baptist Church, so I suppose they were raised to be high and mighty.

"They don't scare me. Damn outlaws."

"Whoa, listen to the bad girl cursing." Dean whistled. "What a rebel."

I took a long sip of my Dr Pepper and scowled at him.

"Are you and Desi going out with anybody this year?" Dean dipped his head, suddenly fascinated with his size twenty shoes. "I see she's googly eyed over the Cowboy Crooner over there."

I forced my gaze away from his unusually large feet, and spied Adam strumming his guitar, humming a tune, and watching Desi—who was indeed watching him back.

"And once again I ask, what's it to you?" I rolled my eyes and walked away, leaving him and his giant feet standing alone by the ice chest.

I spotted Sunny, who chatted with Lenny, the quarterback. I thought how coordinated she must be to move her hips to Hank Williams Junior while holding a conversation. She had on tight jeans and cowboy boots and a T-shirt that said *BOOGIE*.

As I made my way to Sunny, I passed a group of football players who weren't dancing. Instead they were gathered around Mr. Tom, captivated and wide eyed as he talked.

"The house is gonna sit on top of that hill over there." Mr. Tom pointed. "Three stories."

"Whoa," Bubba exclaimed. "That ain't a house—that's a

mansion." There was a round of laughter as they all looked up the hill, imagining Mr. Tom's three-story mansion.

"First I'm gonna get a herd of cattle. If any of you boys want to make some money, I'm gonna need to put a barbwire fence around this pasture here." He again pointed, and several heads turned at once, as if envisioning the barbwire fence. Or maybe they were calculating how much spending money that fence would bring them.

"Cows are expensive, aren't they?" Jesse asked, one of the holier-than-thou twins. "My uncle tried his hand at that and lost a lot of money."

"Yeah," echoed James, his twin brother. "He said he hadn't accounted for the costly upkeep."

Mr. Tom looked at Jesse and James as if noticing them for the first time. "I don't know anything about your uncle, but I think I know how to run a business. I've been with the phone company for over thirty years now."

I didn't hear how Jesse and James responded because I was out of earshot by then.

"Robin, my little goose." Sunny enveloped me in a warm hug.

"Hey, Robin," Lenny mumbled. "How's it going?" For a moment I reverted to the old Robin, the pre-Desi Robin, shocked that the high school quarterback acknowledged me.

"Hey," I said. "Good game."

"I'll say." Sunny beamed. "What a superstar! And so handsome."

I thought Sunny was being overly generous, but whatever. Lenny reddened.

A hush passed through the party as Cowboy Adam cleared his throat and took center stage with his guitar. Center stage wasn't actually a stage—more a patch of dirt next to a pine tree where the stereo system sat.

"First of all, congrats to the Wildcats for owning the Hawks tonight."

A raucous cheer erupted, followed by whistles and a little chant from the cheerleaders. Including Desi, who glanced at me. Winked.

"I'd like to take just a minute to sing a little song I wrote for..." Adam paused rather dramatically. "For someone pretty special." Cheers, whistles, and encouragement spread among the guests.

"That's the one Desi likes," I whispered to Sunny. "Adam."

Sunny appeared surprised. "Is that so?" She sized him up.

Adam tipped his hat before he strummed his guitar. I glanced at Desi, who'd separated herself from the Bouncy girls and moved closer to watch the performance.

I didn't know much about country music, but the tune had a neat melody, and the snappy chorus had everyone tapping their feet and clapping their hands.

"How old is this Adam?" Sunny asked.

"Adam's a senior. He's pretty good, huh?"

She didn't reply. Sunny was watching Desi now.

The lyrics left little doubt who the song was written for, with snippets like "You make me dizzy" and "dazzling Desi," which riled everyone up. Even Mr. Tom made his way to Sunny and offered her a dance and a pinch on the butt.

"Come on, lovey. It's got a nice ring to it." He kissed her on the lips.

Sunny kissed him back, but I could tell something wasn't sitting right with her. Especially as Adam finished his song and took an over-the-top bow. Desi jumped on the little pad of dirt stage and gave him a big hug. Adam responded with a thumbs-up to the crowd.

Sunny leaned over to Lenny, and whispered into his ear. He nodded.

"Good," she said. "Come over Tuesday night. It's taco night."

It was well past midnight, and the bonfire showed no signs of dwindling. The stereo played rock ballads and party songs, and the buffet table still held a steady line. Winston trolled the ground for discarded food and sat on command in exchange for hot dog bites.

Desi and I huddled in a small group gathered around the bonfire. We sat side by side, holding hot dogs attached to dismantled wire hangers over the flames.

"They're sizzling," I said, reaching for my Dr Pepper.

"That means they're done," concluded Dean, who once again appeared out of nowhere.

I tried an eye roll, but it fell flat. Ever since Macho Mitch put something in my Dr Pepper, I couldn't even get annoyed with Dorky Dean. I was happy and so was Desi, who swigged her spiked Sprite and leaned closer to Adam, who sat on her other side.

Lenny walked over, arching his eyebrow. Somebody had given him an old Polaroid camera, and when he snapped a picture of Desi and me huddled by the fire, we grinned, our hot dog hangers in hand. It popped out, and he flapped it back and forth. As he passed it around, he asked Desi, "You need me to fix that for you?"

Desi handed him her hot dog. "Ketchup and mayo please." She giggled as Lenny headed off to do her bidding.

A group of kids who had disappeared behind the old barn at the edge of the property walked up smelling like cigarettes. Sunny and Mr. Tom continued with their slow dance, although I was sure they were aware of our transgressions.

Just as Lenny came back with Desi's hot dog, we saw bright headlights crawling up the drive. They were hard to miss, especially as they were accompanied by a trumpet of muffler rumbles.

And heavy metal music. Even before we saw the driver of the old beat-up black truck, we knew who it was...

"Wolfheart," Ricky swallowed his hot dog.

Mitch drained his Coke concoction, tossed it in the garbage barrel, and headed to Brad Wolfheart's truck. The heavy metal music poured out of Brad's open window, drowning out Sunny's stereo. Sunny and Mr. Tom stopped dancing.

"Who is that?" Mr. Tom asked. "It's a little late to be showing up now."

Sunny put her hand on his chest and spoke soothing words into his ear. I glanced at Desi, who suddenly seemed nervous. A few kids walked over to Brad's truck, traded a few words, and then walked away with their hands in their pockets.

Mr. Tom moved away from Sunny despite her attempts to calm him. "Like hell," he muttered as he stalked to Brad's truck.

"Who is Brad Wolfheart anyway?" Desi asked the group around the fire. "I've heard a lot of stories. When did he graduate?"

"I don't know if he ever graduated," Bubba said. "He's what you call... mysterious."

While we watched the action play out at Wolfheart's truck, Mitch, obviously trying to defuse the situation, spoke to Mr. Tom. But Mr. Tom wasn't having it.

"Turn that racket off," Mr. Tom told Wolfheart. "Act like you got some sense. And what is that you're handing out to these kids like candy?"

By this point, I'd sadly lost every bit of my Dr Pepper buzz. I glanced around, relieved to see that Jesse and James had long since gone, so at least there wouldn't be firsthand testimonials at the podium Sunday morning. While Dolly remained, her version of events would be skewed, as she appeared glassy eyed and wobbly on her feet.

Sunny followed Mr. Tom over to Wolfheart's truck, all the while tugging at his waist, but he firmly shook her off.

Brad Wolfheart mumbled something I couldn't quite hear, and as usual, there was something troubling about him. He had the look of an amused cat toying with an ill-fated mouse. And in this situation, the tall, usually self-assured Mr. Tom was not the cat. "Well, get out of that truck and introduce yourself then," Mr. Tom said. "I'll decide if you're up to no good."

Brad finally slid out of the truck, lit a cigarette, and meandered over to the fire. The party had quieted, and Brad, being Brad, didn't feel the need to fill the silence. Olive skinned and undeniably good looking, Wolfheart had an edgy quality about him, with his thick, blue-black hair and green eyes.

He cut his eyes around the group, pausing a beat on me. I lowered my eyes, reflexively hiding my stomach with my hands. I could feel him checking me out to see if the Dexatrim had made a difference.

Desi suddenly appeared next to me, brushing her thigh against mine as she sat. Her presence settled me. Gave me the courage to raise my eyes to meet Wolfheart's, daring him to call me out.

He didn't. Instead, he turned his attention to Sunny, lingered on her chest, at the words *BOOGIE*. He grinned.

Mr. Tom moved toward him. "Get on out of here, trash. If I catch you near here again, you'll see the front end of my Remington."

Brad didn't look scared at all. In fact, he stood toe to toe with Mr. Tom. Stared him down. Made him blink when he said, "You got a little bit of twisted in you, don't you, old man?"

Mr. Tom went for him then, dove into him and muttered some curse words I'd never heard. A cacophony of screams resounded as several of us squealed aloud, pleading with them to stop fighting.

Mr. Tom and Brad managed to get off a few punches and even rolled around in the dirt before half the football team pulled them apart.

Ricky pushed hard against Brad's chest. "Go on, Brad! Get out of here!"

Finally, Brad swaggered to his truck, barely out of breath. When he drove off, his jacked-up muffler grumbled loudly, along with the heavy metal music he'd turned up for our benefit.

"I'm sorry, Desi," Ricky offered, but it was too late.

The best party ever was officially over.

Chapter Six

Sorting And Packing, For Crying Out Loud
Desi

Why would a girl who didn't own a church dress or know the Lord's Prayer go to church on the heels of the most disastrous party in Shady Gully history? I shook my head in despair, asking Robin for the fiftieth time, "Are you sure I'm not going to get pulled up in front and flogged? Half the people from the bonfire will be at your church."

Robin flashed through my closet. "Here, I found a skirt! And it's gray. It will go with anything."

She'd said I could wear anything to church, but what she really meant was I could wear anything except pants. I grumbled. "Sunny said it was going to be a party people talked about for years. What she didn't say was it wouldn't be in a good way."

"Desi, name one thing that happened that was your fault?" When I didn't respond, Robin pressed, "You didn't tell Brad Wolfheart to show up past midnight and peddle dope, did you? You didn't tell Mr. Tom to get into a fight with him. Although I think it was honorable the way he tried to protect us all from Brad."

"I don't know. I got the feeling it was more a territorial thing."

"But why? Because Brad flirted with Sunny?"

I shrugged my shoulders. "And what about Mitch spiking our cokes? You think Dolly is going to tell everybody?"

Robin turned back to my closet. "That would be stupid, because she was doing it too. Even for her that would be hypocritical." She raked her hands through the hangers. Sighed. "You're right. She just might say something."

"Oh my God, I'm freaking out. Maybe I shouldn't go today. I don't have the right clothes, and I'm probably going to be presented with a scarlet *D* or something."

"A *D*? Why a *D*?"

"'Cause I'm dumb. And I'm damned. Dumb Damned Desi."

Robin laughed. "Dumb Damned Desi is on her way to hell's bells." She hooted. I resisted, which made her laugh harder. "I know somebody who'd give you a scarlet *D* for… dazzling Desi, you make me dizzy." Robin hummed Adam's song.

I cracked a smile. "Stop." I chuckled. "Find me a top."

She went back to ransacking my closet.

I heaved a big sigh. "Besides, Sunny is acting weird about Adam. She said he's too old for me."

"He's a little old. But lots of freshman date seniors."

"I know, but Sunny doesn't like him. And you don't know how she is when she sets her mind to something."

Robin pulled out a white button-down blouse. "How about this? I bet Sunny has a pretty scarf to dress it up."

I reached for it, dragging it on. The result was not nearly as sharp and put together as Robin in her purple dress and gold jewelry. "I like your violet eyeshadow. You look really pretty."

Robin's hands automatically flew to her stomach. She squinted in the mirror, turning from side to side. Frowned.

"Hey, you know who likes you?" I asked.

"Who?" She made a face.

"I'm serious. I think Dean has a huge crush on you."

"What? Dorky Dean? No way." Robin slipped on her pumps, glancing again in the mirror. "It's you he likes, silly. He was hinting around about it, trying to find out if you liked Adam."

"Nope, it's you. And I think y'all would make a cute couple."

Sunny rat-tat-tatted on the door. "I found some pantyhose."

"Yay!" Robin grabbed them, tossed them to me. "Thanks, Sunny. Do you have a cute scarf that would tie in the white and gray?"

Mama gave me the once-over and nodded. "I have just the thing." As she walked out, she added, "Let's get a move on. I promised Mabel y'all wouldn't be late."

I looked at the pantyhose with distaste. "I certainly wouldn't want to be late for my own flogging."

Sunny was visibly impressed when we pulled up to Robin's house. "Oh my! Your home is gorgeous!" The modest, well-maintained brick house radiated hominess and hospitality. Compared to our trailer, which was starting to mildew a horrid green along the edges, the yard's luscious green landscape read fresh and inviting.

There was a definite note of envy in Sunny's tone. I'd hoped Robin hadn't noticed, but she leaned into the front seat and rested her hand on Sunny's shoulder. "I guess it's okay. But just wait until you get your three-story mansion!"

Something flashed across Mama's face then, a burst of disappointment and sadness, making her look surprisingly old and tired. Robin grabbed her overnight bag. "Thanks again for the wonderful weekend and the fantastic bonfire."

There it was again. Sunny was definitely sad. Whether her melancholy was triggered by the brick house or the mention of the bonfire, I didn't know, but either way she was going to have to work through it herself. I had my own problems today.

When I mumbled a goodbye, I resisted the urge to look back at her. I could feel her watching me as I followed Robin to her front door. I held firm, relieved when I finally heard her car fade further and further down the driveway.

Honestly, the whole ordeal of finding something to wear this morning had worn me down. That and the unshakable shame over the bonfire. Maybe Robin had been right, and nothing that happened had been my fault, but I still felt conflicted, because deep down I'd known that a bonfire at my house wouldn't be like a bonfire at Robin's house. And I'd known that with Sunny and Mr. Tom, there was always something, some unpredictable element, better left unexposed. And yet I'd jumped at the chance to have a bonfire. So, in a way, it *had* been my fault.

"You look good, Desi. I like that color on you."

Robin was trying to be nice, but I was grumpy, and the humidity was making my pantyhose stick to my legs. We were just to her front door when she said, "What's wrong, Desi? I never wanted you to feel pressured to come to church today."

"I needed to come, Robin. For me. Maybe God can help me understand things better."

Robin gave me the strangest look. She was just about to say something, when the door swung open and her parents, perfectly dressed for church, ushered us in with great warmth.

Mrs. Mabel looked respectable and churchy, wearing a blue frock and a matching cardigan. Mr. Gene looked perfectly at ease with a dress shirt tucked into his dress pants. His hair was parted on the side and neatly wet down. I almost didn't recognize him in something other than his welding coveralls.

Mrs. Mabel headed down the hall to hurry up the boys while Robin ran into her room to get her Bible. That left me and Mr. Gene. It wasn't awkward though because he asked me how Winston was doing, and I told him how Winston ate one of Mr. Tom's shoes.

"Uh-oh." He laughed. "That's never good."

He thought it was even funnier when I explained how Mama didn't think it made any sense to buy another whole pair of shoes when we only needed one.

"Perfectly logical," he agreed.

"She almost talked a salesclerk at JCPenney's into selling her just one shoe for half price. But then when he asked his supervisor, he wouldn't let him do it."

"Completely unjust." Mr. Gene chuckled. He patted his knee and laughed some more at my story. He laughed so much that when Mrs. Mabel and Robin and the boys came out, I didn't feel grumpy anymore.

For such a popular church, Shady Gully Baptist was simply a square structure with a pitched roof. Sure, the cross on top was very impressive, but the Sacred Heart Catholic Church down the road seemed more imposing.

Nevertheless, the parking lot was packed, and a huge crowd converged at the entrance to the church. When we approached, nothing unusual happened, like a siren or a spotlight or God himself showing up and declaring me a disgrace to all humankind.

To the contrary, every time Mrs. Mabel introduced me to someone, they seemed delighted to meet me and have me as a guest.

Unfortunately, I recognized a lot of kids from school. There was Dean, who offered me a sympathetic look. I saw Daryl, who gave me a thumbs-up; Bubba, who winked at me; and Dolly, who made a big show of reading her Bible. Jesse and James, Dolly's brothers, were there, as well as their dad, the pastor, who greeted everyone at the entrance.

I panicked a little, unsure what was expected of me. "Robin." I clutched her sleeve. "Can't we just go around? Do I have to talk to him?"

She strung her arm through mine just as we reached him. "It will be fine. I'm right here."

The pastor bent to shake hands with Ernie and Max. "You boys behaving yourselves lately?"

When Ernie nodded yes, Max looked shocked. "He's lying, Brother Wyatt. Yesterday he stole my Power Ranger and—"

Mrs. Mabel gave them both the eye, steering them toward Mr. Gene. "Brother Wyatt, I'd like you to meet Robin's friend, Desi."

And there I was. Shaking hands with a man of God. His grip was firm, and his blue eyes never left mine. He made me nervous, and I stumbled through an incoherent greeting.

"It's a blessing to have you here, Desi," he said gently. "I understand y'all had quite the bonfire the other night."

I think I actually gasped aloud. "Uh…"

As I faltered, Robin propped me up, telling Brother Wyatt, "We did. Dolly was the life of the party. So much team spirit." How could Robin be so calm when this man could obviously see into my soul?

He smiled at Robin, then turned his attention to the family behind us.

"You did great," Robin said as we filed into a pew midway through the church. "We sit here every Sunday. One-time old man Jenkins got confused and sat in our seat, and Ernie told him he had to move. Mama almost died."

Robin's rambling comforted me. I decided right then and there that if I did nothing else today, I was going to thank God for my friend Robin. And as long as I had his ear, I was going to promise that if Sunny let me go out with Adam, I would never do anything bad again.

Robin picked up a hymnal and flipped some pages just as the piano player touched the keys. As the choir began to sing, everyone around me stood and to my surprise, started singing along. My eyes cut wildly to Robin, who tapped the opened page of the hymnal. Right there were the words to "Great Is Thy Faithfulness."

I was impressed that Robin knew all the words without having to look at the hymnal. I was also taken by the way others sang with such conviction. And some clearly couldn't sing. Like Ernie and Max. I think Max sang badly to get a rise out of Mrs. Mabel, but the more I observed, I realized she was oblivious, completely consumed in her own worship.

Mr. Gene reached over and gently placed his hand along her waist as he sang, "Great is thy Faithfulness, O God my Father, there is no shadow of turning with thee…"

I was taken aback by the loving gesture and the way Robin's parents, and Robin herself, lacked any inhibition singing in front of others. To be honest, I was mesmerized.

As another hymn began, Robin found the page for me. This time she smiled, urging me to take the book into my hands. By the next hymn, I found the song on my own, inexplicably pleased by this small achievement. Perhaps it was because the songs were beautiful. Or maybe being surrounded by so much unabashed reverence fascinated me. Or maybe, as heady as it was, the idea that there was a God and that he could see into my soul was… appealing.

When the music stopped, the congregation sat. Brother Wyatt took to the podium, and began with what he called "housekeeping business." Topics like the need for volunteers for the church fair, folks willing to sort donations, and help packing lunches for the homeless shelter.

Despite being here for only a short time, I pictured myself packing lunches and sorting donations. It was a ridiculously pleasing notion.

But then everything came crashing down on my momentary bout of whimsy when Robin nudged me. "Just take a deep breath and say your name like you did on the first day of school."

What? I gaped in confusion as the pastor's words broke into my consciousness. "Thank you, Ms. Rogers. Anyone else visiting today? Please stand up and tell us about yourself."

Oh no. God, please, no. I was just starting to like you! Heck, I was even imagining sorting and packing, for crying out loud! No. No. No.

"Desi, go ahead," Robin said. "I'm right here."

But I couldn't. I was frozen in place, and I couldn't breathe. I looked frantically down the pew for help. *Someone save me, please! Great is thy faithfulness? You've got to be kidding!* This was a nightmare!

Mrs. Mabel nodded encouragingly, but that didn't help.

This was worse than not knowing the Lord's Prayer in a room full of judgmental girls. Worse even than shaking a man of God's hand as he asked me about the shameful bonfire, all the while staring me down with his piercing blue eyes. I was an imposter in church, and I'd been found out!

But then my eyes were drawn past Mrs. Mabel to Mr. Gene. His kind expression was in and of itself nothing new. But something else was there. A look of confidence—in me, of all things. Like he knew I could pull this off, like he didn't have any doubt, like he had absolute faith in me.

It spurred me on, and slowly, miraculously, I caught my breath. My legs still shook, but my heart stopped threatening to explode out of my chest.

"Anyone else?" Brother Wyatt asked again, his blue eyes zeroing in on mine.

I stood up, and somehow my legs held firm beneath me. And with the beautiful hymn still on my lips, and with the idea that maybe there was a God who knew my soul, I uttered, "Uh, my name is Desi. That's actually my nickname. My real name is Désireé. I don't know why my mama named me that. It's kind of a weird name."

Encouraged by a few friendly chuckles, I continued. "Uh, we're from New Mexico, and I… we live here now. Oh, and the most important thing is that I'm Robin's best friend. And I… I like your music."

I sat down quickly before I threw up. A splattering of "welcome Desi's" rose from the congregation. The piano player hit a few keys of "Great Is thy Faithfulness" in a sort of musical thank-you.

And it was over. My heartbeat returned to normal, and the shaking stopped, and finally, everyone focused on Brother Wyatt rather than me. Hallelujah.

While I spent most of the time gathering myself, I caught bits and pieces of the sermon. Inspired by Peter 1:5, it had something to do with elders being shepherds of God's flock and youngers submitting to elders.

I glanced at Robin, wondering if she suspected the parents of Shady Gully had met, and requested this particular sermon in response to the scandalous bonfire at Desi from New Mexico's house.

But Robin seemed unfazed, and no one turned around in their seat and looked accusingly at me. As I listened further, Brother Wyatt made the point that the elders weren't supposed to lord it over the youngers but rather be examples to them. This got a few amens, and again, nobody looked at me.

"I want to finish today with 1 Peter chapter 5, verses 6 to 7." He closed his Bible, and his penetrating blue eyes scanned what seemed like every man, woman, and child in the congregation. "'Humble yourselves, therefore, under God's mighty hand, that he may lift you up in due time.'"

He paused again. "Friends, hold this to your heart and let it bring you peace with whatever you're struggling with today. "'Cast all your anxiety on him... because he cares for you.'"

My throat felt thick, and my eyes welled with tears. I looked sideways at Robin, who still seemed unfazed.

But Mrs. Mabel was another story. As she considered me, she had tears in her eyes, and I thought her smile seemed especially joyous.

Still feeling the glow from my captivating morning in church, I was determined to talk to Sunny about Adam. The timing was perfect as Mr. Tom had driven to north Louisiana to shop for cows.

I searched for her in her painting room, finding only a blank canvas sitting atop an easel, with the Polaroid of Robin and me from the bonfire propped beside it. I examined the loopy expressions on our faces, our cheeks flushed from the glaze of the fire. Or from the spiked sodas. We'd never know, I supposed. Regret swept over me as I considered our happy faces just before Brad Wolfheart crashed our party, and Mr. Tom went all Rambo on him.

"Mama?" I returned the picture to its place on the easel, and headed to the kitchen. "Where are you?"

I found her on the back porch, eating a bag of chips and

looking at a magazine. She glanced at me, not really happy. But not sad either.

"What are you reading?" I forced some cheerfulness into my voice.

"Not really reading, kitten." She tossed the magazine aside. "Eating too many of these fattening chips." She handed me the bag.

"Is Mr. Tom going to bring some cows home?"

She shrugged, "Who knows? I'm not sure about this wild hair of his…"

"I hope he does. They're so cute with their long eyelashes and giant brown eyes. And think of the baby cows."

She changed the subject. "Are you still mad at me?"

"Mama, I'm not… I was never mad at you. I'm just confused."

She lit a cigarette. "Let's go for a walk."

Encouraged by the upbeat, enthusiastic tone of her voice, I took the plastic bag she handed me, and followed her down the gravel driveway.

We picked up soiled napkins, paper towels, and empty cans strewn across the yard. "I guess the wind blew the trash out here," I said carefully.

"Or people tossing them out their windows." Ashes fell from her Kool menthol as Sunny gestured. "Let's go this way. I like these big oaks."

I followed, happy to be in the sun, to be with Sunny.

"Some of these people," she scoffed. "So thoughtless."

"Like Brad Wolfheart, you mean? The party crasher?"

Sunny took a long puff of her cigarette. "Is that what you're confused about, Desi? Or is it something else?"

"Well, no. Maybe. I just don't—"

"Because we worked really hard to make it a nice party. And that boy, he was disrespectful and rude. I don't know if it's a cultural thing or what. That's what Tom thinks."

I picked up a napkin and crumpled it into my bag. Thought carefully about my response. "Yeah, Brad is a shady guy." I hesitated. "But I've never seen Mr. Tom so mad. Have you?"

Mama said nothing. Flicked ashes into a ditch. Walked faster. After that I felt bound to add, "Good thing he was there." "It was indeed." Mama seemed relieved. "You know he loves us so much. He wants us to have a good life here." "And it was a really nice party," I said. "Everyone had fun until the bad stuff happened." "Is anyone talking about us?" Mama asked suddenly. "About Tom?" "No." It wasn't a lie. Truth was, I didn't know. "You know, he told me the other day he wants you to call him something other than Mr. Tom." "Like what?" I slowed down. "I can't call him Daddy." "No, you don't have to, but maybe something less formal." I didn't know how I felt about this. Except more confused. "Hurry up, kitten." She picked up her pace. "Can't burn calories being a slowpoke." "Oh, Mama. Not you too. I hear that all the time from Robin." Sunny grinned. "Speaking of Robin, I've decided my next painting is going to be a portrait. I'm going to use that cute one Lenny took of y'all roasting hot dogs." "I saw it on the easel. I like that one." I squeezed her around the waist, feeling optimistic about talking to her about Adam. "I enjoyed church today. I saw lots of kids from school there." We passed a horse pasture with an old dilapidated truck parked strategically between some downed fencing. Barbwire had been carefully strung to both the front and back ends of the old truck, preventing the horses from getting out. "Now that's some country engineering, huh?" Mama chuckled. "Yep. You should paint a picture of that," I told her. Mama nodded. "That Adam boy wasn't at church today, was he?" She caught me off guard. And just when I'd thought things were going in the right direction. "No, he wasn't at church. But I like him." "Desi, he's a senior. You can't date him." "It doesn't matter how old he is. He likes me. He wrote me a song." I hated the pleading tone in my voice, but I couldn't seem to stop it. "Didn't you hear how sweet it was? Even Mr. Tom loved it. He wanted to dance with you. Don't you remember?"

"Anybody can write flowery words and play a guitar and woo a young girl."

"No they can't. Why are you acting like this?"

"Because, kitten, he's the wrong sort of boy for you. He'll be out of school after this year. Why not have a boyfriend who can share in all these fun years ahead?"

"You don't understand. You're not even trying to understand." My face burned, sweat falling across my brow.

"How about someone on the football team maybe? Like that cute quarterback, Lenny? The one who took the picture?"

"No. I don't like Lenny. I like Adam."

"That's just ridiculous," Mama snapped, tossing her cigarette into the ditch. "This Adam you seem so fixated on is a player. He's all flair. Didn't you see how he was hamming it up for the crowd the other night? You're too young to understand it, but it's true. Trust me on this."

"I don't trust you." I was angry now.

Sunny, taken aback, fell silent. "Fine," she said eventually. "But I'm going to tell you something I wish someone had told me. A girl should always, always choose substance over flair."

I rolled my eyes.

"Flair is fleeting, Desi. It's insincere. It's vain. It's selfish. You want a nice young man who is steady, who has character. You want someone who proves himself with his actions. Not with fancy words."

"And you think Lenny is going to be all that? No, Mama. It's my life, and Adam is the one I like. Not boring Lenny."

"Desi!" Mama stopped, out of breath as she tried to keep up with my emotionally fueled stride. "Don't you see that's what I'm trying to tell you?" There were tears in her eyes. "Romance and hearts and pretty words are nothing. Steady and dependable and… yes, maybe boring—that's what matters."

I groaned, turned, and headed toward home.

"Desi." She followed me. "Desi, I only want what's best for you. I don't want you to make the same mistakes I've made."

I stopped, turning to face her, a hundred arguments and questions running through my mind. Finally, I said what mattered most. "Mama, please just spend some time getting to know Adam. I think you'd really like him."

"Fine," she said in a clipped tone, huffing a little from the heat and the pace and the emotion. "I'll do that. But I've invited Lenny for dinner Tuesday night. I think he's a nice young man."

Fury spread through me then, incinerating whatever bliss I'd found earlier in church. "What? Why did you do that?"

"He likes you, Desi. He told me so at the party. And Tuesday is taco night. You love tacos."

I wheeled on her then. Screamed with frustration to the sky and to God, who supposedly knew my soul. I left her there upset, in front of the dilapidated truck fused into a makeshift barbwire fence.

I ran as hard as I could, sweat and anger pouring off me. All this talk about substance and steadiness and actions being better than romance and flowery words and…

I stopped, placing my hands on my thighs, catching my breath. Realization swept over me.

I don't want you to make the same mistakes I've made…

If my daddy was the steady, boring man with substance, what did that make Mr. Tom?

PART II

Chapter Seven

Extra Sugar, If You Please
Robin

It turns out Dean wasn't a total dork after all. True, he dressed way too conservatively. Also true he preferred algebra and physics over art and PE. Plus, he told corny jokes, wore prescription glasses, and recently started taking college courses. None of that mattered, however, because I was crazy about him.

We walked hand in hand to the Wildcat travel bus. He looked down at me, way down, because he was at least a foot taller than me. His grin was even bigger than mine, which was hard to believe considering the amazing news I had to share. Technically I wasn't supposed to share it, but there was no way in hell's bells I wasn't telling Desi. I could hardly contain myself.

"You're shaking," he said. "I challenge you to wait five minutes before telling her."

"There she is." I let go of Dean's hand and rushed over just as Coach Cal passed, thumping Lenny's head.

"Mind on the game, QB," Coach ordered.

Lenny begrudgingly removed his lips from Desi's, and had the grace to look embarrassed. Although the minute Coach was out of range, he kissed her again.

Desi's face reddened. "Hey." When she tucked her hair behind her ear, Lenny's senior ring was in full display on her pointer finger. Secure with the aid of two corn pads, the ring's sapphire stone reflected off the late afternoon sun.

I had no need for corn pads because Dean thought investing in a senior ring was shortsighted and a waste of money. Like I said, not a total dork, but still...

"Guess what?" I clutched her arms.

"She couldn't even wait a minute," Dean told Lenny. "Much less five."

"Okay. Y'all can't tell anyone," I said. "This has to stay between the four of us. Until they make the announcement tomorrow in homeroom."

"Oh my God."

"Desi, yes. Yes. You made the homecoming court!" As we squealed and embraced, Lenny and Dean formed a male barricade, in case anyone was watching.

"I knew it," Lenny told Desi, full of adoration. "Never any doubt."

"How'd you find out?" Desi asked. "Are you sure?"

"Long story. But yes, I'm sure."

Dean nudged me, impatient. "And? Tell her the rest."

I squeezed her hand. "And so did I."

Desi's hands flew to her cheeks, and tears flooded her eyes. "This is the best thing ever!"

Lenny cleared his throat, looking over our heads. "Bouncy girl coming in from the left."

We managed to contain ourselves and appear sober just as Kendra, decked out in her cheerleading suit, waved us down. "Coach Becky wants us to get on the bus."

"Okay," Desi said. "We're coming." She wished Lenny good luck with a kiss, then strung her arm into mine.

As we headed for the bus, Dean asked, "Hey, why don't I get a kiss like that?" Dean had decided three years ago that it was smarter to become the team statistician and preserve his bones and brain for his career.

"Give those numbers hell, babe!" I teased him.

Desi and I floated onto the bus in a fit of giggles. We high-fived Pepsters, cheerleaders, and band members. Dolly, who sat by Ashley, flashed us a halfhearted smile. Still peeved that Desi had been made captain, Dolly stewed in her demotion to co-captain.

As the big blue bus revved its motor, Desi led us in a cheer. After a raucous roll call, she and I snuggled into our backseat bench. Nothing better than a long road trip to plan and fantasize about our dream night on the Shady Gully homecoming court.

Who cared if I'd ballooned to a size thirteen and couldn't button the top button on my Pepster skirt? I was on the homecoming court with my best friend.

Late in the fourth quarter, just after Lenny threw a pass to Ricky, who ran it in for a touchdown, I noticed a man watching Desi. He was standing in the spectator area, cheering the Wildcats on and doing his best to get Desi's attention.

After the chant during the timeout, I walked over to the edge of the bleachers to get a better look. He didn't seem threatening. An older guy wearing a windbreaker, jeans, and bright white tennis shoes. Thinning hair. A bit of a paunch.

Something about him seemed familiar. When he turned in my direction, I gasped. It was Mr. Harry! Desi's daddy! He spotted me and raised his arm in a friendly wave.

But what was he doing here? All the way from New Mexico? Did Desi know he was coming? No, no way. She would have told me. As the time clock ticked down to a Wildcat win, I headed down the bleachers toward Mr. Harry.

Desi and I had gone to Gulf Shores, Alabama, with Mr. Harry during the summer. We'd had a fun-filled week on the beach, baking in the sun by day and touring the city at night. We'd felt safe because Mr. Harry trailed around with us, but gave us our space and let us explore and do our own thing. He generously shelled out money for dinner at fancy seafood restaurants along the beach and bought tickets to cool things like the zoo. One of my favorite memories was Mr. Harry laughing as we climbed up a long ladder to meet a giraffe face to face.

"Hello, Robin," he said warmly just as the crowd erupted at the final second of the game. "Looks like it's a win."

I gave him a hug. "What are you doing here? I can't believe it! It's so good to see you."

"You too," Mr. Harry said. "I just decided to take a road trip and see the country. I had some time off."

"Desi is gonna flip! She'll be so excited!"

"I hope so." He sounded unsure. We both glanced at the cheerleaders, on the lookout for Desi. "I still haven't met her boyfriend. I figured this way I might get an introduction."

When Desi spotted me, I waved. "You'll like Lenny. He's crazy about Desi."

Desi stopped in her tracks when she saw her dad. I noted the surprise, happiness, and worry flicker across her face.

"Daddy." Desi bounded straight into Mr. Harry's arms. "What are you doing here? Is something wrong?"

"No, pumpkin, I just wanted to see you. Like I explained to Robin, I had some time off."

"He wants to meet Lenny," I said. "Oh, and Mr. Harry"—I lowered my voice—"we have some major exciting news for you." When he looked at me expectantly, I blurted, "Desi and I were both picked to be on the homecoming court!"

"That's wonderful. Congratulations, pumpkin." While Mr. Harry appeared thrilled, Desi flicked her eyes at me as if I'd overstepped.

It was then that Lenny approached, sweaty, still in full uniform, shoulder pads and all. Dean followed, neat khakis, blue Wildcat shirt, clipboard in hand. Such a nerd.

"Mr. Harry." I urged Dean forward. This is my boyfriend, Dean."

Dean shook Mr. Harry's hand as I explained. "This is Desi's Daddy."

"It's a pleasure, sir," Dean said politely. "Everyone loves Desi."

He smiled at her, reluctantly moving aside so Lenny could step into the introductions.

"And this must be Lenny." Mr. Harry offered his hand to Lenny. "Nice game, son. Calling that audible in the third quarter was smart. Nice adjustment after seeing their defense at the line of scrimmage."

"Thank you." Lenny, obviously pleased that Desi's Daddy knew football, grinned. "I'm glad it worked. Nice to finally meet you."

Coach Cal blew a whistle as Coach Becky called for everyone to load up on the travel buses.

"Daddy, we have to ride the buses," Desi explained. "I'm sorry."

"That's okay. I understand, pumpkin. I just wanted to see you for a minute. How's your mama?"

"She's fine. But… you can't just turn around and go back to New Mexico. Aren't you going to stay in town for a few days?"

"I'll stay for few days, sure. Maybe Sunny will let me take you all for dinner tomorrow night."

Desi and I talked quietly in the backseat of the dark bus all the way home. No danger of anyone hearing because most everyone was sound asleep. "I wish you hadn't told him about us getting on the homecoming court, Robin."

"Why? He was so excited. He wants to walk you down the football field like all the other dads."

"But that's just it. That's going to cause all kinds of problems with Pop and Sunny. And we don't even know for sure yet. We're going to be so disappointed if Mrs. Shanna May, well, if your source, was wrong."

"She's not wrong." I huffed in frustration. "I still don't get it though. What problems will it cause?"

Desi looked out the window, saying nothing. I gave her a minute, counting to ten, determined to let her gather herself. Ten took forever. "Talk to me," I implored. "Whatever it is, you can tell me."

She shook her head. "You can't understand because your parents would never get a divorce. There's this whole thing that happens when you have stepparents. Pop is going to get mad because he will want to do the homecoming walk with me, and Sunny will be on his side because she wants peace. And I already know what's going to happen to Daddy. Just like always, he's going to be the loser. And it just makes me... so miserable." She lowered her eyes.

I put my arm around her. She was right. I had no clue about the dynamics of divorce.

"And he drove all the way here. You know why? Because he's lonely, Robin. He has nothing. His whole life, the life he had planned for himself, and his family, got ripped out from under him when—"

She stopped.

"When what? You've never really told me what happened."

As the bus stopped at a railroad track, I watched as red and yellow lights flashed across Desi's face, which held more pain than I'd ever seen. "Daddy works at the phone company too. He and Mr. Tom... Pop... worked together in Albuquerque. And..."

"And what?"

"He and Sunny had an affair."

Whoa.

"It was a horrible scandal. My Daddy was... is... still heartbroken. Mama was the love of his life, and I don't think he'll ever get over it. The whole thing was humiliating for him. Can you imagine?"

I shook my head, at a loss for words.

"I don't want you to hate Sunny. You know how she is..."

I nodded, still speechless.

"She's everything to me. No matter what she did."

The next morning my heart flipped when the intercom cackled. Unfortunately, the whole school endured one of Principal

Jethro's long, drawn-out coughing fits before he finally started the homeroom announcements.

As Desi and I traded glances, I did my best to take deep breaths. Now that the moment was here, I couldn't shake the feeling that Mrs. Shanna May had been wrong.

After an especially long and tedious list of announcements—such as admonishing boys who were pushing the hair-length rules, and urging drivers to stay out of the bus lanes—Principal Jethro finally delivered the homecoming news.

"After yesterday's vote, we now have a list of seven lovely young women to make up this year's homecoming court at Shady Gully High." Our homeroom erupted in cheers, as did others, judging from the whoops echoing through the halls.

"Before I read the names, I'm going to explain how this works so there's no confusion," Principal Jethro said in a dry voice. "Tomorrow morning at this time, ballots will be passed out. Each student will vote for one—I repeat, one—young lady as homecoming queen. The winner will not be announced until homecoming night. Now, take time today to congratulate each of these impressive young ladies."

After another excruciating coughing fit, Principal Jethro said, "Dolly…" The names blurred together as my heart raced. "Kendra… Ashley… Denise…" I glanced at Desi, who was as pleased as I that the star of the girls' basketball team, Denise, had made the cut.

Only three more names to go.

"Claire…" Cough. Cough. Only two more names to go. Hack. Cough. "Sorry about that." Principal Jethro cleared his throat. Two more names.

Someone give that man a glass of water.

"Desi…" Cough. Cough. "And finally, Robin…"

Our class clapped. Bubba, seated behind me, patted me on the shoulder.

"Congratulations, ladies." Principal Jethro signed off.

"Nice going, Robin," Bubba offered. "You've come a long way."

I turned around, skewering him with a mean look. But then he leaned over and whispered, "I'm gonna vote for you."

And it began. Twenty-four hours overflowing with gossip, strategy, and alliances that inevitably, and historically, sent the school into a tizzy when the winner was announced on homecoming night.

Desi and I exchanged a smile. Let the games begin…

Bella's was the fanciest of fancy-dress shops in the sixty-mile radius of Shady Gully. Desi and I were determined to have a unique and stunning outfit, different from the frumpy suits our local department stores had to offer. In fact, at the last "court meeting," which was what it had been dubbed by Mrs. Shanna May, Denise and Kendra had ended up buying the exact same mauve suit.

Kendra had started crying, and it was a whole big scene. Mrs. Shanna May, who was coordinating all the homecoming details, had done her best to console Kendra while encouraging the rest of us to pick a color and do our best to stick to it. And most importantly, we were required to let her know as soon as we found our outfit so she could tell the other girls. No one wanted another heartbreaking scene like that again.

Of course, things had worked out for Kendra because Denise kindly volunteered to return her suit and find something else. She said it was no big deal because she'd also liked a red-and-gray suit, and if they still had her size, she'd be happy with that one.

Denise was like that. She cared more about beating her previous time on the sixty-meter run and making free throws and striking batters out than primping for homecoming.

Dolly, on the other hand, told us all flat out she was wearing Wildcat blue, and we weren't to go near anything on the blue palette. Humph. Not sure who made her queen and gave her the right to call dibs on the school color, but there you have it.

Since the general feeling was the title of queen would go to either Desi or Dolly, everyone carefully measured Desi's response to Dolly's pronouncement.

Desi quickly agreed, impressing everyone with her graciousness. She'd even managed to make it look like a concession, but I knew blue wasn't the color she wanted anyway.

In fact, I was pretty sure we were looking at her dream outfit right now.

While Mama and Sunny flitted in and out of the parlor area, Desi and I brought a number of garments into the dressing room at Bella's. I'd tried several on, but nothing worked. Either I couldn't get the waist buttoned, or the sleeves and skirt were too long. When I tried on a boring black suit that almost fit, Mama said hopefully, "We can get it hemmed." But when I glanced at Sunny, she said nothing, so I moved on.

Desi, however, had found a few options in the petite section. They all looked good, but this one, this winter-white belted skirt-suit with a pencil silhouette made her look like a glamorous movie star. Sophisticated and elegant, it stood out from the basic skirt, blouse, and blazer ensembles everyone else planned to wear.

I'd been in the middle of tugging off a horrendous yellow monstrosity when Desi clasped the belt on the white suit. Stunned, I stood gaping at her. "That's it," I breathed. "That's the one, Desi."

Our eyes met in the mirror. She shot me a lopsided grin, flattening the skirt. It had long sleeves with a snazzy notch collar. The big belt accentuated her tiny waist, and the angled, uneven hemline of the jacket was striking.

"You look like royalty to me." I nodded decisively.

"But the slit in the skirt? Is it too much?"

"Only one way to find out." I covered myself with the yellow eyesore, and beckoned for the moms. "Come and see the queen."

Sunny and Mama opened the door expectantly.

"Oh!" Sunny's hands flew to her mouth. "Oh my. It's lovely."

Even Mama was impressed, apparently unbothered by the

slit in the skirt. "It's very pretty." She knelt and fiddled with the bottom. "It will have to be hemmed."

"And the sleeves too," Sunny agreed.

Miraculously, the hostess appeared and exclaimed, "Gorgeous! So gorgeous! You are so tiny." She motioned Desi into the lighted parlor room, helping her onto a boxed platform.

I followed, emotional because the outfit reminded me of a wedding dress. I imagined someday it would be just like this… Desi looking beautiful, stepping onto a pedestal while I watched from the background.

The hostess concentrated as she pinned the outfit so we could get an idea how it would look once altered. "I think the slit will have to go up once the skirt is hemmed."

Sunny agreed.

But Mama cautioned, "Not too much."

"It will be fine," I told Mama. "Don't you think, Sunny?"

Sunny stepped back, appraising Desi with pride. "I think it's perfect."

"She'll need a hat," Mama said.

"Oh yes," Sunny exclaimed. "The hats are fun!"

"I have just the one," the hostess proclaimed. "A gorgeous white one with a tiny veil, like the kind they wear to the Kentucky Derby!"

Mama and Sunny oohed and aahed, and Desi and I could barely contain our excitement as the ladies fluttered toward the hat rack.

"You can totally pull this off," I assured Desi.

She grabbed my hand. "We're going to find you the perfect one too."

"Try this one." The hostess fussed as Sunny returned with the hat. "Don't look yet," she said as she climbed onto the box beside Desi and adjusted it just so. "Now."

Desi opened her eyes and looked at herself in the giant mirror in the women's parlor of Bella's.

"Beautiful," we told her in unison.

And she was.

"May I use your phone?" I asked the hostess.

Everyone looked at me strangely. "I need to call Mrs. Shanna May and tell her white is taken."

On the way home, I was too excited for Desi to be sad for myself. Well, maybe I was a little bummed.

We'd tried and tried at Bella's, but nothing worked for me. Truth was, I was probably a little over a size thirteen now, and there just weren't that many options for a short-sized person like me.

After being off all morning, Mama had to get back to the library, so Sunny suggested we try a few specialty shops on the way home.

"We really need to find something soon," fretted Mama as we let her out at the library. "Because it will surely need to be hemmed and—"

"And I need to pick my color before the only thing not taken is orange," I grumbled.

Sunny said with confidence. "Don't worry, Mabel. I have an idea."

Once we left the library, Sunny put the pedal to the metal and we went flying toward the interstate. "We're taking a road trip, girls. Hang on."

As Desi's mouth formed an exaggerated O, I squealed with a sense of adventure. Sunny flew through an interstate sign that said forty miles to Baton Rouge. I gawked at Desi.

"So here's the deal," Sunny explained. "No two girls are built the same, and there's no shame in that. You, my sweet goose, are gorgeous, and we are headed to a place that designs beautiful clothes for people that are your kind of gorgeous."

"I didn't know there was such a place."

Of course there is," Sunny confirmed with a wink.

Desi giggled, as psyched as me. We made good time and

drove into the big city before midafternoon. Tons of traffic raced in every direction, and we crossed a bridge that seemed to go on forever.

"It says it's the Atchafalaya Basin Bridge." Desi pointed at the sign.

"It means we're almost there. Kitten, grab the map and tell me which street to turn on when we get off." I watched in awe as Desi took the map, followed the path Sunny had highlighted, and concluded, "Looks like you want to take a right on Vance up here."

"Copy that," Sunny said.

"Perfect." Desi eyed the street, then looked back at the map. "Then go about a mile and turn left. The address is 2911 Jackson Street."

I shook my head in amazement. "And you think I'm cool 'cause I know all the words to the hymns at church."

We pulled up to a quaint little dress shop called Extra Sugar, if You Please. The sign in the window said *Plus-Size Clothing for Teens.* "Don't pay attention to that," Desi said.

"I'm not." I just wanted to find my perfect dress and have my own moment on a pedestal.

When Sunny opened the door for us, we entered a nice, cool boutique that smelled like gardenias. The clothing on the mannequins was trendy, like stylish girls Desi's size would wear.

"We need to look at something for our beautiful Robin here, who is on the homecoming court." Sunny smiled at the hostess. "Something with pizzazz."

"Absolutely," the hostess answered in a chipper voice.

We followed her to a special room called *Fancy Wear.* I almost lost my breath as I gawked at the stunning outfits on display.

"Oh my goodness, Robin!" Desi shrieked. "Look at this stuff."

When the hostess asked me what size I was, I mumbled, "I guess thirteen. Maybe bigger." Unfazed, she pulled outfits for my approval.

Sunny grabbed a few things as well. "Let's start her a room, shall we?" Within minutes I was swept away in a whirlwind of colors, styles, and whatever whimsy struck my fancy. I had only to beckon, and it was delivered. The dressing room was extravagant, and the hostess had written my name in chalk.

Surely there was something in this kaleidoscope of color that would fit me.

When Sunny disappeared to use the store's phone to call Mama and Mr. Tom, Desi said, "Robin, look at that. On the mannequin."

"Oh... that color." I stared up at the most beautiful, vibrant emerald-green I'd ever seen. It was a two-piece suit, like Desi's, and the jacket collar was lined in emerald satin, cinched slightly with a button at the waist. The skirt was straight and tapered, not flared like the ones I'd tried on at Bella's.

"Do you have this one in a thirteen?" Desi asked the hostess.

"Let me check."

While Desi raved as I tried on several outfits, both of us were eager to have a look at the green one. When a knock sounded at the dressing room door, Desi opened it expectantly.

Sunny said, "I explained to Tom and Mabel that we were going to be late so take your time—"

"I'm sorry to interrupt," the hostess said. "But we don't have the dress on the mannequin in a size thirteen."

Crestfallen, I flopped onto the dressing room bench.

"What about the one on the mannequin? What size is that?" Sunny asked.

"It's a size eleven."

"Let's try it," Sunny quipped. She turned to me when the hostess disappeared. "Chin up, goose. Don't you worry."

When the clerk brought the green dress, Sunny reached for it, carefully taking the top off the hanger. "This is lovely."

After Desi closed the door, Sunny gently eased the top along my shoulders. I held my breath, pleased when it seemed to fit.

"Look how pretty," Desi said. "That green makes your eyes look so dark and beautiful."

Although it felt uncomfortably snug, I managed to fasten the cinch at the waist. I let out a nervous gulp. "So far so good."

Sunny unzipped the skirt and handed it to me. When I slipped it over my hips, the lining felt smooth along my legs. "It's lined and everything," I exhaled, turning so Desi could zip up the skirt. "Please tell me it will zip," I begged.

"Yeah, almost," Desi replied, but I could tell there was a problem. "I'm having trouble with the clasp, that's all."

"Let me see," Sunny said, taking over.

I felt confident suddenly, the way Sunny shifted my body towards the mirror. The way our eyes met as we all considered me in the stunning emerald outfit.

"It's beautiful," she said. "It complements your coloring and it pops with pizzazz."

"But will it zip?" Tears filled my eyes.

Desi joined Sunny, and together they wrestled with the zipper clasp.

"It's close," Desi said.

"Not to worry," Sunny assured. "A seamstress can do something with this."

The hostess, who'd peeked through the door, looked skeptical. "I'm not sure there's enough material to take it out much."

I took my eyes off the mirror just long enough to see Sunny give her a brutal look. "It's very close." When the hostess disappeared, Sunny said casually, "I've been having the same issue with my buttons lately." She smoothed the jacket over the skirt. "It's beautiful."

"I love it." My voice was unsteady. "It's just perfect, and I love it."

"Me too," Desi agreed.

"Homecoming isn't for three and a half weeks," I pronounced as tears spilled from my eyes. "I can lose enough weight to fit into it—I know I can."

Desi hugged me from behind, and Sunny smoothed the dress again, calming me with her motions.

After a moment Sunny looked at me in the mirror. "I can

get you in this dress, Robin. But you have to promise me you'll ask your mama."

"I'll do anything," I said.

Chapter Eight

Bucket Of Lard
Desi

Saturday night in Shady Gully and Lenny and I were doing our goodbyes. Him leaning against his old Pontiac, a hand-me-down that his dad had given him on his seventeenth birthday. And me leaning against him, my arms wrapped tightly around his neck while his locked behind my back. Kissing him was heaven.

His lips were gentle, probing. Which sort of summed up Lenny. Gentle. Kind. But always curious and searching.

"The lights are on in your mom's room," he said.

"So," I mumbled into his neck as I breathed in his deliciously unique scent. "Who cares?"

I didn't. The stars were out, and our background music was the steady sound of cicadas humming somewhere in the swampy woods around our trailer.

When he chuckled, his mouth vibrated against mine, and I drank in his sweet breath. Kissed him harder. He groaned then, lifted me off the ground, and pressed himself against me.

I moved against him, slowly at first and then quicker, the magic familiar to me now. Soon I gasped into his neck and shuddered. After a moment he kissed my forehead and gently placed me back on the ground, so that I was looking up into his deep-brown eyes.

"I'm sorry…" I said shyly.

"No, you're not." He grinned.

"No, I am. I feel bad. For you."

He shook his head, as if it were nothing. My pleasure. His frustration. And always, his graciousness.

"I love you, Desi. You know that, don't you?"

"I do." I nodded firmly. The porch lights flickered a few times, and I sighed. "I hate going in there."

"Have things been bad lately?"

I shrugged.

"You did the right thing. Your dad has the right to walk you down the field for homecoming. Don't feel guilty."

"I know, but I do. I just hate it all. The negotiation that it turned into."

Lenny agreed. "Still, Harry got the best end of the deal, I think. Giving up graduation isn't that bad. It's boring compared to homecoming."

The lights flickered again. Was it my imagination, or did the flickers seem particularly frantic? "I better go."

"Night." He kissed me again. "You want me to pick you up for Mass tomorrow? Or are you going to church with Robin?"

"Yep," I said as I headed inside. "To both."

Sunny was in her nightgown when she met me at the door. She was in a highly agitated state. Her hair was plastered to her head on one side and still curled and sprayed on the other. Black mascara streaks covered her cheeks, and her eyes were swollen. She'd obviously been crying. And she was obviously very, very drunk.

I followed her into the kitchen, unsettled by her condition. The bedroom door was closed, and there wasn't a peep from Pop. "What happened? Are you all right?" I glanced at Winston, who watched us intently from his spot on the sofa.

"No, I'm furious." She took a long puff of her Kool menthol.

"He's such a disappointment." She raised a shaky hand in the direction of the bedroom. "I've given up everything for him. Everything!" She lowered her voice. "You should have seen the big shot in his element tonight. Boasting about himself, and his sycophantic underlings fawning over his every word. The big boss, hamming it up for his followers. It was nauseating."

Sunny and Pop had gone into Belle Maison for a dinner party, and as best I could tell, the party consisted of phone company employees and their spouses.

Mama had worried all week about what to wear and how to do her hair. "But what happened?" I wanted to know. "What went wrong? You looked so pretty and happy when you left."

I watched as she unrolled a paper towel and blotted tears from her eyes. "I can't... I can't compete with these young women. And you should have seen her, Desi. She was so skinny, and she giggled at his stupid jokes. Fluttering her eyes at him."

"Who? Who did?"

Mama looked exasperated. "It doesn't matter, Desi! Some-body's wife. I don't know. It could have been anyone. She was seated next to him at dinner, and I got stuck on the other side of the table. And oh, how they laughed. He hung on her every word, and it was... it was..." Mama rubbed her face with the rough paper towel, smearing mascara and raising red welts on her cheeks.

"Well," I said, removing the paper towel before she rubbed her skin raw. "She was sucking up—"

"Exactly! But he fell for it. He's so shallow, so full of himself. You should have heard him." More tears.

I pulled a box of Kleenex from the pantry and blotted her face and eyes.

"And then," she went on, "he has the nerve to come home and try to get romantic with me. The nerve of him. Obviously, this little twit got him all worked up and he thought he would just—" She stopped, her anger turning into despair. "Oh, everything is such a mess. It's all gone so wrong."

I handed her another Kleenex. How dare Pop hurt her this way? My beautiful, special Sunny, so full of joy and light and love, and he had the audacity to flirt with another woman.

I shook my head, outraged. "Well, I'm going to have a word with him tomorrow."

"No, Desi, no." She sobered up suddenly. "You can't do that. Especially now with everything going on with Harry. This competition between them." She reached under the cabinet by the sink, pulled out a bottle of vodka, and poured some into a glass. "And you know, you and Lenny, you haven't helped anything."

"What? What did we do?"

"You broke his heart, Desi. He hasn't been the same since you let Harry barge back into our lives. And Lenny, after all Tom's done for him, he's suddenly getting all righteous—"

My anger flared, so I struck a blow in a way I knew would hurt. "Vodka isn't going to help. You're going to feel terrible in the morning."

"I don't care. It's helping right now." And she wept again. "When I think of all I gave up for him. To come here, to this godforsaken place. People don't even read around here, Desi. Much less know about history or art."

"Mama, let's go to my room and sit down." She wouldn't budge though. And she wouldn't let go of the bottle of vodka.

"He used to tell me about this big house he was going to build me in God's country. That's what he called it. Shady Gully, God's country! Humph!" Still clutching the bottle, she waved her hands to emphasize her point. "And now that he's gone and fallen in love with his damn cows, losing money right and left, we'll never get out of this trailer. I will rot here because he's getting into debt, wasting all our savings on his selfish wild hair."

I coaxed her to the table, made her sit down. Finally, the tension in her face eased. She took a deep breath, sipped her vodka. In the silence I thought I heard movement from the direction of the bedroom. I got two aspirin out of the cupboard and put them on the table. "Here. Take these, Mama."

"I know," she wept. "I'm going to feel terrible tomorrow. And Desi, I tried to start the painting of you and Robin, and I've just lost it. I can't do anything right anymore, and I'm getting fat and—"

I put the aspirin in her hand, even as tears flooded my eyes. I was enraged and conflicted and felt so utterly powerless. "Open your mouth and take these. Good. Now, drink." I handed her the vodka.

The bedroom door creaked. As I turned, full of pent-up anger, Sunny gripped my arm, squeezing so tight it would leave fingerprints. "Desi, just let it be. I can handle this."

I wheeled on her. "It doesn't look like it to me."

"You don't understand. Just let it go—"

"Sunny," Pop called out in a rugged tone. "Come here, lovey."

Mama rolled her eyes. But she got up.

"Mama, no. Sleep in my room."

She downed her vodka, put out her cigarette. She looked newly determined. "Go to bed, Desi. And don't worry." She kissed me on top of the head and left me sitting there at the table, staring at her empty glass of vodka.

I wish Robin were here. Or Lenny. I felt devastated and furious and not sure what to do with my emotions. Had I started all this? Had I caused this emotional turmoil?

Hoping to shake off some of my frustration, I made a peanut butter and jelly sandwich. Just one piece of bread rolled in half. I stood at the kitchen sink and ate it with a glass of ice-cold milk, pinching off random pieces of bread for Winston.

I stopped chewing suddenly when I heard… something. It sounded like crying. Yes, soft, emotional sobbing. They must be talking. I hoped she was laying down the law. I took another bite of my sandwich.

Now I heard something else. A groan. A whimper. The trailer actually shook when someone bumped against a wall. My mother, my Sunny, my once vibrant and shiny heroine, had lowered herself to having sex with the very man who'd hurt her.

The moans and sighs of passion disgusted me. They weren't even trying to be quiet. I threw what was left of my sandwich in the trash, signaling Winston to follow me down the hall. Anything to get away from the throes of sex reverberating from their bedroom.

I felt embarrassed for Sunny. And yes, even ashamed. How could she sink to this? Why was she so eager to beg and scrounge for whatever scraps of affection were thrown her way?

Never, I swore to myself as the moans from the bedroom filled me with revulsion. Never, ever would I disgrace myself like that...

We had just crossed state lines when Robin told Sunny and me, "Claire asked why we were skipping school today, and I told her we had to go to the seamstress for a fitting."

Sunny sported oversized sunglasses, bright-red lipstick, and a trendy scarf in her hair. "Well, that's sort of true." She winked at Robin. I watched as they sang along to a popular song on the radio, sharing a moment of solidarity. I wasn't feeling it.

Other than a severe hangover, Sunny had bounced back from her drunken meltdown quite nicely. She and Pop were all lovey dovey the next day, and she'd even encouraged me to be especially nice to him. A little oodling might help, she'd urged, since he was still stinging from my casting him aside for Harry.

"What about the skinny woman who was fawning over him?" I'd asked. "And the cows and the boasting and the lack of fine art in Shady Gully?"

"Kitten," she'd said, "it was all a misunderstanding. I was tired and feeling insecure, and I overreacted." This was possible. I'd seen her respond to Harry similarly over the years. She'd nurse some perceived slight or imagined offense until it grew into week-long bouts of misery. But she was happy now, and even a few residual rays of Sunny's happiness were enough to brighten the dreariest of days.

And happy she was, fueled no doubt by the brisk fall weather and the hope that today was the reagent to a new beginning. "I don't think I've ever been to Natchez, Mississippi," I said. "Are we sure this is legal?"

Sunny gave me the eye. "Of course it's legal. Don't be silly."

After a moment she asked Robin, "Are you sure Mabel said she was fine with this?"

"Yes," Robin said. "She's absolutely on board."

There wasn't a doubt in my mind. Robin was lying through her teeth.

To say the waiting room was overflowing with people would be an understatement. Not only were all the seats occupied, but the walls were taken, strangers leaning against one another, resting shoulder to shoulder along the dirty Sheetrock. Wheelchairs and their occupants were propped willy-nilly in the middle of the floor, not an inch of linoleum to be had.

We were each given a folder with paperwork to fill out, with instructions not to return the folder to the front desk, but rather wait until we were called. Of course, this made absolute sense, because bodies going in crisscrossing with bodies going out would have resulted in a traffic jam too great to contain.

Sunny suggested we take our folders and join the group waiting on the sidewalk outside. Most definitely. Too many anxious bodies crammed into too tight a space reeked of body odor and desperation. When we could barely find a spot on the concrete sidewalk to ourselves, I glanced longingly at our car in the parking lot. "We don't belong here," I said with sudden indignation.

"You don't," Robin said. "And Sunny, neither do you. But I do."

Robin looked around, scanning the varying degrees of hopelessness, self-loathing, and shame... and decided these were her people.

"That's ridiculous. You don't belong here, and I'm starting to wonder if the green outfit is worth it."

"That's easy for you to say," Robin snapped.

Sunny looked up from her paperwork. "Okay, girls. Sit down and fill out your forms. This will all be over soon."

I looked at the long line outside and cringed when I recalled the sad waiting room. "I wouldn't bet on it."

"Uh-oh. It says if you're under eighteen, you have to have a parent or guardian sign." Robin held up the consent form.

"That's what I'm here for," Sunny said. "Give me yours too, Desi."

Begrudgingly I opened the folder. "What's this? They already have the prescriptions written out? Stamped with a signature?"

"Yeah," Robin answered. "You're supposed to just fill out your name and the date. It's asking my weight. I think I lost a pound since we went shopping."

"Don't put that yet," Sunny instructed. "They'll weigh us."

We waited for what seemed like hours. The brisk fall air had vanished, replaced by stifling humidity and strong winds. "All we need now is for it to rain." I groaned.

Sunny gave me a dour look when the doors to the clinic burst open. A herd of folks poured out and made their way to the parking lot. I was astounded so many people had been stashed somewhere else in that building, somewhere beyond the sad waiting room.

A nurse with a whistle around her neck came out and waved the outside group in. I followed Robin and Sunny, who suddenly found a little spark in their step. *Good*, I thought, *let's get this over with*. The nurse, a mean-looking old bag, found it necessary to blow her whistle when the chitchat among the newcomers grew too loud.

"Listen up," the nurse said, blowing the whistle again. "Everyone line up single file. Have your sheet ready, and step on the scale on the way in."

I glanced at Sunny to see if she was as mortified as I was, but she seemed resigned.

"Mama, this is—"

"It's a means to an end, Desi. Come on." There it was. The look. I fell in line, following the rest of the herd single file as instructed, lest the nurse get riled up again and blow her whistle. One by one we shuffled in, looking ahead at the scale as if it were an instrument of doom.

Sunny reached it first. "One thirty," the nurse said. "Write it down and move into the auditorium."

Auditorium? Was there going to be a band?

Robin turned to me. "I'm so scared, Desi. You go first." I was going to argue with her, but the mean nurse gave me the evil eye, so I jumped onto the scale ahead of Robin.

"One fifteen." She looked at me. "Write it down and get going."

Cruella motioned for Robin to get a move on. "We don't have all day. Up on the scale." She looked at the number and seemed a little too pleased to report, "One forty-five. Wow."

That did it. The *wow* was entirely unnecessary.

We found Sunny in the auditorium, and we, along with at least sixty other people, had our personal consultation with the good doctor. His name was Dr. Schmidt, and he was a creeper. Emaciated looking, he wore black horn-rimmed glasses and sniffled excessively. His hair was dirty blond and scraggly, like he was too busy to comb it. Of course, with his patient load, one could understand.

"Quiet. Quiet, ladies." His voice was snarky, and I didn't know why it bugged me that he said *ladies*, but it did. There were a few men here. Not many, but still.

He gave the nurse a look, and she raised her whistle to her lips. On the ready. But we, the patients, were quick learners and quieted down before it was necessary to discipline us.

"Now," Dr. Schmidt began in his condescending, clipped voice. "You are all here, why?"

Heck if I know, I thought. One fifteen was more than I thought, but I could pass on the peanut butter sandwiches if it meant never having to endure this again.

"Because," the doctor said, "you are fat! You eat too much, and you don't exercise, and you are all going to die. Why? Because you are fat!"

His skeletal frame circled a rolling table offstage. With great effort, he hauled the table to center stage so everyone could see a towel draped over something mysterious. It reminded me of a prize or a magic trick when the host or magician whipped off the sheet to an amazed crowd. But somehow, I doubted the big reveal would uncover a diamond necklace or tickets to Hawaii.

"Now. Think about what you had for breakfast this morning. Did anyone have an apple? What about a banana? Anyone?" No one replied. "Of course not. Why?"

Some in the audience actually said, "Because we are fat."

"Right," agreed the doctor, pleased. "You probably had pancakes and bacon and muffins and... what else?"

"Peanut butter," a woman said. "It has protein in it, and it's healthy."

"No," Dr. Schmidt disagreed with exasperation. "Peanut butter is no better than this." He yanked the top off the mysterious object on the rolling table. A giant can of Crisco. "Do you know what this is?"

A few mumbles of "fat" and "what you fry chicken in" made the rounds.

"This," proclaimed the doctor, "is a bucket of lard. And that, ladies, is what you are. A big, fat bucket of lard."

I looked over at Sunny and Robin, because at this point I'm thinking, *There are more of us than him, and with this group of healthy women we could take this moron down! And Cruella the nurse too!*

But Sunny remained stoic. A means to an end, like she said.

But Robin... Robin lapped it up. This quack was getting to her, and it enraged me. "Robin," I whispered furiously, "he's an idiot. Don't listen to him."

She barely acknowledged me, her eyes never leaving the stage. She was completely mesmerized.

"Now," he went on. "I can help you. I can make you healthier and your quality of life better. But you must do what I say. Why?"

"Because we're fat..." The followers chanted the madman's mantra.

"These three pills are going to change your life."

Someone from the audience, a heavyset lady in a wheelchair, asked, "What are they? I take a lot of other medication, and I want to know if they mix."

"If they don't mix," Dr. Schmidt said, "you should get off the other meds because your excess weight is going to kill you faster than anything else." He looked annoyed that she'd interrupted.

I looked at Sunny to see if she was as outraged as I was and felt a wave of relief when she shook her head in disgust.

"A thyroid pill," he began, "a fluid pill, and an appetite suppressant." He placed the three bottles on the rolling table next to the bucket of lard. "You decide. This?" He pointed to the pills. "Or this?" He pried the top off the Crisco and turned it over. We all watched, enthralled, as the thick goop of lard slimed its way onto the tabletop. "Don't be a bucket of lard!"

The "because we are fat" chant didn't really fit here, so no one said anything. "That's all," he said in a bored voice. "Go. Take your medicine. Eat right. Exercise. Come back in ninety days, and we will weigh you. We'll see if you're still fat." He walked off the stage.

To my horror, a few people clapped. When Robin put her hands together, Sunny clasped them in hers and said, "Let's hurry. Maybe we can beat the crowd to the pharmacy."

It was dark by the time we got the prescriptions and headed back to Louisiana. Sunny lit up a Kool menthol as soon as we reached the car. I leaned over to Robin, who was beside me in the backseat. "Where'd you get the money for the pills?"

She looked at me for a long moment before saying, "I stole it out of Ernie's piggy bank." When I reacted with shock, she made a face. "No, you goof. I saved up my allowance."

I didn't respond. Just gazed out the window, lost in my own thoughts. Sunny and Robin seemed to also embrace the quiet, and the car ride was tranquil for a long while. Perhaps we all needed some time to process the notion of being herded in like cattle, thoughtlessly rounded up, and weighed for auction. Or maybe images of the crazy little man and his whistle-blowing assistant lingered. Whichever it was, I felt utterly disheartened by this day and the level of humiliation people were willing to endure just for a pill that was probably bogus anyway.

We finally crossed state lines and were winding our way through a little town, when the flickering neon lights offering burgers, pizza, and fried chicken caught my eye.

"Hell's bells, I'm starving," I said.

Robin swung her head in my direction, and Sunny flicked some ashes out the window.

"What?" I said. "Y'all can't tell me that pizza doesn't sound good right now?"

I didn't know why, but I was feeling just ornery enough to goad them. "Lots of hot, melty cheese and salty pepperoni and buttery crust—"

Nothing. And then… my enchanting Sunny let out her joyous cackle and immediately, the day's tension dissolved. When Robin finally grinned, the tightness in her face disappeared. I cheered as Sunny put on her blinker.

Robin fidgeted next to me. "But… what about?

"Tomorrow we start," Sunny said. "Tonight we celebrate with pizza. We deserve a reward after this day."

Before heading to the pay phone, Sunny ordered Cokes for us and a beer for her. "You girls go ahead to the buffet. I'm going to call everyone and let them know we're running late."

"Oh." Robin mulled that over. "No need to call Mama. I told her we'd be late."

Once Sunny disappeared, Robin and I piled our plates high with pizza. "You're going to get caught, you know." I nudged her affectionately as I manhandled an extra piece of pepperoni onto my plate.

"Maybe not. If we can just keep Sunny from talking to Mama for a while."

"How is that even possible? With homecoming around the corner?"

We headed to the table where our drinks were waiting. The ice-cold Coke made me smile. It also reminded me I had a full bladder. "Be right back."

On my way to the restroom, I overheard Sunny on the pay phone. I started to walk over, to get her to ask Pop to let Winston out before it got too late, but I stopped in my tracks.

"Oh, you know how it is with these girls," Sunny told Pop. "The fitting went on forever, and those two could shop all day."

So there you have it. Everybody was lying.

We started hashing out the numbers as soon as we gathered in the booth. "My scales at home must be off," Robin bemoaned. "One forty-five is even worse than I thought."

"I bet you'll lose five pounds the first week." Sunny sipped her foamy beer. "And that will encourage you, and before you know it, you'll be down another five."

"How do you know so much about this?" I frowned at Sunny.

"I know," Robin agreed. "You're so skinny."

"Oh, I'm not." Sunny tusked. "I need to lose a solid ten pounds. I've been feeling so horrible lately. Hopefully, the pills will give me a boost and I'll be able to paint again."

"She's going to paint us." I nudged Robin. "Remember when we were holding our hot dogs on hangers at the bonfire? Before our freshman year?"

"I love that one," Robin said. "Just paint me skinny, Sunny."

I toyed with the crusts of the six slices of pizza I'd devoured, feeling stuffed. Maybe it was all the talk about pounds and strategies, but suddenly I felt compelled to throw out my number for discussion.

"I weighed one fifteen." I glanced at Robin and Sunny, but they didn't comment. "That's not bad, is it?"

"I would give anything to be one fifteen," Robin said.

Sunny looked over her mug of beer at me. "You're just fine, Desi.

I bobbed my head up and down, not finding Sunny's tone convincing. That was when I realized there were seven gnawed pizza crusts on my plate, not six. Unsettled, I said, "I guess it wouldn't hurt to try the pills for a few weeks. Maybe get super svelte for homecoming."

Robin nodded distractedly, then pressed Sunny, "How do you do it, Sunny? Is it because you're so tall, or do you have a secret?"

Sunny looked thoughtful. "I don't know, girls. I think a lot of times we eat too much not because we're hungry but because we're searching for something to fill us up. We need a lift in our mood, something to soothe the voids in our lives."

Robin and I were both spellbound by Sunny's honesty. It felt like we were right on the edge of something. Some epiphany. And who better to enlighten us than Sunny?

"If I have a secret, it's this." She held her mug up. "I do this instead of eating. It lifts my mood, and it's not as fattening."

With that, she downed the last of her beer. "Let's get on the road. You both have school tomorrow."

Chapter Nine

Orange Station Wagon
Robin

I stood in front of the full-length mirror captivated by the sight of me in the emerald-green outfit. For the first time in my entire life, I believed anything was possible. I could become a highly acclaimed newscaster or a journalist in New York City. I could become a movie star. I could be on the cover of a magazine.

I could even, I thought as I cocked my jaunty green hat at an angle, become the Shady Gully High homecoming queen. I thought my chances were good actually. I couldn't believe the number of students who went out of their way to tell me they'd voted for me. They said they hoped I won because I wasn't stuck-up like the other girls.

Also, and this was the biggie that gave me a flutter in my stomach, Mrs. Shanna May refused to tell me who was voted queen. In the past she'd been more than happy to spill the beans, so why not this time? It had to be because she didn't want to spoil the surprise for me.

I could just imagine it. The announcer would call out my name, and everyone would be shocked. Especially Desi. That I felt bad about, but just once I'd like the applause to be for me. Lenny, the captain of the football team, would put the crown on my head, and there would be pictures, lots of pictures, of me and my court.

"Robin." Mama knocked on my bedroom door. "Hurry up. I want to see."

I opened the door and stood back so Mama could take in the whole view. She said nothing at first, but the awestruck look on her face and the tears bubbling in her eyes told me all I needed to know. She was pleased with the final fitting before homecoming.

"Do you like it?" I asked.

"Oh, I love it. You look beautiful." She did a little stroll around me, bent to check the hem, and swiped a piece of fuzz off the collar. "It's almost too big for you." She placed two fingers into the waistband of the skirt, astonished at the gap. "How much weight have you lost?"

"About twelve pounds."

"Well... wow." She shot me a lopsided smile. "It really shows."

"Thanks, Mama. I really love the dress. I think it's even prettier than Desi's, don't you?"

"I think you're both going to be stunning."

A whistle of approval sounded from the hallway as my dad peeked in, reacting with surprise. "Well I'll be..." he gushed. "How did I get so lucky? I'll be the envy of all the other dads. It will be an honor, my beautiful daughter, to accompany you down the field."

"Isn't she pretty, Gene?" Mama couldn't take her eyes off me.

A stampede of mischief and energy roared down the hallway in the form of Max, who gawked to see what all the commotion was about. "Whoa..." he said, clearly searching for words. "I guess you don't look as ugly as usual."

Daddy flicked his ear. "What's that behind your back?"

"Nothing." Max and Daddy enjoyed a game of keep away until Daddy retrieved the package from Max's hands. "It's a package," Max teased before disappearing down the hall. "For Robin, the leprechaun!"

"Oh! I'm so happy it's finally here!" I grabbed the box, ripping into it with excitement. I carefully removed the tissue paper, pleased to discover the gold gilt-edged pages were even more delicate than

I'd imagined. The debossed title, contrast stitching, and ribbon marker were all flawless. As was the dark-blue leather. "It's perfect."

"How did the engraving turn out?" Mama asked.

I gently placed the Holy Bible into her hands. The ornate brass nameplate read *Desi* in custom print.

"She'll love it," Mama said.

I agreed.

It was dark, and we could hear the crickets and the cicadas buzzing in the woods behind the abandoned bleachers at the old ballpark. Basically, the lover's lane of Shady Gully, everyone called the place Cicada Stadium.

Since it was a weeknight, Dean and I had the place to ourselves. A little igloo rested on the blanket beneath us, and the fall breeze kept the temperature pleasant.

Dean tidied up with a washcloth and zipped his pants. He rolled onto his back, put his hands behind his head, and sighed. "You're the best," he told me with a lazy grin. "When are we gonna—"

"Not yet," I told him. "I'm not that kind of girl." We both laughed, because lately I'd been very close to being that kind of girl. But not quite.

"You're just so sexy. If you keep losing weight, I won't be able to find you."

I smiled in the darkness, pleased that he was delighted with the new me. I settled next to him and rested my head on his chest. Completely confident in his devotion to me, now and forever.

"Life is good. It's gonna be especially great for us." My fingers tickled his shoulder.

"It is," he agreed. "Did I tell you I finally got my college applications done? I sent three of them out today."

"Really? Where?"

"This round of apps was all in state. Northwestern in Natchitoches. LSU, of course. And Tulane, in New Orleans."

"I like New Orleans."

He nodded. "Yeah, that would be cool, huh? I need to see who gives me the best break on tuition though."

"You'll get scholarships, I'm sure of it. And you already have so many credits with the pre-college courses you took this year."

"Yep. I'm hoping I get a full scholarship because Mom and Dad won't be able to help much. If at all." He sat up, reaching into the igloo for a Gatorade.

"Better fuel up," I teased him. "You'll need all those electrolytes to record stats for tomorrow night's big game."

"Dang straight." He grinned. "Want anything?"

I sat up, asking shamelessly, "Were you able to get the beer?"

Dean nodded as he pulled out a bottle of Miller Lite. "Yeah, I snuck one from my dad's garage fridge. I hope he doesn't notice." He unscrewed the top and handed it to me.

I took a long, delicious sip, and as it went down, I relished the slight burn in my stomach. "It's so good. You want a sip?"

Dean didn't, and I wasn't surprised. Once a nerd, always a nerd. I watched as he inhaled a ham sandwich. Began working on the brownies. "Mom made you a sandwich. I told her we were studying at the library tonight."

I didn't want a sandwich, but the brownies were a little tempting. I took another sip of the ice-cold beer. No way was I messing up on my diet tonight. Not with homecoming tomorrow. "I'm not hungry, but that was nice of her to send her hard-working boy off with nourishment."

He chuckled. "Are you nervous for tomorrow?"

"Nope." And right now I wasn't. The buzz from the beer made everything seem less daunting. Sunny had been right about her secret, and between that and the adrenaline rush from the diet pills, life and its possibilities were boundless. I impulsively threw out, "I'd like to travel someday. And for sure live somewhere else besides Louisiana. You?"

"Oh yeah." Dean propped himself on his side with his elbow.

"Maybe we could go west? I could find a job in New Mexico. Desi says it's beautiful."

"I loved Santa Fe when we went with Harry," I told him. "It was kind of a hippy town. Way smaller than Albuquerque, which I liked, and it had the cool snow-covered mountains in the winter and the gorgeous sunsets all year long."

"I remember the pictures y'all took from your trip," he said. "They were from some neat place in the mountains. I remember because I thought the trees were nice. They had these intense yellow leaves. What were they?"

"Aspens. They were everywhere. The whole place was magical."

"Yep, I want to travel too," Dean confirmed. "See the world."

"With all the money you're gonna make, we'll be able to afford all the fancy hotels and restaurants, just like in Santa Fe," I gushed. "Spas and trendy cars and fine dining."

"Sounds like a plan," Dean said bashfully. "Only Michelin-starred restaurants for us."

"I love you," I said, feeling high on life and even higher on the future. Dean kissed me on the lips, lingered. "What if…" I said when the kiss ended.

"What if what?"

"What if I got homecoming queen? Wouldn't that be something?"

Dean smiled. "I voted for you."

When he didn't expand on that, I prompted, "And?"

He offered me a perfunctory peck on the lips. "I wouldn't get your hopes up, Robin. You know Desi's going to be queen, right?"

It took me two hours to primp and fuss over my hair and makeup, and another hour for Mama to round up and spit shine the miscreants, and thirty minutes for Daddy to hook bow ties onto their button-down shirts. Overall, it was a good team effort, and we managed to pull into the parking lot of Shady Gully High on time.

The weather was unusually beautiful for a fall night in Louisiana, and there was a buzz in the atmosphere. The band practiced their opening number in the distance, and the Corvettes and Z28s lined up at the starting station behind the Future Farmers of America building. Mama was armed with a camera and fluttered about taking pictures of everything while I tried to find Desi.

"Let's do one with you and your daddy," she commanded.

I flashed a genuine grin as I posed with Daddy, who looked rather dapper in his gray suit. Posturing with the little demons, however, was another matter. To Mama's chagrin Max seemed intent on doing the two-fingered rabbit ears over my head, while Ernie's bow tie was hopelessly askew. Mama had to stop and adjust it repeatedly, and the whole process lasted forever. And still, I couldn't find Desi.

Coach Becky flitted around with her own camera, snapping a nice shot of our whole family. "You look beautiful, Robin." Then, taking it a step further, added in a low voice, "Your outfit is the classiest I've seen so far."

As I was having a fabulous time, I enjoyed the double takes from the faculty as well as the surreptitious looks from the other girls on the court. Everything was perfect, except I couldn't find Desi.

Mrs. Shanna May approached, her face carefully made up with extra eyeliner for the special occasion. "My lordy mercy, Robin, you look ravishing, if I have to say so myself." After she hugged me, I hesitated a moment, hoping she'd give me some kind of sign. Maybe a whisper in my ear or a little wink. But nothing.

Dolly, of course, wore her Wildcat blue and sported freshly highlighted hair. She pranced around with an air of royalty, while Kendra, adorned in mauve from her hat to her shoes, followed her around like a servant. The only thing missing was a train on Dolly's ensemble for Kendra to hold reverently.

Denise looked lovely in her red-and-gray suit, even though she stood on the balls of her feet as if she were on a basketball court. Ashley wore wild purple, and good gracious, Claire had on a yellow get-up with a crazy feathered hat that made her look like a canary.

"Let's do a group picture, girls," Mrs. Shanna May instructed. "A before shot."

As she rounded us up, I reveled in the moment of shock and amazement as the other girls took in my striking green outfit. I truly had never felt so vindicated in my measly little life.

"Wow, Robin," Denise said. "You look great."

Kendra locked eyes with Dolly, as if asking permission before offering a compliment. "Pretty color."

I smiled, soaking in all the praise. Eventually Dolly said, "It's nice."

Mrs. Shanna May dished out instructions to the court and their entourages. "All right, dads, why don't y'all head over to the cars and jump into the passenger seat? Your daughter's name will be on the glittered sign on the car. We did our best to match the colors to your daughter's colors."

Regardless who overheard, Dolly said, "I already know I got the blue Camaro Z28. It's Mitch's brother's car."

Of course, I thought. *It's all about connections.* Every year around homecoming, the faculty reached out to alumni, especially those known to have fancy cars with moon roofs. Most of the time they were able to divvy them out accordingly, but sometimes strings got pulled.

We lined up and took pictures amid whispers and mumbles about Desi. I tried not to panic, but I was worried. Things had been tense with Mr. Tom and Sunny and Mr. Harry. Earlier this week, while on the phone with Desi, I'd heard a whole argument play out as Mr. Tom threatened not to come to homecoming at all.

"This is what it's been like all week," Desi had said, holding the phone out for me to hear. "Listen to them."

"Well fine." I'd heard Sunny sobbing. "But nothing is going to stop me from being there."

"Go then," Mr. Tom had shouted back at her. "You and Harry and Desi can get cozy like a little family again. I'll stay home since nobody wants me anyway."

Yikes.

Eventually, Desi couldn't take it anymore. She'd shut her bedroom door, raised the volume on her stereo, and we'd talked on the phone for hours. I did my best to be supportive, but like she'd told me long ago, I couldn't really relate since my parents and my family were one unit.

Speaking of which, I heard one of the miscreants rushing over to me now. "Robin, wait. Robin!" Ernie, his bow tie hanging on his collar by a thread, held a bouquet of pink roses.

"I saved up my money." He thrust them at me, obviously pleased with his own generosity. But also a little proud of me, I could tell.

"Thanks, brat. They're very nice." I kissed him on the cheek.

"Over here." Mama waved, her camera poised.

Afterward, when Mama and her camera had moved along, he gave me an extra hug. I was touched, even though he messed up my hat a little when he squeezed me. He whispered in my ear, "I hope you win. I think you're the prettiest."

I found it a little hard to swallow as I watched him run off, especially when his dress shoe trod across the ill-fated bow tie after it tumbled to the ground.

Mrs. Shanna May approached and asked in a low voice, "Robin, do you know where Desi is? We're going to have to get the cars rolling soon."

"There she is!" Coach Becky pointed, and sure enough, there was Desi.

To say the sea parted might be a bit much, but the parking lot behind the Future Farmers of America building certainly did. As Desi made her way to us, the swell of approval was palpable. Mothers cried out in awe, children followed her as if she were Pied Piper, and even the drummers did a little number as they lined up. There were catcalls, whistles, and cheers, and a feeling among the crowd that now that she was here, homecoming itself could start.

She waved to everyone, glowing like a radiant candle with an abundance of grace. It wasn't until she came up to me and hugged me that I knew something was terribly wrong.

"You look magnificent," she told me. "You're so beautiful, Robin." And for a moment, as she focused on me with genuine appreciation, her eyes didn't seem so puffy and her mascara didn't seem so smeared.

Mrs. Shanna May instructed Mr. Harry to join the other dads while lining up the court to take another group picture.

"Are you okay?" I asked Desi, "What happened?"

She smiled on the outside as the photographer took several pictures of the now complete homecoming court. Finally, when it was over, she turned to me. "No. The ride over was terrible. Pop decided to come along, and he was being so nice and—"

"This way to the cars, girls." Mrs. Shanna May beckoned to us. "Are you excited?"

We both smiled but managed to stall and trail behind everyone.

"And then Daddy snapped at him," Desi continued. "I couldn't believe it. I felt sorry for Pop."

"How's Sunny?"

"How do you think? She got caught in the middle—" She stopped. "Oh…" Desi's face fell when she saw her car. "Oh no…"

I half expected to see an orange station wagon but instead saw a beautiful, sparkling white Corvette. And there stood Cowboy Adam chatting casually with Mr. Harry. When Adam looked up and locked eyes with Desi, his boyish grin widened.

"Robin, here's your car!" someone called to me.

I was torn. While I felt compelled to accompany Desi to her fate, I was eager to embrace my own destiny. I admit, I was relieved when I was swept away toward my own silver convertible. My name was written on a sign with emerald-green glitter, and my daddy reached for my hand.

I didn't know the driver. Some old guy who'd graduated a long time ago. But I loved his exquisite car, polished to a pristine shine that reflected like a mirror off the stadium lights. It was an untainted classic that stood out from all the others, and when Daddy and the driver lifted me on top of the seat, I forgot all about Desi.

Until I saw Lenny bounding toward her car, his arm piled high with red roses. He was in his uniform, shoulder padded and all, and seemed hurried, giving the impression he'd finagled hard to sneak out of the pregame locker room.

I saw his face the moment he spotted Adam. He slowed his pace. I watched from a distance as he gave the roses to Desi, shook Mr. Harry's hand… but I didn't see the rest.

Because that was when the cars revved up their engines. Homecoming had begun… and I felt like a queen.

The cars made their way slowly around the stadium to the sound of festive cheers. Maybe it was my imagination, but I found the applause especially loud when the announcer called my name. I waved to everyone, enjoying myself immensely.

When it was over and we'd made it to the fifty-yard line, I said to the driver, "That was so much fun! Can we go around again?" Daddy thought that was hilarious, and he and the old timer shared a chuckle.

I glanced at Desi before the ceremony and was pleased to see that she was happy, not at all traumatized. I ventured over for a quick hug before Mrs. Shanna May hurried us to our assigned spots.

As the announcer started the ceremony, each girl waited for her name to be called before walking with her dad to the other side of the fifty-yard line. I was astounded at how quickly my turn came and glad that Daddy was there to hold me steady.

As we made our way down the field, the announcer told my story, boring things like what classes I took, and what my extracurricular activities were, and what my plans were for the future. When I'd filled out the form for Mrs. Shanna May, I'd been stumped by that question. I was absolutely clueless about my future.

"Robin is excited about her future and says the possibilities are endless as long as you have a good attitude. She's exploring many options, and will surely be a success and make her mark on our community," reported the announcer.

The audience clapped. I smiled. That sounded way better than clueless.

Naturally Dolly's future sounded more impressive. She wanted to go to college and become a lawyer. Coincidentally, so did Kendra and Ashley. Denise wanted to go to college and coach women's softball one day. Claire wanted to either go to culinary school, or be a postal carrier. Rather random, but that was Claire.

When Desi's turn came, all eyes were on her and Mr. Harry. Desi beamed as she gracefully glided down the field. She had a way of making everyone believe her smile was just for them.

I knew though. When she looked at me, I knew we were linked well beyond this day. When the announcer spoke about Desi's future plans, he said, "Desi considers friendship one of God's greatest gifts, and she wants to leave us with a Scripture from Ecclesiastes 4, verses 9 to 11. 'Two are better than one, because they have a good return for their labor: If either of them falls down, one can help the other up. But pity anyone who falls and has no one to help them up.'"

Desi's eyes stayed on mine through the whole reading. It was there, in Ecclesiastes, that I'd placed the ribbon in her Bible.

When the class song started, the audience rallied. And then the time had come. After a long, drawn-out drum roll, the announcer said, "I'm pleased to announce that Shady Gully's homecoming queen is—"

My heart pounded in my chest. Daddy settled me as my legs began to shake.

"Desi—"

The crowd erupted, and everything else the announcer said

was drowned out. The football players cheered. Dean high-fived another statistician. Sunny broke down on the sidelines. Mama handed her a handkerchief.

And then Lenny, emotional, as he carried the crown to Desi. After Mr. Harry took off Desi's white derby hat, Lenny placed the crown on her head. And when he bent to kiss her, the crowd cheered.

Finally, she looked my way. I left Daddy's side and ran over to embrace her. I loved this friend of mine with all my heart.

"Oh, Robin." She cried happy tears. "I can't believe it! I'm so excited!"

I hugged her again. Happy for her. And yet, a part of Ecclesiastes ran through my head over and over. "But pity anyone who falls and has no one to help them up."

No one would be helping me up tonight, because they'd all be too busy celebrating.

Chapter Ten

Pieces Of Pie
Desi

Early morning Mass at Sacred Heart Catholic Church baffled me. No matter how hard I tried, I couldn't remember when I was supposed to stand, kneel, genuflect, or sing. Even the Peace Be with You's caught me by surprise.

I loved it though. And I knew it meant a lot to Lenny. The church's cathedral ceilings and colorful stained-glass windows were beautiful, and the image of Jesus crucified on the cross at the head of the church was powerful. I found my eyes drawn to it repeatedly during Mass. The ceremony itself seemed more somber than at Robin's church. While I appreciated both churches for their differences, I loved them equally for the sameness in their message, that Jesus was the Christ.

A shuffle sounded as the kneeling benches were unfolded and I took my place next to Lenny. I side-eyed him as he knelt with his hands clasped and his head bent in prayer. I wondered what he was talking to God about in that moment.

Unfortunately, I probably had an idea. Things between us had been strained the last several months. Ever since homecoming. How was it that one of the best nights of my life was the catalyst to this rocky patch between Lenny and me?

It was Adam, of course. Adam had shown up like a white

knight in a Corvette and stolen Lenny's moment. Poor Lenny. He'd walked up in his Wildcat uniform, armed with his roses, only to be trumped by Adam with his shiny car and his hand clasped in my father's. Lenny had looked stricken, as if in that instant his role as my boyfriend had been usurped and his status as the team's hero had been stripped. He'd thrown five interceptions and fumbled the ball twice in the big game. The inference was clear—Adam got under Lenny's skin.

Unfortunately, Adam seemed emboldened by the negative effect he had on Lenny, and since then, he popped up everywhere. At impromptu parties at Cicada Stadium, where he always seemed to have his guitar handy. At Wildcat ball games, where his very presence correlated with Lenny's plummeting stats. And even here at Sacred Heart Catholic Church.

I spotted Adam's shaggy red head sans the cowboy hat ten pews ahead of us. Even worse, just as the kneeling benches rumbled back into place, Adam glanced at me. And winked.

I prayed Lenny hadn't noticed. He'd been furious when Adam started invading his *territory*, as he called it. "He's nothing but a holiday Catholic, only showing up on Easter and Christmas, and now he's gonna come every Sunday to gawk at my girlfriend!" Lenny had let out a string of curse words, then punctuated them with a defiant threat, "If I have to, I'll take him down on his way to Communion."

At Father Patrick's prompting, we stood and shared the Peace Be with You's to those surrounding us. Afterward I put my blue leather-bound Bible on my lap. I never seemed to use it at Mass, but I liked the feel of it close.

The sermon encouraged us to examine our own hearts for wrongdoing, using one of the psalms as a reference. It got me to thinking about homecoming night and how I'd kind of liked Adam being there. I'd enjoyed him witnessing me in all my glory. I'd never forget the way he'd said "Congratulations, Desi" with that little-boy smile of his... it was like he really saw me and believed me to be special. Sometimes I wasn't so sure Lenny did.

The Communion prayer drew me back to the present. "This is the Lamb of God, who takes away the sins of the world. Happy are those who are called to his supper."

Ashamed of my distraction, I passionately recited the response, "Lord, I am not worthy to receive you, but only say the word and I shall be healed." Perhaps a little too passionately, because several heads pivoted in my direction. Unabashed, the prayer reminded me that the only one I needed to impress was God, and for the rest of Mass I resolved to temper my vanity.

During Communion I watched closely as Lenny clasped his hands in front of him and flowed along respectfully with the other worshipers. Adam included. I was relieved, as I had visions of an all-out brawl over the bread and wine.

Everything remained civil though, and I watched, fascinated, as Father Patrick placed a wafer on each person's tongue and blessed them with reverence. I observed the ceremony, unsure about my own place, or right, to Communion. The requirements here at Sacred Heart seemed stricter, especially if you weren't officially Catholic.

At the end of Mass, Lenny reached for my hand and led me out into the early morning sunshine.

"It was good today. I liked what Father Patrick said…"

Lenny nodded agreeably, while scanning the congregation for Adam.

"Do you want to come to Robin's church with me?" I asked, hoping to distract him.

After a moment he said yes. "I'd better. He might show up there too."

The air smelled like spring. Like change. It permeated the hallways at school, lit up the brightness in some of the senior class's eyes, and the fearful fade in others. The faculty and parents seemed to breathe a little easier, their responsibilities slipping away with each student measured for a cap and gown.

For me, change never meant anything good. In my experience, it always signaled disruption and trouble.

But right now, Robin was here, and Winston tracked us through the trailer, and all was well. We had the place to ourselves because Sunny and Pop were meeting us at school for graduation.

"Sunny wanted to show it to us after graduation," I confided to Robin. "But we could peek now. If you want."

"I want! Let's do it." We tentatively opened the door to Sunny's painting room, as if whatever we found there, whatever it revealed, was not only a symbol of our high school experience, but a foreboding of things to come.

"It's going to be awesome," Robin mumbled.

"Yeah," I agreed. "Sunny's been painting like a madwoman, so it would be finished by graduation." But I was nervous. If disappointing, would it be a bad omen for our future? Although Sunny insisted she'd been at her creative best lately, I worried that her artistic drive was a little manic and over the top. Ever since she started taking the diet pills, her emotions wavered between extremes.

Sort of like Robin, who was almost the same size as me now. She too seemed happier than ever, but there was an element there that bothered me. But then again, maybe I was just jealous because I was missing out on all their hyper-happiness. I had tried to take the pills, but because they made me feel jittery inside, I'd ended up dividing them between Sunny and Robin, who were more than happy to take them off my hands.

Robin and I tentatively approached the easel, noting the cloth covering. "We have to put the cloth over it exactly like she had it," Robin said. "Or she'll know."

We took a moment to memorize the details of the covering, and then Robin, unable to wait a second longer, yanked it off.

The background was a soft gray with scattered shades of midnight blue. The bonfire roared with vivid fiery colors, like burnt orange and maroon and yellowish red. The people around us, sitting next to us at the time, like Adam for instance, had been reduced to shaded blurs on the canvas. It was a skillful trick used to draw the eyes to Robin and me, the stars of the painting. Our faces were alight with joy, our smiles infectious. It was stunningly, impeccably drawn, and artistically shaded, but even more than that, the feeling it evoked brought us back to that night. To our happiness and enthusiasm as we were on the cusp of our high school experience.

"It's too perfect," Robin breathed. "We shouldn't be looking at it."

"I know. I feel bad now."

"Your mom is so talented, Desi. My gosh, it's a masterpiece. It's actual art."

I nodded, speechless. After a moment we carefully re-covered the painting.

"We better get dressed," I said in a quiet voice.

"Yeah, you're right." And then Robin asked with a grin, "Where's Sunny's vodka?"

Although Robin put twice as much vodka in her glass, I was the one feeling wobbly. "I can't make these pins stay." I giggled as I tried to make the graduation cap stay on my head. "There. Got it."

The second I removed my hands, the cap fell.

It was side-splittingly funny. "Here. Let me do it." Robin snickered as she gave it a try. "This is so fun. Why didn't we drink more vodka all these years?"

"Because we're squares."

"What? Speak for yourself. I'm a rectangle."

Robin's razor-sharp sense of humor sent me into another bout of hysterical laughter. And once again sent my cap spiraling to the floor. Winston, who'd been watching closely, snatched the cap and ran down the hall. "Oh no!" I gave chase. "Winston, stop!"

After Winston shrewdly parlayed my graduation cap for a

doggie treat, we breathlessly returned to my room. "Seriously, Lenny and Dean are going to be here to pick us up." I looked at my watch. "In five minutes."

"Crap!" Robin said, but she didn't seem alarmed. "Hey, I know what we can do." She pulled some diet pills from her purse. "Take these."

"No, I can't take those. They make me bouncy."

Robin popped the pills into her mouth. "Desi, seriously, with the vodka, they make you feel so good." She chased the pills down with the cocktail. "Do you realize tonight is the last night we'll ever have to see the Bouncy girls?"

We locked eyes and smushed our foreheads together affectionately. "I'll drink to that," I said. But I didn't take the pills.

Despite our imbibement, Robin and I managed to walk on stage and receive our diplomas.

After the ceremony, students and clusters of parents took photographs and huddled outside the auditorium. I was on my way to Sunny and Pop's circle, when Ricky pinched me on the arm and whispered like James Bond. "Party at Cicada Stadium in thirty minutes. Be there."

"Have you seen Lenny?" I asked.

"He's over there taking pictures with his grandparents," Ricky reported. "As soon as he can escape, he's headed your way."

I gave Ricky a thumbs-up, moving toward Sunny, where she and Pop were holding stage with a few other parents. "She's the apple of my eye," Pop said. "She adapted to this place and the school in no time. We're so proud of her."

I burrowed between him and Sunny, giving them both a hug.

"And on top of that," Pop bragged, "she's as pretty as a picture."

Heat rose on my cheeks as the other parents agreed.

"Thanks," I said to everyone. I went in for another hug, feeling happy tonight, the freedom of high school suddenly tangible. "We're going to a party," I whispered to Pop and Sunny.

"Well, that's to be expected," teased Sunny in a louder than usual voice. "It is graduation night, after all." When she gave me a big smooch, I couldn't help but wonder when she'd hit the vodka. "Have fun and be careful, kitten."

Lenny bounded over, a fresh look of freedom relaxing his features. He returned Sunny's wholehearted embrace, and shook Pop's hand. "Are you ready?" he asked me.

"Here's my advice, son," Pop told Lenny. "Don't do anything I wouldn't do."

The adults chuckled and then bid us goodbye. I gave Sunny another kiss, told her I loved her, and we took off.

Once we found Robin and Dean, we cheerfully piled into Lenny's Pontiac and nudged the volume up to high. "I think my parents were a little looped too." Lenny laughed. "Word is a whole bunch of them shared some bourbon in the Blue room."

"Cheers to our folks." Dean lifted an imaginary glass. "Now all they have to do is pay for college."

Robin rolled her eyes. "Oh, have mercy, no school talk tonight! Let's party!"

We rolled out of the parking lot, windows down, singing along with Kool and the Gang to "Celebration!"

When we arrived at Cicada Stadium, the party was in full swing. Loud, festive chatter soared to the treetops, and ice chests overflowing with beer lured the crowd. It was perfect. Except that Adam was already on stage, his guitar tuned, and his cowboy hat perched atop his head. There was no way Lenny could miss him.

Bubba and Daryl, beers in hand, ran over to us like it had been decades rather than minutes since they'd seen us. "Lenny! Desi! Whoa! We're out of prison! We're free!"

They handed us beers. Lenny took one and guzzled most of it in one gulp. His mood, only minutes ago celebratory, had become agitated. I passed on the beer, but Robin took one. She was in her happy place, humming and already moving to the beat of the music.

"Check out Claire over there by the trees," she told me. "I think she's puking."

"And there's Brad." Dean lowered his head in the direction of the ever surly Wolfheart. "Looks like he's passing out party favors. Good thing your Pop isn't here." Dean grinned at me.

When the song ended, Adam struck up another upbeat tune, and everyone cheered.

"Let's dance." Robin dragged Dean onto the dirt dance floor.

Lenny finished his beer and motioned to Ricky, who retrieved another one from the ice chest and tossed it over. "Nice catch, QB."

"You want to dance?" I brushed Lenny's hand, hoping a little oodling would settle his mood.

"No," he said firmly. "I want to drink."

Dolly apparently had the same goal, because she staggered over with a Solo cup in her hand, enveloping me in a hug. "Desi, you know… you know I've always loved you so much. You're so freaking fantastic."

I got a little buzzed just from smelling the whisky on her breath.

While Lenny raised his eyebrows, I tried to be nice. "So are you, Dolly. Cheering has been fun all these years."

"I know. I can't believe it's all over. I'm going to miss it. And you. I just love, love, love you." She hiccuped. "You've got… what do you call it, Lenny, when someone is… sophisticated? What's that word?"

"Class?"

"Yeah, that's it." Dolly thanked Lenny with a sweaty hug. "You've got class, Desi. That's definitely it."

It was then that the song ended, and Adam tapped on the microphone. My heart flipped because he stared straight at me. "Some of y'all might remember this little ditty I wrote when y'all were just baby freshmen. But now y'all might think of it differently since y'all are all grown up."

The tune, when the beat started thumping, filled me with panic. Adam casually strummed his guitar and softly crooned the "Dazzling Desi" song, all the while never taking his eyes off me. He was almost daring me to acknowledge him, only I was too busy eyeballing Lenny, whose face flushed redder by the second.

And then in a flash, Lenny threw his beer can on the ground and cursed. "That's it!"

"Lenny, stop!" I begged.

But he was already on stage. Within seconds the tune went awry and after one last offbeat squeak of the strings, Lenny ripped the guitar from Adam's hands. I watched in horror as Lenny raised it high above his head.

"Lenny! No!" I screamed.

But it was too late. Lenny smashed the guitar onto the ground with the kind of gusto usually reserved for spiking the football.

"Oh no."

Adam jumped up and threw a lopsided punch. Lenny easily ducked it, then connected with a vicious uppercut that brought a gush of blood across Adam's jawline. Some in the crowd starting hooting, picking a side, like at a boxing match. While others like Ricky, Bubba, and Daryl did their best to pry them apart.

"Long time coming," someone muttered through the mayhem.

Eventually, bruised and bleeding, Adam and Lenny were separated. It seemed everyone was just catching their breath when flashing blue and red lights appeared in the distance.

"Cops!" someone shouted.

Some ran off into the woods, and others made a mad dash for their cars. Amid the chaos I watched in horror as Lenny calmly walked over to Adam and threw one last punch, knocking him soundly to his knees.

Furious, I yanked Lenny's arm and shook him by the shoulders. "Stop it! You're acting like a fool! Stop it!"

"He had it coming, Desi. He's lucky I didn't kill him!"

"I don't even recognize you right now."

All at once we were swarmed by Dean and Robin, who hurriedly ushered us to the car. Dean slid behind the wheel of Lenny's Pontiac, and we sped out of the abandoned ballpark.

We stared numbly as others frantically piled into vehicles and peeled out at a frenzied pace.

On the way home, Robin and Dean remained silent as Lenny and I shouted at one another. I was beyond angry when Lenny refused to admit his part in the disaster. "I've had enough," I yelled.

"Just calm down, Desi," Lenny pleaded. "Try to understand. He was making a fool of me."

"I think you were doing a good job of that all on your own. I can't believe you let him goad you like that."

"I just couldn't take it anymore!"

"Neither can I!" I cried.

And just like that, it was over. The party. High school. And Lenny and me.

Mama and Pop were already asleep. I tried to swallow my sobs as I made my way to my room. Winston had waited for me, and his little tail wagged as he led me down the hall. He had no clue my life was over.

I put on my old raggedy nightgown, turned off my light, and slipped into bed, not bothering to brush my teeth. I wrapped myself tight like a mummy under the covers, and I cried and cried, heaving in misery, my face wet and swollen in agony.

Winston was licking my face, the only thing visible to lick, as the door creaked open. "Hey, sweetheart," Pop said in a quiet voice. "What in the world is the matter?"

"I just..." I cried, emotions pouring out in ragged, incoherent words. "Everything was so great at first... at the party... but then Adam was there, and he was singing that stupid song." I tried to catch my breath.

"Adam the cowboy?" Pop asked, kneeling beside my bed, propping his elbows on the covers. "Why was he there? Where was Lenny?"

"Lenny was there... but Adam showed up too. That was part

of the problem. It was so bad." I wept some more, unable to control myself.

Out of somewhere Pop pulled out a handkerchief and wiped my eyes. "Oh now, it can't be as bad as that. Don't you cry anymore now." Through the darkness I could see Winston's shadow as he lowered his head against his paws and settled down to sleep.

"It was that bad. Everybody was drinking. Lenny too. And he usually doesn't."

"It was graduation night," Pop consoled. "We figured there'd be a little of that."

"Where's Mama? Is she…?"

He nodded. "She passed out a few hours ago."

"I really wanted to talk to her tonight."

"I understand," he said. "Why don't you tell ole Pop about it."

"At first it was fun." I finally hiccupped. "But Adam started in with that song. You remember from the bonfire?"

"Oh." Pop chuckled. "That 'Desi, you make me dizzy' number? Yep, I remember." He continued to blot my eyes, but my tears kept flowing.

"Pop, you don't understand. Lenny went after him. Jumped on stage, and they started fighting. Like serious fighting."

"Oh boy."

"There was blood and hollering. And Lenny…" I sobbed. "Lenny busted Adam's guitar into a million pieces."

"He was angry, I guess. Guys get that way if they feel someone is trying to take their girl away." Pop wiped a tear as it dripped down my cheek onto my chin.

I just couldn't stop crying, but telling the story felt better, like I was less alone.

"It was so embarrassing though. I was so mad at Lenny." I crumbled as I remembered the rest. "And I might be in trouble because the cops were on the way. We could see their lights."

"Don't you worry about that. I know people. You won't get into any trouble. I'll make sure of that."

"Can you really? Everything just got so out of hand. And I

think… I think I broke up with Lenny." I let go with a fresh round of sobs.

Pop sighed, gently tugging the covers down so he could blot my tears as they streamed down my chin onto my neck and chest. "Desi, sweetheart, I know you don't believe this, but you'll be all right."

"I don't think so."

"Boys are like… well, think of them as pieces of pie." Pop's hand shook as he got a little emotional. Trying to help me calm down. Trying to make me understand. "There are lots of different delicious kinds of pies, right?"

I nodded, sniffling loudly.

"There's apple pie, blueberry pie, pecan pie, and you know you have to try all kinds of different slices of pie before you decide on which one you want for the rest of your life. Does that make sense?"

"I think so. But I like Lenny, and I don't know if I want any of the other slices." I broke down again, realizing I'd just broken up with my favorite slice of pie.

"No, no." Pop ran the now soggy handkerchief down my chest, over and over, blotting my tears. "Please don't cry, sweetheart," Pop said, shaking. "I'm right here." He was probably growing tired being on his knees.

The more I tried to get control of myself, the more I cried. Pop continued to wipe my tears, gently tugging the covers down, dabbing lower to wipe fresh tears.

He breathed heavier. Shook more.

Winston lifted his head. Something… something was wrong. My heart did a flip. No. I was being stupid. I tried hard to catch my breath, to calm down. But I couldn't move my arms because they were pinned under the covers.

"Thanks, Pop. I get it now." But he didn't move away. I added in a stronger voice, "About the pie."

But he still wasn't leaving. In fact, he seemed more upset, more worked up. I could barely make out his shadow, but I could see him moving the cloth along my chest. He tugged the covers lower and lower.

He probably didn't realize what he was doing. It was dark. Surely I was wrong. This couldn't be happening.

"It's okay, Pop. I think I'm okay now." But I couldn't turn away, couldn't move because I was a trapped mummy under the covers. All except the top where he'd moved the covers to wipe the tears.

And now... was that? No, it couldn't be.

I felt the handkerchief on my nipple. Pop was moving it back and forth like he was wiping tears. But I wasn't crying anymore!

"I just love you so much," he breathed.

"Okay." I tried to pull myself away, but his elbow remained on my nightgown. I couldn't move. "Thanks, Pop. I'm okay now."

"Like I said, you're the apple of my eye. You're my girl."

Whatever this was... I wanted it to end. It had to end!

"I love you. Do you love me?"

What should I do? Should I scream? Of course not, that would be silly. I was probably wrong and being stupid. It was dark, and he couldn't see, and this was probably all my imagination, and I was just being stupid, stupid, stupid.

Yes." I pulled away again. *Oh please, God, I'm sorry for being so stupid. Just please let it stop.*

He breathed hard then, and a ragged tremor went through him.

"Pop's gonna always take care of you. You know that?" Uneven breaths, one after the other, and then one final shudder.

Winston raised his doggy head beside me, let out the tiniest of sounds. Almost like a low growl.

Pop finally lifted his elbow off the covers.

I managed to free my arms then. Scooted away.

Finally, he moved the handkerchief somewhere I couldn't see, lower, more toward the floor. Fiddled with it a minute. And then, with an effort, he pushed himself up off the floor. His knees cracked.

"Good night, sweetheart." He sighed, and mercifully, left the room.

For a long time, I stared at Winston. I stroked him, focusing on his dark button eyes and his lolling tongue and nothing else. My mind was blank. I wanted it to be blank. Nothing. Nothing. Nothing was in my heart. And finally, the fluttering stopped.

I turned over then, and reached on my nightstand for the Bible Robin had given me. I held it tightly to my chest. Stared blankly at the reflection of the moon through the shades in my room. I wasn't sure how long. Thinking about nothing was hard work.

Eventually I fell asleep, listening to Winston's soft snores beside me.

I dreamed of guitars and handkerchiefs and slices of pie...

Chapter Eleven

Evil Trickery
Robin

Lenny was driving me crazy. Sure, his muscle was coming in handy as he loaded boxes into the back of the U-Haul rental trailer, but his incessant yakking and agonizing over Desi stretched my last nerve.

"Lenny!" I snapped, "put that box in the back. It's got breakables in it."

"I see it, Robin. Right here. It says *dishes*. I got it." Forlorn, he traipsed through the hot trailer and placed the box in its proper place. "You don't have to be so mean."

I sighed. "I just don't understand. Y'all are back together now. What's the problem?"

"I don't know. That's what I'm trying to find out from you."

"She's just tired, Lenny. She's got that new job at JCPenney's, and she's busy working long hours, and—"

"You're the one who's busy. I mean, have you really talked to her lately?"

"Of course I have. She practically spends the night here every night." I glanced over at Dean, who lugged another box from my house to the U-Haul. "What's that box say?"

Dean was tired and sweaty, but on a mission. He put the box in its proper section. "*Paper goods*. Goes in front."

Sometimes I found his practical traits adorable.

"But you know, Robin, our apartment isn't that big," Dean said. "And I'd like to bring a few things of my own. Things like—oh, I don't know—paper and pens and books?"

"Don't be ridiculous," Lenny quipped.

I shot them both a look, hushing Dean, "Don't say that so loud. Mama or Daddy might hear."

"Do you really think they don't know y'all are sharing a place?" Lenny asked.

"I think they have an idea, and I think they aren't pleased," I explained. "But why rub it in?"

Dean had received a full paid scholarship from Northwestern University in Natchitoches, which covered his tuition and most of his housing expenses. Things that wouldn't be covered, like food, gas, and day-to-day expenses, would be coming out of our own pockets.

Dean, because he was so brilliant, had found a decent-paying intern job in the Business Department. I, because of Mama's library connections, had snagged one of the coveted on-campus jobs at the university library.

Mama had managed to get a glowing letter of reference for me from the director of the State Library Association. The job only paid minimum wage, but it would likely be enough to cover the additional cost of a two-bedroom apartment on campus.

Our parents had reluctantly agreed to let us "room" together until we got settled in Natchitoches. Mostly because it was economical. But also because Dean had made it clear that as soon as he could provide properly for me, he planned to marry me. To prove it, he'd bought me a promise ring, with a ridiculously tiny diamond. Once his career took off, he vowed, he'd replace it with one that could cut glass.

Whatever that meant. None of this I cared about. I was just thrilled to be getting out of Shady Gully, Louisiana. Except, of course, the part about leaving Desi.

"Did you know Mitch and Dolly are getting married?" Lenny asked, straightening boxes. "I just don't see that."

"Oh, I do," I said. "They're both good looking and shallow and absolutely perfect for each other."

"But it's not like that with me and Desi. I really love her."

"You better get a grip on your obsession with Adam then. Everybody is still talking about the throwdown at Cicada Stadium. Jesse and James supposedly used it as a bad example in their Sunday school class."

"What?" Lenny was annoyed. "Those two are worse than Dolly."

Dean agreed. "That family covets their morally superior image."

"Yeah." Lenny nodded. "Anyway, Mitch and Dolly are building this house on Piney Lake. They're subcontracting it themselves. Desi saw the plans and said it's gonna be nice."

"They're building a house here?" I asked, "What happened to law school?"

Lenny shrugged. "Beats me."

I popped the trailer's side. "Is that everything? Are we ready?"

Dean looked at his watch. "We're ahead of schedule. We'll have just enough time to unload in Natchitoches and—"

"We need to be back by six, when Desi gets off," Lenny said.

Dean gave him a thumbs-up as we climbed into the cab of the big truck. Lenny behind the wheel, me in the middle, and Dean riding shotgun. I turned the volume up on the radio as soon as we hit the interstate.

"So," Lenny said, turning the volume down. "I know Desi isn't eighteen yet, but if I get that job offshore, I think I'm gonna ask her to marry me."

"What? Where are y'all going to live?" Dean asked.

"We'll find a place. If she says yes." Lenny glanced at me. "There's this old trailer on Coke's Landing. It's not much, but I checked it out, and we can get it pretty cheap. It would just be a starter place anyway."

"You better make sure of that," Dean said. "You don't want to put her in a situation like her mom. It's been how many years, and Mr. Tom still hasn't built that three-story mansion?"

"Yeah. That's not happening," Lenny said. "I feel sorry for Sunny."

I sat between them as they went back and forth about what Desi deserved and how Lenny would provide for her.

"You have to get her to marry you first," I said.

"Exactly," Lenny agreed. "That's where I need your help."

I groaned inwardly. This was going to be a long drive.

We made it back to Shady Gully in time to clean up and change clothes and head to the mall in Belle Maison, where Desi worked. At exactly six o'clock, Lenny headed into JCPenney's to retrieve her.

"That poor boy," I said to Dean. "He's gonna be devastated if Desi tells him no."

"She might."

"Why do you say that?"

"I don't know," Dean said. "It's Desi. Do you really see her settling down with someone around here?"

I didn't respond. Just watched thoughtfully as the glass doors of the department store opened and Lenny and Desi walked out, hand in hand. Desi wore a skirt and a silk blouse and black pumps. On the surface she seemed okay, smiling and laughing with Lenny, but there was more there. Lenny was right—she seemed off.

"She looks nice," Dean commented. When I looked at him, he added, "Happy, I mean."

Once in the backseat, Desi smiled, and just like Sunny, her presence seemed to make the air lighter. I was going to miss her. But I couldn't wrap my head around that right now. Couldn't dwell on it, or I'd chicken out altogether.

"How was the apartment?" she asked.

"Cool," I told her. "It's got a cute little yellow kitchen. I was thinking about accenting with light blue."

"Really? I saw some cute light-blue kitchen towels on sale in the Household Department today. We could get a good deal on them if we use my employee discount."

"That's perfect."

Dean and Lenny tuned out for a little while as we chatted about color schemes and vacuum cleaners. Finally, Dean said, "You realize, Desi, you're actually the first one of us to earn a paycheck. That's impressive."

"I agree," she said, "but that doesn't mean I'm treating tonight. And I'm starving."

We all laughed.

"I'm treating," Lenny said. "What's it gonna be?"

"Mexican," Desi said.

"Great," I said. "I can get a margarita."

We found a booth and ordered nachos. I used my fake ID, compliments of Brad Wolfheart, and ordered a giant margarita. I watched as they all plowed into the nachos. I had absolutely no desire for food. My food was the three-pill trifecta—thyroid, appetite suppressant, and diuretic. That chased down with my delicious lime and tequila concoction was all I needed. Or wanted.

I was utterly content. Except for the nagging worry I'd run out of my magical trifecta when I moved to Natchitoches. Although Desi didn't take diet pills herself, she promised to keep going to the doctor with Sunny to get them for me. She insisted it would give her an excuse to drive up and see me, but I felt guilty.

I knew she disapproved of me taking them. She said I had lost enough weight and didn't need them. It's true—I was down to one twenty, and finally had an inkling of what normal people experienced all the time.

Like looking into a mirror and not cringing in shame. Or pulling on your blue jeans without doing body contortions. How about the simple pleasure of being able to breathe in your clothes? And the joy of letting your boyfriend touch you wherever he wanted without angling yourself in a flattering way or sucking in your gut.

The pleasure of thinking about things other than weight, like blue kitchen towels for instance, was a freedom I'd never enjoyed. Quite simply, living without being consumed with self-hatred was a whole new world for me, and no way would I ever risk losing it.

"Earth to Robin," Desi said. "The waiter wants to know what you want to order."

"Oh, I'm fine just munching on these." I grabbed a chip. "Thanks." I nipped off a bit of the chip, then casually discarded it on my plate as the waiter moved on to take Lenny's order. I went back to sipping my margarita.

To say I felt superior wouldn't be true, but as I watched Desi, Lenny, and Dean devour hundreds, if not thousands of calories, I did feel I had an element of power over them.

That night, Mama had made up the cot beside my bed for Desi, and carefully hung her church clothes in my closet. Now that Desi spent the night almost every Saturday night, Mama's routine became as practiced as ours.

We'd moved to the big bathroom in the hallway and were washing off our makeup and brushing our teeth when Desi said, "I have the whole weekend off next weekend. Maybe I can go with you and help you decorate your new apartment?"

I spit out toothpaste. "Let's do it. Just us. I don't think Lenny and Dean understand the concept."

She nodded.

"You know, it's a two bedroom, and you can come anytime. It's not like I'm gonna be using that extra room."

She looked at me, only a little shocked. "I figured. The way y'all were making out tonight."

"Us?" I made big eyes. "What about y'all?"

We chuckled, towel dried our faces, and gathered our makeup bags. When we opened the door, Desi and I both squealed as a big gray snake jumped out at us. Turns out it was a rubber snake launched by the youngest miscreant, Max.

"Brat!" I threw a wet washcloth down the hall at him. "He's so annoying."

Desi laughed. "I wish I had a brother. Or a sibling."

"You have me." I smiled at her as we went into my bedroom and locked my door.

"Thank God for that."

I lowered the setting on my lamp as we crawled into our respective beds. I was just gearing myself up to approach the Lenny thing, when she said, "Robin, I need to tell you something."

"What?"

"I just want to start off by saying I wouldn't be where I am now if not for you. And your whole family really."

I waited, unsure where this was going.

"I know that Sunny believes in God, because she quotes the Bible all the time and gives me good advice and uses the Bible to make her point. I think she's tried, and Daddy too, but I never..." Desi wiped a tear.

"Desi, what's wrong?" I sat up, brightening my lamp.

"No, don't do that."

I dimmed my light again.

"I was never exposed to church as a kid. That's why I didn't even know the Lord's Prayer, which I'm ashamed of—"

"That wasn't your fault."

"And I'll never forget how you came to my rescue that day. Or how you and your family welcomed me to your church, and I'm... I'm just really grateful."

"You know Mabel wouldn't have it any other way." I chuckled in the dark.

"Robin, tomorrow, at church, I want to be baptized. I want to be cleansed."

I hesitated, searching for the right words.

"I've come to know Jesus, and I believe he's my Lord and savior, and I want to proclaim it publicly. With you and your family. Tomorrow."

"Desi, that's wonderful. I'm so happy for you. Should we call Sunny and Mr. Tom so they can come?"

"No."

"But it's a big day and—"

"No, I'll share it with them in my own time. I just want to do it tomorrow. With you. And it has to be tomorrow because… because next Sunday you won't be here." She started to cry. "You'll be in Natchitoches starting your new life."

I jumped out of bed and joined her on the cot. Held her close as she cried.

"I don't know how I'm going to survive without you, Robin."

"You will," I said firmly. "You're way stronger than me. You always have been." We rubbed our foreheads together like we had so many times before, and I wiped a tear of my own. "I'm scared to death to move to north Louisiana," I confided. "With Dean. Away from you and my parents and even the brats. Sometimes I can't believe I'm even doing it. I mean, who do I think I am?"

"You're brave, and you're going to do great," she said. "You have to go, Robin. Even though I'm going to be lost. The one thing I know for sure is that this is something you have to do. It's the right move and the right time."

"Yes," I said. "I like your conviction, but I'm not so sure." I crawled under the covers with her, resting my head on the pillow. "It's not that far. I want you to come visit a lot."

"I will. Whenever I get can get off work."

"Desi, you know there is a JCPenney's in Natchitoches. You could move there with me. Wouldn't that be awesome?"

As she mulled it over, I felt a stab of guilt for poor Lenny and his dreams of the old trailer at a pretty good price on Coke's Landing.

"Unless," I begrudgingly said, "you want to marry Lenny."

"What?"

I could see the curve of her smile in the dark. "That boy has got it bad for you. He's ready to sweep you off your feet and take you away from your mama and Mr. Tom." I chuckled.

I wasn't sure, but I thought I felt a tremor run through her. I held her close and pulled the blanket over us. "But it's your life, and you can do whatever you want, so don't let the poor little lovesick lad pressure you."

"I won't." And then, "Have you been baptized? I'm kind of nervous. I wish we could do it together."

"Yep, I was baptized when I was in sixth grade. It's nothing to be afraid of. It's a good thing."

Mama got teary eyed the next morning when I told her Desi wanted to be baptized. She stuck close to her like a mother hen, helping her get dressed, praying over her, and even giving the miscreants the eye if they got too close with their evil trickery.

Desi was rather emphatic about not calling Sunny and Mr. Tom, so Mama dropped it, even though it went against her grain. On the way into church, she whispered in Brother Wyatt's ear. He cut his eyes toward Desi and signaled her over.

I watched as he bent low to talk to her. She nodded. For some reason I found myself holding my breath. Didn't release it until she smiled.

I didn't remember there being such a fuss when I got baptized, so all the twittering made me nervous.

Desi bounded over. "What about my clothes? Are they going to get wet?"

I squeezed her affectionately. "Are you kidding? Mabel is always prepared for baptisms. She keeps extra shorts and T-shirts in her car."

Desi grinned, and oddly enough, as soon as the service started, she visibly relaxed. She sang the hymns without looking at the hymnal. She flipped her Bible to the right section at all the readings. And when the time came, as the choir sang after the sermon, she lightly brushed my hand. "I have to go now."

I bent my forehead to hers, moved by her transformation over the years. The girl that couldn't recite the Lord's Prayer now rose and slipped away with a look of determination and peace.

I, however, twitched anxiously. As the hymn ended, Brother Wyatt returned to the podium and gazed upon the congregation. "I hope you all don't mind staying a few extra minutes today so we can celebrate a baptism."

"Amen!" someone shouted, and others echoed in response. A round of impromptu clapping erupted.

I felt more than I saw Dolly turn all the way around in her seat, curiously eyeing the empty space beside me. Brother Wyatt cleared his throat. "Many of you know Sister Desi, who came to our humble church here in Shady Gully a few years ago. We're blessed that she was called by the Lord to learn more, to deepen her relationship with Jesus."

The lights clicked on over the baptismal pool to the left of the church. Desi, with Jesse on one end and James on the other, padded into the water. All three wore shorts, baggy T-shirts, and no shoes.

My first thought was annoyance with Brother Wyatt for appointing his sanctimonious sons to do the honors. While I tried my hardest to swallow my very un-Christian thought, I couldn't help but notice that Mama's expression tightened as well. Desi looked unfazed though, obviously caught up in the significance of the moment. Even the outlaws on either side of her appeared solemn and respectful.

"From 1 Peter 3, verse 21." Brother Wyatt quoted, "'And this water symbolizes baptism that now saves you also—not the removal of the dirt from the body but the pledge of a clear conscience toward God. It saves you by the resurrection of Jesus Christ.'"

All heads turned toward the baptismal pool. I noticed that even Mitch, who had been half asleep next to Dolly, suddenly sat up with interest. I also saw Dean sitting with his parents, leaning forward, his hands clasped prayerfully.

Jesse said to Desi in a shaky voice, "Based upon your profession of faith in the Lord Jesus Christ, I now baptize you in the name of the Father and the Son and the Holy Ghost."

Just like that, they gently laid her into the water. When I saw her face again, her hair was wet, and her radiant smile ignited the room. She raised her fists in the air, full of joy, and the congregation cheered.

Afterward there were chicken salad sandwiches and strawberry cake in the church hall. Just like Mama, the elder ladies were always ready for a spur-of-the-moment baptism. Desi was prayed over, hugged on, and flooded with well-wishes.

Lenny had come straight from Mass, and while some of the hard-liners gave him the eye, most everyone was too blissful to discriminate.

Jesse walked over to me, Bible in hand. "It's a blessed day, isn't it, Robin?"

At the sound of his pious tone, I jabbed my fingers into my eyes to keep them from rolling. "Blessed indeed, Brother Jesse."

Taken aback by my irreverent sarcasm, Jesse stumbled. While I enjoyed watching him flounder, I admired his counter. "I hear you and Dean are off to Northwestern this week." He gave me a long, judgmental look.

I bobbed my head up and down. "Yep, we are."

Naturally, we both turned and searched the room for Dean. We spotted him as he stood next to Desi, smiling, his head bent low with interest.

"Well," he said wryly. "I'll be sure and pray for you."

Just as he meandered away, Desi bounded over and wrapped me in a big embrace. "Thank you, Robin. I love this church. I'm so happy."

"Me too," I told her. "Do you want to hang out this afternoon? Eat some more chicken salad?"

"No. My head is clear now." When I looked at her curiously, she added, "I know what I have to do."

"What?" I asked, unsure.

"I'm going to talk to Sunny."

Chapter Twelve

The Sunshine In Sunny
Desi

Athick layer of smoke greeted me as soon as I walked into the trailer. I found Sunny not in her painting room but sitting Indian-style on her bed. Chain smoking.

Tom wasn't around, so that meant I had her to myself. Which was what I wanted. But I was prepared either way. Winston ran over to me, his stubby tail wagging ninety to nothing. I picked him up, gave him a hug. Felt a little sad that he reeked of cigarette smoke.

"Hey, Mama." I set Winston down and opened a window.

"Kitten, where've you been all day?"

"I went to church with Robin."

"I know. I just figured you'd come home earlier since you spent the night last night."

"Yeah, well. Something special happened at church today."

"Oh?" Sunny raised one eyebrow. "Do tell." Her "oh how scandalous" look fell flat, which also made me sad.

Instead of sitting at the foot of the bed like I usually did, I sat in a chair against the window. Sunny looked at me oddly.

"It's the smoke," I explained. "It's a little intense."

She groaned, irritated. "Oh, not you too. I'm so sick of everyone picking on me. If I want to kill myself smoking, I will." Her defensiveness set me on edge. "What happened at church?"

I took a deep breath and summoned up some of the resolve I'd felt earlier. "I got baptized."

Sunny's expression froze in a combination of hurt and shock. She remained silent, obviously buying some processing time. "Well…"

"I've been thinking about it for a while now. And I wanted to do it before Robin left."

Sunny just nodded. It bugged me that she wasn't saying anything. "Mama," I prompted. "What? Do you have a problem with it?"

"No, of course not." She lit another cigarette, even though there was one already lit in the ashtray. "I'm happy for you. I think it's good. I guess I failed you in that department. Among many others."

"That's not true," I told her. And I meant it.

When she realized she had two lit cigarettes in the ashtray, she angrily smashed the shortest one into smithereens. I couldn't help but notice the bags under her eyes and her dull, thinning hair. My Sunny looked worn down lately, and despite all the trips to the diet doctor, she was thicker around the middle than I'd ever seen her. I could tell she wasn't happy.

And I was about to make it worse.

"I guess Mabel and Lenny and all your loved ones were there. A shame I didn't get an invite." She took a long drag on the Kool menthol and made a big show of blowing smoke in the opposite direction from me.

"It was kind of spur of the moment," I mumbled. Feeling guilty. And sad. And angry. All of that jumbled together in a toxic knot in my stomach. "Mama, there's something else. And I don't really know how to tell you this. I'm sorry."

Sunny looked at me with resignation. As if she expected nothing but bad news from me today. "Just tell me."

I inhaled, sent up a silent prayer. "Something happened with Tom, something—"

She scrunched up her face in annoyance. "And what is with this 'Tom' lately? What happened to Pop? What the heck is going on with you, Desi?"

"It was the night you were passed out after graduation." I plowed ahead, determined now more than ever. "He came into my room and he did something. To me."

"Oh, for heaven's sake. What are you saying?" She was furious. Her hand was shaking. And to my absolute horror, her fury was directed at me.

But again, I forged ahead, steadfast. "We were talking about Lenny. It was the night we broke up—"

"Desi, I know all about that. Tom told me. He said you were hysterical, and he talked you through it until you calmed down."

"What?" I felt my face go hot. "That's not what happened, Mama! He's lying to you!" I stood up, erupting with frustration. "He started out being nice, acting interested in why we broke up, and then he—"

"He what, Desi?" She uncrossed her legs and angled herself to face me. "And be very careful here. What you say now you won't be able to take back." Her whole body trembled with emotion. For a second I was afraid she was going to have a stroke or something.

And then a wave of understanding swept through me, and I calmly settled back into the chair. I knew what this was, and I knew what she wanted from me. But I couldn't.

"I'm sorry, Mama. I can't pretend it didn't happen. And I can't let you pretend either. It happened. He—"

"What exactly happened, Désirée? What are you telling me? That you and Tom had sex?"

"No! Heck no. I would never—"

"Well, what then?"

I had to look away from her. I couldn't bear the pain in her face. And suddenly I doubted myself. I doubted it all. I was flooded with the confusion of that night. What if I was wrong? What if I was just being stupid? Did I really need to ruin her marriage?

Sunny seized on my flash of weakness then and threw it right back at me. "You've always been more than happy to oodle him if it meant getting something you wanted. Whether it was a dog, a bonfire, or a new outfit." She sucked impatiently on her cigarette. "You are partly to blame for whatever... whatever you think... happened."

I searched her face. Begged God to show me a hint of the colorful, joyous Sunny of days past. But it was all gone. My beloved, shiny Sunny had been snuffed out, extinguished.

I took a deep breath, fully committed now. "I don't *think* anything happened. I *know* it did. At first, I thought it was a mistake. Because it was dark. But it wasn't. He touched me. He played with my breast, Mama."

"And you let him? How could you let him?" I watched as she stood up, unsteady on her feet, and stormed into the bathroom. Slammed the door.

I sat stoically in the chair for a few minutes. Listened to her cry.

What a disaster. I'd been so horribly wrong. I'd imagined that putting the deed out in the open would be like my baptism, that it would cleanse me and give me the chance to start fresh. But this... this wasn't that. This felt even worse than it had the night Tom came into my room.

Nothing had been gained by telling her. I'd only broken her heart, and now she'd broken mine. I squeezed my eyes shut as I felt the sting of her accusations. Of her blame.

I looked down at Winston, who maintained his post at the closed bathroom door. "Come on, boy." He followed me into the kitchen and watched as I packed up his bowls and food. Next I went into my room and packed clothes, toiletries, and my Bible. I stopped only to call Lenny.

When I heard the crunch of tires on gravel, I was horrified to see not Lenny, but Tom's truck rumble down the driveway. I didn't feel brave anymore. Nor did I feel Jesus anywhere in my heart or in my head or in this trailer. It was just me and the remnants of my once wonderful mama... and the very man who'd uprooted us and smothered the sunshine in Sunny.

I heard him come in, followed by a cacophony of crying and shouting. I stayed in my room until finally I saw Lenny's old

Pontiac roll down the driveway. I loved Lenny in that moment more than I ever had before. I motioned for Winston to follow, and we made our way down the hall.

I stopped as I passed the painting room. My resolve dipped when I took in the sight of all the colors and memories on canvas. All the laughter and hope that had once blossomed inside this space seemed as dingy now as the walls yellowed with smoke. I swallowed my tears, took the painting I'd come for, and shut the door behind me.

Lenny was in the living room, looking like a cat in a room full of rocking chairs. "Take Winston to the car," I told him, anxious to get him out before the crying and shouting from the bedroom revealed too much.

"But are you gonna be okay?"

"Yes." I handed him Winston's leash. "Just go." Lenny wasn't a part of this drama. Maybe someday he would be, but right now he knew nothing except that I was coming with him. I knew instinctively that it would be enough. "Please go."

And he did.

Mama was sitting on the bed again, her face ravaged with grief. Tom was pacing. When I walked in, I held up the painting of Robin and me from the bonfire. "Can I take this with me?"

"Where the hell are you going?" Tom ranted. "I suspect off with that boy?"

I didn't answer him. Nor did I look away.

"Your Mama told me about your ridiculous claims. You need to tell her that you're wrong. That you misunderstood."

I said nothing. Then watched as the last ounce of hope drained from Mama's face.

"I don't know what your agenda is, young lady," Tom sniped, "but I just have one question for you. Is breaking your mama's heart worth it?"

I glared at him. "That's on you."

"Get out," Sunny said.

Tom and I both looked at her, unsure whom she meant. When

she raised her chin toward Tom, I felt the smallest of victories. "Just leave us for a minute," she told him.

Tom stormed out of the room. I waited then. For her to say something. Do something. I needed direction from the person I loved most in the world. *Please, God, let her still love me.*

"I don't really know much about the Bible," she said, gazing miserably out the window. "Just the high points, I guess. Like you, I never had anyone to teach me or push me to learn. But I'm glad you were baptized today, Desi."

She spoke without anger. Her tone now was one of defeat. "It heartens me to know that... whatever happens to me, you'll always be loved. You've found someone who loves you even more than I do."

"Mama, Lenny and I—"

"I don't mean Lenny, Desi. I mean Jesus. His love is perfect. Not flawed like mine. I'm sorry." She shook her head with regret. "It's horrible to think that a whole lifetime of love has brought us to this..."

I really didn't know what she wanted me to say. I didn't understand. Was she saying she didn't love me anymore?

When she got up and hugged me, I clung to her, never wanting to let her go. But she pulled away from me. "You go with Lenny for a while." She led me to the door. "Give me some time to work through this."

I wanted to fight for her. "I've got a job now, Mama. We can go somewhere—"

"Desi." She breathed heavily, dropping her head with a sigh. When her eyes landed on the painting in my hands, she smiled. "And of course you can have that. I want you to have them all."

PART III

Chapter Thirteen

An Expensive Barolo After All
Robin

Everything was bigger in Texas. At least that's what people said with a slow drawl, followed by a knowing wink. I, for one, was definitely on the bandwagon.

Dean pressed a button on the dashboard of our Mercedes, and the moon roof opened to reveal a cluster of stars in the dark-blue sky. Was it my imagination, or were the stars even bigger and brighter here?

After only a couple years at Northwestern University in Louisiana, Dean switched gears and allowed himself to be lured to the business school at Trinity University in San Antonio. He graduated with flying colors and got his master's in finance at the University of Texas, in Dallas.

In between all that studying, he managed to take time off to marry me, and even, as shocking as it was, took a whole week for a honeymoon in Los Cabos, Mexico. After that it was back to the books, and my husband the Brainiac focused on taking Dallas by storm.

We lived in a high-rise apartment in the city for a few years. A beautiful place with floor-to-ceiling glass windows overlooking downtown Dallas. Not a stitch of yellow or a light-blue accent to be found.

Just when I thought it couldn't get any better, Dean was hired as the CFO at a giant pharmaceutical company based in Dallas. And at that point, another upgrade was in order.

Dean pulled the Mercedes up to the stunningly landscaped entrance to our subdivision. Butch, the security guard, waved us through with a tip of his hat. I let my head fall back on the leather seat, squinted up at the stars, deliriously happy with my life.

"It's gorgeous tonight." I brushed my hand lightly against Dean's thigh.

He grunted his agreement, apparently still distracted by one of the highly important conversations he'd had at dinner with one of the highly important executives he'd schmoozed. Silly me, thinking I could get his attention with a trivial thing like stars.

And finally, after a short tour glittered with massive homes and twinkling state-of-the-art landscape lights, we pulled into the long, curvy driveway that led to our humble abode.

To say it had curb appeal would be an understatement. While modest in comparison to some of the other homes in the subdivision, it had all the bells and whistles, starting with the paved brick driveway. Water trickled from the fountain in the landscape as we drove up.

"I love that sound," I mumbled, still feeling the effects of the vintage wine the waiter had brought in from the restaurant's esteemed wine cellar.

Dean nodded.

Dark trim complemented light-colored bricks, sweeping up two stories, culminating in an elaborate pitched roof. "Home sweet home," I said as Dean pulled into the three-car garage and pressed the button to close the moon roof. "I sent a picture of our house to Desi," I tried again.

"Good," Dean said. "You should get her to come visit soon."

I smiled as I followed him through the garage. "She'd have to bring the two kids. She doesn't go anywhere without them."

"That's usually the way it works." He entered the code on the security system. "Did you tell me, or did I dream that she was pregnant again?"

"Yep. Another one on the way."

"Wow." Dean looked bemused as we entered the house. "Well, we definitely have room." The floor lights reflected off his shiny shoes as he padded across the designer ceramic tiles. "Gonna brush my teeth. Good night."

I sighed. Poured myself another glass of wine to take onto the veranda. I sipped the wine and watched the stars until I concluded that the stars were definitely brighter in Texas.

When my alarm went off the next morning, I woke up in a fog. My head pounded, and I wanted nothing more than to roll over and go back to sleep. Still, I told myself, I had a job to do. Dean wasn't the only one with responsibilities.

No one could accuse me of not doing my part in our quest for upward mobility and success. Being an executive's wife wasn't as easy as it looked. Today was book club day, and after I'd suffered through all five hundred pages of that literary slop, uh, masterpiece, I was determined to get my due.

Unfortunately, what I saw in the mirror wasn't boosting my confidence. My face was puffy, as was my belly. After I washed my face and peed a few more times—fluid weight was a real thing—I approached the scale with trepidation. Like always, my heart did a little flip as I stepped on.

"Oh crap!" I gasped. "What the heck?" How was it possible to gain two pounds in one day? I weighed 112.2, and I was especially insulted by that nasty .2. After all, I'd only eaten five bites of steak, and I'd made sure they were lean bites. Also, I'd made a point of cutting my baked potato in half and then picked at it through most of the meal. I had three bites, tops. I racked my brain, wondering what I'd done.

"The mushroom." My voice echoed in the marble bathroom. I remembered it now. I'd been chatting with the COO's date, an insipid blonde who happened to be twenty years his junior, and I'd popped the stuffed mushroom into my mouth without thinking.

And now I was paying the price. I tugged on my skirt, flush with panic when it bunched at the waist. Tucking in my blouse was another lesson in humility, as the image reflected in the full-length mirror was the classic picture of dowdy. No, this wouldn't do at all.

Makeup was no match for my puffy eyes, as my eye shadow looked horrendous. Tears welled up as I castigated myself. Why today? Of all days. The snotty book club ladies were going to see me as a little "patate"—or potato—as the Cajuns in Louisiana called little fat girls.

I'd starved all week to be at my peak weight for book club today. And then that stupid business dinner had ruined everything. Maybe I could lie and say I was sick? Not going at all was better than presenting myself negatively.

In the end, I put myself together as best I could, loaded my fat self into my Volvo, and drove to the mansion on Adams Path. I smiled pleasantly as I followed a few elder, junior-league types into the house.

While the house was incredible, the table setting was stunning. Silver coffee server, china coffee cups, and catered petit fours on crystal serving trays. As the book club rotated hosts monthly, I calculated the cost and envisioned the possibilities upon offering my own home.

I relaxed a little as several of the older ladies were friendly, and suitably impressed when I told them what my husband did. The younger gals, however—the ones my own age—sized me up and took a hard pass. They stuck together, never giving me an opening to approach.

They were all shiny blondes and brunettes, trim and decked out in Antonio Melani suits. I felt frumpy and lumpy in my skirt and blouse and regretted not calling in sick.

Eventually we were seated, and to my surprise one of the

designer-suited shiny blondes sat next to me. For a moment I delighted in the notion that maybe, just maybe, I could find a friend. I missed Desi so much, and I was lonely for a female comrade.

The aged, although quite distinguished, speaker settled down in a chair by the fireplace and chatted about the five-hundred-page book. Honestly, she was as boring as the book.

Shiny Blonde leaned into me and whispered, "I'm Cara."

I nodded in a friendly way. "I'm Robin. Nice to meet you."

"What do you do?" she asked.

I stuttered, totally unprepared for the blunt question. "I... well, I'm a housewife. My husband works at—"

But when she turned her attention back to the speaker, I knew I'd lost her. No way the old lady speaker was more interesting than me. Even if I was...

Nothing.

When I got home, I traded in my uncomfortable clothes for a pair of shorts and set out to walk laps around my neighborhood. Our subdivision was shaped like a giant football field. One jaunt around was supposedly a mile.

I dwelled on book club for half a mile, deciding that Shiny Blonde Cara was as bad as a Bouncy girl. The whole exchange reminded me of school, pre-Desi anyway. I wondered what Cara "did" and why she'd decided I wasn't worth the effort.

I started to imagine how impressed Cara would be when it was my turn to host. Maybe she'd regret her pettiness. I walked faster and faster as I mentally worked out what I'd need to cater and serve the book club in dazzling fashion.

As I approached mile two, I felt better. Way better.

And then I passed a house that was about the size of ours, sans the bells and whistles. I heard laughter and noted a small little girl tossing a pink ball to a woman my age. I assumed it was her mother.

The little girl waved at me. "I got a pink ball."

"I see that," I said, slowing down. "It's very pretty."

"Do you want to play with us? This is my mommy." The mother walked over, reaching for the child's hand so she wouldn't dash onto the road.

"I can't right now," I said. "But maybe another time."

The woman grinned. "I'm Nancy, and this is Cindy. We just moved in."

"I'm Robin. Nice to meet you both."

"Come on, Mommy. It's your turn. Come on."

Nancy shook her head, clearly exhausted. "She's a handful. I don't know how I'm going to handle another one." She patted her stomach, which looked as flat as a board to me.

"Oh… are you?" I asked.

"Yes, ten weeks. We're hoping for a boy this time."

I congratulated her and promised the little girl I'd come and play another time, even though I had no intention of doing such a thing. Nancy was pleasant, but we had nothing in common.

As I continued to walk, I realized I'd dismissed Nancy just as Cara had dismissed me. I pondered this as I walked another quarter mile. By the time I made it to my long, curvy driveway, I had another thought.

I gasped. Put my hands on my belly.

The clerk at the pharmacy shot me a judgmental look as she rang up the bottle of wine and the pregnancy test. She couldn't have been more than twenty. What did she know about life anyway?

I took my time driving home, careful to follow the speed limit and grateful for every red light—all while the Eagles belted out "Life in the Fast Lane." By the time I returned, and keyed in the security code, I'd convinced myself I was mistaken.

I ignored the test, left it in the plastic bag on the granite island bar. Instead I poured myself a glass of wine and brought it and my daily journal to the veranda. As I flipped pages, I found myself distracted by my blossoming weekly weight averages. I'd vacillated for a while between 110 and 111, but for the last few weeks I'd maintained a whopping 112.

Frustrated, I reached for my wine and held it to my lips. Held it there for another long moment. I sighed so loud the birds at the bird feeder flew off with an indignant swish. I set the wineglass down and went back to my journal.

Like clockwork, Dean and I had done our thing on the usual days. Only weekends, of course, because Dean was too stressed out during the week. I sighed again when I realized that my period was indeed a few weeks late.

"Crap," I mumbled. But I couldn't be... I was on the pill.

I picked up the wine, and once again held it to my lips. Thought about the diet pills I took every day. The trifecta of thinness. Fluid, thyroid, and appetite suppressant.

But what if I was... that couldn't be good for... whatever it was.

I thought about the bold, precocious little girl and her pink ball.

I closed my journal, carrying it and my wine inside. I thought about pouring the wine down the sink but didn't. It was an expensive Barolo, after all.

I set it on the counter and headed to the bathroom. I really had to pee.

Desi's phone rang and rang. I hung up, irritated. Where was she? What in the world could she be doing? I dialed her number again. Waited.

"Hello?" Finally, I heard Desi's voice on the other end of the line. Gruff and hurried.

"Where were you? What are you doing? I've been calling forever."

Desi chuckled. "Hey! I'm here. I just didn't hear the phone. Maybe I need a beeper like Lenny."

"Is he there?"

"No," Desi said. "Offshore for five more days." Lenny had

landed the offshore job he'd wanted years ago, and he and Desi had married quickly after. From what Desi said, Lenny had worked his way up the ladder and was paid very well. Still though, laboring on a rig drilling for oil in the Gulf of Mexico was dangerous work. Usually he worked seven days on and seven days off, and right now Desi sounded gloomy about the separation.

"What's up with you?" she asked in a chipper voice.

I took a deep breath. "Well, I need to tell you—"

"Luke, stop!" Desi shouted. "Don't you dare walk on that floor. I just—" The phone slammed down, followed by a muffled round of discipline. And then, "Sorry. I just mopped the floor, and he came in all muddy."

"How is he? And little Peter?"

"Oh, they're good. Petey is already twenty-one months now. Can you believe it? Anyway, what's up?"

I frowned. "Desi, why are you mopping floors? I thought you were supposed to be taking it easy. Are you still sick?"

Desi groaned. "Yeah, every morning. But thank goodness the sciatica has eased up a bit."

Sciatica? Good grief.

"Anyway," Desi went on, "I just have so much to do. We're growing out of this place, so I've got to clean and clear some stuff out."

"How about Merry Maids or something? I can arrange that for you. Tell me how I can help."

There was a longer than usual pause. "We're fine, Robin. We've decided to put the baby in our room, and Luke and Petey will room together. I just need to get it all organized."

I couldn't imagine. "When's the baby due?"

"I told you. A little over a month."

A husband, two kids, one on the way, and…

"How's Winston?"

I could almost feel her smiling across the phone line. "Good. I sent you a picture. His face and snout are white. He's an old man now."

"Wow," I mused. "So much has changed. All these things going on in your life. Lenny, the kids, now another baby. You've got to tell me things, Desi. I can't keep up."

I could hear her talking to Luke again. "Desi?"

"Yes, I'm here."

"Desi, I have some news." Maybe it was the way I said it.

"What is it? Did y'all find a church? I know y'all have been looking."

I could tell I had her full attention now. "No, not yet. We're still visiting," I could hear the tone in my voice change, grow more serious. "Desi, it's something else. I'm freaking out. I haven't even told Dean yet." Finally, her wheels were turning, and she was almost there. Four. Three. Two.

"Robin! Oh my gosh, you're pregnant!" One!

"The test said yes. But I don't really feel like it. Except that…" My voice broke. "Except that I'm getting fat. Desi, I can't get fat again. I just can't. What am I gonna do?"

Chapter Fourteen

Lair Of Luxury
Desi

Well, there went my brief window of serenity between cleaning the floors and Petey waking up from his nap. I'd spent the whole thirty minutes reassuring Robin while she melted down. The effort had been futile, as I'd expected, but I had to try.

And what was this bit about my not telling her things? I told her everything—most everything—but she just didn't listen. She was too consumed with counting calories and recording her weight and living her fancy life.

I picked up Petey and strapped him into the stroller while responding at the appropriate points throughout Luke's directives. "Mommy," he announced with authority. "Winston wants to come on our walk. He just said."

"Okay. Are you sure he's not too tired?"

"Nope," Luke confirmed. "I'm sure. I think he wants to run."

I looked at Winston, slow and arthritic, and highly doubted that. However, the ole boy was hopping around and turning in excited circles, so I consented. "Okay. Can you make sure he's a good boy?"

"Yep." Luke turned to Winston. "Let's go, Winston. To the mailbox. Follow me." Winston trotted behind our little caravan, oblivious to Luke's instructions.

I stopped to water the hydrangeas on the front porch. They were blooming and looking healthy, along with my gladiolas and daisies. I had worked hard to plant them in colorful tubs and situate them perfectly around the wicker furniture. Lenny had power washed the trailer before he'd left, and everything looked bright and inviting.

Thinking about how hard Lenny worked, both offshore and here at home, made me miss him even more. Our trailer might be little, and it was true we were outgrowing it, but Lenny always made sure everything was clean and in working order.

Merry Maids. That had been Robin's solution. A house cleaner. She had no clue, I thought, growing more and more exasperated. She worried about getting fat, while we worried about housing our family and paying bills. She had no idea what it was like to barely make ends meet and be isolated all the time.

As I led our little parade to the mailbox at a leisurely pace, I got lost in Petey's melodic string of baby babbling. His happy prattling made my heart swell, and soon my everyday worries faded away.

"Winnie… Winnie… Win…" he jabbered as he watched his big brother, Luke, keep old Winston on the straight and narrow.

"This way," Luke told Winston.

Already panting a little, Winston cocked his head as Luke told Petey, "Ya know, PeePee, soon you'll be in charge of Winston 'cause I'll be in school learning."

Petey giggled, nodding as if he understood.

When we got to the mailbox, Claire, who had foregone culinary school to be a postal carrier, had drawn a smiley face on green construction paper for the boys.

"You have a letter." I handed it to Luke, enjoying the wonder on his face as he marveled at the missive with great importance.

I reached for the stack of bills then, sighing as I flipped through the electric bill, the water bill, and the gas bill. But then there was a letter from Robin, *Photos, Do Not Bend,* it promised in her familiar scrawl.

As exasperated as I was with her, I couldn't help but smile. I missed her so much. I would give anything to have her with me right now. What fun it would be to share our pregnancies. Dishing over baby names and double baby showers.

I ripped into the envelope and pulled out several color photographs. "I wanna see! Let me see!" Luke grabbed my elbow, pulling me down to his level. Then Petey, feeling left out, started to whine.

I squatted on the ground and went through the photos with both of them. The first was a photo of Robin looking glamorous at some ritzy shindig. Dean stood beside her, looking reserved as usual.

"Oh, she's pretty, Mama," Luke said. "Is that your bird friend?"

"Yes. That's Aunt Robin," I muttered at the irony, noting Robin appeared extremely birdlike and frail. The pregnancy would be good for her. She'd have to get off those stupid pills, and once she had her baby, she'd be more consumed with motherhood than dieting.

The next photo featured elaborate landscape lighting framing a magnificent house against the night sky. "Oh, look PeePee," Luke said. "It's a castle. Mommy, see the castle."

"Yes." My goodness, how did she and Dean ever find each other in this sumptuous lair of luxury? I was stunned by the extravagance of Robin's home. There were a few pictures of the inside, and the last photo spotlighted a dove in a bird bath beside an elegant back porch. This must be the veranda Robin talked about from time to time.

"Oh, pretty birdie," Petey said.

"Yes, it is, isn't it?" I kissed his little head, then herded our posse back toward the trailer. I couldn't help but contrast the way I lived with the way Robin lived. Luxury versus necessity. Weight issues versus money issues.

I didn't fret too long, as a car barreling down the road caught my attention. Once I made sure Winston and the boys were safely next to me, I glanced at the driver, and knew my day was going to get worse.

Dolly sat behind the wheel, and after we traded friendly waves, she pulled the car to a stop along the country road. All the highlighting and dying had turned her hair brittle and straw-like, but the way she'd teased it into two little pigtails made her look like she was in high school again.

"They are so precious!" Dolly cooed over the boys with phony, over-the-top affection. "And shoot, you are so gorgeous, Desi. Everyone's been a little worried about you since weren't at church last Sunday."

"I'm feeling better. I've had some complications this time around." I patted my stomach, aware I'd gained a lot more weight with baby number three.

"Oh no, that's terrible. Is there anything I can do to help?"

Impulsively, I pulled out Robin's photos. Anything to divert her pity. "Look, I just got these from Robin." As she gawked at Robin's home, I enjoyed the look of shock and envy as it flashed across her face.

"Wow," she said. "Is that her house?"

I nodded emphatically. Suddenly my day was picking up a little.

"Nice." Dolly eventually tore herself from the photos and handed them back to me. "You know, we're probably gonna be putting ours up for sale soon."

I'd always found Dolly and Mitch's cozy white-siding house on top of the hill at Piney Lake enchanting. "Are y'all moving?" I asked.

Mitch had a job as the guidance counselor at Shady Gully High, which was kind of ironic considering what a conceited dope he'd been in high school. Nevertheless, it probably paid well, and certainly gave them options if they wanted to move.

"Yeah, I don't know. We're thinking about building again." She was being vague, which was typical of Dolly. "Anyway, if you know anyone who's in the market, send 'em my way."

"Okay."

"Or," Dolly said coyly as she turned toward her car. "Y'all could even look at it if you want. We're motivated to sell."

After she drove off, the boys chattered incessantly as Luke led us down the driveway. There was a spark to my step as I toyed with the idea of Dolly's beautiful house, of our kids growing up there. Up on that glorious hill with the pristine white siding and all those pine trees overlooking the lake.

Of course, I was being ridiculous, because there was no way we could afford it, even if they were "motivated to sell," an obvious dig at our financial status.

But still, Lenny and I often talked about the pros and cons of my going back to work after the baby was born. Another baby meant more expenses, and an extra salary would help. However, Lenny always pointed out, the cost of daycare negated the advantage.

It just wouldn't make sense, we'd always agree.

Unless, Lenny always responded, Sunny could take care of the kids.

And that was always the point the conversation ended.

Quiet was underrated, I thought as I rested my head on Lenny's chest. The sky was dark and heavy with clouds, and the curtains ruffled against the breeze passing through the opened window. My eyes drifted closed as I reveled in the pleasure of having the boys asleep and my husband home.

"It seemed like more than seven days this time," I whispered.

Lenny rolled toward me, placing his hand on my giant stomach. "Probably you were more anxious 'cause he's getting close."

"He?"

"Or she." I could hear the smile in Lenny's voice. "Be kinda nice to have a little princess in the mix. Pink shoes, baby dolls, Daddy's girl…"

"Temper tantrums. Pouty faces. Dramatic tears." I chuckled. "God, I hope it's a girl." We laughed together, shushing ourselves, afraid we'd wake the boys.

For a long moment there was nothing but the sound of our

breathing. Counting down the seconds to make sure the silence lasted. Finally, Lenny said, "It wouldn't hurt to take a look. At Dolly's house."

"I don't know." I propped myself on my elbow, squinting through the dark. "I sort of hate to deal with her. You can't trust half of what she says."

"That's being generous. I was gonna go with a quarter."

"Exactly."

"But again, it doesn't hurt to look."

"I don't know what kind of price equates to 'motivated to sell,' do you?"

"No clue. But I'll talk to Mitch tomorrow. Maybe we can run by in the afternoon. Maybe we can rule it out. But we'll never know if we don't look. You never know—you might hate the inside."

"I doubt it," I said wistfully. "Okay. Let's look. But if it's out of our range..." He'd closed his eyes, and I felt the need to put an exclamation on my point. "I'm serious, Lenny. I'm happy to go back to work, but I can't put the kids in daycare."

His chest rose in an exaggerated sigh. "I saw Sunny at Sprite's Quick Stop at the crossroads on my way home today. When I picked up your butter pecan ice cream?" He grinned. "I knew you'd be happy to see me, but I knew you'd be *really* happy to see me if I had butter pecan."

I shook my head. "What'd she say?"

"She was getting cigarettes. Asked after the boys. Said she misses them."

"She sees them," I said defensively. "She came at Christmas."

"Desi, it's coming up on Easter. She lives three miles from here. I don't understand what the falling out was about, but I wish you'd tell me."

I pulled the covers up tight. Closed my eyes.

"She looks bad, Desi. I'm serious." Lenny knew me well enough to know I was done with the discussion. Eventually he shut his eyes, and five seconds later he began to snore.

I opened my eyes in the dark, fixated on the fluttering curtains and the sound of the thundery breeze. Wondered what my Sunny was doing three miles away at this very moment. I turned over, angrily swiped at a tear. The wind was wild tonight. A storm was surely coming.

Mitch and Dolly welcomed us with open arms and chocolate chip cookies. They pulled us in, leaving the door wide open, and led us right to the island bar, where a plate of warm cookies waited.

"Here you go," Dolly offered, once again with the girly pigtails. "I bet you boys are hungry." We'd told the boys to be on their best behavior, but they eyed the cookies ravenously.

"Just one each." I gave them the eye. They looked past me to Lenny's looming presence, and I knew at once they'd behave. Dolly prattled on about the flooring and the windows and the molding, but I only heard bits and pieces of it. I was lost in the airiness and brightness of the house, utterly dazzled with the clean lines and the stainless-steel appliances.

I played it cool when I saw the state-of-the-art dishwasher and the fancy microwave, but Lenny saw my eyes widen. He picked up Petey and followed Mitch to the covered back patio.

"Come and see the master bedroom," Dolly said. I grabbed Luke's hand, and off we went, enjoying a glimmer into how the better half lived.

Not us though. Surely there was no way. I glanced through the huge plantation-shuttered window and caught a peek of Mitch and Lenny chatting on the patio. I tried to read Lenny's expression, but he had the world's best poker face.

"Mama, look!"

I turned as a dark-brown blur rushed into the house via the opened front door. "Doggie!" Luke squealed with delight. "Can I pet it, Mama? Please?"

"Dusty, come here, boy," Dolly hollered.

"Oh, is he yours?" I asked.

Dolly bent to pet the scruff of the German shepherd's neck. Apparently, it was. I had a moment of anxiety as Luke reached over to pet the dog, but it seemed friendly enough.

"Come and see the other bedrooms," Dolly said with a smile.

In a twisted way I wanted to find something wrong with the house. That way we could "rule it out," like Lenny said. Unfortunately, each room made me love it just a little more. In fact, I knew this house would forever be the baseline by which I judged others.

When we joined Lenny and Mitch on the porch, I let Luke run around in the fenced-in yard. Petey sat in the grass and clapped, for his brother, for the doggie, and probably even for the house. No poker face on that one.

Dolly gave Mitch a look, and almost on cue he said, "Why don't y'all take your time and look around. We have to run an errand—"

"Oh no, man, that's okay," Lenny said, making a move to leave.

"No, no. We insist," Dolly said. "Take your time getting to know the place."

I quickly rounded up the boys. "Oh, don't be silly. We're grateful you took the time to show it to us."

But they already had their keys and were walking to the garage.

Lenny frowned, "Should we lock up?"

"That would be great," Dolly said. "Bye, kiddos." I realized then that Dolly had no idea what my kids' names were, nor was she interested.

"Well," Lenny whispered when they left. "That was weird."

Nevertheless, it was nice to have the freedom to roam, to ooh and ahh over the amazing features of the place without seeming too eager.

"Let's live here," pronounced Luke. "It's cooler than our house."

"We'll see," Lenny said. He looked at the dog, puzzled, "Are we supposed to leave this guy in or out?"

I shrugged. We opted for out. Gave the boys one more cookie

before loading them into the car. When we got to the end of the driveway, we took a moment to linger, to gaze a bit longer at the house that seemed almost too good to be true.

I went into labor two weeks later, as the last of a ferocious string of storms passed through Shady Gully. Between the bad weather and the baby coming early, Lenny was in a state of panic. Once he dropped the boys off at his parents' house, he gave Ricky, his old wide receiver, a heads-up. Ricky was now a sheriff's deputy and was more than happy to light up his squad car and lead us to the hospital in Belle Maison. We made it in record time.

Despite the challenging pregnancy with the sciatica and the excess weight I'd gained, the baby came quickly, without much drama. This was a good sign, considering Lenny had finally got his little princess. She was a perfect little cherub, and we named her Micah, which meant "He who resembles God" in Hebrew.

She took to my breast quickly, and as I watched her nurse, with Lenny by my side, I was moved with tenderness for this little girl. Yes, I'd been overjoyed with my boys, but this, this delicate little slice of heaven, had seized my heart the minute I'd laid eyes on her.

Just when I drifted into an easy state of bliss, the door to my hospital room swung open, and my happiness jumped another notch. Robin and Dean stood there, like cherries on top of the most perfect cake. Robin's arms were overflowing with red and pink roses, which she immediately handed off to Lenny as she enveloped me and Micah in a giant embrace.

"She's so beautiful," Robin cried. "I love her already."

Looking at my best friend's face triggered so many sentiments, and soon I was crying too.

"And it begins," Lenny said, shaking Dean's hand. "The female bonding. Soon they'll morph into a superpower and take over the world."

Dean grinned. "Yeah. What a way to go, huh?"

"Yep," Lenny agreed, looking pleased.

Dean patted the baby's head. "She's perfect." He slid a chair over for Robin to sit and added, "Congratulations."

I smiled through tears. "And to y'all too."

Dean patted Robin's little baby bump affectionately. "It's heady stuff. Having twins."

"Twins? Are you serious?" I was astonished. Robin bent her forehead to mine, and we had a moment with little Micah right in the middle of us.

"I'm freaking out. I'm so scared," Robin said. "Can I hold her?" Robin gently took Micah into her arms, and she looked quite natural and maternal. "Oh my," she said suddenly. "Just think if I have girls. They could be besties like us."

While we were lost in our own world, Lenny pulled Dean aside, and the two chatted in earnest.

"I can't believe you're here," I told Robin. "I'm so happy. Seeing you hold my little girl like that… it makes me very emotional."

Robin brushed her fingers lightly through Micah's wispy scalp hair. "It's amazing how they just fit perfectly in your arms, isn't it? I'm getting so excited," she gushed. "But Lord, how am I going to handle two?"

Dean hovered, interrupting with a sweet kiss atop Robin's head. "Lenny and I are gonna go grab a cup of coffee. Want anything? A cinnamon roll? A biscuit?"

"I'm good," she answered, never taking her eyes off Micah.

"Are you sure?" Dean persisted. "You haven't eaten all day."

"I'm okay," she told him. "Y'all go ahead."

When they left, I gave her a firm look. "Robin, you can't be worrying about your weight now. You know that, don't you? No dieting—"

"I'm eating right," she insisted. "I promise. And no more diet pills. I've just had a time with nausea."

"I did too. In the mornings. But it gets better."

The door creaked, and we looked up expectantly, thinking

Dean or Lenny had forgotten something. It opened slowly, hesitantly. And then Robin gasped. "Oh!" She turned to me, the shock evident on her face. And then back to the door. "Sunny, come in. Come see your granddaughter."

"Well…" Sunny stammered, "I don't want to intrude." And then Mama saw Micah, and she faltered. "Did you say granddaughter?"

"Yes." Robin rose and carefully walked the baby over. "Isn't she beautiful?"

Lenny had told me Sunny looked bad, but I was hardly prepared for her striking deterioration. Her hair had thinned so much that even the colorful scarf she wore couldn't hide the bald patches. Her face was haggard, and her skin was pallid and ashen. She'd gone to some effort to apply makeup, but sadly her effort appeared drawn on and haphazard.

Robin, clearly uncomfortable, suggested, "Come sit down in my chair."

Sunny approached me with a hesitance that broke my heart. *Oh Sunny,* I thought sadly, *what has become of us?* "Mama," I said, opening my fingers.

She immediately clutched my hand. "A little girl…" She bent to brush her lips against my cheek with a kiss. "There's nothing better."

"Her name is Micah," I told her.

"I love it. It's different," Sunny said. "Like Désireé. I can already tell she's going to be unique. Special. Just like her mama."

"Here." Robin placed Micah into Sunny's arms.

My eyes flit nervously to Robin, and instinctively she understood. She hovered close then, her hands at the ready in case Sunny grew wobbly.

"She even looks like you, Desi," Mama said. "She's going to have a wonderful life."

"I remember when you told us that," Robin said. "It was the day you put makeup on me and told me about Napoleon's lover, Désireé."

"I remember that day like it was yesterday." Sunny's chuckle held a hint of her lively laugh from a long time ago. I had to look away from her. I couldn't bear seeing her like this.

"I heard Mr. Tom retired, is that right?" Robin asked, desperate to fill the awkwardness. "Is he enjoying it? Or is he driving you crazy?"

"Both, I suppose." Sunny focused on the baby, as if she were trying to memorize her features in case she never saw her again.

Guilt flooded me. Now I was the one feeling uncomfortable. "Guess who's expecting twins?" I prompted.

Sunny glanced at us both with raised eyebrows. Finally landed on Robin. "Twins?" Sunny swallowed, "That's wonderful. My girls. All grown up and having babies of their own."

Robin shrugged. "Well Desi is an old pro now. But I don't have a clue."

"Oh, you learn as you go," Sunny said. "You'll make mistakes here and there. Just hopefully... not big ones."

Micah suddenly let out a half-hearted wail—otherwise the silence would have been painful. Sunny handed her to me and we all watched, mesmerized as she instinctively latched on to my breast.

"You see there," Sunny said in a shaky voice. "A lot of times your babies figure things out for themselves."

Chapter Fifteen

Dim Those Lights
Robin

Dean had hired a housecleaner, a decorator, and a caterer for the party. He wanted this to be just another day for me. No stress, no fuss.

As if. Only a man would think it was that simple. I'd had to ask Nancy, the neighbor, if she and her precocious little girl with the pink ball would come and sit with the twins for a few hours. All so I could get my hair done, and attempt to find a semi-flattering outfit for Dean's little meet-and-greet.

My main priority, however, was assuring the babies were rested, fresh faced, and perfectly adorable for the guests. After all, they were the reason for the party. They were five months old now, and everyone couldn't wait to meet Sterling, who came first by a minute, and his little sister, Violet.

I'd been away from them now for exactly two hours and thirty-five minutes, and I felt the sharp pang of separation. I'd settled for a frumpy dress just to speed the shopping process up, and I'd let the hairdresser cut my hair short because it had been quicker.

Even with the sleepless nights and the spit up and the all-day crying marathons, the physical ache of being away from them was worse. Tick. Tock. I put my foot on the Volvo's gas pedal.

No one understood their needs like me. Not even Dean. How Violet had to be placed just so when she napped so she could keep Sterling in sight. How Sterling would cry when Violet did that trumpet-like whining melody, and how the trick was distracting her before she got to the last note… or you'd have a full-fledged symphony of bawling.

When I finally drove up our driveway, the caterers were unloading, and Dean had made it home with the liquor. The florist's van pulled in right behind me.

Dean set a box of vodka down and opened the car door for me. "Wow, your hair looks good." He gave me a perfunctory peck on the cheek.

"Have you seen the babies yet?"

"No. I was just on my way in."

When we walked in, Nancy was playing jacks with little Cindy on the kitchen floor, which meant the babies had been swaddled correctly and were still napping. Excellent.

Dean and I exchanged expressions of relief. As I followed his long, lanky frame down the hall, I felt a wave of apprehension for him. While he'd resisted the idea of a get-together for months, tensions with his boss had pushed him into setting a date. He hoped that by hosting a party he'd appear more engaged and mindful of office politics.

We inched the door open just enough to see that Sterling and Violet were snuggled together, nose to nose, still sound asleep. We still marveled at the differences in them. Violet was longer, and her hair was light like Dean's, while Sterling's was dark like mine. As we watched them for a minute, the anxiety and the physical ache I'd felt earlier tumbled away.

"See. They didn't even know you were gone," Dean whispered.

He was delighted with the babies. Even with the night feedings and the double diaper duty, Dean always seemed unflappable. Even now as a huge crash echoed through the house, Dean simply tiptoed out of the room. I, however, hurried over as Violet's mouth puckered, and trumpet sounds racked her little body. I swept her into my arms, but was too late, as she made it to the final note. Right on cue, Sterling revved up for his part in the sobbing duet.

The party was a huge success. Sterling and Violet were perfectly adorable in their matching outfits. Sterling's shirt said *Born First*, with an arrow pointed to his face, while Violet's said *Show Off*, with an arrow pointed toward her brother. They giggled and made cooing sounds and were passed around like baby dolls. Dean's boss, Ben, the CEO, insisted we open his gift before feeding them. Sure enough, he got kudos for his clever gift of bibs that read *Drinking Buddies*. I winked at his wife, Beverly, knowing fully well she'd been the clever one.

The weather was balmy, so folks armed themselves with glasses of rosé and gin and tonics. Several unattached younger women with long, bare legs lingered on the veranda. These young women made no effort to speak to me, apparently deeming me insignificant. After all, who had time for a dumpy mother of two wearing a frumpy dress when you had powerful, married men fawning over you and laughing uproariously at your every utterance?

Apparently, it seemed, Bouncy girls existed in all walks and stages of life.

Even Dean made a cheery show of topping off the lithe beauties' wineglasses. As his over-the-top attentiveness triggered my old feelings of inadequacy, I impulsively snatched a glass of chardonnay off a handsome waiter's tray. "Thanks," I regarded him with a smile. But he quickly moved on, no doubt in search of someone more relevant.

The wine burned my throat and warmed my stomach. I closed my eyes and savored it, my first drink since I'd found out I was pregnant over a year ago.

The COO's girlfriend, a bubbly blonde who was much younger than him, offered me a hug on her way out. "I don't know if you remember me, but I'm Maggie, Rich's girlfriend."

I vaguely remembered her and was honestly surprised they were still dating. "Of course, I remember you. How've you been?" "Just fine. Your home is lovely," she gushed. "And the babies were such angels. My goodness, you must feel so relieved."

"Thanks..." My expression must have reflected my puzzlement over the latter part of her comment.

"Oh, I just mean you've got a boy and a girl now, so you don't have to have any more. You're done!" She giggled, turning to search for Rich, who was a few steps behind her.

A big, congenial guy, Rich went on about how nice it was to see me. "And those kids, uh Sterling and Velvet...just beautiful."

Dean, ever the good host, patted Rich on the back and ushered him to the door. As our eyes met, we mutually agreed not to bother correcting Rich's name gaffe.

Eventually everyone cleared out, and we were left to ourselves. While the cleanup crew bustled around in the kitchen, we fed and bathed Sterling and Violet. They were as exhausted as we were, and once they fell asleep, we took a fresh bottle of rosé to the den.

"What'd you think of Ben?" Dean sprawled on the love seat, his long legs dangling over the side. He placed his glass of wine on the mahogany coffee table. "Too cool for school, huh?"

I laughed. "Does anybody even say that anymore? You're such a dork." I used the balls of my feet to nudge my rocking chair in motion. The rocker had turned into my favorite chair, where I rocked my babies when they were fussy and where I marveled at them as they fell asleep.

"Hey, I'll own up to my dorkiness. But that's beside the point." He raised his long arm into the air. "Tell me what you thought of the A team. And before you say anything, I loved that show, but in this instance, I'm referring to the administrative team."

I shook my head. "I liked his wife, Beverly."

"Yeah. I wonder what she sees in him."

"I wonder what Rich sees in Maggie. She's a little shallow and empty headed. And what was up with all those little floozies with the short skirts? They didn't seem like executive material to me."

"They work in administration. Assistants, like that. I had to invite them."

I sipped my wine, sniping in a low voice, "Yeah, I see you struggled through."

Dean rested his wrist on his forehead. "Not this again. You have nothing to be jealous of. I thought you were over all that."

I said nothing. Sipped again. "What's your problem with the CEO?"

"He's a figurehead. He's on various boards, and he attends charity dinners, but he's absolutely clueless about what goes on day to day." Dean sat up. "And he compensates for his insecurity by injecting himself into things he shouldn't, like trying to talk about finances at board meetings and getting things so mixed up that board members come to me afterward in a panic. I have to calm them down and explain to them that Ben is awesome, and he just got his facts wrong, and all is well. It's time consuming and frustrating, and the worst part is that the only reason he's doing it is to appear relevant. It's a joke."

"I'm sure they see through all that, Dean. Just ignore him."

"I can't just ignore him. Finance is my territory." Dean slumped back into the love seat. "You just don't get it."

Usually, venting made Dean feel better, but there was an extra hint of restlessness in him tonight. "I'm sorry," I told him.

"It just never changes. Everybody's a yes man, and the more they do that, the more puffed up Ben gets. It's a cycle. Nobody challenges him."

"I don't want you to be miserable."

"I'm not miserable. Especially when I'm with you and the munchkins. And the money is great. I'm just not sure this is where I need to be."

I flattened my heels to stop my rocker. "What do you mean?"

"I don't know. Come sit by me." Dean patted the love seat.

With raised eyebrows, I set my wine on the coffee table and settled next to him. He tugged me closer, so we were thigh to thigh. "There are other opportunities, you know? I get calls from headhunters at least three times a week."

"What's a headhunter? Like on *Gilligan's Island?*"

Dean laughed at my lame reference, and then grew serious. "Recruiters hired by companies and corporations to help them find the best candidates for executive positions. All over the country. The world even."

"I'm not moving to Saudi Arabia, Dean."

"What about to Denver? Or California? New York?"

I looked away from him. Not because I didn't find those places intriguing, but because I couldn't wrap my head around moving with five-month-old twins. "But I love our house. Don't you love it here?"

"Sure," Dean agreed. "But we wouldn't even consider moving unless it was a substantial increase in salary. And there are great houses everywhere. Even—"

"Even where?"

He picked up his glass and drained the pink wine. "What would you think about going back to Louisiana?"

"No. I mean, I don't know. Why? We said we didn't want to live there."

"Yeah, but that was when we were kids. Lately I've been thinking, with us loaning the money to Lenny and Desi to buy that house…" He shrugged. "Maybe it wouldn't be so terrible to go back home again. Think how cool it would be for our kids to grow up together."

"And what? Go to Shady Gully High? I thought we wanted more opportunities for our kids?"

Dean nodded. "I know. You're right. And realistically there aren't any CFO jobs in Shady Gully. It would be more like New Orleans or Baton Rouge."

"I don't know." This whole conversation had taken an unexpected turn, and my head was too fuzzy to process it all. Part of it sounded great, to be closer to Desi, for little Violet and Micah to grow up together. But part of it sounded like running back home because we couldn't cut it in the real world.

"It's just something to think about." When Dean pulled me closer, I let myself lean into him, determined not to say anymore until I understood it myself. "Have you talked to Desi lately?"

"A little," I said. "She's excited. Just busy getting their place cleaned and fixed up to sell."

"Yeah, that's what Lenny said. He's doing some roof work and replacing the AC. They've made it a cute place. It'll be a nice starter home for someone."

"Yep, it will." I took a long sip of rosé and set my glass down. "Desi's trying to set up a time with Dolly so she can get into the house and measure the windows because, get this, she's going to make curtains herself." I chuckled. "Can you believe Desi sews?"

Dean laughed. "Wouldn't surprise me. It's Desi."

Just then the housekeeper popped her head in. "All done. It's clean like you never had a party."

We went into the kitchen to thank her and her staff. While Dean wrote her a check, I was overcome with appreciation as I surveyed my big, beautiful, and squeaky-clean kitchen. What was Dean thinking? How could we move back to Shady Gully after living in a place like this?

We went around the house, turning off the big lights, and following the mini-lights built into the sides of the lower wall to our master bedroom. As we brushed our teeth, I felt relieved that our social obligation was done.

"Are you glad it's over?" I asked Dean.

"Over the moon." He kissed me lightly on the lips. "Now we don't have to have another party until our next set of twins."

"Ha! Very funny!" I splattered him with water from my toothbrush.

As we slid into bed and turned our lamps off, Dean asked, "Have you decided if you want to come to Shady Gully for the closing? There's talk of trying to get a half-baked reunion going."

"I don't know. I hate to leave the babies. We'll see."

"It's not for a couple of months still. Dolly and Mitch keep pushing the closing date back. I've got all the finances together, so I'm ready when they are."

I leaned in and pinched his flat belly. "Isn't it so great that we can help them? Make this house happen for them?"

"It is, but I think Lenny is struggling with the idea of us loaning them the money."

"But why?"

"I don't know. It's a man thing, I guess. A pride thing." Dean yawned. "I want him to be okay with it. I mean, it's easy for us to do. We're blessed, and it feels good to do it."

"It really does, doesn't it?" I rested my head on Dean's chest. "They shouldn't feel bad. I mean, it's still a loan. No interest, but a loan all the same."

"Yeah, but I was thinking…"

"What?" I squinted at him in the shadows.

"I'd like to maybe gift them the down payment. It would drop their monthly notes even more, and I'd just like to do it. What do you think?"

"Let's do it," I said, my voice thick with emotion.

"I'll get the attorney to figure it in, estimate their monthly notes for closing." Even in the dark, I could see Dean calculating figures. "I doubt Lenny's gonna examine the numbers that closely. Hopefully, he won't even notice and won't get offended."

I grinned and reached for him in the murky shadows, "Maybe I will go. Desi's gonna be so happy when she finally gets to walk in those doors. It will be fun."

A week later as I returned from a walk around the neighborhood, Desi called. I let her message go to the answering machine as I wrestled Violet out of the stroller. Sterling, who was always the first to get out, felt it necessary to assist, which made the whole process harder.

Violet kept pushing his hand away, which made him furious. This went on until he laughed at her antics. Then she giggled. I tried to free her from the buckle, but soon I was laughing as well, adding to their pandemonium.

Eventually we freed Violet from the stroller and settled into the living room with a handful of saltine crackers and vanilla wafers. Propped on the couch beside me, they held their sippy cups and babbled happily.

As I dialed Desi's number, I listened to them coo, watching as drool and crumbs pooled on their *Drinking Buddies* bibs.

"Hey," I said cheerfully when Desi answered.

"Hey," she said back, sans the cheeriness. "You won't believe this."

"What?"

"She won't let me in. She keeps saying she won't be home this day or she's having company that day, or this day isn't good because she needs a mental health day—"

"Dolly schedules mental health days?"

"I don't know. I made that up. But maybe she should. I just don't get it. Is she mad because we bought her house?"

"Okay." I spoke in a calm voice, partly because I didn't want to get the babies riled, but also because Desi was uncharacteristically frantic. "Slow down and tell me exactly what happened."

"I wanted to go and measure for the curtains. Remember I told you that?"

"Yep."

"And she keeps making excuses."

"I thought Dean told me y'all put something in the contract about that, right? About them allowing y'all to get in from time to time to measure for furniture or window treatments or whatever."

"We did. Just like Dean suggested. But it's pointless if it's never convenient for her."

"That's not right," I reasoned. "Before they were so casual about y'all staying as long as you wanted and even encouraged you to stay without them there."

"Right. Before we signed the contract. Now it's a different story. I'm telling you, I think she's mad because she has to move now."

I grew angry just thinking about it. Poor Desi.

"Lenny is furious. They're doing the same thing to him. He wanted to bring a plumber over Wednesday afternoon—it took him forever to line one up—and Dolly said they could come, but only for five minutes because she had to go somewhere."

"What's wrong with the plumbing?"

"Nothing. Lenny just wanted to see if down the road we might be able to install a garbage disposal. He wanted the plumber to see how involved it would be, how much it would cost us. Anyway, Lenny told Dolly it might take a little longer than five minutes, but he'd be happy to lock up when they left. Do you know what she said?"

"I'm almost afraid to hear."

"She told Lenny no, because she didn't feel comfortable with laborers in her house when she wasn't there. I kid you not—that's exactly what she said."

"Oh my. What is going on with her? That's just mean."

A beat passed as Desi sighed hopelessly. "I guess we should have known. Done our due diligence. Remembered who we were dealing with."

Sterling had settled down, and lazily rested his head on the propped pillow while Violet nibbled on his toes. They both watched me closely. When I grinned at them, their expressions flooded with assurance.

"I'm so angry," Desi went on. "And hurt, honestly. I'm to the point I won't humiliate myself anymore by asking. We'll just wait until closing."

"That's not fair."

"No, it's not."

"Doesn't closing have to be in so many days or the contract is null and void? Or something like that?"

"Yeah. It's set for two and a half months from now."

Violet's eyes drooped with exhaustion. Apparently, Sterling's toes were close enough to a pacifier to put her to sleep.

"You know what's so bad?" Desi asked. "I finally got up the nerve to share the news with Sunny. I even asked her to go see the house with me. She was so excited. You know how she's always wanted a house."

"I do. What was Dolly's excuse that time?"

"I don't remember. She had an aerobics class or something."

"She's a horrible person," I said angrily. "And yet she acts so sanctimonious and holier than thou."

"Yeah. Speaking of holiness, have you and Dean found a church home yet?"

Now it was my turn to make up excuses. "Uh… we've been to a few, but nothing fits. And with the twins…"

"I understand. I've got three little energizer bunnies myself. You should see Micah. She's such a prissy little thing now."

The more Desi talked about the kids, the more I wavered on the notion of moving back to Louisiana. Forcing myself to shake it off, I waded into unchartered territory. "How is Sunny these days?"

"The same," Desi said sadly. "She's overjoyed at whatever scraps of love are thrown her way."

Dare I push this? While Desi had always been vehement in her refusal to talk about the dustup with Sunny, this sounded like an opening. "Desi," I broached slowly, "whatever happened—"

"Robin, don't—"

"Okay, I won't push, but just let me say this." When she didn't protest, I went on. "Whatever happened, no matter how horrible it was, don't let it diminish the beautiful relationship you had with Sunny. Part of what makes you special is her and vice versa. You two shine the most lovely, bright light on one another. Whatever happened, it's just Satan trying to dim those lights."

"I agree," Desi said finally. "And that's why I'm so disappointed in Dolly. This would have been a good chance to show Sunny some love."

Chapter Sixteen

Filthy Microwave That Did Me In
Desi

Micah's little snores hummed through the intercom speaker perched atop the kitchen bar, while the boys quietly colored on the back porch.

On my hands and knees, I was in the process of scrubbing the grime off all the baseboards in the trailer. The couple who had bought our place were moving to Shady Gully in a few weeks, so I had time to make it squeaky clean and as inviting and cozy as possible.

A box of yellow rubber gloves and a blue bucket filled with bleachy water sat next to me. So far, I'd been through three pairs of gloves, and even with those, my hands had gone from itchy and red to full-fledged blistered and chapped. I huffed as I pulled a fresh pair of gloves from the box and wrenched them onto my stinging hands. Winston watched me from the comfort of his doggie bed, looking as exhausted as I felt.

Outside, the boys bickered over the merits of red violet, debating whether it was more pink or more purple. Fortunately, they came to a peaceful compromise, before moving on to sea green.

It was hard to concentrate today. This was the day I would finally set eyes on my beautiful new house on Piney Lake.

Dean's flight into Alexandria was due around midday, and

unless there was a delay, he was all set to meet us at the lawyer's office in Belle Maison for closing this afternoon. I scrubbed a little harder on the baseboard under the sink as my heart catapulted with anticipation.

When the doorbell shook me out of my reverie, I quickly yanked off my gloves and hurried to answer it. Sunny stood on the other side of the screen, with a giant package in her hands.

"Mama." I opened the door.

She'd made an effort with her clothes and her makeup, and I sensed in her an air of well-being and contentment.

"Good morning, kitten. Did I interrupt anything?" She took in my cracked hands. "My goodness, what did you do to your hands?"

"Oh, I was cleaning. I'm fine." I ushered her in. "What's that?"

"It's a surprise. Sort of a housewarming gift." When she handed it to me, I could feel the outline of a picture frame. "Everything looks spotless. I thought you and Lenny found buyers already."

"We did. I just want to make sure everything is nice. Lenny's going to repaint the baseboards, so I'm trying to get the muck off."

Sunny walked to the sink and set her purse down. She took in the stove grates and oven racks I had soaking in hot, soapy water. "You've always taken such good care of your things." She nodded, as if she were making a point to herself.

Just then the patio door slid open, and Luke and Petey raced each other to get to Sunny first.

"Nana!" Petey exclaimed.

Sunny delighted in the attention, and for a brief moment, I saw a flicker of the old Sunny.

"What's in the bag, Nana?" Luke asked. "Did you bring us a surprise?"

"Yes, of course I did. But this is for your mama. For your new house."

While Luke fixed his eyes on Sunny's car, Petey moved excitedly toward the package. "Open it! Let's see!"

I knelt and carefully tore away the thick brown paper as Petey's hot breath warmed the side of my cheek.

When I had cleared the paper away, I found myself face to face with my past. I couldn't have been more than seven years old. Mama and Daddy stood behind me, all of us aglow as Far-olitos lit up the dark skies of downtown Santa Fe. It had been Christmas Eve and one of the most wonderful nights of my life. Daddy had coaxed Mama into breaking tradition, and we drove up to Santa Fe for the legendary Christmas Eve Farolito walk. Farolitos, little lights made with tea candles, sand, and paper bags, lined the rooftops of old adobe buildings throughout the art district of Santa Fe. Folks sipped hot chocolate while strolling in and out of art galleries along Canyon Road, home of some of the country's finest art collections. Street musicians sang Christmas carols as families bundled up in festive hats and scarves and warmed themselves by tiny bonfires, called luminarias, which smelled like pinon logs.

It had been a street musician who'd taken our picture. My cheeks were flushed, and there was a thick sheen of chocolate on my upper lip. Mama's eyes were sparkling, and her nose was red from the cold. Daddy's eyes squinted as his happy cheeks pushed them up into little slits.

We had been so happy that night. I found myself wistful for the little family in the painting. Their faces so confident, so sure of the countless nights of happiness and joyous celebrations ahead.

"Mama," I breathed. "Look at us…"

"Do you like it?"

"I love it. The colors, the background. Look at our faces. You did a beautiful job."

"Good," she said in a thick voice.

"Can we go get our surprise now? Is it in your car?" Luke interrupted. Once Sunny told him it was in the backseat, he sprinted off, Petey right on his tail.

"I wanted you to remember the good times," Sunny said to me then.

I looked at her. "I do. I always will."

She nodded, as if relieved. When she glanced at Winston, who was almost sound asleep, she frowned. "He didn't even get up to follow the boys. He looks so tired." Mama bent to pet the old dog, and as they exchanged looks it seemed a jolt of empathy passed between them.

"Harry is getting married," She said pensively.

It took a minute for the shock to wash over me. And even then, I looked to Mama for further explanation. How could that be? Sunny was the love of his life. He would never get over her. "What? Why?"

"I don't know, Desi. I guess you'll have to ask him." Mama looked sad, and for some reason that irked me.

"Well, why should he be heartbroken forever?" I asked. "He has a right to a life."

"Of course he does."

"I mean, you're the one who left him."

"That's true."

"He waited for years, hoping you'd come around—"

"Yes, Desi." Mama finally reacted. "You're right. I broke his heart. I destroyed his life. I'm aware."

After the initial satisfaction of her reaction faded, I felt deflated. "Who is she? How did you find out?"

"He wrote me a letter. Some woman named Connie."

I saw Luke and Petey outside, running around blowing bubbles at each other. "I'm glad for him."

"I suppose deep down I am as well. I just regret that my bad choices, or the culmination of them, have hurt you and Harry." Mama fidgeted, no doubt itching for a cigarette. "I guess that's what I get for picking style over substance."

"Your motto," I harrumphed.

"It's true."

"Well then, stop doing it."

Sunny looked at me, taken aback.

"I'm serious, Mama. You're doing it now. You're picking Tom over me. Over your grandkids."

"I'm not," Sunny denied.

"Then why don't you leave him? I don't understand," I said with rising anger. "Why aren't you furious with him?"

"It's not that simple—"

"It is that simple."

"Where would I go? What would I do? I've made such a mess of my life, and it's too late for me to start over, Desi."

We stared at each other, frustrated, hurt. At an impasse.

"The best thing I ever did in my life was having you," she said. "I want you to always know that." Mama's eyes clouded as she watched Luke and Petey play outside. "Now that Harry's happy, and you're doing so well with your beautiful kids, your wonderful husband, and moving into a big new home…"

"There's room for you in that home, Mama. Just pick me."

Mama kissed my forehead tenderly. "I pick you, Desi. Always know that. And knowing you're happy is everything. And I'm grateful that you've kept this between us. It's the only thing that's helped me function without humiliation. Without shame." She took a long look at the painting, seemed momentarily adrift in better times.

Poor Sunny, I thought, utterly confused.

"Why on earth would I ever tell anyone, Mama?" I couldn't hide the pain in my voice. "Because it's humiliating, that's why. And shame? I have to live with the shame of what happened every single day of my life."

A long moment passed as Sunny watched her grandsons chasing bubbles outside. "I'm sorry, Desi. If it makes you feel better, the guilt haunts me every day."

"So what then?" I demanded. "He just wins? Is that it?"

Sunny's face was ravaged with hopelessness and defeat. "I don't know." She picked up her purse. Stole one last glance at the Farolito painting, at our joyful, unknowing faces. "I'm not sure anyone does."

Dean's flight landed early, so he was already at the law office when we arrived. After he and the real estate attorney did some brainstorming, we were pleased to learn our monthly notes were going to be lower than we'd thought.

"That's great news," Lenny said. "Maybe we can swing this without Desi having to go back to work."

"Yeah," Dean commented. "That would be ideal."

My heart leapt at the thought. Despite scouring my hands raw and the troubling encounter with Sunny earlier, my day was improving. Particularly since Dolly and Mitch opted to send a proxy to sign the official closing documents. It turned out to be Kendra, who was an assistant at another law office in Belle Maison.

"How've you been?" I asked pleasantly.

"Great," she said in a clipped voice. "Sorry Dolly and Mitch couldn't make it. They moved out of town."

"Really?" Lenny said. "Where to?"

Kendra didn't seem inclined to elaborate, so I added, "I hope everything is okay."

Kendra focused on the paperwork in front of her.

Lenny raised an eyebrow, clearly skeptical as we began to sign papers. Everything went smoothly as a lot of talk revolved around the scandalous arrest in the local news. I'd been so busy cleaning and planning our move that I'd barely had time to check the weather, much less the news of the day.

"This guy is going to do some time," said David, the good-natured attorney. His eyes were blue, his smile warm, and his demeanor hopeful. Apparently, a huge Yankees fan, David had a Derek Jeter jersey encased and framed on the wall.

"This quack was practically running a pill mill, from what I understand," Dean commented. As I watched Dean and David banter back and forth, I was struck by Dean's transformation into a self-assured, professional executive. "Wasn't he based somewhere around Natchez?"

"Yeah," David replied. "He's charged with multiple counts of unauthorized practice of medicine, gross negligence, overprescribing controlled substances, and reckless endangerment. A basket full of felonies."

As realization swept over me, I forced myself to focus on the document on the table, but my hands had gone clammy, and the pen kept slipping in my fingers.

"I read one lady with heart disease died." Dean shook his head. "Our good Dr. Schmidt is in serious trouble. And rightly so."

"Agreed," David quipped. "Drugs like phentermine and amphetamines have serious side effects and should be carefully regulated."

While I was busy making an effort to concentrate on the paperwork, I noticed something with the numbers…

Just as I was about to question it, David, the affable attorney, tossed a few keys on the table. "Congratulations folks," he said with a grin. "You just bought yourself a house."

As we drove to the new house, I forgot all about the creepy fat doctor, his whistle-wielding nurse, Cruella, and even the funny closing numbers. Instead my thoughts were consumed with new beginnings and what lay beyond the key I held in my hand.

"We're ahead of schedule," Lenny said after glancing at his watch. "That'll give me a few extra hours before I have to hit the road for New Orleans."

"I can't believe you have to leave for offshore this evening," Dean said. "Seems like they could've been more flexible with your schedule."

"They were. I was supposed to be there three days ago." Lenny said as he turned into our driveway on Piney Lake. "Check it out, Desi. Home sweet home."

As we pulled in, I thought how handsomely the lake framed our white-siding house on the hill. My heart swelled with anticipation. "I'm so excited. If only Robin were here."

Dean whistled. "Wow, that's beautiful."

"Not bad, huh?" Lenny looked pleased.

"It's like a picture," Dean agreed. "And trust me, Robin is

disappointed she couldn't be here, but Violet's inner ear issues are making her crazy. She's convinced she's the only one who can get her through it. Nevertheless, she sent me armed with this." Dean opened a fancy leather carrier and pulled out an expensive-looking Nikon camera. "She wants a play-by-play."

After Lenny parked, he retrieved the garage opener from the big envelope with the paperwork. He clicked it, and just like that, the door lifted to my dream house.

"Nice big garage," Dean said.

It was. Even if there were garbage bags, broken lawn chairs, and random plastic throw-outs piled on one side. "Let's go inside." I could hardly feel my legs underneath me as I put the key in, turned, and opened the door.

I knew something was wrong immediately. The first thing I saw was a plastic bottle of soda lying sideways on the hardwood floor. The lid hadn't been properly secured, and sticky brown soda had leaked all over the oak planks.

"Well… that can be cleaned up," I muttered.

"Nice wood though," Dean offered.

As we walked down the hall, I couldn't help but notice how our feet made imprints on the scratched, filthy floor. I said nothing, until a glance in the small office revealed a lone lightbulb hanging from the ceiling. "Lenny, wasn't there a ceiling fan there?"

I could tell by his tight expression that there had been. Okay. Whatever. The kitchen would be beautiful no matter what. When we turned the corner the kitchen windows shone brightly against the granite bar. Unfortunately, the granite bar was carelessly scattered with…

"Sprinkles?" asked Lenny. "Are those sprinkles like from a cake?"

Multicolored, festive candy dustings littered the granite. And the floor. Although on the floor they mingled with cheerios and fruit loops. I watched despondently as ants made a home atop a pile of cast-off cereal.

"Okay, so they weren't the best cleaners. But it's beautiful," Dean ventured lightly.

Lenny said nothing and headed off to the bedrooms. When I heard him curse, I followed with a sense of trepidation. The smell wafted through the hallway before I even got close to the bedroom. Almost afraid to look, I slowed. Full of dread.

"They let the dog crap and pee all over," Lenny said in an angry, clipped voice. "We'll never get that smell out."

I fought off the small waves of hysteria that were building inside me, and I blinked hard to fight back the tears that gathered at the corners of my eyes. Then I made my way to the other bedroom. Once again, the smell forebode the mess there as well. I felt Lenny's presence behind me. "This carpet will all have to be replaced."

Dean, notably more subdued, suggested, "Let's take a look at the master."

"The flooring is wood in there, at least," Lenny sniped.

We walked through, and despite scratches and missing paint on the walls, the room looked fine. The bathroom as well, although a huge orange rust stain covered the white countertop next to the sink. "I don't remember that," I said in a small voice.

I headed back to the kitchen, determined to discover something hopeful. Surely the stainless-steel appliances would console me. But alas, I saw that the oven and the stove were corroded with grease and grime, and reeked of stale dinners.

But I was still standing. Still optimistic. Until I opened the microwave. "Oh no," I gasped, dropping my face into my hands.

"Good lord," Dean said. "Did they actually cook in that?" The turntable was crusted dark with dried pepperoni and food remnants. The sides of the microwave itself were smeared brown with grease and chunks of cheese and crust. Something moved, and we watched, horrified as a roach skittered out… sluggish, but well fed.

"That's a health hazard," Dean noted. "I can't believe they ate food from this."

"It should be white," I mumbled. When Dean and Lenny looked at me in confusion, I explained. "The turntable. It's supposed to be clean. Pristine. Instead it's grimy and dirty. Tainted." I dissolved then, the nasty microwave mirroring my own dishonor and disgrace.

After all I'd been through in my life, it was a dirty, filthy microwave that did me in—just plain leveled me like a freight train.

Lenny and Dean had taken the car to pick up some cleaning supplies, and since it was clear I'd be here for a while, Lenny arranged for the kids to spend the night at his parents' house. We all knew, however, that this kind of job would take more than an evening. I was both appalled and saddened by Dolly's thoughtlessness. It was customary, proper, and *honorable*, to have your home cleaned before turning key.

The men returned in two cars, with sandwiches and a six-pack of beer. Lenny seemed more positive, although I was sure a lot of it was for my benefit. We sat on the dirty wood floor and ate ham and cheese on rye. Dean and I clinked beer cans while Lenny stuck with Coke.

"How long do you have before you have to go?" I asked him.

"About a half hour," he said. "And I don't want you to kill yourself doing all this. I hired somebody to come out this weekend. After that's done, we'll go from there. Get a quote on carpet and all."

"Yeah." Dean nodded. "Lenny's right. Take it step by step. The bones of the house are great. All this"—Dean glanced around the dirt and grime, sprinkles and fruit loops, spilt Coke, and dog waste—"All this can be fixed."

"I just don't understand." I took a long drink of the cold beer. "Didn't they know leaving it like this was shameful? I mean, even with our little humble home, I knew instinctively that it was common decency to make it nice for the new folks."

"Well, we messed up too, Desi," Lenny said. "We didn't do our due diligence. We knew who we were dealing with."

"Still," I protested. "Even for Dolly, this is disgraceful. I just don't understand why. What did we do wrong besides buy their house? A house she practically dangled in front of me?"

"I don't know." Lenny shrugged. "But the lesson here is this— just because somebody lives in a big house doesn't mean they have integrity."

Dean agreed. "Lenny's right. When it comes to class, you've either got it or you don't."

It was well past dark, hours after Lenny had left for south Louisiana. By now he was likely in a helicopter being transported to a giant oil rig in the Gulf of Mexico, his home for the next four days.

Meanwhile, Dean and I soaked the oven racks and stove grates in hot water. Dean had even detached the exhaust vent over the stove when we discovered it too was slick and corroded with grime and filth.

The more we worked, it seemed, the more we found to discourage us. I looked at Dean, his gangly arms elbow deep in brown, grimy sink water. "I'm sorry, Dean. I'm so embarrassed about this."

"What are you talking about?" His glasses were askew, covered in smear and soot, forcing him to tilt his head at a goofy angle so he could see. I resisted the urge to laugh, and instead reached for his fancy camera, quickly snapping a picture for Robin.

"You helped us get this house, went out on a limb for us, and it's turned out horribly. I'm mortified."

Dean shook his head and stared into the nasty water. "Desi, I didn't go out on a limb."

"It's just too much though." I glanced at him sideways. "And I know you reworked the numbers and paid the down payment."

"Don't worry about the numbers," Dean insisted. "I'm serious. Robin and I are glad to do this for y'all."

"But how can we ever return the kindness?"

Dean's response was drowned out by blaring music and

honking horns. I went to the window, locking on to Bubba and Daryl, as their arms swayed outside the opened windows of a Ford pickup. "Party hardy." Daryl waved, swilling beer from the passenger side.

Dean laughed. "Am I having a flashback, or did he just say, 'party hardy'?"

"Unfortunately, yes." I threw a hand towel to Dean, and we headed outside.

Bubba hopped out of the driver's seat, wrapping me in a giant hug. "Desi, look at you. There's even more to love now."

I swatted him and gave him a mean look. "It's baby fat. What's your excuse?" I pinched his beer belly.

"Yo, Deano!" Bubba hollered. "Did you cure cancer yet? Invent a flying car? I got money riding on you saving the world one day."

As we laughed comfortably together, the years slipped away.

"Where's your other halves?" Daryl asked. "We got a bonfire raging over at Cicada Stadium. We're trying to round up all the stragglers."

"Lenny's offshore," I told Daryl. "We just bought this house."

"I heard that." Bubba grinned. "Nice hut. What'd y'all do, run Dolly and Mitch outta town? Word is they up and disappeared."

I bit my tongue, determined to temper my anger.

"Yeah, there's a story there somewhere," Daryl chimed. "But no worries tonight, huh? Come on. It's gonna be a blast."

Dean and I watched as they started the truck and pumped up the radio another notch. Before they pulled out, Bubba hollered, "Y'all ain't there yet?"

We watched them go, and then silently walked back inside and took in the muddy-brown soap water in the sink.

"You know," Dean said. "All this will be here tomorrow."

"True." I felt like a rebel. "I have no kids tonight."

"Ditto."

We giggled like teenagers. "Let's refresh the soap water and hit the road."

~

It wasn't until about the eighth person commented on my weight that I started to feel self-conscious. While most folks saw me every week at church, it seemed the change was shocking for those I hadn't seen in years.

I pledged to go on lots of walks around my new neighborhood and cut back on the butter pecan ice cream, which come to think of it, I ate regularly even though I was no longer pregnant.

I saw lots of folks from school, including Denise, who had lived up to her homecoming aspirations, and become a softball coach at a small college in south Louisiana.

Ricky, the deputy who had cleared a path for us to the hospital when Micah was born, walked around with a red Solo cup, reeking of whisky. He told everyone they couldn't leave until he checked them with the breathalyzer.

Claire was there, still wearing her USPS shirt and gossiping with what was left of the Bouncy girls. Most of the blond beauties had moved on to pastures greener than Shady Gully. Even Dolly apparently.

I sipped my vodka and tonic, determined to forget about Dolly tonight. I wished Robin were here. Whether it was the disappointing day, the reminiscent vibes from high school, or the vodka, I felt her absence keenly.

"Dizzy Desi," drawled a voice behind me. "You're looking good, girl."

I took a moment to prepare myself before turning around. "Oh, hey Adam." Super, super casual. "How's it going?"

"Great. I'm about to sign a recording contract up in Dallas. Did a little gig down in Biloxi a few months ago."

"Cool." Again, super, super casual.

"You're even prettier than you were in high school," he said, not taking his eyes off me.

I straightened my blouse, suddenly mindful of my weight gain. "Well I... gained a little weight." So much for being super casual, I cringed inwardly.

"It suits you. It surely does."

"I heard you got married?" Definitely not super casual. "And you have kids?" Gracious, I was the lamest person on earth.

He nodded. Smiled. Apparently not interested in elaborating. He just kept staring at me and smiling like he had me all figured out.

Desperate to flee, I searched the crowd for a familiar face. My eyes landed on the shadiest of shady characters, Brad Wolfheart. He sat on a log all alone, smoking under a towering pine tree.

"Nice seeing you, Adam," I said over my shoulder as I made my way to Brad. I should have felt better leaving Adam in the dust, but I didn't. I could feel him staring a hole in my back, the outline of his cocky smile imprinting my flesh like a tattoo.

I sat next to Brad, taking in a heavy whiff of whatever he was smoking.

"You look a little wound up, girl," Brad snarled.

"A little."

He offered me the joint. I declined, guzzling the rest of my vodka.

"How's Sunny doing these days?"

I looked at him sharply. "She's fine. Why?"

"Saw her at the gas station a while back. With Tom. She didn't look so good."

I let that settle for a minute. Looked again at the joint. And suddenly Dean appeared out of nowhere. All limbs and glasses and awkwardness. "Hey, Brad," he slurred. "Great to see you, buddy."

Oh brother. I pulled Dean down beside me on the log before he fell over and injured someone.

"You want another drink, Desi?" Dean asked. "I think I do."

Brad laughed. Took a puff. Amused with us, I could tell.

"I've got twins now, Brad. Did you know that?" One drink in and Dean was Mr. Sociable. "Here," he said. "Let me show you. I've got a picture right here in my wallet."

Of course, Dean dropped his wallet and half the contents fell out. Credit cards and all. I got down to pick them up and handed Brad the picture of Sterling and Violet.

"What are you smoking there, Brad?" Dean asked. "Is that marijuana? You better not let Ricky see that." Dean laughed, just plain cracking himself up.

But even Brad laughed. Handed the picture back. "Cute kids."

"Yeah, they're the best. And Robin, she's the best. We have the best life."

Brad nodded again. Took another drag before he stood up, handing the joint to Dean, "Congratulations, man." Brad then looked pointedly at me. "Enjoy."

Brad disappeared, like a panther prowling for a rabbit in the crowd.

I looked at Dean. "Let's go for a walk." I pointed toward the trail behind Cicada Stadium, known as Hummingbird Trail, where a few couples and small groups strolled about.

"Yeah, let's go." He hopped up with surprising agility. "What am I supposed to do with this?"

"I don't know." I raised my eyebrow at the joint. When we hit the trail, a pleasant breeze whipped the pine trees into backbends, and the half-moon reflected festively against the vintage stadium lights.

All in all, the day was ending okay.

Dean put his arm around me in a warm hug. "You're the best, Desi. You know that?"

The next morning, I woke up in my trailer to the piercing sound of a phone ringing. Over and over again. I was going to get up and get it. I really was. But I fell back asleep. And then it started ringing again.

When I sat up, I noticed two things at once. My head was exploding inside my skull. And I wasn't alone in bed.

Dean was sleeping beside me.

The urge to throw up competed with the need to stop the ringing hammering my skull.

"Hello." My voice was thick, crackly, and my mouth was dry.

As I listened to the voice on the other end of the line, that of my dearest friend in the world, my heart broke in a hundred pieces. I couldn't speak, found myself utterly lost for words, and crushed beyond measure. "Robin..."

Dean's eyes flipped open. He rustled the covers as he rolled over.

"Oh my God... Robin..." I couldn't breathe. Found myself heaving desperately for air. Somehow, with God's grace, I managed to hand the phone to Dean. "You have to talk to her," I mumbled in a hoarse, whipped voice.

"What?" He sat up. Took the phone. Looked at me with panic in his eyes. "What?"

"Her parents were in an accident this morning. They're dead."

Chapter Seventeen

To Save An Apple Fritter
Robin

W e went back and forth on whether to bring the twins to Louisiana for the funeral. Dean had offered to fly back home and help me get them—and myself—together, but I decided it would be too much.

It was all too much. Losing my parents was too much. Leaving my babies was too much. In the end, I reluctantly agreed when Nancy, the supermom from our neighborhood, offered to keep the twins for a few days. After all, Sterling and Violet never really knew Mama and Daddy. This thought, of all the ones cluttering my mind, filled me with overwhelming sorrow.

As I again checked my flight's boarding time, I regretted not letting Dean come home and console me, but that would have been silly. I just had to hold on. Soon I would have Dean and Desi to lean on, and I wouldn't feel so alone.

Dean's skill set was best served in Shady Gully now anyway. Ernie and Max would appreciate his pragmatic, logical style with the funeral details as well as the autopsy particulars. Because there were no other cars involved in the accident, an autopsy was required to determine exactly what happened. The assumption was that Daddy, who had been driving a car filled with cakes and desserts to help Mama set up for the church fair, had had a heart attack and lost control of the car.

I looked around the Dallas airport, my sight landing on a young couple with a teenage son. He wore flip-flops, droopy shorts, and slumped belligerently in a terminal seat, his eyes disinterested and half-closed. He looked ornery. His parents looked worn.

Now I could see the other side clearly. I had been this kid once. And my parents, despite my ungratefulness and lack of respect, they'd mostly seemed happy. In fact, the church fair had been Mama's favorite time of year. She'd work all day at the library, and then come home and suit up in her *Bless my Heart* apron, and set about building her delicious desserts. She'd bake for days and days, all her secret recipes for delicacies such as banana pudding, blueberry crunch, peanut brittle, and white chocolate fudge. By the end of the week, all her specialties would miraculously pile up on the table and overflow to the bar and even the living room end tables.

Each year on the morning of the church fair, Mama and Daddy skittered around the kitchen in the wee hours. Whispering purposefully like robbers in the dark, they hustled back and forth, opening and closing the refrigerator, snapping Tupperware shut, and rolling out aluminum foil. How many times had I heard them those mornings, trying to be quiet, but the eagerness in their voices giving them away? Finally, I'd hear the car start up and off they'd go. To sell Mama's baked goods at the church fair.

She always sold the most, and although she said pride was the devil's tool, I think she would have been crushed if anyone had ever beaten her record. Because Daddy knew this, he made it his mission the week before the church fair to grant her every wish, and entertain her every whim.

I used to think their lives were routine and boring. Now I think they were living out one of the world's greatest love stories—right in front of my ungrateful eyes.

Although my doctor had given me a prescription for Xanax before leaving Texas, I hadn't taken any as I was too consumed with leaving the twins, and detailing their care for Nancy. And now that the flight was approaching the runway in Alexandria, I knew I'd have reinforcements waiting at the terminal.

When I saw them, Dean and Desi, all the grief I'd been holding back flooded over me, and I ran into their arms, feeling at once safe and loved.

Dean bent his head to mine and kissed me. "I'm sorry, Robin. I'm so sorry." He seemed unusually strained, and I realized that he was also grieving my parents.

"It's okay," I said. "I'm okay.

Desi pulled me into her arms and broke down. The only words I could make out were intermittent murmurs of grief. "I hate this. I'm so sorry."

"I know." I patted her tenderly. "I know. It's going to be okay."

We walked to baggage claim, and Dean retrieved my luggage. "How are the kids?" he asked. "It seems like I've been away from them forever."

"They're okay. They cried when I left them at Nancy's." I held Desi's hand as we made our way to the parking lot. "Is Lenny going to be able to make it for the funeral?"

"Yeah. He got permission to leave a few days early. Between that and the closing, he's been home more than offshore."

"How's the house? Is it wonderful?" Dean and Desi exchanged glances. "What? Did Dolly do something awful at closing?"

"No. It's a long story," Desi explained. "For right now let's just get you settled. Do you want to stay at my place or… at your mom and dad's?" Tears fell steadily down her face.

"I think we'll stay with you." I looked at Dean. "Don't you think? I mean, I know I'll need to go there at some point, but I just don't think I can do it now."

Dean nodded his agreement. "Ernie and Max said

they'd come by later. They're broken up. The autopsy results came back."

"And?" I half expected to hear that Daddy had looked away from the road to save an apple fritter.

"It was a stroke. A bad one apparently. He veered off the road, and your mom was likely focused on his distress. They probably never saw the tree."

"You know on Shady Lane right before the church?" Desi asked. "That big tree on the curve?"

"I had no idea they were that close to the church," I said as I scooted into the car. "They almost made it."

Desi sat in the back, and I sat next to Dean in the front.

He reached over and touched my hand. "The police said the car was loaded with sweets. For the fair."

"Yeah. I've been thinking about the church fair all morning."

"Me too." Dean pinched the bridge of his nose.

It occurred to me at some point during the drive to Shady Gully that of the three of us, I was the only one who hadn't cried. Of course, after they told me about the condition of Desi's new house on Piney Lake, I realized they'd had a rough few days.

"It's all going to work out," I reassured Desi. As we pulled into the driveway of Desi and Lenny's trailer I was struck by the pretty green plants on the porch and the coziness of the place. "And the reunion? At Cicada Stadium? How was that?"

Dean shrugged, "It was okay. Same old scene, just older characters." He picked up my bags and brought them inside. "I drank too much."

"Yeah, me too," Desi said as we followed Dean inside. She clicked the blinking light on the answering machine, and Lenny's voice announced he was on his way home, and he'd probably make it after midnight."

"Where are the kids?"

"They're at Lenny's parents."

I watched as Desi quietly put together a giant plate of nachos and put them in the microwave. For all Desi's earlier emotion, she seemed unusually subdued now. That was fine with me. I was exhausted. I settled on the floor to pet Winston, who didn't look long for this world. This made me inexplicably sad. Just like the memories of Mama and Daddy sneaking out on church fair mornings, I seemed oddly moved by the old dog's weary eyes.

"Here come Ernie and Max now," Desi said as she glanced out the window.

Sure enough, the sight of my two favorite miscreants stirred a profound wave of grief within me, and I hopped up, desperate to embrace them. I sort of fell into their arms, which were strong and sturdy now. They were grown men, with their own families, and as they folded me into their tight circle, something loosened up inside me.

In that moment I wasn't Dean's wife, or Violet and Sterling's Mom, or even Desi's friend. In that moment I was an integral link in a family's shared history. Everything from the toddler years to the miscreant years to the teenage years. All of it was contained inside of us, and we saw it in one another's eyes. The history. The bond. It was ours alone.

When Dean walked into the room, the air thickened. Max and Ernie backed away from me. Awkward, all business now.

Desi placed the nachos on the table. "Y'all sit down. Help yourselves." Strange that even Desi seemed suddenly uncomfortable.

While we shared a few Gene and Mabel stories, the conversation felt forced.

"Brother Wyatt's gonna say a few words at the funeral," Ernie said. "I figured you'd want to say something too. I put that in the program."

"Yeah, I do. Of course." I looked at Max, who was somber. "What about you?"

Max shook his head, uncommitted. "We'll see." He hadn't eaten any nachos and hardly said a word to Dean. He was being polite to Desi, but the mood unsettled me. There was something going on beyond grief.

"All right, well." Ernie stood up. "We're gonna head out." He kissed me on the cheek and enveloped me in another hug. "If you need anything, you know where to find me." He shot Dean and Desi a look, and he and Max headed toward the door.

I stood on the doorstep and waved goodbye. Max gave me a lingering look. "I love you, sis."

Whoa. Something was definitely up.

Dean lay beside me, fast asleep, breathing deeply. I, unfortunately, tossed and turned. I just couldn't turn my mind off. I worried about seeing the murderous tree by the church tomorrow. I worried about whether Nancy remembered to give Violet her ear drops. I worried about what I'd say at the funeral and what I'd wear. I worried about finding Mama's recipe for her legendary white chocolate fudge.

Eventually I gave up and found a Xanax in my purse. On my way to the kitchen, I passed Desi's bedroom and heard the shower running. I headed into the kitchen and poured myself some ice water. The clock said it was close to midnight. Lenny would be home soon.

I swallowed the pill and prayed for oblivion. On the way back to my room, I hovered at Desi and Lenny's bedroom door. I would give anything to talk to her long into the night, like when we were young girls and she slept on the cot beside my bed. I fondly recalled the way we'd mumble back and forth, until eventually one of us wouldn't answer, having finally surrendered to sleep.

The shower was running strong though, so I turned away, trusting that the pill would do as advertised by the doctor. I took a couple of steps and stopped.

Something was off. I went back and peeked in again, searching for whatever I'd seen that nagged at me. As usual, her room was spotless. The bed was tightly made, the end tables were dusted…

And on Lenny's end table was the oddest thing. Something he would never use. For any purpose whatsoever. Because he didn't wear glasses. And neither did Desi.

Headlights reflected off the windows then, and I could see the outline and hear the familiar sounds of Lenny's truck. I walked toward the night table and picked up the wadded premoistened towelettes and the ripped package of Zeke's eyeglasses cleaner.

I carried them down the hall and shut my door just before Lenny came in from the garage. I looked at the familiar wrapper and towelettes in my hand. I walked over to the nightstand where Dean slept. And placed them next to his others.

I sort of floated into church the day of the funeral, greeting people like a robot, and saying thank you as they offered various snippets of sympathy. *I'm sorry. They're in a better place now. Their faith was inspiring. Such a gentleman. Such a selfless woman. They will be missed.*

All the while my eyes flitted back and forth between Desi, my best friend, and Dean, my husband. After years of falling short, my experience in the executive setting had sharpened my intuitions. In essence, it had been my training ground, and my strategy was simple. First, I'd scope out the room, and identify my threats. Then I'd monitor Dean's body language through the evening, noting who he engaged, and how quickly he moved on. Because I knew him so well, I could gage his patience for chitchat, read the sincerity of his smile, and most importantly, his response to flattery.

The difference was, I didn't expect to have to do it today in front of the whole Shady Gully community. And certainly not on the day my parents were buried.

He brought me a cup of water. "You okay?" he asked.

I drank the water, despite it all, grateful for his attentiveness.

Maybe there was a reasonable explanation his stuff was on Lenny's end table. I knew he'd spent the night, and I understood it wouldn't do for him to go stumbling into his parents' house in the early hours of the morning after a night of drinking. I guess I'd just assumed he'd slept in the kids' room, like we'd done last night.

Angry suddenly, that my focus was on something other than my parents, I pivoted to the many people who came to show their respects. Occasionally someone outside of the community would offer some unexpected anecdote that took me out of my own head. *Your Daddy took my shift every Tuesday so I could go to chemo with my wife. Your Mama gave the best book reviews—she'd have us in stitches every time.*

Sunny and Mr. Tom showed up. Oddly, they were on the opposite side of the room from Desi. Sunny looked worn and defeated. Her black suit looked crumpled and outdated. Mr. Tom looked a little better, but his demeanor was stiff and on edge.

As Sunny approached, weariness and smoke spilled off her in waves. She seemed especially frail. "Oh Sunny," I whispered as I embraced her. "I miss you."

"Oh, my sweet goose, I miss my girls as well," she said.

"Those were good times," I told her. "With you and Desi. You were such fun and so good to me."

She placed her hands on either side of my face. "Let me tell you something. Your mama, she was the good one. Not me." Her lips trembled then. "I'm going to miss her."

Mr. Tom nodded, patting me sweetly on the shoulder, and just that quickly he and Sunny disappeared into the crowd.

The whole exchange disturbed me, left me feeling disquieted and adrift. I roamed the room, saw Claire and Ashley watching me, whispering. Even Bubba and Daryl seemed off today, offering their condolences but unwilling to hold eye contact. Grief? Sadness? Maybe. But I had become good at reading a room, and I had a bad feeling.

My parents had died. That was heavy enough. I shouldn't have to endure the whispers and the surreptitious looks of pity. It hung in the air. It tainted the celebration of my parents' lives. And that I couldn't forgive.

In the end I couldn't speak. I begged Max to take my slot in the program, and he did, quite graciously. He and Ernie, my little monsters, had both done Mama and Daddy proud.

Brother Wyatt did as well, refraining from his usual hellfire and damnation sermon, and I was grateful for that. Instead he talked about Mama and Daddy's loyalty. To the church, to our family, and to one another. "Living your life as a testament to the Lord isn't always easy," Brother Wyatt said. "Gene and Mabel just made it look that way. I believe the way they died was in itself a demonstration of their faith. One last act of devotion to God, to community, and to one another.

"They were on their way to set up Mabel's table for the church fair. Always the first ones to arrive every year. Before sunrise." Brother Wyatt smiled as he looked up and down the pews. "And, Lord, I just gotta say it—Mabel's blueberry crunch and apple fritters were something to behold. Am I right?"

"Amen! Praise the Lord!"

"That's right. She baked with joy because she loved the Lord. And Gene, well, we all know how sincerely he gave himself to the Lord, to his wife, and to his family. But let's just be honest—the week prior to church fair, he gave a little extra to Mabel, right?"

Laughter spread, and chuckles mingled with emotional amens.

Brother Wyatt grinned mischievously. "We all know who was gonna sell the most baked goods that day, don't we?"

"Amen! Hallelujah!"

"Come on, now!" Brother Wyatt said again, "We all know it!"

A splattering of applause soon erupted in full-out cheers. Never in my years of coming to Shady Gully Baptist Church had I seen such an outburst. Mama would have been appalled. But I thought, as I clapped along with everyone else, she would have been a tad flattered.

Claire zeroed in on me after the service. It was in the church hall, as folks shared stories about Mama and Daddy and visited with one another over sandwiches.

Desi was setting up a dessert table, and Dean was chatting with his parents and Coach Cal. Claire undoubtedly chose that moment because she knew from experience that isolated prey was easier to manipulate.

I braced myself. Smiled somberly as she offered her condolences, obligatory under the circumstances. And to her credit she waited a good two minutes before she lowered her voice and said, "You're doing really well... considering."

I said nothing. I wanted her to elaborate. To verbalize what I feared in real words. Claire didn't fail me.

"I know you heard, right? I mean everybody was there and saw them."

And there it was. I couldn't unhear it now. Still I refused to help her.

"You know how it is at Cicada Stadium. Everybody was drunk, but I think Wolfheart gave them pot, so they weren't thinking straight."

Now this shocked me. Desi, who wouldn't even take diet pills, and Dean, who usually ordered sweet tea at five-star restaurants. Pot?

"It just kind of happened, I guess, because you weren't there and Lenny wasn't there, and well, everybody is so used to seeing them together, but then they were holding hands and well, they went missing for a while. I'm so sorry, Robin."

Dean saw me talking to Claire. Or rather, listening. Just as I could read his expressions, he could read mine. He tucked his head in and elbowed his way across the room. But Desi beat him to it. She had a piece of fudge perched on a napkin. "Here, Claire," she said. "I thought you could use something to put in your mouth right about now."

"What?" Claire scrunched up her face. "You have nerve. How could you do that to your best friend anyway? And the same night as her—"

Even Claire had the decency to stop there. She glared at Dean as he finally made it across the church hall to us. He glared right back at her. "You don't know what you're talking about, Claire. You need to mind your own business."

"Everybody saw y'all holding hands, Dean. Don't get mad at me. Robin is my friend, and she has a right to know the truth."

"We didn't hold hands," Desi argued. "Dean put his arm around me."

"Whatever," Claire snapped. "I guess that makes it okay. And I'd love to know what Lenny says about all this, huh?"

I blocked out the white noise of their bickering, focusing instead on Lenny, who appeared oblivious as he chatted with Ricky, James, and Ernie. Good ole Lenny. Nothing ever seemed to faze him. Or had he even heard yet?

I left them like that. Desi, Dean, and Claire, hashing out who had crossed what line and who was the better friend. While they tallied up my fate, I walked outside.

Drawn to the cemetery, I sat on a bench and watched silently as the gravediggers shoveled dirt onto my parents' graves.

It didn't take long for Dean and Desi to track me down. I watched as they padded over the manicured grass toward me. Puzzled once again that Lenny was absent from such a pivotal point in all our futures.

Dean, a man on a mission, started out with a fervent denial. "You know Claire is about as trustworthy as Dolly, right? Robin, I swear to you, nothing improper happened between Desi and me."

"Then why wouldn't you tell me about it? Why wouldn't you at least warn me about the perception around town, so I wasn't blindsided at my parents' funeral?"

Dean sat next to me on the bench. Dropped his face into his hands and ran his fingers through his hair. When he looked at me, his hair unruly and his glasses askew, a wave of grief, betrayal, and loss swept over me.

"We were," Dean said as Desi flopped down in the grass, church dress and all. "We talked about it. But because of your mom and dad, we thought it best to wait."

"Dumb move," I snapped. "And I saw your glasses stuff on Lenny's end table. So don't even try to lie. Not here in front of Mama and Daddy's grave."

"He's not," Desi said. "He's telling the truth. We were idiots. Drank too much. Smoked some crap Brad gave us."

"Was that before or after y'all were holding hands?"

"We weren't holding hands," they said simultaneously.

"Oh, that's right. It was an arm-around-the-shoulders thing. Silly me."

"Okay," Desi snapped. "Here's the truth. And I'm swearing it ten feet from your parents. Okay?" There were tears in her eyes, and she had that innocent, slightly naïve look that I'd grown to love. "We were messed up because your nerdy husband can't handle his liquor, and sure as heck can't handle a joint. Ricky took pity on us and brought us to my place. We stumbled in, and I swear, I didn't even know where Dean landed until the phone rang the next morning."

"That's about it," Dean said, appearing almost relieved. "I just passed out."

"Well," I said. "Why act so guilty then? And why is half the town convinced y'all are cheaters? Even Ernie and Max seem skeptical."

"If we acted guilty it's because we realized the timing was horrible," Dean explained. "And as for Ernie and Max, just like everyone else, I guess it depends on whose version they heard, and which one sounded better."

We turned to the sound of footsteps. Lenny. Finally. "What's up?"

Dean sighed. "Would you tell Robin that all these rumors floating around are unjust and not true?"

Lenny looked at me, really looked at me, and I searched his face for the tiniest speck of doubt. I saw none. "Robin, don't let these gossipmongers get to you. Especially not today."

For some reason, Lenny's matter-of-fact, no-nonsense attitude was more convincing than Dean and Desi's vehement denials.

"Ricky is my good friend, right? He brought them home. He told me about it, and Desi told me when I got home. It's all ridiculous." Lenny glanced at Desi, chuckling. "As if? Seriously, trust me, Robin. We're stuck with these two losers who can't hold their liquor."

I almost laughed, but didn't.

Lenny patted Dean on the shoulder. "Hey, come help a minute, okay? James needs a hand taking down the tables and chairs in the hall."

Dean stood up. Looked at me for a long moment. He bent to kiss me, but I turned away. He brushed my forehead with his lips, then followed Lenny back to the church hall.

That left me and Desi. I sighed deeply. Watched the gravediggers. Desi joined me on the bench and watched with me. After a long while I asked, "Where'd y'all disappear to?"

Thankfully, Desi didn't try to play dumb. "We walked on Hummingbird Trail, which was sort of a challenge because I was trying to hold your husband up. Eventually we sat on a rock and talked."

"About?"

"About you, Robin. Dean is really, really happy with his life. He loves you. I give you my word. Nothing happened."

I wanted to believe her. I really did.

But I didn't.

Somewhere deep in my soul, I'd always known Dean had a thing for Desi. It was obvious the first day she walked into Coach Cal's class, and he'd hung on her every word.

I'd always sensed it, the lift in his voice whenever he said her name. His eagerness to befriend Lenny and thus assure the four of us remain a regular thing. I'd just refused to face it because I wanted so badly to believe I had something special that stood apart from Desi. But I'd always lived in Desi's shadow. Dean had seen it, known it. That was clear when he'd found the very notion of my beating her for homecoming queen laughable. I guess he'd been right after all. As if, like Lenny said.

I'd been nothing more than a consolation prize. I was nothing more than a means to an end. A way for Dean to keep Desi in his life.

Desi's eyes hadn't left my face, pleading for confirmation that I trusted her, believed her.

But I didn't. So I stood and walked away.

Chapter Eighteen

Smorgasbord Of City-Slicker Neopolitan
Desi

My boss was a twenty-year-old Bouncy girl. Could it get any worse? Here I stood, a mother of three, asking a bleached-blond aerobics instructor with rock-hard abs for permission to leave work early to pick up my kindergartner.

"Well," Heather said. "I really need you to let me know beforehand so I can get coverage." Her heavily mascaraed eyes widened as she stressed the implications of being shorthanded in the JCPenney Cold Weather Accessory Department in May. "I don't know, Desi. I just don't know." I watched as Heather pondered the great importance of her decision, clearly burdened by the depths of her power and standing. "And there's nobody else who can go pick Michelle up?"

Breathe. Count to ten. One. Two.

"It's Micah, and no, my husband is offshore until this evening." I waited, looking as meek and pathetic as possible. "And she got sick. Suddenly. I couldn't let you know beforehand."

"Well, okay. But I'll have to dock your pay."

I grabbed my purse and left, giving the Empress plenty of time to revel in her power and supremacy. Within minutes, I was headed out of Belle Maison toward Shady Gully. Poor Micah, I sighed, suspecting her tummy ache had more to do with separation anxiety than a stomach bug. Losing half a day's pay wasn't good, but I couldn't take the chance that she might actually be sick.

Once Micah had started Kindergarten, I'd gone back to work part time, leaving work each day in time to pick the kids up after school. It was a compromise, as Lenny said, which meant extra money without the expense of daycare. It worked great, except that I was exhausted and frazzled and felt like I wasn't doing my best job as a mom or as an employee in the Cold Weather Accessory Department. However, if Micah made this a weekly thing, Heather the Hottie would likely use her authority as Empress to send me straight to the guillotine.

Money was tight these days, and I really needed this job. We sent a check to Dean every month for the house payment, but it seemed that the house of my dreams had created a plethora of extra expenses. Like a new roof after we discovered leaks the first time it rained. Like a new air conditioner after a hot summer revealed the original unit had been undersized from the beginning. Like a new stove after incorrect electrical wiring had shorted out and nearly caused a house fire.

We handled all those excess expenses on our own, never dreaming of mentioning them to Dean. He and Lenny talked occasionally, exchanged pleasantries, but we'd agreed it best to keep our money troubles to ourselves. Under the circumstances.

Like the fact that Robin hated my guts. Sure, I sent her and the kids' birthday cards, and she sent Christmas cards and gifts for my kids. It was all very cordial, like the kind of relationship you had with a great-uncle or a distant cousin you never saw, and you couldn't quite recall if they'd died a few summers back or if you'd just dreamed they did.

I'd also tried to call Robin on occasion, but the conversations were always uncomfortable and short because she had somewhere else she had to be.

Regardless of what she thought I'd done, I was devastated she could so easily rid herself of me. But her life was full of fancy cocktail parties and intellectual conversations with sophisticated people. No doubt she was jet-setting here and yonder having facials and massages and living the high life. What did she need me for anyway?

I went to church every Sunday, praying constantly for God to change her heart, but nothing changed. It hurt to lose people you loved, like Robin and Sunny, not from death but from their own choosing. Their outright rejection, their dismissal.

The worst part was hearing that Robin and Dean had flown in to visit her brothers or Dean's family. Or catching a glimpse of Sunny and Tom getting gas or turning into the post office. Everyone was living their lives like I'd never existed. Everyone else was moving forward, and I was just stuck. I felt discarded, and it shattered me.

And then I'd see my little girl, and all was right with the world again.

I saw Micah sitting in the Elementary school office way before she saw me. She was sitting in a giant chair, and her huge bookbag was on the floor beside her. She had her head down, and appeared dejected and miserable.

I quickened my pace. As soon as I turned the corner and entered the office, Micah's lips curved in a humongous smile. I knew instantly I'd been had.

"Mommy! It was forever. Forever, forever, forever till you got here." She crashed into me, her little arms not quite able to encircle my girth. "Why did forever pass? Where were you?"

"I was at work, pumpkin. You know Mommy has to go to the mall and work at the big store, right?"

"Yep," she said. "With the pink Barbie buggy. Can we go there now?"

"No, I just left there because the office called and said you were sick."

"Oh." She tugged on my sleeve. Pulled me lower and cupped her hand over her mouth. "They lied."

I gave her an exasperated look as I signed her out on the office clipboard. "Let's go."

"Can we get ice cream?" She beat me to the car.

Luke and Petey still had another hour before they were done, so it wouldn't make sense to bring her to Lenny's parents and go back to work. "Want to go to the Cozy Corner?"

"Yep." She handed me her bookbag. "I want strawberry."

I drove less than a mile before we reached the hamburger joint at the center of Shady Gully. It was a warm day, and the sun was out, so I decided to enjoy the unexpected time with Micah. After ordering burgers and fries, I put my sunglasses on and settled at a picnic table.

"I just want ice cream. Can I get chocolate?"

"I want you to eat a little of your real food first."

"Ice cream is real, Mommy." Micah's legs dangled off the bench, and she kicked them back and forth. "Do you know Mindy?"

"From your class?"

"Yep. She got a dog. He's so cute. He has this much hair." She held her arms wide. "Mindy brought a picture today, and his name is Bubbles."

"Stay right here. Don't move." I went up to the counter and picked up our food. Spread the burgers and fries out on the table. "Here. Eat your fries at least."

"Why can't we get a dog?"

I took a bite out of my burger, stalling. Micah had been too little to remember Winston, but his passing had been hard on all of us, especially Luke. Lately Lenny and the boys had been campaigning for another pup, and apparently Micah had picked up on it.

But I just wasn't up to it. I didn't have the will or energy to take on any more responsibility. Besides, Winston was one of a kind.

"We'll see, pumpkin. Eat your food." I finished my burger while Micah played with her fries.

As vehicles hustled in and out of the Cozy Corner, the hub of lunch time cuisine in Shady Gully, a familiar truck slowed at the four-way stop sign. I prayed it would keep going, but it just wasn't my day.

I quickly wadded up my burger wrapper, disgusted with myself as I realized not only had I devoured my burger, but half of Micah's. I rubbed my tongue over my teeth as Adam hopped out of his big red truck. He'd long since traded in his white Corvette for his signature four-wheel drive.

I scrutinized him as he meandered over to the counter and placed his order. Still tall, with a little more weight around the middle. And still sporting his boyish "life's just a game and I get to roll first" grin.

"Are you ready?" I asked Micah.

"No! You promised!" Her face reddened with the outrage of a regularly bribed kindergartner. "I ate all my food. You promised. I want strawberry."

"Okay, okay. Shhhh." I hurriedly gathered our trash into one bag.

"No, I think I want chocolate," she whined. "Maybe vanilla. Mommy, don't throw the trash away. We're not leaving!"

Adam and his big, bold belt buckle moseyed over with his bag of lunch. And a bowl of ice cream sprouting a spoon and a cherry. "Well howdy, ma'am," he said to Micah. "Is this seat taken?"

Micah looked completely baffled. But make no mistake, she saw the ice cream. She nodded shyly.

"Well, thank ya, kindly," Adam said. "As a token of my appreciation, I'd like to present you with this here prize-winning ice cream." Her eyes widened as he placed the bowl in front of her.

"Mommy, it's… *every* color." She looked at Adam to confirm that he was indeed real and not just a figment of her imagination.

"It surely is. It's what the city slickers call Neapolitan. And that there is a Shady Gully cherry, which makes it extra special. Like magic."

Micah tentatively stuck the spoon into the ice cream. After the first bite, she dug in with gusto.

Adam grinned at me. "And you, my lady, could I offer you a fry?" He popped one into his mouth.

I shook my head. "You're too much."

"That I can't deny."

"I heard you got married again." For heaven's sake, why oh why did I have this compulsion to grill him on his romantic status every time I ran into him? "A couple more kids?" *Stop talking now, Desi.*

"What can I say, Dizzy Desi? I reckon I'm still searching for the right one." He took a huge bite of his hamburger, glancing at Micah, who had made the chocolate disappear, and was now halfway through the strawberry. "And you? Still set on breaking my heart?"

I didn't respond. Apparently finally gaining control of my mouth.

"The one that got away." He sat back, appearing melancholy. "That's what you are. You're like… unfinished business. Maybe I'll write a song about that."

I chuckled. Okay, so maybe I giggled.

"Got me a tour coming up," Adam said. "A big one. My manager says my new tunes are gonna bust the charts wide open."

"Wow. Where's the tour?"

"South Louisiana. Houma. Thibodaux. Thereabouts. Wrapping up in the Big Easy."

We turned as the gravel crunched under the wheels of another Cozy Corner customer. "Great," I said under my breath.

Adam laughed. "What? You got something against Wolfheart?"

"Seems I recall you warning me off of Brad and his clan, saying girls like me should steer clear."

Adam threw his head back in an all-out chortle. "That's true. But something tells me you're a little more experienced now."

I broke eye contact first. Focused on Micah, who looked dangerously sated. "You ready, pumpkin?" I gathered her napkins, and put them in the food bag. "Now what do you say to the nice man?"

"Thank you for the magic ice cream."

Adam made a show of tipping his hat, which Micah thought was funny. As we got up, he drawled in a low voice, "I think I just came up with a perfect title for that song."

"What's that?"

"How about… 'Unfinished Pleasure'?"

I shook my head, picking up Micah to rush her along.

"It's got a nice ring to it, huh?" Adam grinned, heading to his truck.

I turned toward my car, hiding my scarlet face as I settled Micah into her seat. Brad Wolfheart appeared, opening the driver's door for me. "How ya doing, Desi?"

"Good, Brad. How are you?"

"Not bad. Have you heard from Robin lately?" He reacted when I flashed him a dirty look. "What? I was just asking. She called me a while back looking for some—"

I angled myself in front of Micah's line of vision. "Looking for what?"

Brad scowled. "Man, what is with you? I try to be friendly, but every time I see you, you are so wound up. You need to chill."

"I can't chill, Brad." Feeling suddenly frazzled. "I have a crappy job, and I work for an arrogant bimbo, but I have to work because I have a house that is a money pit and I have three kids that want everything, including a damn dog, which I can't handle and I don't want because I miss my old dog, and I live in a nosy town and everybody is up in my business and making snide remarks about me losing my best friend because a hateful gossip told her lies and I…" I couldn't breathe because the waistband of my pants was cutting me in two. "And I'm getting fat!"

Brad pursed his lips. "That all?"

I rolled my eyes. Unbuttoned my top button as I slid into the car. As I turned the key, the engine cranked up. Brad still lingered outside my window, looking shell shocked. "Sorry, Brad. It's just been a bad day."

"I can see that," he said. "But I'm telling you, I got something that can take the edge off."

"No thanks. Last time I did that, my life fell apart." I shifted into reverse.

"Just saying. That was a long time ago. It's way better stuff now." He moved aside as my car started moving.

I was almost to the school to pick up the boys when Micah said. "Mommy, my tummy hurts."

"Not now, Micah. And you're seriously going to have stop pretending—"

I never finished the sentence because a kaleidoscope of vanilla, chocolate, and strawberry swirled like a tornado and in slow, excruciating motion slid down every crevice of my car. The windshield, the gear shift, the glove compartment... the cracks between the seats and the console. Micah spewed a smorgasbord of city-slicker Neapolitan... and I'm pretty sure the magic Shady Gully cherry landed in my purse.

Lenny had fallen asleep in his recliner, watching a cop show I'd seen a hundred times. I switched the channel, pausing on a cooking show featuring a woman making a chocolate soufflé. Naturally she was a size two and had long, flowing tendrils and shiny pink lip gloss.

"That looks good," mumbled Lenny as he woke up.

"Yeah." I sighed dejectedly.

"What's wrong, Desi? The kids are all sleeping. Even Micah's stomach seems settled. For the moment."

"I know. And tomorrow I get to get up and do it all over again."

Lenny looked back at the TV, watched as the chef created a base for the soufflé by folding a rich chocolate sauce into an egg white meringue. Or maybe he was watching the sexy chef. I picked up the remote and turned the TV off. "What are you doing tomorrow? If you can pick up the kids, I'll see if Heather will let me make up the hours I lost today."

"I can take them, pick them up. Whatever you need." Lenny reached over the cluttered end table, offered his hand. "What's wrong, Desi?"

From the love seat, I returned the gesture, squeezed his back. "I don't know. I'm just in a rut, I guess. I'm tired, but I'm bored too. I was thinking maybe we could go on a little vacation. Maybe take the kids to see Harry in Santa Fe? He and… Connie… bought a house there."

"Well, if you're gonna pitch it, pitch it like you mean it."

"I'm trying to like her. I really am."

Lenny nodded, understanding without further elaboration. "We can't afford plane tickets, but we could drive. I'd have to get the car checked out. And see if I can switch schedules with somebody."

I looked at the black screen on the TV. "I don't know. Might be more hassle than it's worth."

"Or maybe you and the kids could go?" When I said nothing, he added, "Or maybe a road trip all by yourself is what you need."

Without warning, tears fell from my eyes. Lenny let go of my hand, sat up, and clicked his recliner closed. "What you really need is Robin."

"Lenny, there's no point in going there."

"But it's true."

"Yeah, it's true. But what good does that do me? She doesn't want me."

He sighed and lifted himself out of the recliner. His hands automatically went to his back, which ached for days after he returned from offshore.

"I just don't get how she could abandon me." When Lenny got up, I twisted my head toward the kitchen as he downed an aspirin with a glass of water. "I mean, if she really thought Dean and I had a fling, why is she still with him? Why am I the one who gets cast aside?" I was getting myself worked up, and it annoyed me that Lenny was going through the motions of going to bed. "It's just like Sunny. All over again."

He stopped then. Just as I knew he would. "What do you mean by that, Desi?" He waited for a solid minute before giving up, switching off the tiny light over the sink. Which infuriated me. "And you," I went on. "Weren't you even a little bit jealous? You never even questioned me. Or Dean."

"Why would I do that? I trust you. I trust Dean. I know it was all lies."

"How do you know? What if I told you it was true? Would you fight for me? Or just say 'As if,' like you did then? You'll never know how much you hurt me by shrugging off the whole thing without even being a little jealous."

Irritated now, Lenny banged around making coffee for the morning. "Do you want me to be jealous? Would that help? Do you want me to go punch Dean in the nose?"

"Maybe." I was being irrational. I knew it, but I couldn't seem to rein myself in. "I mean, is it so hard to believe that someone would find me attractive? I know I don't look like I did when we got married, but—"

"Okay. That's enough. You're being silly, and I'm tired."

"For your information, I've had offers. I'm still desirable. Wanted."

Lenny scooped coffee into the basket, totally ignoring me now.

"So you're just going to make the coffee and go to bed? You're done then?"

"I can't talk to you when you're like this. I don't know what you want me to say. Whatever I say, it's going to be wrong."

I met him in the kitchen. "I'm so frustrated. I feel abandoned. I'm bored. This is not how I wanted my life to be."

"What did you want?" He huffed, completely exasperated.

"I don't know. I wanted a theater group or to go to a book club. Heck, Robin has a book club, and she doesn't even go for the right reasons."

"Start a book club then."

"Nobody around here would come. That's not the point, Lenny. I just… I don't know. I wanted more. This isn't how I dreamed my life would be."

"You think this is how I planned it all out? You think I didn't have bigger dreams than busting my back on a platform in the middle of the Gulf of Mexico? I wanted to be a college football star and go to the NFL, but that was never gonna happen, so this is my life. And you know what, Desi? I guess I just don't hate it as much as you do."

Lenny punched the timer on the coffeepot. "It's good, honest work, and it's wreaking havoc on my body, but I get to come home to you and the kids. And that's enough for me."

He flipped the big kitchen lights off. "And it's everything to me."

I stood there in the dark kitchen, vacillating from the satisfaction of getting him riled up to the shame of hurting him.

The latter won out. The final exclamation point on a crappy day.

As was our custom, we waited until the last possible minute to pay the monthly bills. In this case, payments due the roofer, the AC guy, and the electric company were overdue, but not yet in the penalty phase. Lenny had called the bank this morning, confirming that his paycheck had indeed cleared, and given me the go ahead to write the bills.

All good news until he reminded me, "You probably need to drop them at the post office on your way to work. That way they'll be postmarked today."

"Can't you do it?" I complained. "You know I hate going there."

"I could, but I'm dropping the kids off at school." He looked at his watch. "And they're running late. And you have to go by there anyway on your way to work."

I let out a giant sigh to emphasize my displeasure.

"You don't have to talk to Claire. They're already stamped. Just put them in the box."

Fine. It was too early in the day to be overwhelmed (that would come later), so I kissed the kids and hugged my husband and set out to conquer the day. It could always be worse. I sent up a prayer of gratitude—at least my car started.

Shady Gully was nice in the early morning hours. Spring was in the air, and there was a light mist on the grass, and pink blooms on the azalea bushes. I passed a few old folks sipping coffee on their porches. They waved.

There were more cars at the post office than I'd expected. Hopeful that I'd get lost in the early morning shuffle, I grabbed the stamped envelopes and set my sights on the USPS mailbox at the first entrance. With luck I could slip in and out.

I heard her big mouth echoing from the main vestibule, doing what she did best. "The family is in turmoil," Claire said. "From what I hear, they're divided about Dolly and Mitch."

"Forgiveness versus condemnation, huh?" snapped a voice I didn't recognize. "Do they even know where they ran off to?"

"I have a feeling the forgiveness side does, but it's a mess, especially with Brother Wyatt talking about retiring soon." I heard packing tape being rolled out and the hacking of a mailing label being printed. "That'll be $17.20 to go first class. Is that okay?"

"That's perfect," said the patron.

Despite the clear sounds of the exchange coming to a close, I lingered at the mailbox with the envelopes in my hand. *Put them in and go, Desi.*

"It's all gonna blow up soon," Claire said. "Probably when Jesse and James kill each other."

"That poor family," bemoaned the woman. "Thank the Lord it's been kept quiet all these years. Jethro is so surprised. And relieved."

Jethro? As in Jethro the principal of Shady Gully High?

"You know how Shady Gully is," Claire lamented. "Word travels fast."

Yeah, you know more than most, Claire. I dropped the letters into the mailbox, and high-tailed it to my car.

I'd just about made a clean break, when another vehicle pulled into the post office and a long, muscular arm flagged me down through the open window.

"Desi! Hey!" Denise, a pleasant face from homecomings past, carried a nice-sized box in her arms. "How are you?"

"Good. And you? I heard your team's softball season is going well so far."

"Yeah. I had a few free days before the big tourneys start, so I dashed up to see my folks. I'm glad I ran into you."

Something about her expression worried me. "Oh?"

"Is your mom doing better?" She must have read my expression because she elaborated. "My good friend is a paramedic, and she said they had a call out here a few weeks ago. I was surprised to hear it was your mom. My friend said Sunny was in bad shape, and would be in the hospital for a few days."

"Oh…" I couldn't muddle through what I was hearing. How could this be? What had happened? And how dare Tom not contact me?

And most of all, what if… ?

Fury and panic rose inside me as I stumbled back into my car, managing a half wave in Denise's direction.

"Desi? Are you okay?"

I started the ignition and drove in the opposite direction of work, all thoughts of Heather the Empress falling away with each mile to Sunny's house.

I was shocked by the state of disrepair and neglect when I pulled into Sunny's driveway. The trailer itself looked out of balance, as one side sunk dangerously low to the ground. Carpenter bees had set up colonies all along the gutters, and mildew had turned the color of the trailer from white to spoiled avocado green. I cared not that Tom's truck was here. I was going in one way or the other.

After maneuvering carefully around the rotted wood on the front steps, I banged on the door once, and walked in. The overwhelming smell of smoke and decay nearly took my breath away.

"Mama! Sunny!" I had my fist up, ready to bang on the bedroom door, but it was already ajar. The plaintive sounds of misery and torment seeped from the room. With a sense of foreboding, I pushed the door all the way open. I could see Sunny slumped on her pillow, the bed rumpled all around her, and Tom slapping her face repeatedly.

"Lovey! Lovey!" he wept.

Rage consumed me. "What are you doing?" I grabbed the

back of his shirt and pulled him off her. "Why are you hitting her like that?"

"I'm not hitting her! I'm trying to wake her up! I can't get her to wake up!"

"Move!" I pushed him aside. "Sunny," I said, taking in her ashen complexion, her fluttering eyes. "Mama, wake up. Open your eyes."

I turned to Tom, "How long have you—" I spotted all the prescription bottles on her vanity. "What is all this?"

"I think she took them. She takes a lot of stuff sometimes. But I found these. I think she saved them up."

"So you found her like this, and your solution is to pat her on the face until she wakes up? You imbecile! Get the phone! Call 911!"

Tom looked this way and that, as if unable to comprehend my instructions. I cursed as I ran to the living room and dialed the phone, stretching the long, curly cord back into the bedroom. Tom hovered over Sunny, weeping. I pushed him aside and handed him the phone. "Tell them to hurry."

"Mama." I gently took her in my arms and spoke in a calm voice. "I'm here. We're getting help. It's all going to be okay." As I listened to Tom mumbling into the phone, I used the damp bed sheets to wipe the moisture from her brow. Her skin felt clammy, sickly cold. "Please wake up, Mama." I gently smoothed her face, which seemed even more gray than it had a few seconds earlier. Fury, fear, and panic coursed through me.

"This is all your fault." I sneered at Tom. "Everything. It's all your fault. This should be you. Not her."

He scoffed at me, biting back a response.

When I turned back to Sunny, I saw foam coming from her mouth. "Oh, lovey," Tom moaned. "Look at that. Oh, lovey." His dramatic wailing struck me as insincere and affective. I grabbed the phone from him.

"Go," I told him. "Go wait outside for the ambulance. Flag them down."

"Why don't you go flag them down? You can't kick me out of my own house. I'm staying here with my wife."

I took my eyes away from Sunny for only a second. "Get out now."

"The hell I will. You go."

Before I placed the phone between my shoulder and chin, I glared at him. "I will take you down, old man. I've got years' worth of hate boiling inside me. I. Will. Take. You. Down."

Tom skulked out of the bedroom. I heard the screen door bounce closed.

"What can I do?" I asked the 911 operator.

"They're almost there," she assured me.

So, I held Mama. Got into bed next to her and gently put one of my arms beneath her head, encircling her frail shoulders. I clutched her hand with the other, whispering into her ear, "Please, Mama, not like this. Please… I'm so sorry I hurt you. I need you."

Her eyes fluttered, and for the briefest of moments I felt a faint pressure against my hand. "You are my very best thing," I told her. "I love you so much. Please don't leave me now, Mama."

But she did. I felt it the moment the life drained out of her.

Her spirit had always been so intensely bright, so beautiful and lively, that when it returned for just an instant, I felt a flicker, a current run through her body. And in that one glorious flash, all the anguish was stripped away, replaced by all that was good, pure, and true about Sunny.

And then it was gone. As if she'd passed through only to reclaim it and take it with her on her journey.

Somewhere where it was finally free to shine.

PART IV

Chapter Nineteen

Plum-Sized Proteins And Spirits
Robin (102.0 Pounds)

T he move almost killed me. In fact, the more I thought about it, maybe that was Dean's intention all along. He denied it, of course. Claimed he was frustrated with his boss, Ben, and that he was simply "done" with the pharmaceutical company. The timing was right, he'd insisted, as one of the headhunters had found a perfect place for him. One of the biggest accounting firms in the nation, Dazé & Nolan, needed a regional CFO at their East Coast headquarters. The position would not only double Dean's base pay but would offer several incentive bonuses. It was the big leagues, Dean contended. All we had to do was move to Lexington, Kentucky.

The kids had thrown a fit. Granted they were self-absorbed teenagers, and admittedly a tad entitled, but the degree of outrage they expressed was remarkable. Violet exclaimed in dramatic fashion that she would run away and join a band.

"What band?" Dean had asked, since our daughter had never shown interest in anything other than statistics and algebraic formulas.

"I don't know," she had railed. "But they'll be the most dangerous and sketchy band ever!"

Sterling, on the other hand, had responded with a casual,

"Sorry, but no thanks. I'll stay here and crash with my buddies. Graduate high school with my friends here in Texas."

Dean had become furious then, told us all we were ungrateful and that we didn't appreciate the fact that he was the one who had to go to work day in and day out, just so we could continue to "live the dream."

At that point Violet had started to cry, and for a whole minute Sterling maintained a look of thoughtfulness. And then they went off and did a very dangerous thing. Individually, each was a force, but together, they were Batman and Robin. Luke and Leia. Sherlock and Watson.

They approached us a few days later and announced they'd be willing to move (which was awfully accommodating of them), but they wanted us to seriously consider a highly acclaimed boarding school in Asheville, North Carolina. They actually used the words *highly acclaimed*. They lauded the school's excellent college prep courses and guaranteed the elevated curriculum would lead to opportunities at a variety of ivy league colleges. Also—they put the cherry on top—Asheville wasn't far from Lexington.

"Okay." Dean had agreed, knowing they had colluded with their friends and done their research and several other parents were likely getting the same North Carolina pitch. "We'll consider it."

I strongly disagreed, but anything to get the move moving, so to speak.

"Great. Perfect." Sterling was pleased.

So while Dean flew back and forth to Kentucky for meetings, and the kids were busy wrapping up their sophomore year in high school—and plotting their course to independence—I was left to pack up our lives in Dallas.

Violet refused to let me throw anything away, while Sterling said everything but his guitar could go to charity. Over a period of a month, I sorted, packed, and labeled like a madwoman.

After a few trips to Lexington, Dean and I found a beautiful home with a sprawling two acres of rich green grass, called *bluegrass* in Kentucky. The property bordered a horse farm, and as the owners encouraged us to spoil them, Dean had taken to the noble creatures immediately.

By the time the moving company showed up, I was ready to leave the crowded, polluted city behind and embrace the horses, hills, and bluegrass of Kentucky.

I was more than ready. I was excited. Just like Sunny used to say, moving was a chance to set goals... and reinvent yourself.

The landscapes in Lexington made me miss Sunny. The rolling hills covered in striking green grass, the horses grazing in misty pastures at sunrise, all framed by black fences and towering trees, moved me in a visceral way. It was the kind of scene Sunny would have painted in stunning fashion.

I took lots of photos and posted them on Facebook. Some I texted directly to Desi. We'd spend hours debating the merits of each, trying to decide which would have caught Sunny's fancy. One in particular, a gorgeous chestnut Mama horse and her baby, a shade lighter, with long legs and white socks, caught our eye. I'd snapped the photo just as the bold youngster dared to venture off a few feet from his protective Mama, and she'd raised her head in stern warning.

"That one," Desi said. "Sunny would have painted that one."

When Sunny died ten years ago, it had given me an excuse to go to Desi. To let the fact that she and Dean did whatever they did... go. Or at least try to. The jealousy and suspicion were always there, rearing up randomly, and robbing me of my peace, but Desi had needed me, and I couldn't let her grieve alone.

The suffering had been horrific. It was never determined if Sunny meant to kill herself, or if she'd overdosed accidentally, but the result had been the same. Long tormented by the estrangement with Desi, Sunny had finally succumbed to her heartbreak.

Desi, also devastated by the ordeal, had kept Sunny at a distance, denying her a part in her life. And in her children's lives.

Now haunted by guilt, the defeat in Desi's voice grew worse every time I spoke to her. I could see the regret in her face as pictures popped up on Facebook. I noted the hopelessness in her posture, and read the surrender in her weight gain. My friend was miserable and depressed.

When I mentioned I'd found a doctor willing to prescribe diet pills, and offered to get her some, she'd declined. Admittedly, I was relieved since I needed them for myself. I also suggested she find a doctor in Belle Maison, and floated the idea of antidepressants, but she'd mumbled about money, forcing me to drop the subject.

My computer dinged as I scrolled Facebook, signaling Violet had posted from North Carolina. The Dynamic Duo had won the boarding-school battle, and now my babies were over two hundred fifty miles away. My pretty little girl posed with three other girls, each wearing white lab coats, while holding up test tubes in a science classroom. An older, bespectacled man lurked in the background, sporting a bewildered expression. Apparently, I wasn't the only one puzzled by this generation. Violet looked happy, and I was glad I could at least lay eyes on her, as Sterling was less enthused about social media.

I scrolled some more, finding pictures of Max and Ernie, their kids, and my sisters-in-law, all apparently gathered at a crawfish boil. They also seemed happy.

A wave of sadness washed over me when I thought of how seldom I saw my siblings and their families. They were always busy, and I was glad their lives were full, but it still hurt when after traveling miles and wading through airports, they often put me off, claiming previous obligations and commitments. How had that happened, I wondered? And what part should I be playing in furthering Mama and Daddy's legacy? It seemed so wrong that distance and indifference could consume a family whose patriarch and matriarch were so devout, so defined by their love of family.

I looked at my watch and realized I'd wasted enough time

scrolling. The big gala was tonight, and putting myself together was more of a challenge than it used to be. I'd found an off-the-shoulder dress, bold for my age, but everything had to be just right for me to pull it off.

I threw my carrot and celery sticks in the garbage and headed to the scales.

Dean was distracted when he got home. "Just work stuff," he'd quipped while reaching for his tuxedo. I spent some time bolstering his ego, fastening his cufflinks, straightening his tie. "You look great," I smiled.

He raised his eyebrows, picked up his phone, and walked out. I sighed, hurt by his indifference.

I looked at myself in the mirror. I wasn't pleased. I looked like an old lady in a young girl's dress. As short as I was, I needed to lose another ten pounds to avoid looking dumpy. To make it all worse, I'd been having trouble with my contact lenses in Kentucky, and had no choice but to wear my glasses. All the bluegrass, I supposed.

I stood there studying my reflection in the mirror, deciding nothing was worse than appearing as if you were trying too hard. Since I didn't want to look like a fool, I unzipped my dress.

Dean beckoned. "Let's go, Robin. We're already late."

We hardly spoke a word on the way to the gala. How dare Dean already express frustration with his new job! After uprooting us and moving us across the country! Sure, I'd been apprehensive at first, but I'd jumped on board and been supportive. And now he was unhappy again. Being a supportive wife was a thankless job.

As we headed downtown, we passed a massive church that would probably have covered over three blocks in Dallas. I watched as policemen directed traffic in and out, and people of all ages offered cheery waves to one another. In the center of the massive structure was a giant cross.

It was nothing like Shady Gully Baptist Church, but I felt a sharp void nonetheless, a pang for something lost. "I guess that's what would be considered a megachurch, huh?"

Dean nodded. "Yeah, I hear good things. Darla and some of the other folks at work say they really walk the talk. Back up what they preach. Give back to the community."

"North Lake Christian Church." I noted the writing on the center building. "Maybe we should visit."

"Yeah, maybe," Dean said, swiping his phone at the red light.

A photographer snapped our picture as soon as we walked into the ballroom. We ordered drinks and perused the auction items. Although there were a few beautiful paintings of Kentucky landscapes, I thought they paled in comparison to Sunny's work.

"You look so pretty, Robin," complimented Darla, Dean's assistant. "Off the shoulder suits you!"

Darla was a heavyset young woman with a big smile and girlish dimples. She had a pixie haircut, which fit her perfectly.

"Thank you. You look beautiful as well." Pleased that she was the one working with Dean on a day-to-day basis, I added, "This is such a lovely venue."

I watched as Dean wandered over to greet another circle of people. Shaking hands, smiling, networking.

"Have you met Annie, Rick's wife?" Darla motioned to a mature woman holding an untouched glass of pink wine. As Rick was the CEO at Dazé & Nolan, I smiled enthusiastically.

Annie shook my hand, and grinned in a genuine manner. "It's so nice to finally meet you. Your husband raves about you and the twins."

"Thank you, Annie. It's a pleasure to meet you."

Darla headed off as Annie and I traded pleasantries. Annie was sharing a story about her grandchildren, when I noticed a sleek, elegant young woman approach Dean, place her hand lightly on his back, and lure him aside. The two began a serious conversation, heads bent close.

"Excuse me," I said to Annie as I moved toward Dean and the mystery woman. I hovered there for several agonizing seconds before Dean finally turned and acknowledged me.

"Oh, Gayle, I'd like you to meet my wife, Robin." Dean turned to me. "Robin, this is Gayle, the director of human resources."

I shook Gayle's hand, noting the absence of a ring on her finger.

"It's nice to meet you," she said.

As we chitchatted, Dean reached over and shook another tuxedoed man's hand, who in turn joined our little group. While the man barely acknowledged me, he raised his eyebrows pleasingly at the lovely Gayle.

"Tank," Dean said, "this is my wife, Robin." Tank, a robust man with a mischievous grin and thinning hair, shook my hand. "Tank is the COO at Dazé & Nolan."

"It's a pleasure," I said, but Tank barely acknowledged me as he seemed much more intent on how "nice Gayle cleaned up." Dean and I sipped our drinks throughout Tank's obsequious appraisal, until we were finally able to excuse ourselves.

The rest of the evening progressed in a similar fashion. Introductions ensued, people deemed me insignificant, and quickly moved on. I realized that the smiles and the compliments were reserved for the beautiful people. They were the centers, and everyone gravitated toward them with the single-mindedness of a bulldozer. Whoever was in their way was cast aside as irrelevant. Quite literally, I learned, as one young man crashed into me on his way to deliver a drink to a striking brunette. "Oh, I'm sorry, ma'am. Are you okay?" And when had I become a *ma'am*?

Relieved when the night was over, I enjoyed the silence on the way home. Unfortunately, Dean was keyed up. "Tank is a bit of a blowhard, but he's got some good ideas and he commands respect."

"I can see that," I said. "What about Gayle? She certainly seems popular."

"I don't know. I don't know her that well."

"I'm sure you'll get there." It must have been my tone that set him off. Or maybe he was just feeling guilty?

"Don't start, Robin. Just don't." He put his blinker on, picking up speed once he turned. "I just can't deal with that now."

"Oh, I'm so sorry. I forget how important you are." He didn't respond. "I wouldn't be this way if you didn't have a history."

"A history? You've got to be kidding me." Dean looked sideways at me, headlights reflecting off his glasses. "You're impossible, you know that? What do you want from me? What do you want me to do?"

"I want you to be honest. I want you to finally come clean about Desi."

"Do you want me to say it's true? Is that what you really want? Because I will. And I'll beg for forgiveness. Heck, let's give that a try, since telling you the truth hasn't worked."

"I guess I don't really care if it's true or not anymore. But I'll never trust you ever again."

Dean, angry now, tightened his lips and became sullen. He glanced at the giant church as we passed it on the way home. "Like you ever did."

I ignored his remark, fixating on the enormous cross that lit up the night sky. And then I turned away from it, overwhelmed with a cloying feeling of shame.

The long drive home had drawn me deeper into my warm, familiar blanket of self-pity. It was my usual pattern. I'd start to feel better about myself, and think I was okay. And then foolishly dip my toe out of the confines of my isolation, out of my comfort zone, only to confirm that I was indeed inadequate. Only the beautiful were revered, and I quite simply didn't measure up.

Yet I had a new plan. A goal, as Sunny used to say. I'd up my daily dosage of the trifecta to three instead of two. And I'd cut my daily treat of five almonds out of my diet completely. I'd skip the wine too. The calories were too high, and it was time to get serious.

By the next function, I'd be so noticeably thin that people couldn't possibly look through me. Even Dean would have to acknowledge me. The kids as well. Despite being so completely self-absorbed, my family would finally have to recognize me.

I squinted as the garage lights clicked on and Dean parked the car. Still agitated, he threw his keys onto the foyer tray as we walked inside. "I think we should go to counseling."

"What? I'm not doing that. That's ridiculous."

"Why is it ridiculous?" When I didn't respond, he put his hands on his hips. "Robin, I've never cheated on you, but I'm starting to think you want me to—it's like you're trying to drive me away."

"Why would I do that?"

"I have no idea. Maybe so you can say you were right all along?"

I scoffed as I walked into the kitchen, shaking an aspirin out of the bottle.

"Good night," Dean said.

I mumbled back, distracted as I searched the back of the bottle to see if there were calories in aspirin.

Dean was out of town, and I had the whole house to myself. I ran on the treadmill in the morning and again in the late afternoon. I wouldn't even have to pretend to eat tonight, since I was alone.

I was just about to prepare a basket of apples and carrots and walk across the pasture to feed the horses on the neighbor's farm, when the phone rang. Thinking it was Dean, I answered in a nonchalant voice.

But it was Sterling. And my heart flipped. "Hey, Mom, what's up?"

"Hey! How are you? Is school okay? Have you seen Violet?" I couldn't stop myself from rattling off questions like an interrogator, but the sound of his voice had a way of dousing the fumes of my hopelessness. "I miss you so much, baby boy."

"Oh, c'mon, Mom." I could almost see him rolling his eyes. "Where's Dad?"

"He's in Chicago. Some team-building nonsense, I think. What's wrong?"

"Nothing. I just wanted to ask him something." I sensed I was losing him, and he was already thinking of ways to let me go. "What have you been up to, Mom?"

"I'm good," I answered. "I was about to go feed Sam and Ellie's horses."

"Oh cool." I could tell he was smiling over the phone. "Did the mare have her baby yet?"

"Yes, she did. He's so cute. Ellie named him Kuzco because she said he looks like a llama."

Sterling laughed. "I loved that show. *The Emperor's New Groove.*"

"Yeah, how many times did we watch that?" I chuckled. "Have you seen Violet?"

"No, Mom. It's not like I have classes with her or anything."

"Oh, well, I know. I just thought—"

"All right, I'll let you go feed them."

"No, no. It's okay. I can do that later."

"No, I need to call Dad real quick."

"Okay. Well…" I admonished myself for saying the wrong thing. Again. Driving him away just like Dean said. I guess I had a knack for that. "Well, I love you, baby." I wanted to ask him if he'd got the care package I'd sent or if he was coming home for the upcoming long weekend, but it was too late. I'd blown it.

"Bye, Mom." I berated myself as he clicked off.

I tried not to dwell on my failure and instead filled my basket with treats for the horses. By the time I reached the fence line at the end of the pasture, I was out of breath and a little dizzy.

The horses eagerly approached the fence and flicked their tails with appreciation as they gobbled their treats. Kuzco, the feisty colt with the large brown eyes, studied me as he chewed. While I scratched the soft, fuzzy coat along his neck, I noticed the beginnings of a rainbow as it came to life atop Sam and Ellie's barn. I instantly felt my pocket for my phone but realized I'd left it on the bar. The fact that I had no one to share this beauty with left me feeling sad and regretful.

Exquisite moments like this, bursting with such overwhelming loveliness, sometimes made me question my own brokenness. Caught in this stunning picturesque instant, it was hard not to wonder if a lot of my anguish was of my own making.

I sipped herbal tea and scrolled Facebook late into the evening. I was surprised to learn that the gala raised over $30,000 on the auction items alone. I zoomed in on a photo of the foundation president holding a giant check, smiling for the camera. While the amount raised was impressive, I was disappointed because I hadn't seen anything bid worthy. I opened another screen and googled landscapes and oil paintings. My eyes widened as thousands of links pulled up.

I went to the kitchen to pour myself another cup of tea, trying to ignore the hunger pangs as I traipsed through the living room back to my office. I noted that while we had accumulated some nice pieces of art over the years, we had blank wall space to spare.

I browsed through some impressive art, but nothing caught my fancy. One link led to another link, and soon I discovered that the way to buy art was via fine art exchanges, all anonymous and done by brokers.

My eyes were getting heavy when my phone buzzed with a text. Dean, saying good night. *Going to bed*, he said. I responded with, *How was dinner and the evening in general? Long*, he replied, *and boring.* The phone rang.

"I hate texting," he said. "Why are you up so late?"

"I'm looking at paintings. Did you know the gala raised over thirty thousand dollars on auction items?"

"I heard that." He yawned. "Did we buy anything?"

"No." I clicked the mouse and absently opened a new page. "Have you heard of fine art brokers? Is that a thing?"

"Yeah. I think they're sort of the middleman between buyers and sellers. They keep it anonymous, discreet and all that. What did you have for dinner?"

"Uh… why?" I sounded defensive, but since when was Dean monitoring my calories?

"Just asking. I worry you don't eat when I'm gone." I could hear his exasperation. "Anyway, I had some kind of protein. I think fish. It was the size of a plum. Served with two dollops of some kind of green sauce smeared on the plate. I'm starving."

"I'm sure it was delicious." I chuckled, genuinely amused. I suddenly missed him very much. "Did Sterling call you?"

"Yeah. One of his buddies is selling a car."

"And he wants to buy it?"

"He does. I told him we might try to drive down in a few weeks because you were missing them."

I laughed. "Yeah, right. More like you are."

"Maybe a little. Anyway, pick a weekend you want to go. Book a nice hotel, some fancy restaurants. It would be nice to get the gang all together."

"Yeah." I smiled. "It would."

When we hung up, my heart swelled. With love? Happiness? Again with that fleeting twinge, that notion that I'd lost chunks of my life and subjected myself to needless doubt—

And then Facebook summoned me with a ding, so I mindlessly obliged and switched screens. I scrolled to see what was new. There was a new post with pictures from Micah, but I didn't click on it.

Instead, with a sense of dread, I clicked on a newly posted photo from Annie, the wife of the CEO of Dazé & Nolan. She wasn't my friend in real life, but she was on Facebook. She and her husband, Rick, were in the picture. So were Tank and a woman I assumed was his wife. Darla and a few of the other executives' assistants were there as well. They were all gathered around a table in a glitzy restaurant, plates laden with protein the size of plums and dollops of smeared sauce.

Oh look, and there was Dean, smiling, not looking bored at all. And next to him was none other than Gayle, the superbly cleaned-up human resources director wearing a curve-hugging purple dress spilling over with cleavage.

I was furious. Hurt. And felt foolish for my momentary lapse of sentimentality. Here they were, the gang all together. Wasn't that the phrase Dean had used? Only I hadn't been invited to partake in the plum-sized protein and spirits, and apparently Gayle had stepped in for me.

I quickly closed Facebook, hoping to avoid making a snide comment under the picture. I stared at the black monitor for a solid minute before searching *how to tell if your husband is cheating.* Along with several advertisements for private investigators, a long list appeared. Body language was number one.

I jumped back onto Facebook, enlarging the picture, but something drew my eye to the side of the screen. Nothing to do with cheating or body language or plum-sized food. It was a photo of a painting from the art brokerage website I'd been searching. I gasped aloud. It couldn't be…

I zoomed in, my heart pounding in my chest. "Oh my God." I noted the price and hit Purchase. "I can't believe this," I mumbled. "But it is…"

There was no mistaking the turbulence of the ocean, the deep-blue waves with expertly painted white caps. And the ill-fated ship against the hazy moon. How could I ever forget this painting? It had been on an easel next to the Battle of Waterloo scene Sunny had been painting that afternoon.

That magical afternoon of makeovers, Napoleon and Désireé, and fairy tales. After all this time, how had Sunny's painting made it to a fine art exchange?

I started to text Desi but realized it was too late. Besides, what would I say? I scrolled through the pictures Micah had posted earlier. She and her brother Peter, who was starting his senior year, and Luke, who was now in college. Where had the time gone?

Another photo of Micah looking fabulous in her Shady Gully High cheerleading uniform. She was the spitting image of Desi at that age. Perhaps like Desi, Micah would rise to popularity and win homecoming queen her senior year. This saddened me, for some inexplicable reason.

Especially when looking at Desi next to her beautiful, vibrant daughter. Her clothes were rumpled, her grin was forced, and her eyes reflected nothing but agony.

There was a time long ago I might have delighted in this, felt a little victory after living in Desi's shadow for so many years. Not to mention what happened with her and Dean.

But the defeated and weary look on my friend's face now had nothing to do with the way she looked on the outside. The torment she felt was deeply rooted on the inside, knifing through her much like the blue waves were tossing that ill-fated ship around the turbulent ocean.

Chapter Twenty

Winston In A Frame
Desi

Saint John's Hospital in Belle Maison was a nice hospital. The rooms were nice, and the cafeteria was nice. Even the nurses and the doctors were nice. But if I had to stay here one more day, I'd slit my wrists.

While Lenny slept through most of the last three days, I perched in the uncomfortable chair next to his bed, at the ready with ice chips. The doctor came by daily to admire his handiwork, and this morning, he'd given us the okay to go home. Now we were waiting to be discharged.

My phone rang the same time Luke walked into the hospital room. Robin. Deciding to call her back, I embraced my eldest child. "Hey, honey." Now old enough to fight in wars and buy a drink, Luke looked every bit the grown man. Polo shirt tucked into belted khakis. Conservative short haircut. He reminded me of Dean.

"How was school?" I asked.

He made a face. "Mom, it's college. Why can't you say, how were classes?" Luke had moved into his own apartment, and was "going to classes" at the local college in Alexandria. He also worked a part time job to pay his tuition. Lenny was thrilled at the notion his son would someday have a job that wouldn't ruin his back.

227

"Sorry. I'm not college educated, so I don't know how to talk."
Luke ducked his head, feeling guilty. "What did the doctor say?"
"He said your dad is managing the pain well, so that's good.
When we get home, we have to focus on minimizing the pressure
on the back while the"—I looked at the medical term on the
release papers—"lumbar spinal fusion solidifies."
"That's doable. I'll come by. Give you a break."
We turned as Petey and Micah walked into the room. Micah,
pretty and petite, was dwarfed by Petey, her long and lanky
brother. She was dressed to perfection even after a full day at
school, while Petey had dirt on his jeans and under his finger-
nails. As usual, despite being under the hood of a car all day, he
maintained a skip in his step and a sparkle in his eye.

As soon as Petey graduated from high school almost two years
ago, he'd moved into a trailer with one of his buddies. He also
landed a full-time job at the one and only auto shop in Shady
Gully. Like Luke, Petey had done well in school, but unlike
Luke, he had no interest in continuing his education. "I'm done
cracking the books," he'd justified. "I'd rather work with my
hands. I don't have a problem working for the Man, especially
if it means I get to settle here in Shady Gully and get a home-
cooked meal at Mama's a few days a week."

Luke hadn't pushed Petey. He'd always been fiercely protective
of both Petey and Micah. He'd fight any battles they picked or
found themselves in, and I thought Luke secretly dreamed of
getting a college degree and using it for good here in Shady Gully.

"Hey, old man." Petey grinned at Lenny as he stirred. "Enough
laying around now. What do you think this is?" He squeezed
Lenny's toe. "A vacation?"

Lenny grinned when he heard Petey's voice. As did most
everyone. Petey was my little charmer. He had a way about him
that drew people in and held them close. He reminded me of
someone else I once knew.

"Hey, Dad." Micah kissed Lenny on the cheek. "I heard you
get to come home today."

"About time," Lenny grumbled. "This hospital bill is gonna put us in the poor house."

Micah leaned in and whispered in my ear, "I need to talk to you." Her expression hinted at the dramatic. But that was the norm with Micah.

Just then a pretty nurse with raven hair came in, followed by an aide pushing a wheelchair. "Your limo awaits," she said. She handed me some paperwork. "Just need your autograph, ma'am, and here are the prescriptions he'll need. He's likely to have some residual pain, so we want you to have this ready." She was attractive, and both Luke and Petey admired her curves.

Petey squinted at her name tag. "Tammy Jo. Now that's a great name."

Luke folded his arms, amused as he watched his brother's moves.

"Well thanks." Tammy Jo blushed, turning to me. "If you want to go to the pharmacy and pick those up, we'll have him ready to go downstairs." She pivoted back to Petey, "What's your name?"

"I'm glad you asked," Petey grinned. "My mama named me after the great apostle Peter. He was the feisty one, in case you were wondering."

"Oh, that's good to know." Tammy Jo chuckled. "And what does everybody call you?"

"Dweeb," Micah said.

"I used to call him PeePee when he was little." Luke unfolded his arms.

Petey shrugged. "You, my dear Tammy Jo, may call me anything you like."

"I'd go with dweeb," Micah said.

Tammy Jo laughed and patted Lenny's leg. "How do you put up with them?"

"It ain't easy." Lenny's chuckle turned into a cough.

Tammy Jo told me, "You can just pull your car around to the entrance of the hospital. We'll meet you there in about fifteen minutes."

I signaled to Micah, and we headed down to the pharmacy. She asked, "Is Daddy going to be able to go back to work?"

"Not tomorrow, no."

"I don't mean tomorrow. I mean ever?"

I sighed. "I don't know, honey. The doctor says he's doing well, so we'll just have to see how it goes. Why?" I handed the prescription to the pharmacist and had to sign some papers as the pain meds were considered narcotics.

"I just found out how much cheerleading camp is gonna be."

My heart dropped. We simply could not afford three hundred dollars now. We were already overdrawn, and the bills were mounting. Plus, I had taken a leave from work to get Lenny through this surgery.

"I know it's a lot, Mom, but I have to go. I'm head cheerleader."

"When is it due?"

"We have to pay four hundred now and—"

"Four hundred? Good gracious, it went up. It used to be three hundred."

"Mama, that was a hundred years ago. It's eight hundred now. Half now and half when we get to Natchitoches."

I had no words. So I focused on the pharmacist. Watched the little pills as the machine counted them out. If only I could just run away, escape… but where would I go? And what would happen to my family?

I barely listened as Micah prattled on. It was only going to get worse as homecoming rolled around. If Micah made the court, how on earth would we swing that expense?

I thought briefly about Robin. About doing something I swore I would never do. Ever. No, I wasn't that desperate. Yet.

"Mama? Are you listening?"

"Yes, of course." I handed the cashier my credit card and prayed it wouldn't be declined. "You were talking about cheerleading uniforms. How much is that going to cost?"

Micah looked stricken. "Not much. Just the material. Dawn's Mama is gonna sew them to save money."

As we headed to the elevators, I felt guilty for snapping at Micah. "We'll figure it out, honey. Don't worry."

Micah let a moment pass before succumbing to her love of random chat. "Everybody is talking about which church they're going to Sunday. Dawn's family is going to Brother James's, but Rachel's folks are going to Brother Jesse's. Crazy, huh?"

"Yeah," I replied.

"Both churches look exactly alike. And they're right next to each other. Everybody at school is laying bets on where Brother Wyatt will go."

When we walked outside, we watched as Luke carefully steered Lenny's wheelchair toward the vehicle, and Lenny gazed up at the sunshine as if it were the risen Lord himself.

"Oh, he's so embarrassing," Micah scoffed.

"Who?"

She was looking at Petey, who peered over Tammy Jo's shoulder as she entered her number into his phone.

I was taking inventory in Luke's old room. I had Sunny's paintings divided into three piles. One for those I didn't want to part with, one for those I couldn't bear to part with, and finally, those I'd pass on to the kids one day. The last pile was the biggest, but the more our expenses grew, I found myself making hard choices.

The light from the bedroom window illuminated one of my favorites, a shack on a riverbend. It was jumbled with yellows and oranges, and the dilapidated shack was painted rustic red. As usual, Sunny had done a wonderful job with the river, blending tans and blues into a muddied texture that seemed sprung from another era. I snapped a picture with my phone.

No, I couldn't part with this one.

I selected another one from the ones I didn't want to part with pile. It was a bowl sitting atop an old-time credenza. It contained an apple, an orange, and a lime, but they paled next to the little toy car haphazardly strewn amid the fruit. It told a story of a home, a family, and a little boy. I loved this painting. Why hadn't I ever asked Sunny what it meant to her? How had she imagined this family behind the bowl? And the boy? Was he precocious or shy? Had he been trying to hide his toy car? Or had he hastily dropped it into the bowl as he galloped off to another adventure? I snapped a picture with my phone.

No, I couldn't part with this one either.

On and on it went, the depths of my sadness plummeting with each new picture I snapped. There was a tap at Luke's door, and Lenny shuffled in and took in the sight of the paintings. And my tears.

"Missing your Mama today?"

"Yeah," I said. "Do you need another pill? Are you hurting?"

"No. I'm doing good. I'm weaning myself off. Just wanted to tell you Petey is bringing over a pizza, so you don't have to cook tonight."

"Good." As Lenny started to leave, I said, "Lenny? Did I tell you I saw Tom and his new wife at the gas station last week?"

He leaned onto the frame of the door for support.

"They were holding hands. At the gas station. Isn't that disgusting? He was prancing around wearing a button-down western shirt, and she was laughing at something he said…"

"What'd you do?"

"I rode home on fumes so I didn't have to talk to them. Her name is Wanda. She has red hair and…" I swallowed. "It just makes me sick that he's happy."

Lenny nodded. "Well, I reckon you could have run over them and that would have been the end of that." He was trying to make me laugh, but I was too tense.

"I wonder if he still has any of Mama's paintings."

"I thought he gave them all to you."

"That's what he said. But I wouldn't put it past him."

Lenny ambled over to the rocker I used to rock Luke in and sat gingerly. "Nothing's stopping me from rounding up the boys and going over and taking a look."

I took in the sight of this hobbled man ready to spring into action out of devotion and sheer love for me. I was so humbled I looked away.

"Desi, I know you don't want to talk to me about it. You never have, and I've let it be. But"—Lenny scratched the stubble on his chin—"I'm not so dumb I don't have an idea what happened."

I swatted a tear away. Looked at the floor, at Mama's paintings spread around the room. All that I had left of her. "It was just a fight."

"No. I don't believe that. I believe Tom laid a hand on you. Or worse."

My shoulders sagged with the heaviness of a lifetime of shame.

"Just so you know, I've wrestled with the idea of… hurting him. Especially when I was younger. Even now if I think about it too long, I get stirred up and want to make him suffer. At this point it might even be a fair fight, considering the shape I'm in." He reached over and lightly brushed my fingers. "But I still think I could take him."

I eyed him with a crooked grin. "I think so too."

"What I've never understood is, what happened with Sunny?"

"She didn't believe me," I said vehemently. "She picked him."

"That's nonsense. She never picked him. She settled because she didn't know what else to do. She hated him, Desi. It was clear in everything she did. All that hate rotted inside her, poisoned her, and eventually killed her. But I don't think she felt she had any other options."

"But she did. I told her she could move in with us."

"I know. And I agree she made a bad choice. But we've all made dumb choices, right?" Lenny shook his head regretfully. "Sunny was amazing. Special. All that. But she was the most fragile person I've ever known. She wasn't strong like you."

"I'm not—"

"Yes, you are. This has been your cross to bear. You've carried it around all these years, held it close, embraced it even. And look at you. You're the most wonderful mother, the most beautiful wife, and the most loyal friend."

We heard the rattle of the front door opening. "Delivery!" Petey bellowed. "Come and get it while it's hot."

Then the sound of Micah's sneakers as she squeaked through the garage door. "Did you get extra pepperoni?"

"No. For you I got pineapple and anchovies."

"Gross!" Micah groaned. "You're such a dweeb."

As I helped Lenny up, we shared a parental chuckle. He squeezed my hand and made his way to the kitchen. Before following, I flipped through the pictures I'd taken of Sunny's paintings, indecisive. Just then my phone buzzed with a text. Wolfheart.

I entered my security code. *You sitting tight?* Brad had texted. *Or you need anything?*

My fingers hovered over the letters on the mini keyboard. Finally, I typed, *I'm good for now.*

Robin's problems were in another realm. Granite versus butcher block, which apparently was very trendy now. "I don't know," I told her.

"Desi, look again. Come on." She moved her phone closer to the samples, and I endured another round of bullet points on each. I was at a red light and had my phone mounted on the dash. "I like the granite."

"Really? I do too. But then I keep thinking, it's just a basement."

I resisted an eye roll, lest FaceTime betray me. "Then go with the butcher block." The light turned green, and I was on the move again after chasing my tail all morning.

"Okay." The view on the phone shook before Robin's face appeared. "That's enough of that. How is Lenny?"

"Lenny is good. Are you actually wearing lip gloss and full makeup at ten in the morning? What planet are you from?"

Robin laughed. "I'm going into Louisville later. And you're one to talk. You've already been to Belle Maison this morning."

Yeah, I thought dismally. And I got a flat-out rejection from Heather Hard Body at Penney's, who'd suggested I reapply for my old job when my family "situation" was less chaotic. "What's in Louisville?" I asked Robin. "Have you already run out of places to shop in Lexington after two years?"

"No." She laughed. "It's just something I thought about doing when we first moved here. I should have done it sooner."

"Consider me intrigued." I ran my hand through my hair, catching a glimpse of my sloppy appearance in the rearview mirror.

"What's up with you?" Robin changed the subject.

Nothing good, I thought miserably. A meltdown at the Belle Maison Post Office after mailing six of Sunny's paintings to my Fine Arts Sellers Club. I'd ended up parting with both the toy car in the fruit bowl and the shack on the river painting—as well as four others. "Uh… Micah is on the homecoming court," I told Robin. "Petey has a girlfriend."

"That's exciting."

"Yeah." I put my blinker on and turned into the last pharmacy in Belle Maison before the Shady Gully exit.

"Anyway, tell me about Lenny. Is he bored?"

"Yes, he's losing his mind. We got into a fight this morning because I opened a new pack of coffee before the old one was empty. And he's been watching cooking shows, so at dinner he says things like, 'I like the texture of the radishes. They balance the smoothness of the aioli.'"

"Aioli? Wow. He's practically a master chef." Robin laughed. "Where are you now? Sounds like you just went into a store. You're out of breath."

"At the grocery store," I lied, switching off FaceTime, huffing as I placed the empty oxycodone prescription bottle on the pharmacy counter.

The clerk pushed the be-aware-that-this-is-a-narcotic form over for me to sign.

"Yeah, he's ready to get back to work," I told Robin. "He's going to take a supervisory role on the next offshore tour. Hopefully, it won't be too much strain on his back."

"Is that necessary? I mean, if y'all need money—"

"—no, we're fine." *Of course we need money.*

Why else would I be selling away my memories? And it wasn't easy. Because Lenny was home all the time, I had to sneak around, quietly carting Sunny's art into my car while he was preoccupied or in the bathroom. There were things that Lenny just couldn't handle, and the extent of our money problems was one of them. He'd practically been doubled over in pain before the kids and I made him go to the doctor. And getting him to agree to have the surgery had been another battle.

The pharmacy clerk took the cash I gave her and handed me the receipt. The other thing Lenny couldn't handle was the extent of my… habit. And that's all it was really. I just tended to get a little nervous when I didn't have stash on hand. Occasionally I'd buy weed from Brad, as it helped me relax when I had a night to myself, like when Lenny was offshore, and the kids were busy.

But now that Lenny was home all the time, and the bills were piling up, I'd been feeling tense and edgy. Wound tight, as Brad would say. And those pills of Lenny's were just wasting away because he insisted he didn't need them.

I hadn't meant to take any, but one night I just couldn't make the bad thoughts go away. I tried saying the Lord's Prayer, I tried reading my devotional, and I even tried listening to worship music. But as hard as I tried to hold on to the memory of Sunny's bright, shiny face, the image was devoured by the excruciating last moments of her broken life.

And then I took one pill. Just one. And I found oblivion.

"Desi. Where are you now? Put me back on FaceTime."

"I'm headed back to Shady Gully." My hatred of FaceTime increasing by the minute, I begrudgingly mounted my phone and turned her on again. "You look gaunt," I snapped. "Like you're starving. You're not taking those diet pills again, are you?"

A kaleidoscope of emotions flitted across Robin's FaceTime face. I really was losing my mind. Lashing out at Robin wouldn't help anything. "Have you heard from Ernie and Max lately?" I asked nicely, "What's their take on the dueling churches?"

"No. I get a 'Happy Birthday' text or a 'Merry Christmas' text, but we don't talk often. Can you believe that? I'm fresh out of Shady Gully sources."

"Word is Jesse's leading on the number of cars in the parking lot, but James landed Brother Wyatt's attendance the first Sunday, so I guess it's a wash."

"Where'd y'all go?"

"We flipped a coin. Landed in favor of Jesse. But when Lenny saw that it was called Jesse's Church of Christ, we went next door to James's Church. Lenny's roots are Catholic, remember, so it's all getting to be a bit much for him."

"Poor Lenny," Robin said.

Eventually Robin signed off to go to her mysterious meeting in Louisville, and I made it to the Shady Gully exit. I processed the pros and cons of my morning. I lost my job and I lost six more of Sunny's paintings. But I had money to pay bills and a bottle of pills to ward off the bad thoughts. Much like the dueling churches, my morning was a wash.

Micah was at cheerleading camp for a week. Luke was in the midst of finals. And Petey was either on his way to the small town of Naryville to meet Tammy Jo's parents or hanging out with his friends in Shady Gully. I was helping Lenny pack for his first trip offshore since the surgery.

"I put in the heating pad in case you start aching," I told him. "Remember, you can make it cold too, if that feels better to you."

"I got it. I'm gonna be fine. Oh, did you put my Harry Bosch book in?"

"I can't believe you're a reader now." I patted his suitcase top. "Yes, I put it in. You'll be able to see who did it."

"Oh, no worries there. Harry always gets his guy." Lenny's brow furrowed. "You think I should take a few of those pills with me?"

I held my breath, kept my face normal. "Yeah, just in case. Are you hurting?"

"No, I feel good. Just thinking, in case of an emergency."

"I'll go get them. I moved them a while back." I casually walked out of the bedroom, leaving Lenny to pack his underwear and T-shirts. In Luke's room, behind some of Sunny's old paint supplies, I gathered a handful of the pills from the bottle. In the kitchen I sealed them in a bag and brought them to Lenny. When I walked back into our bedroom, I gasped.

Leaning against the bed was Winston. In a frame. I'd never seen it, but the painting captured his little egg-shaped head and his long, droopy ears. His tongue lolled, and his smile was crooked. Sunny had captured his essence perfectly.

"Oh… Oh Lenny. Where did you—"

"I wanted to surprise you. I was gonna leave it where you could find it this week. But you know me, I'm kind of impatient."

I knelt next to the painting, held it up, pulled it toward my face. "I never knew she did this," I cried.

"Me neither. The boys and I paid Tom and Wanda a visit yesterday. Looked through his closet, the shed in the back."

"What did he do? Was he hateful?"

"No, he was meek actually. When we found this in the laundry room, the old reprobate was even contrite."

"Thank you, Lenny." My sobs were soundless, just tears falling at will. "I love you."

"I love you too, Desi. And rest assured, you've got all her paintings now."

I stood up and held on to him for dear life. Several minutes later when he set me aside and whispered that he'd better get on the road, my heart broke in two.

I swallowed half of one of Lenny's pills with a glass of iced tea. It was early evening, the sun was setting, and I'd set the painting of Winston against the wicker chair on the porch. I kicked my feet up on the ottoman and watched the sun set, hoping relaxation and the notion of my childhood dog would ease me into oblivion.

It didn't. Maybe because I wanted it so badly. Maybe because I'd only taken half a pill. I wondered if Lenny had made it safely. I wondered if Petey and Tammy Jo had decided to go to Naryville or hang out here with his friends. I wondered about Micah, my little shining star at cheerleading camp in Natchitoches, Louisiana.

I closed my eyes and prayed that the tingling burn in my stomach would spread and settle my qualms, run off my bad thoughts. To hurry the process along, I picked up my phone and called Robin. It took forever for her to answer, and when she did, it was obvious I'd interrupted something. She seemed unusually distraught, along with another ingredient I couldn't identify. Resolve? Fear? She finally told me she couldn't talk, but that she'd call me later.

"Okay." I sighed, sweating in the Louisiana humidity. I raised my housedress to my thighs and fanned my chubby legs. The dress was an ugly tent of a thing with orange and yellow flowers, but who cared? It didn't bind me up and make me miserable. Eventually, I was going to have to lose weight. I guessed.

I dialed Harry's number. It was an hour earlier in Santa Fe. I'd like to hear his voice, hear him call me pumpkin again, even if I had to go through Connie to do it. But the line rang and rang there as well. "Okay." I sighed again, gulping my sugary tea, checking the time on my phone.

A text chimed, and I saw Connie's moniker. She explained that Daddy was asleep, and she hated waking him since he'd been feeling bad lately. Wow. So that was how it was gonna be. I'd have to go through Connie the Gatekeeper to talk to my father.

I worried that he was sick, that he was aging. I needed to do better checking in with him. I'd add him to my growing list of worries and regrets. Along with Lenny's health, paying bills, and losing enough weight to make breathing in this humidity easier.

I set my glass of tea down and stared at Winston for a minute. When he didn't respond, I picked up my phone and sent a text.

Hey, I typed, *what's up?*

Several minutes went by before I decided heck with it—I'd take the other half of Lenny's pill and have some ice cream. And then I heard a ding.

Wolfheart said, *Meet you at Cicada in twenty.*

Chapter Twenty-One

The Before
Robin (98.4 Pounds)

W hile I sensed the boredom and neediness in Desi's voice, I simply couldn't talk to her. I promised I'd call later, and I would, but first I had to deal with the drama in my own household.

Not only was Dean out of town—again—but Violet and Sterling were about to get on the road to return to North Carolina. "It's so late," I told Sterling, worried they'd be driving in the dark hours of the night. "Why don't y'all just stay here tonight and leave early in the morning?"

"Mom." He rolled his eyes. "The traffic will be worse then, and besides, 'Rambler' likes night driving." Not only had he named his new car, but apparently it had its own preferences and partialities. I just raised my eyebrows and returned my focus to Violet.

After what she'd told me earlier, I knew I needed some time with her. And I could tell by the way she fidgeted that she was upset. I looked firmly at Sterling, took in his thick dark hair and handsome, muscular frame. "Fine," I told him. "But I need Violet to help me with something first."

When Sterling scoffed, Violet made a big show of mocking me as well. After an impressive performance, she followed me into the sitting room in the master bedroom. "Mama," she said, "why are you making a big deal of this?"

"I'm not. It's not."

She plopped her Dr Pepper can on the mahogany coffee table and folded her lithe, lanky frame onto the down feather loveseat. "Whatever."

"Violet, you are a beautiful young woman." I moved the Dr Pepper can onto a coaster. "You're being silly."

"I'm just not going to go." She stubbornly tucked a strand of wispy, dirty blonde hair behind her ear. "Dances are dumb anyway."

A cute boy had invited her to a dance at school. It was spur of the moment, so she was flummoxed because she had nothing to wear. In Violet's case, this was probably true. She was like her father. Smart, logical, and no nonsense. There would be no space in her closet or in her focused, driven world for something as frivolous as clothes.

She'd been flipping through the cocktail dresses in my closet, happily chattering about this boy's shy smile and cute dimples, when she saw something she didn't hate. "Wow, this isn't horrible."

It was a $1,500 Antonio Melani dress. "I'm glad you like it." It was a simple black dress, timeless and elegant. "You could wear it with those red ankle straps we bought you at Christmas."

"That's what I was thinking." She grinned, stepping into the dress, and turning for me to zip her up. "It's a little short on me, Mama. You're such a shrimp."

"Yes, but it's perfect to show off your long legs," I told her. "That's the way the girls wear everything now anyway." I tugged on the zipper, but it wouldn't go all the way up.

"Zip it. Come on."

"I am. Hold on." It wouldn't zip, and I knew she'd be disappointed. My mind had already moved to alternatives in my closet when I realized she was troubled. "Don't worry. I have other outfits."

"No, you don't. Nothing like this. I'm just too fat."

"Violet, that's ridiculous." She was tall like Dean and perfectly curvy. "You just need a different size. Maybe I can have it altered. How soon do you need it?"

She twisted with irritation, insisting I unzip her. "It's so embarrassing. I can't even fit into my mom's clothes."

"It's because I'm so short—"

"And skinny."

"No," I said emphatically. "That's not it."

"It's okay," she quipped, already pulling on her blue jeans. "Lance is a dork anyway."

But I saw tears in her eyes when she stormed out of my room.

As I sat now and looked at my beautiful daughter on the love seat, I was stricken with the fear that history was repeating itself. Violet chugged her Dr Pepper and returned it to the mahogany coffee table, once again ignoring the coaster.

How could this be? Had all my dieting and obsessing over my weight caused this? I'd been a horrible example. My mind raced with the best way to address her insecurities. Nothing had worked for me. Mama had always brought up God and church and assured me that Jesus loved me just the way I was, but that hadn't worked. Sunny had got me diet pills, and that...

Had it worked? If I'd never got the diet pills, I'd probably be as big as Desi now. So yes, it had worked. And yet my life had been defined by my weight. My days were determined by the scales. If the results were good, I'd get out and embrace the day with a little optimism. If not, I'd close the curtains and spare the world the disgust of having to see me.

So maybe the blessed trifecta hadn't worked after all. Maybe my wise mother, Mabel, had been right all along. I felt a pang of guilt for never telling her about my trip to the fat doctor. She'd have stopped me in my tracks for sure.

"Violet, you're beautiful. And smart. Please don't allow these negative thoughts to enter your head. It's just the devil telling you lies."

She looked at me strangely, and I realized I sounded just like my mother. And yet I couldn't seem to stop. "I've been thinking, you know that little church right off campus? You and Sterling should go."

"Oh geez, Mama. I don't hang around with him at school."

"Well, you and some of your girlfriends then. And next time y'all come, I think we should all go to that big church downtown. As a family." Even when Violet's eyes widened in shock, I pushed on. "Jesus loves you just the way you are. He made you exactly the way he wants you."

I swear, those words came straight from Mabel.

"Yeah, I know that, Mama. But how does that help me now? In this life? In this world? When I'm such an amazon compared to all the other girls. I feel like everyone is always looking at me and laughing at me."

"Violet, feelings aren't reality." *Preach it, Mabel.* "They're probably looking at you because you're so smart." I was rather enjoying preaching what I myself didn't practice, but my sermon was interrupted when Sterling hollered from the kitchen.

"We're burning daylight! The sun has set! Let's go!"

Violet jumped up, eager to end the conversation.

"Use the credit card, go to the mall down there, and find yourself something beautiful. Violet, you should go to the dance with this boy."

"I don't know." She shrugged. "Bye, Mama." She seemed suddenly fine, as if she were already on to the next thing. What a blessing, I thought. Maybe I'd overreacted and she wasn't at all like me.

I settled down with a glass of wine and my phone. I was just about to click on Desi's face, when another number popped onto the screen.

It was a Louisville number. From Columbo, Inc. My heart dropped. I'd almost forgot about hiring the private detective. I answered tentatively, "Hello? Xavier?"

"Yes, ma'am. How are you?" He sounded muffled, as if he were in an airport. "I didn't catch you at a bad time, did I?"

"No. Not at all. Do you... have something?"

"Yes, ma'am. I'm sorry to say, I do." He cleared his throat. "Actually,

I know it's short notice, but I'm on my way to Lexington now. For another job later. But I could meet you somewhere in town."

I was having trouble finding my voice. I couldn't really believe it. All this time, deep down I never really believed Dean would cheat on me.

"Or we could wait until another day. I've got some time Tuesday."

"No. I'd rather meet tonight. In fact, Dean's out of town… but," I said in a squeaky voice, "I guess you already know that." I attempted a casual chuckle, but it came out as an anguished cry. "You could just come here. To my home."

"Okay. Are you sure?"

"Yes. I'll be here. Xavier, can you tell me who she is?"

"Uh, ma'am, I'd rather wait until I can sit down with you. I promise I'll be there in fifteen minutes."

Fifteen minutes. Those fifteen minutes were the most agonizing and torturous I'd ever had, and yet, they were a precious gift too. I savored them. Like a parent who was oblivious until they got that call in the middle of the night. It was the *before* to a life forever more defined as the *after*. After the accident. After the red and blue lights flashed outside my house and the knock on my door divided my life in two. Forever more distinguishing The Before from The After.

I sat quietly at the kitchen table. Unable to drink the wine I'd poured for my conversation with Desi. I found myself doing something I hadn't done for years. Praying.

Maybe it was looking into a mirror and seeing myself through the insecurities in my own daughter. Seeing the falseness of them. Seeing the destructive power in them. Afraid my baby girl would be consumed by the lies of them.

Maybe it was my mother's voice and words and will stepping in to speak and act when I couldn't. Whatever it was, I prayed for grace and strength. In a twisted way, I was even grateful.

Now that the fears that had defined my life had finally been realized, I could surrender. And in surrender I found freedom. So when the knock on my door came, I was ready.

And I opened it to My After.

Xavier sat at the table, sipping the sweet tea I'd offered. I sat next to him, my wine still untouched. I eyed the folder in front of him with dismay. "Let's hear it," I said. "Is my husband having an affair."

"Yes, ma'am. It appears as though he is." He opened the folder and handed me an envelope. "I have some pictures for you here." I gazed at the envelope but didn't pick it up. "I also have some cell phone records. The calls between this number"—he tapped the document—"and your husband's have increased substantially lately."

"How long?"

"The phone records would suggest well over a year. But like I say, the frequency has picked up in the last"—he glanced at the file—"month or so. That would suggest—"

"Something just… blossomed," I said calmly.

"Yes, ma'am. Also, the photos suggest they've taken a few trips together."

Now I was curious. My hand shook as I reached for the envelope. When I opened it, I sucked in a ragged breath. "No… this can't be…"

Darla.

A photo of them coming out of the airport. Embracing, her arm around his waist. His head lowered, gazing at her with intensity.

A photo of them getting out of a rental car, locked in a hug.

A photo of them at a park, not here in Lexington, but somewhere else. Dean on a bench, his head in his hands, her head on his shoulder.

A photo of them entering the Hyatt Regency in Cleveland.

Xavier cleared his throat awkwardly. "I assume you know who this is, ma'am?"

"Yes. She's his assistant. They work very closely together."

"Yes, ma'am. I'm very sorry. I was hoping for a happier conclusion."

I chuckled cynically. "How often does that happen?"

"Not often, to be honest."

The irony, of course, was that I'd dismissed her because she was heavy. I felt like such a fool. How they must have laughed at me, at how they'd duped me all this time. And all these events! How amused they must have been watching me carry on like a... like a wife. All the while knowing they had the upper hand.

I poured myself a second glass of wine. Or maybe it was a third. I couldn't be sure. I'd called Desi repeatedly. Once every fifteen minutes, but there was no answer. I glanced at my watch, knowing it was an hour earlier there. But still...

Where could she be?

Darla. Of all people.

I honestly had no idea how to proceed. I supposed I'd need a lawyer. Maybe one of those man-hating woman lawyers. One who'd been scorned herself and understood my pain. One who'd seized her second chance at life and was fueled by punishing every cheating, lying man out there.

It suddenly occurred to me I was going to be a very rich woman. Of course, I already was, but this would be wealth of my own. I could do whatever I wanted, anything...

What could I do? *Nothing. You have no talents or gifts.*

What would become of me? *You will be even more insignificant and more irrelevant than you are now.*

Where would I go? *Who cares? Nobody, that's who.*

What about all these years? Were they worth nothing? *Not a thing. Wasted years.*

Panic and rage coursed through my body. I picked up my phone and pressed again on Desi's face.

Please answer, I prayed. *I need you.*

Chapter Twenty-Two

We're Just Trash
Desi

Cicada Stadium was deserted, which suited me fine. It was dark now, and the only light came from the moon and the lightning bugs. Unlike the steady drone of cicadas, they were quiet creatures, just fluttering around like little lanterns in the night.

Brad still had his beat-up truck, which he'd pulled deep into Hummingbird Trail, its headlights mingling against mine as I drove into the old ballpark. He was sitting on a stump, already smoking. While still pencil thin, I noticed more gray streaking through Brad's otherwise blue-black hair. "Hey," I said as I walked over. "I can't stay." I handed him the money, and he handed me the product.

"What? No hey, kiss my ass, or nothing? You could at least sit and chat for a minute."

I sighed, clearly hesitant.

"Here." He held out the joint. "A freebie. You know how at Bath and Body, if you buy one, you get one free?"

It seemed such an odd thing for him to say, I couldn't help but laugh. The very thought of Wolfheart in town, much less at a store like Bath and Body, was weirdly comical. "Just for a minute."

"What'd you take? You already look dazed."

I settled next to him on the stump, raising the joint to my lips, breathing in the soothing promise of it. "I'm just tired. And I have a night to myself. The kids are busy and—"

"Where's Lenny?"

"Back offshore. A different role. Easier I hope."

"I always liked Lenny. He was cool. For a jock." He took the smoke when I offered it. "Now Tom was another thing altogether. But you know that already."

I didn't reply.

"How's Robin? How's she liking Kentucky?"

"I think she likes it." I subconsciously felt for my phone, realizing I'd left it in my car. "Although you never know with her. She hasn't asked you for anything lately, has she?"

"No, she's got everything she needs there." We sat quietly for a few minutes, oddly content in each other's company.

"Brad, can I ask you something?" When he shrugged with indifference, I asked sincerely, "How'd you get into this? You've been doing… what you do, as long as I've known you. I'm curious."

He let out a soft roll of laughter. "I guess I never had anybody tell me I could do anything different." He blew out smoke, his green eyes turning into slits as he grinned. "It ain't all that bad. You learn a lot of secrets. Usually the bad ones."

"Is that so?" I reached again for the joint. "Like what?"

"They wouldn't be secrets if I told you, now would they?"

"Come on. I bet you Claire knows way more secrets than you," I teased.

Brad roared with laughter, slapping his thigh. "She's something, isn't she? A piece of work, that one."

We fell into a comfortable silence.

"I got one for you," he said. "And it's one I think you'd be interested in." When I looked at him with curiosity, he put his finger to his lips. "It's been kept quiet a long time though, so you can't tell."

I cocked my head at him. "Dolly and Mitch?"

"The big kahuna. The scandal felt throughout Shady Gully."

"Tell me." I leaned in. Ashamed at how badly I wanted to know.

"He got run off, plain and simple. And truth be told, he's lucky that's all that happened to him."

"What do you mean? What did he do?"

Brad reached over. I handed him what he wanted. He took a big puff. "Remember he was working at the school? Guidance counselor or something. Of course, everybody knows the only reason he got the job was because he was a big shot in high school. Anyway, Mitch liked all the attention he got. From the young ladies. And when I say young, I mean young."

"Oh no." My heart dropped.

"Yep. He had a thing with a student. Not just flirting. He told her he was in love with her. Was gonna leave Dolly, and as soon as she graduated, they were gonna run off and live happily ever after." Brad offered me the last bit, but there was nothing there, so he ground it into the dirt with his boot. "He probably would have got away with it too, except she got pregnant."

My hands flew to my mouth. I tried to process all the resentment I'd directed at Dolly over the years. I guess you just never really knew what someone was going through. But it all made sense now. The bizarre reduced-price sales pitch, the make-yourself-at-home showing, and then the isolation. And finally, the fleeing. Leaving all the damage behind.

"But what happened to the girl? How have they kept this quiet all these years?"

"That's simple, Desi. It's because she didn't matter." Brad gazed off into the distance, thoughtful. "She's one of my people. From across the creek. There was no way we were going to raise a ruckus, now was there? We didn't want the law involved, snooping in our business."

"And they took advantage of that."

"That they did. After all, they're pillars of the community. And we're just trash."

I let that sit for a minute. Then finally asked, "How is she? The girl? Did she have the baby?"

"She's my sister's kid, and yeah, she had the baby. A girl. Almost eighteen now."

"Like Micah. I'd been about to have her at the time."

"That's right. They're all piled up in a tiny shanty, living with my sister's boyfriend. They collect a government check but still can't manage to keep the electricity on. That's a whole other story."

"What about Mitch? Does he help at all?"

Wolfheart shook his head. "What do you think?"

"Wow." I was reeling. "I wonder where they went."

"Up north, is what I hear. Arkansas, I believe."

I stared out at the lightning bugs. Processing this revelation after years of wondering what the catalyst had been to us making the worst financial decision of our life. "The repercussions are staggering, aren't they? What Mitch did affected so many lives. The least of which being Dolly's family."

Brad chuckled. "Yeah. I'm not a church-going man, but I heard one side is preaching hell and damnation, while the other side is preaching forgiveness."

"And which side do you fall on?"

Brad seemed contemplative. "A little of both, I suppose."

We both squinted suddenly as headlights appeared in the distance. "Oh crap," I muttered. "I need to get out of here."

One by one the headlights doubled, then tripled as another generation of rebels sought Cicada Stadium as a venue to express their independence. "Look at that," Brad muttered. "Business is picking up tonight."

"That's nice for you, but how am I going to get out of here? Somebody might recognize my car."

Brad dug into his pocket and handed me his keys. "Take my truck and go that way, past Hummingbird Trail. Not as much traffic, and it will lead to the main road."

"But…" I panicked when I heard one of Petey's favorite songs spilling from a truck that looked a lot like his Ford. "What about my car? And if I take your jalopy, are you sure it can make it through all that thick brush?"

Brad stood up, reclaiming his keys. "My jalopy hasn't let me down yet. But I tell you what—follow me in your car, and I'll do my best to clear the brush and lead you out to the main road."

That was when I heard the laugh. That crazy, infectious, lovable laugh that lit up rooms and commanded a fun-loving audience. Petey.

"Okay." I didn't really have a choice. I jumped into my car and tried to focus on Brad's dim taillights as his truck trampled through the brush ahead of me. Even with his jalopy's help, limbs slammed into my windshield with surprising force. I realized now this path had served as an escape route all these years. Naturally Brad had known about it.

Apparently, others had as well, because when we finally made it to the gravel road behind Cicada Stadium, there were a few trucks already lined up, waiting to enter. Still, traffic was lighter than at the regular entrance.

I waved my thanks to Brad and watched as he turned around and made his way back to the stadium. I guessed it was just another night on the job for Wolfheart.

I was well on my way when I noticed headlights shining behind me. Too dark to identify the vehicle, I could only make out the outline of a truck.

It was difficult to navigate the curves along the gravel road, especially with all the rubble on my windshield. I prayed it was only debris, and not real damage. Real damage that would cost real money.

My pulse quickened. All I needed was to wreck my car on the way home. I had visions of having to call Ricky and him arriving in his deputy's car to rescue me, and then having to turn around and arrest me because of the marijuana in my purse.

I cursed in a shaky, slightly impaired voice. I really had to get myself together, but this truck behind me wasn't helping. The bright headlights shimmering in my rearview mirror made it impossible to see. But what if something was wrong with my car? What if I'd hit something? Or dragging something?

Fright compelled me to slow down. The flickering behind me continued as the truck slowed down as well. And then I saw the truck more clearly... and the driver.

I jeered with annoyance. Put my foot back on the accelerator. "Not now." I gripped the steering wheel, wanting more than ever to get home. But Adam sped up as well, and his flashing headlights blinded me. Distracted, I rounded a curve too quickly and almost slid into a ditch.

"That does it!" Furious, I pulled onto an embankment on the right side of the road that held a big garbage dumpster. Beyond that was a pumpjack which mechanically lifted oil out of a well. I could hear the rhythmic grinding of gears as I threw my car into park.

Adam pulled in beside me and turned his engine off. His big cowboy hat was visible in the fading lights of the cab of his truck.

"What are you doing?" I screamed. "Are you crazy?"

He stepped out of his truck wearing his signature grin. "Dizzy Desi, were you slumming at the stadium with Wolfheart?"

"No. But why are you flashing your lights in my face? Are you trying to get me killed?" I slammed the door as I slid out of my car.

"Aw, come on now, pretty girl. You know I'd never do that." He walked over, managing to appear contrite. "I didn't mean to scare you." He stood over me now and nudged his hat back a notch so he could see me better. "Nice dress."

"Adam." I planted my fists on my hips. "I need to go."

He didn't reply, didn't move a muscle, just continued to look at me while I remained frozen. And then his mouth slowly turned up in a knowing grin. "Seriously, Desi? What are you doing out so late? On this gravel road in the middle of the night? It's not safe."

"I'm fine," I said in a squeaky voice. But I wasn't.

"Are you lonely, Desi?"

"No," I said too quickly, the silence so thick it magnified the back-and-forth rotary motion of the pumpjack in the background. "I'm fine."

"What are you looking for out here? What are you searching for?" He moved in closer, towering over me, his demeanor undeniably masculine and possessive. "I think you're lonely. And you're searching for something. I think you're just like me." He closed the gap between us.

"Adam…"

"You ever wonder about us? How we'd be together?" His voice was like a dove's coo, full of desire and promise.

"No, I really don't wonder about that at all."

"I don't believe that," he said, his finger lightly brushing under my chin. "'Cause I think about it all the time. I think it's fate, you and me. I think that's why we keep running into each other. What'd I tell you that day? About what we are?"

I was having trouble breathing.

"As soon as I saw you walk onto that school bus years ago, I knew." He leaned in a little closer. Pressed me against my car. "I knew this was gonna happen." His face was so close I could feel his breath. "Come on, Desi. What are we? I want you to tell me."

"No," I breathed. "I don't know what you mean."

"Yeah you do." His lips brushed mine. I closed my eyes, felt the tease of oblivion.

"You're so beautiful. I've never wanted anyone so much. You're always in my head." He kissed me again, a little more hungrily. "Say it. I want to hear you say it."

While my brain said no, the sound that came out of my mouth was a soft moan. And when he deepened the kiss and moved his hands down the side of my body, I moved into him, dipped my head back, and let him have my neck. I felt his soft whiskers brush against my ear, then along my throat.

When he groaned, "What are we?"

I whispered back, "Unfinished business."

I felt the hardness between his legs push closer into me, and

I wanted nothing more than to go slack, to open myself up completely to him.

"No." His lips moved against my hair. "We're unfinished pleasure."

As his lips found mine again, I surrendered to his soft touch and drifted away with the back-and-forth motions of the pump-jack in my ears.

"Unfinished… pleasure," Adam hummed into my ear. "Long… lost… treasure…"

Vaguely aware Adam had unzipped his jeans, I felt powerless. Too much pot, too much oxy. I couldn't seem to find the strength—or the will—to be present and accountable in the moment.

But then I opened my eyes for just a second. And that was all it took. I saw the pumpjack moving up and down into the ground, heard the grinds of the motor as it drilled for oil. And I thought of Lenny.

My sweet Lenny. Loyal and kind. Flowery words, no. But he was on an oil rig in the Gulf of Mexico with a banged-up back because he was the kind of man who *showed* me he loved me. Over and over again—through his actions.

"Gonna find my… treasure," Adam sang as he lifted my skirt, shifted my panties aside. "Be rich… forever… unfinished pleasure."

I stiffened and pressed my hands against his chest. Pushed.

"Come on, Desi. You know you've been dreaming of this too."

"No." I pushed again. "I really don't want this." He was so tall, and the weight of him trapped me against my car. "Adam, stop," I said. "I'm serious."

"What the hell?" He moved back then, enough so I could see his twisted, angry face. "What's wrong with you?"

"I want to go home," I pushed him again, nudging him back a few more inches.

"Why are you being such a bitch? Are you bipolar or something?" He still had his hands on either side of me, pressed into my car.

"This is wrong. You're wrong. Seriously, when are you going to grow up? I mean, how many wives have you been through?"

I shook my head with regret. "And I'm wrong too. But this…
no." I glared at him. "Just no."

He sneered at me then. Moved back. "You know, there was
a day I'd have killed to have my way with you, but now…" He
looked me up and down. "You're a fat ass. I barely got a hard on."
He cursed as he tugged his zipper up. I ignored him, did my
best to smooth my dress out. And then I saw headlights reflect
against the pumpjack and the garbage dumpster. Someone was
coming around the curve.

Adam hopped into his truck. "You missed your chance. I'm
done messing with you. You'll regret it when I make it big
in Nashville."

The other vehicle stopped at the embankment. Flicked its
headlights a few times. When I turned, I saw Brad Wolfheart's
old black truck. Emboldened, I said to Adam as he started his
pickup, "I won't hold my breath."

Adam revved his motor and peeled out onto the gravel road.
I watched his truck until his lights disappeared. Once he was
gone, I started to shake. Mortified at what I'd almost done.
Ashamed of wallowing in my self-pity. Disrespecting my body.
Cheating on my family.

"Desi," Brad Wolfheart called. "Are you okay?" He walked
over slowly. "Just had a feeling I needed to check on you when
I saw Adam turn his truck around at Cicada."

I turned toward Brad, tears bubbling up in my eyes. "Brad,
thank you. But"—I held my hands up in a stop gesture—"I just
need to be…"

Brad stopped. "I got that. I'm going to go sit in my truck.
When you're ready, I'll follow you home. You okay to drive?"

"Yes," I sobbed as a wave of remorse swept over me. "Yes." I
got in my car and gazed out my rubble-crusted windshield.
Reached for my purse, which was full of marijuana. I rolled
down my window. "Brad?"

"Yeah?" He came over.

"Just take this. Please. I don't want it." He looked at me a long moment and then nodded. Reluctantly took the product and headed back to his truck.

Just before he got there, he assured me, "Take as long as you need, Desi. I'll be right here."

I watched him settle into his vehicle. Grateful not only that he showed up, but that he was mindful of my dignity. I sat until the sound of my frantic breathing quieted. Looked at the pumpjack. The dumpster. Unfinished business indeed.

I startled when my phone rang. When I picked it up, I saw that Robin had called back... twenty times. "Hello."

"Desi." Robin's voice was thick with emotion. "Desi, where've you been?"

"I... I... oh, Robin."

"What's wrong? What's happened? Is Lenny okay?"

"Yes," I sobbed. "It's me. I'm not okay. I did something horrible. I can't even tell you. Oh, Robin, I hate myself."

"What happened? Have you been drinking? You sound like you're in some kind of stupor. I've been calling and calling."

"It was Adam," I cried. "He followed me tonight, and I don't know why..." I trailed off. She gave me a minute to pull myself together. "You know how he always made me feel so... I don't know... cherished? Special? Tonight I was weak and I... I hate myself. Oh, Robin, what am I going to do?"

I went on for another minute before I realized she hadn't spoken. My phone must have died. "Robin? Are you there?"

"Yes. I'm here." Her voice cut like steel. "Is this how it was with Dean?"

"What? Robin, no."

"Tell me," she said in a measured voice. "Does it give you a thrill, a feeling of power to go after other women's men? Or do you do it just for the fun of it? Just because you can?"

"That's not... Robin, no—"

"You know, I've wanted to believe for a long time that nothing happened between you and Dean. But now I know. You have a pattern. This is how you are."

I dropped my head onto the steering wheel, heaving in misery. "I don't want to hear your crying, Desi. There's nobody to blame but yourself."

Chapter Twenty-Three

The After
Robin (97.0 Pounds)

"*I don't want to hear your crying, Desi. There's nobody to blame but yourself.*" That's what I told her. And I meant it. But the words haunted me all night.

After I got a text from Sterling saying they'd made it back to school safely, I'd had another glass of wine and drifted off into nothingness. My dreams were filled with lingering visions of Desi making love to a tall man in a cowboy hat, but when his face was revealed, it was Dean. The two of them laughed and laughed, and then suddenly Desi began to cry. Only it wasn't her—it was me. And in the dream Dean turned to me and said, "But you know, Robin, Desi is always going to be the queen."

These horrible, taunting images circled my unconsciousness all night until they finally erupted into a pounding head and a dry throat. I stumbled into the kitchen and took an Aleve and drank a glass of water. An hour later, after a few cups of coffee, I felt better. And because I was dehydrated, the scale surprised me with a favorable number.

Newly energized, I dug up our financial papers in the basement safe. After making notes and doing some calculations, I put together a nice little folder of my own. I arranged it on the ottoman in the living room, right next to Xavier's folder. As soon as Dean sat in his recliner, he'd see both folders. *I hope she was worth it*, I'd say—along with a string of one-liners I'd practiced in my head.

Since he was due back home in a few hours, I took a shower and made myself as presentable as possible. My eyes were puffy from a night of crying, but I made use of the best concealer money could buy.

The scene in my head, the one where he sank to his knees and begged forgiveness, was upended when he came home early. I'd just hit Decline on Desi's tenth call of the day, when I heard the garage door open. Suddenly I wasn't ready, wasn't feeling so bold when I saw him slump through the door, his tall body bent and worn.

"Hi. You're early," I mumbled.

"Hey, babe." He set his briefcase next to his desk. Dropped his keys in the foyer tray and reached for me.

Despite the way I'd imagined greeting him, with indifference and the hint of a sneer, I fell into his arms.

"How are you?"

"Fine," I answered in a clipped tone. Now, I was back on script.

"I'm exhausted."

I bet, I thought angrily, but didn't say anything.

"How were the kids? Did y'all have a nice visit? I hated missing them."

"We had fun. Sterling named his car Rambler."

When Dean let out a genuine bellow, I fought back tears. "That's funny. I guess as long as he hasn't spray painted it on the side yet, we're safe."

When he followed me into the kitchen, I glanced at the folders on the ottoman, not quite as ready for The After transition as I'd thought. "You want some tea? A sprite?"

"No. Uh, maybe a glass of wine?"

"Seriously? It's not even three o'clock."

"I know. But it's been that kind of few days." He looked defeated. I refused to buy into it though. I opened a Bordeaux and poured him a glass. Topped off my iced tea.

My heartbeat quickened as he headed straight for his recliner. No! Not yet! I suddenly wanted things to be normal for a little while longer. But it wasn't to be.

"What's this?" He reached for the financial folder I'd put together.

"Nothing. Don't open that." I snatched the folder away from him, handing him the wine. He didn't protest. Instead he took a long, Dean-sized sip of the wine. He closed his eyes and leaned back in the recliner.

"It's good to be home," he said.

"Is it?" I demanded with an edge in my voice. Once again, back on script. My phone went off, and he looked at me in confusion when I put it on silence. "It's Desi. I'll call her back. Right now we need to talk—"

"I have something to tell you," he said. So that was what the wine was for then, to gear himself up so he could ask for a divorce. My heart sank, as this was most definitely not the way I imagined the scene playing out.

"I'm sure you do," I snapped. "In fact, I already know." I picked up Xavier's folder, with the pictures, and angrily shoved it into his hands. He took his time opening the folder. Calmly flipped through the photographs. His expression never changed, even as he put them all in a neat little pile and placed them back into the folder. "It's not what you think."

I snorted. "Right. I think it's pretty obvious." I was all set to go through my spiel, but his tranquil manner baffled me. He drained the last of his wine and went into his office. Seconds later he reappeared with his own folder.

"Before you open this, I want you to know I love you. And I'm sorry if you're mad. I didn't mean... for it to turn out like this."

I opened the folder and flipped through the pages. One after the other until I couldn't read any more, my vision was so clouded with tears.

"I have stage four pancreatic cancer." When I looked at him in shock and confusion, he continued. "I wanted to understand all of my options before I upset you. Darla's father is a renowned oncologist at the Cleveland Clinic. I didn't know that until she shared it with me. Anyway, she helped me connect with him, and yes, she was there. But those pictures..." He rubbed his temples. "They make it look like it's something more, but it's not. She was really just being a friend."

"They ran tests there?"

He nodded. "It's metastatic. And the last test showed that it's already spread to my lymph nodes. And my lungs."

"But... you were fine. You've been fine. I don't understand." I could hear the note of hysteria in my tone.

"I know. It's fast moving. Started with some back pain and nausea. I guess I knew something was wrong, but I was swamped at work. Eventually I had some tests run, and even though the cancer markers were bad, I still hoped... I wanted to believe. That's why I got a second opinion."

"But how could you not tell me, Dean? Why would you let Darla accompany you through this and not me? I'm your wife!"

"I know. And I wouldn't have, except for her dad. She reached out to him, and he called me himself, invited me up for a battery of tests. I just wanted to wait until I knew for sure."

"But... but..." I wept. "You should have told me. I should have known."

"Robin, babe, I would have. There were times I really wanted to, but—"

"But what? I don't understand."

"You know how you are. Come on, babe. You are the center of my world, but sometimes I just can't get through to you. No matter what I say, you think the worst. You imagine the most horrible scenarios, and you fret and worry—"

"But that's because I'm so afraid of losing you. Of losing everything. I'm just so afraid. And now I have a reason to be."

"I was hoping for the best. Obviously. I was hoping I never had to tell you this. You're so frail. Why would I put you through this until I knew for sure?"

"But this can't be. It's not fair. It doesn't make sense."

"It doesn't. But it is what it is. And now"—he reached for my hand—"I want you on this journey with me. I need you. You're the only one I've ever loved. I know you don't believe me, but I swear it's true. I'm just not good at expressing how I feel. It's not that I don't love you… it's just that I'm a nerd." He laughed.

And then tears gathered in his eyes. My strong, pragmatic, and logical husband, who always had the answer for everything in bullet-point fashion, was vulnerable. Even worse than that. He was dying.

I could hardly absorb it all. Dean wiped his eyes and reached for the other folder I'd put together. "What's this? Divorce papers?"

"No," I said, taking the folder. "It's nothing."

He reached across his recliner and placed his large hand gently around the back of my neck, pulling me closer. Kissed me. "I gotta be honest. I'm a little scared."

I clasped his hand. "Me too."

Darla's Dad recommended Saint Joseph Hospital in Lexington. It was affiliated with the Cleveland Clinic and the oncologist, Dr. Herbert, was first rate. He was compassionate and soft spoken, generous with his time, and his deep-blue eyes exuded intelligence and expertise. The staff, the nurses, and the aides were more than friendly and competent. They were caring and allowed Dean his dignity. In the end though, it was hopeless.

The cancer had spread, the last scan showing that the disease had not only attacked the lungs but now raged war on Dean's peritoneal cavity. The recommended treatment was palliative care, aimed at relieving the symptoms and improving Dean's quality of life. Easing his pain, making him comfortable… for however long he had left. The doctor couldn't give us a specific amount of time, but as I read between the lines, it sounded more like months rather than years.

In order to avoid this grim news, I suggested dinner options on the way home. "I could do chicken breasts. Do you think your stomach could tolerate that?"

"I guess we're gonna have to tell the kids," he said.

"I could do them without the sauce. And maybe a salad. Or broccoli. Dr. Herbert said to get lots of fiber."

"We can't put it off any longer. Remember how you felt when you found out? Mad because I'd taken so long to tell you?"

The Before, I thought. It had been such bliss. I'd just been too stupid to realize it. "Or maybe just a little soup? With some ham and cabbage?"

"Robin?"

"I know. You're right. I'll see if they can come home this weekend." I struggled to keep my voice strong. Capable. Brave. Something I was not.

Dean looked out the window. "The soup sounds good."

"Okay." My mind was spinning with dinner details, hospice care preparation, and anything… that would keep me from feeling.

As I made it over one of the rolling hills of Kentucky, covered in a thick blanket of vivid green bluegrass, it was impossible to miss the cross. "Dean," I said as we closed in on the massive church.

Like a beacon it stood, high on the hill, overlooking the grazing horses, the black fences, and the buildings and businesses of part of the city. I was drawn to it like a child who'd ventured off too far on her own, now eager to return to the safe and loving arms of her parents.

"What do you think?" I asked, putting on my blinker.

"It's not Sunday."

"I know. But maybe we can just go in and sit for a while."

"Okay. Let's do it." His voice cracked. "Back to our roots, huh? Full circle."

"Maybe so."

I parked in the huge parking lot, mostly empty now, and helped Dean out of the car. "I can do it," he insisted. "I'm not to that point yet." I hovered close to him though, as we made our way to one of the many entrances. "It's kind of a dump," he joked. "Compared to Shady Gully."

As soon as we entered, a woman in a red T-shirt rushed over. "Hi! I'm Veronica. How are y'all?" She wore glasses and had thick, short dark hair. Her smile was warm and genuine, and her heartfelt welcome set me at ease. The writing on her T-shirt said *Forgiven*.

"We just thought we'd stop by," I said.

"It's not Sunday," Dean added.

"No, it's not," Veronica said. "But it's a beautiful day, isn't it?" Her simple response made it seem perfectly normal that we'd stopped by, and further, that if we hadn't, it would have been a shame. "Would y'all like some coffee? Or a donut?"

We could smell the alluring aromas of both, but Dean politely declined, his hand moving involuntarily to his stomach.

"We just thought we'd sit... for a bit. If that's okay," I said.

"It's more than okay." She led us to the place I was hoping for, the room at the center of the building, with the cross. Although it wasn't a room at all. It was more like an auditorium. Like at an indoor concert or sporting event.

"Wow," Dean mumbled. "This is something."

Veronica directed us to a comfortable seat, not too many steps up, but high enough to take in the scope of the building. Right in the center, we overlooked the stage, the sound booth, and of course, the cross atop the baptismal pool. A dim light reflected over the water, while the lights illuminating the stage were brighter, showing an array of musical instruments and sound equipment.

When we sat down, Veronica told us, "Timothy is in his office today. He'd want to meet you. If that's okay. If not, that's fine too."

I had no idea who Timothy was, but I liked that she wasn't putting pressure on us. I focused on Dean, made sure he was settled in his chair. These weren't hard wooden pews like in Shady Gully. These seats had nice cushions and soft backs and even plenty of room for his long legs.

When Veronica walked away, giving us our privacy, Dean grinned, "Wow." He was like a little boy full of wonder. An image of him in junior high flashed before me, all limbs and glasses and earnestness. "Look at those flat-screen TVs up there." There were at least three, and like everything else here, they were massive.

"Wow," Dean repeated.

We watched as a few musicians bounded onto the stage. They laughed and kidded with one another, clearly comfortable together. As they queued up the sound equipment, a beautiful woman with the most amazing long, brown hair smiled at us. She too wore a red T-shirt, hers sporting the words *Alive* across the chest. "Hey, welcome." She hummed to herself as she waved, seemingly happy in her own skin.

"I hope we aren't interrupting something," I fretted to Dean.

"No, I'm sure it's fine, or Veronica would have told us." He looked up at the ceiling, like a kid at Disneyland. "Maybe they'll sing a song."

I was thinking this had been a mistake, when a man approached, a friendly smile on his face. "Hi, guys. I'm Timothy, one of the pastors here at North Lake."

"I hope we're not intruding—"

"This place is great," Dean said.

"Not at all," he told me. And to Dean, "Thanks." Timothy was tall, with expressive blue eyes. His hair was shaggy, and I couldn't help but notice the tattoos lining his arms. He was not at all what I'd expected, and I wondered why I'd never googled the pastor at North Lake.

"We've been meaning to stop by," Dean said. "Just… you know."

"I do know. I totally get it." He added, "No judgment here." He placed his hand on Dean's shoulder. "How are you?" It wasn't just a fleeting sentiment. He really looked at Dean.

"Well, I guess I've been better, to be honest." As Dean spoke, Timothy glanced at me. "I hear good things about this place though. Some of the folks I work with—" Dean stopped.

Timothy offered gently, "I understand that you don't know me, but if you feel like sharing, I'm here to help." Timothy eyed the musicians on stage, as well as a few teenagers who'd piled into the sound booth. "We all are. We're a community here at North Lake."

"I was going to say I work at Dazé & Nolan here in Lexington," Dean told him. "But I guess I don't anymore," Dean looked at me, hesitant now that his identity had been stripped away. "I'm sick. I just found out, so I officially retired today."

Timothy nodded. "I'm sorry to hear that. Is the prognosis hopeful?"

"No," Dean answered. "Pancreatic cancer usually isn't. But no."

"I'm sorry." Timothy looked at me. Really looked at me like he'd gazed at Dean a second ago. "I'm glad the Holy Spirit led you here today."

I said nothing as tears slid down my face.

"Tell me," Timothy said. "Do y'all have children?"

"Yeah, we do." Dean grinned. "The Dynamic Duo. Twins, Violet and Sterling."

"They're in North Carolina now," I added. "At school. We haven't told them yet." I held Timothy's gaze, imploring him to take this burden away from us. Which was silly. What could he do? Just because he was a man of God didn't mean he could perform miracles like Jesus himself.

"Maybe we can help with that," he said. "We have counselors on staff here. They counsel people with drug addictions, people going through divorce or having marital problems. We also have support groups for people who are sick." He glanced at Dean. And then he looked pointedly at me. "And counseling for their families as well."

I couldn't speak. I simply stared numbly at the kindness in Timothy's face.

"And"—he grinned—"if it's something we can't handle, we have a mighty big following here." He glanced around the auditorium, which held an enormous number of seats. "Our community, or as we like to say, our bench, is deep. And we're here to help. If you want us, we're your family. You're not alone."

"That's nice," Dean said. "We appreciate it."

"If you want to come to Sunday services, we can have someone come out and pick you up."

"We can get here on our own," I told him.

"Bring Violet and Sterling," he said. "We can all pray together afterward. Maybe it will help. And if this is going to be a financial burden on you," he added, "we can assist in that way as well."

"Oh no," I insisted. "We're fine."

A beat passed, and he asked, "Would it be okay if I prayed with you?"

Dean reached for my hand, and I held his tightly in my lap.

Timothy thanked the Holy Spirit for leading us to North Lake, and he prayed that God bless us and strengthen us, as we'd been given this cross to bear. He prayed for our children, that they'd find peace and a deepening of faith through this challenging journey. He asked God to open our hearts, to allow the love and support offered from the community, from our family, and from our closest friends. He prayed also that God would show him ways to better support us, that he give him the words to ease our suffering, and that God use him as a tool to help us through this daunting and heartbreaking season.

"Jesus, it's in your name we pray," Timothy finished. "And all God's children said—"

"Amen," we said.

Timothy prayed silently for another few seconds, and then he looked up and clasped our hands. "If you want to hang around for a while and listen to our Creative Team rehearse, feel free. Those knuckleheads aren't half-bad." He teased. "Or if you just want to be quiet, they can rehearse another day."

I was flabbergasted that they'd even consider holding up a big production for the likes of Dean and me.

"No, I'd like to hear the music," Dean said.

After Timothy left, we sat together in the comfortable seats and watched as the sound booth and the musicians coordinated their numbers. Most wore red T-shirts with phrases like *Redeemed* or *Free* across the fronts. I was amazed at the pink- and blue-haired teens; the tattooed young adults; the nose, lip, and eyebrow rings. Poor Mabel would have surely had a stroke. And yet it was undeniable, and there really was no other way to say it—these people exuded joy.

A talented man with a buzz cut and thick-lensed glasses strummed a few riffs on his guitar, evoking an impromptu burst of enthusiasm from the group. An attractive young man, slim with a blond mohawk, belted out the chorus of a random hymn to spontaneous and robust praise.

And then the beautiful girl with the thick, long hair waved at us again. She spoke into her microphone. "Hey there, I'm Millie. We're glad you're here. Sometimes our first song is pitchy, so we hope we don't chase you off." The band members chuckled.

As the song began, I was immediately drawn in by the smooth, melodic tone of Millie's voice. She sang of storms, sorrows, and heartache, and how Jesus called us to lay it all at his feet. The poignant lyrics combined with her passionate delivery brought me to tears as her voice rose with emotion.

Dean gripped my hand tightly. "I think the Holy Spirit did lead us here today."

Dean had had a bad few days. Maybe he was anticipating the kids' upcoming visit. Maybe it was the new medicine. Or maybe it was just the poison eating him up on the inside.

The doctor had lined us up with Saint Joseph's outstanding hospice care service, and after one trip, Dean had made a new friend. Billy was a big, brawny nurse with long dreadlocks and a sense of humor.

I was grateful for his strength, because Dean was becoming too much for me to handle physically. But even more so, I was grateful for Billy's upbeat demeanor. His lightheartedness was sunshine amid heavy darkness.

"All right." Billy chuckled as he rolled in the hospital bed on wheels. "I'm gonna put this right here next to the missus's bed. That way you can reach her if you're feeling romantic." When Dean threw his head back and laughed, Billy nodded, "That's right. You know what I'm talkin' about."

Billy liked to read murder mysteries, and he was forever telling Dean about the twisted plotlines of his current book. While I'd never seen Dean pick up a novel in his life, every day as soon as Billy would arrive, Dean would ask about the latest developments. "Did that bonehead detective ever figure out the poison was in the dog food?" Or "Something is off with that artist guy—his fascination with ears is a little unsettling." And off they'd go, Billy pushing Dean's wheelchair onto the porch, catching him up on his whodunnit.

It was at these moments, when I was alone, that I thought of Desi. When Timothy had prayed about us opening our hearts, allowing support from our closest friends and family, I knew I should call her.

Had it only been a week since my world was upended with Dean's diagnosis? To think, my biggest worries had been whether my husband was cheating, the destructive actions of my best friend, and if the scales gave me the okay to step out of the house on a given day. My Before. It was so shallow.

I was ashamed of all the time I'd wasted. Of the life I'd wasted. Mine. And Dean's. But I couldn't dwell on those thoughts. Heck, I could barely linger on the fringes of those thoughts before I broke apart. So I busied myself putting sheets on Dean's hospital bed, preparing a bland and tasteless meal for lunch, and putting medicine in Dean's pill case.

And then I picked up the phone. Desi needed me as much as I needed her. She was in trouble. Her marriage, her psyche, and even her health.

Timothy had talked about counseling.

Maybe she and Lenny could use a trip to the Land of the Bluegrass.

Chapter Twenty-Four

A New Season
Desi

Lenny's trip as an offshore supervisor hadn't gone well. He'd come home in pain, worn to a frazzle, and discouraged. And that was before he got a look at me. Or the damaged car. Or suffered through my excruciating confession.

It hadn't been pretty. I'd spewed everything in a long, drawn-out crying jag. I'd ranted about Tom being the catalyst to my bad behavior. Maybe subconsciously I'd begun my confession with that to gain sympathy. If so, it hadn't worked. Lenny had only stared at me in confusion.

I admitted I smoked pot occasionally with Wolfheart. I came clean about sneaking his pills. I explained, in agonizing detail, what happened with Adam. I even told him about selling Sunny's paintings.

Lenny stood there through all of it with his hand propped on the bar for support. Finally, when I'd hemorrhaged enough shameful admissions to the point of exhaustion, he'd quietly walked into the living room and gingerly lowered himself into his recliner.

He eventually asked in a low voice, "Can I have one of my pills? Or did you take them all?"

After I gave him his pill, he closed his eyes for a long time and let the medicine do its work. Just when I thought he'd fallen asleep, he said, "What about Winston? And you and Robin at the bonfire?"

It took me a moment to realize he meant the paintings. Of all my transgressions, this was the one he wanted to address. "I still have those. I could never part with those."

"Selling away your mama's paintings," he said in a numb voice. "That's just sad." I saw no point in telling him the majority of the money had gone to pay bills, so I remained silent.

"Swiping my medicine, smoking pot," he went on. "That's not you, Desi." He rubbed his temples. "What Tom did, that's despicable. But what you do now, that's on you." He closed his eyes. "You have to decide if you're gonna let Tom ruin the rest of your life." He drifted off then, his eyes tightly closed.

I started to speak, but he shook his head, as if he just couldn't hear anymore.

"What happened with Adam…" he said eventually. "I guess I've gotta decide if I'm gonna let that ruin the rest of mine."

"Please forgive me," I said as remorse washed over me. "I'm sorry. I'm going to do better. I want to be better."

But this time when Lenny's eyes closed, they rested heavily on his face. I watched him sleep for a long time. As his eyelids twitched sporadically, I was overcome with guilt for hurting him, for exacerbating his pain. Eventually I covered him with a quilt and let him sleep. I figured he was entitled to a little oblivion.

For days it had gone on like that—him sleeping in his recliner, and us circling each other in an atmosphere ripe with pain and regret.

And then Robin called. And everything changed.

Lenny didn't like flying under any circumstances. But especially when his world was teetering on the edge. The edge of what, exactly, would be determined in the coming months. Destruction? A breakthrough? An epiphany maybe? Perhaps that was being too optimistic.

"We'll take what we can get," Lenny told the flight attendant. "Nuts, pretzels. Whatever you got." He turned to me. "I gotta take one of my pills."

As I dug into my purse, he quipped, "You want a couple?" It was a joke. Sort of. He was still angry. He was still hurt. And yet he insisted that counseling might be just what we needed. He was even curious about the megachurch. He told Robin that if they'd stopped by a church just to sit for a spell in Shady Gully, they would have had church signs and flags planted in their yard by the time they returned home.

Lenny took his pain pill with a big gulp of water. Grimaced. He hated them. Hated the feeling and the very idea of taking them. I never had to worry about him getting hooked on oxy. Fortunately, I hadn't been on that kick long enough to even miss them. Now the weed, that was another story. I missed it terribly. I wanted desperately to unwind, block out, and escape. But there was no time for any of that now. We were going to help Robin. And Dean. And if we were lucky, maybe even ourselves.

"Well look at that," Lenny commented as he looked out the window. "I've never seen grass that green. "Look, Desi. Isn't that something?"

I peeked over him as the plane descended. "It's beautiful."

"There's a horse! Heck, I see three of them by that barn!" He reached for my hand, squeezed. I squeezed back, loving him for putting his whole heart into this trip. Into being there for Robin and Dean. Into working on our marriage.

As if he read my mind, he gave my hand an extra squeeze. "We're gonna be all right, Desi. Everything is gonna be all right."

I almost didn't recognize Robin waiting for us at the baggage claim. If not for Lenny enveloping her in a warm hug, I'd have thought she was a much-older woman. Her skin was stretched taut and thin, and her once big brown eyes were sunken into her face.

Lenny tugged her into his chest. "If you get any skinnier, you're just gonna go poof"—he gestured with his hands—"and disappear into thin air."

Robin managed a pained grin for Lenny, but when her eyes met mine, she crumbled into a wash of tears. Lenny and the other passengers looked on as her frail frame shook in my arms.

As the baggage rolled into view, the airport speakers boomed with a bugler playing "First Call," like at the beginning of the Kentucky Derby. While Lenny got a big kick out of that, he was even more delighted when a greeter expressed her southern hospitality with a tray of chocolate delicacies.

"Bourbon balls, anyone?"

"Yeah." Lenny pointed at Robin. "She'll have two." He reached into the tray and handed the chocolate to Robin. "Here. Eat this."

Robin watched as Lenny grabbed our bags. "He seems like he's doing okay," she whispered to me. "All things considered."

"We're okay," I said, holding her gaze. Reflexively I opened my mouth to ask how she was, but we both knew the answer to that, so instead I linked her arm in mine.

"So how are the kids?" Robin clicked the remote to her fancy car in the parking garage.

"Good," I answered. "Luke is enjoying school in Alexandria. And Petey is staying at the house with Micah while we're here. He said to stay as long as we wanted."

"His roommate is a slob and he's tired of TV dinners," Lenny explained.

When Robin handed him the keys to her Volvo, Lenny's face lit up. "You don't have to ask me twice." He made a show of opening the back doors for us and getting us settled in. "Just call me Leonard, the chauffeur." He punched in the Home button on the GPS, and we left the dark garage for the bright sunshine and the rolling hills of Lexington.

"How's Dean? Is he having a lot of pain?" I asked.

"He's… well." She swallowed. "Billy is keeping up with his pain, so we're good on that front."

"Billy is the hospice guy, right?" Lenny asked.

"He's Dean's buddy, yes. He's my angel." She leaned into the front seat and pointed. "Look, there's North Lake."

Lenny whistled. "That is some kind of stairway to heaven." He raised his eyes to the rearview mirror. "Desi, why don't you take a picture of that and text it to Jesse and James."

Robin asked, "What's new on the *As the Bible Turns* soap opera of Shady Gully?"

"I guess Dolly is still banished." I shrugged. "As long as she's with Mitch."

"I think I'm gonna ride a horse while I'm here," mused Lenny as we passed yet another pasture of noble-looking equines.

"Maybe that would flip your back into working order," Robin quipped.

Lenny laughed, and for a few blessed minutes it felt like old times.

Lenny and I did our best not to gawk at Robin's sprawling home as we drove along the curvy driveway. But our best wasn't good enough.

"I hope you've got a few maps inside," Lenny joked. "You know where it says, 'You are here.'"

"Oh no, whose car is that?" Robin looked stricken as we parked. "Something is wrong."

Unsettled by her panic, Lenny and I followed as Robin dashed inside.

When we reached the front porch, we encountered a large man with dreadlocks, a man with tattoos all over his arms, and a man in a wheelchair. They were playing rummy.

"Oh." Robin's relief was palpable. She turned to us. "Come on. Dean will be so happy." As Dean whirled around in his wheelchair, I was shaken to the core. He'd always been thin, but now he looked emaciated. His hair, it seemed, had turned white overnight. And he looked sunken and gaunt. Yellow and... deathly ill.

"Who's winning?" Robin asked as she stood behind Dean's wheelchair and snaked her arms around his neck.

"Your husband. He's a shark," Billy ranted. "Ain't nobody can beat him. Even preacher man, here. And he's got the good Lord on his side."

"Awww, look," Dean squeaked. "It's my lifelong friends. Fellows, you're looking at my history standing there."

As I bent into an enthusiastic hug around Dean's fragile frame, Lenny seemed frozen in place. He was stunned, distraught, and unable to speak or move.

The man with the tattoos hopped up and introduced himself. "I'm Timothy. Y'all must be Desi and Lenny." He shook Lenny's hand and discreetly coaxed him toward Dean. "I feel like I know y'all, I've heard so much about you."

"Yeah, me too," Billy chimed. "My man Dean tells me y'all got some wicked card game called Bouré in Louisiana. Ya gotta teach me so I can keep this shark here from getting too cocky."

I pivoted away from Dean when Billy took me in his arms and hugged me. But behind me I heard the moment Lenny finally pulled himself out of his shock and embraced his friend. His sobs mingled with Dean's as their reunion resounded with sadness. I found myself unwilling to do anything other than burrow my head deeper into Billy's big chest.

"It's all right," Billy comforted. "I gotcha."

Later, as we all sat and enjoyed some lemonade and Robin's special zucchini bread, Lenny taught Billy the finer points of Bouré. "Better watch out, Dean. I got the hang of this now. Better bring your A game." Billy winked at Timothy. "And don't be taking notes, preaching on revenge this Sunday. A man's gotta do what he's gotta do."

"I know where you sit, Billy." Timothy chuckled. "I'll be looking right at you."

With some effort, Dean pushed himself up on the arms of

his chair and cleared his throat. "Robin, did you know Billy's nephew is one of the keyboardists at North Lake?"

"No, I didn't. We'd love to meet him."

Robin tensed as Billy's expression transitioned from good-natured jokester to capable nurse. Focused, Billy adjusted the oxygen tank beside Dean's chair.

"Yeah, he thinks he's all that," Billy said before turning to Robin. "All right, it's time to get the missus over here and see if she paid attention to my lively tutorial."

"Oh, is it time?" Robin hopped up and looked at the indicator on the tank. "So when it reaches that level…" She mumbled to Billy. "I unscrew this…"

"Good. That's good. But you gotta get your new tank ready to go first."

"That's right." As Robin started lugging a heavy tank over, Timothy jumped up to assist. "No, don't." Robin waved him off. "I have to learn to do it myself."

We watched as she twisted a lever on the new one, unhooked the empty one, and switched Dean's tank. When she finished, she tenderly placed the plastic tubes back into his nose. Billy nodded his approval, gave her a high five.

"Now tomorrow I'm gonna teach y'all," Billy said to Lenny and me. "And there will be a quiz."

As everyone laughed, Timothy said his goodbyes, taking an extra moment with Dean. I was a little taken aback when he asked me to walk to his car with him.

"It means so much to them that you're here," he said as we stood in the driveway next to his car. "I understand it's difficult seeing someone you love go through this."

"It is." I nodded. "But we wouldn't have it any other way. They're really excited about your church. About you. I think it came at the right time for them."

Timothy's blue eyes lit up with wonder. "God's timing is amazing, isn't it?" He opened his car door, fished through some folders, and handed me a pamphlet. "All this is online as well, but Robin mentioned you were going through a hard time. Even before the news about Dean. I just want you and Lenny to know that if you'd like someone to talk to, feel free to come by my office. Or check out any of the counselors in the pamphlet. We're willing to help. Totally free."

"Oh." I nodded, embarrassed. "Things have been a little rough. And to be honest, my church at home isn't helping lately. In our small town, if you have a disagreement with the preacher, folks just up and build their own church. Preach their own message."

Why was a I sharing all this with this tattooed stranger? Was I that needy?

"Sometimes when bad things happen in your life, no matter how faithful you are, you need a little help climbing out of the muck." Timothy looked thoughtful, as if speaking from personal experience. "I've found that it really helps to get one-on-one attention. To get objective advice from someone you can be honest with, someone you can talk to without feeling judged. Seems like it would be a good opportunity to do that while you're here."

"Okay." I glanced down at the pamphlet. "Thank you."

"And, Desi," Timothy added, "you're not a bad person because you're struggling to connect in church lately. It happens to all of us. Me too." He raised his chin toward the sounds of laughter sweeping from the porch, "Just don't tell them that." He reached for the pamphlet in my hand and scribbled something on it before handing it back to me. "Just something that came to mind. Might be encouraging."

"Thanks."

"See you in church Sunday. Or maybe sooner." Timothy stuck his tattooed arm out the window and waved before heading down the driveway. I waited until he was out of sight before glancing at the Scripture he'd jotted.

Matthew 11:28–30: "Are you tired? Worn out? Burned out on religion? Come to me. Get away with me and you'll recover your life. I'll show you how to take a real rest."

A real rest sounded good right now.

Apparently, the Kentucky bluegrass was getting to me, because after all this time, I'd just told a perfect stranger what Tom did to me. Ruth, one of the counselors at North Lake, had kinky brown hair, old-fashioned wire-rimmed glasses, and a thick southern accent. She didn't have to coax or press the trauma out of me either. I just spilled it in a perfect little pile for her.

"I'm sorry that happened to you, sweetie." Ruth pushed her glasses higher up her nose. "And I'm sorry about your mom. It sounds like losing her the way you did was even more traumatic than Tom's abuse. Quite simply, he didn't matter to you. But your mom, she was very important in your life."

"She was everything to me."

"And she died before you could make peace with her."

"Yes," I said. "And I'm so mad about that. I hate myself for that. I hate myself even more than I hate him. And believe me, I despise him. The way he prances around town with his new wife. Can you believe he remarried less than a year after Sunny died? Sometimes I think we should move so I don't have to ever see him again. But… Mama's buried there, so I could never move."

"I understand that. But where is she really? Do you feel her with you, in your heart? Tell me how you think of her now."

I admired the pictures of Ruth's grandkids all over her office. "Oh, I think of her every day. And I hear her voice. I've heard that's the first thing people forget."

"I've heard that as well."

"I dream about her almost every night. At least four nights a week." I couldn't seem to stop talking. Maybe it was her kind, matronly face, or maybe the volcano inside me had been bubbling, eager to erupt for a long time. "I didn't, for like three months after she died, and it was terrible. I kept praying for God to bring her back to me in my dreams. I wanted her to come back and tell me what to do now that she was gone, how to… reinvent myself." Unwilling tears fizzed up. "That's what she'd say. It was her way of starting over again. She made it sound fun. That's how she was. She made everything shiny. I guess that sounds cheesy."

Ruth smiled with empathy. "Not at all, sweetie."

"Until him. He stole her from me. I'll just never understand why she stayed with him."

Ruth nodded. "You had married Lenny, had a family of your own. Maybe just knowing you were happy was enough for her. Or maybe she felt so guilty for bringing you into the situation with Tom in the first place, so she felt like she was serving a kind of penance and letting you go was her punishment." When I said nothing, she pressed, "Tell me about the dreams you have about your mom."

"When I finally dreamed of her, it was more like a nightmare. It wasn't her coming to me one night, telling me she was happy in heaven and here's what I should do." I swiped a tear away. "It was just the opposite. She looked decrepit and gray and… dead. I thought it meant she was in hell."

As I fought back a desperate sob, I was aware of Ruth coming around her desk and sitting in the chair next to me. She handed me a Kleenex. "Tell me about the dreams you have now."

"Oh." My voice was thick. I blew my nose. "They're different now." I looked at Ruth, astoundingly eager to share. "Now she's beautiful. She's wearing bright, cheerful colors like she used to." I laughed through tears. "She's drawn on her 'smoldering-but-oh-so-subtle' beauty mark along her cheek. That's what she used to call it." I laughed out loud, embracing the memories I'd suppressed for so long. "And it's so weird, but in my dreams, I'll be talking to Micah and Luke or to Petey, and she'll suddenly just be there sitting across the kitchen table from us. And the kids will be having a conversation with her, like of course, that's Nana. Like she's been with us all along. I love those dreams so much. When I wake up the next morning, I feel so happy. Throughout the day, details will come back to me, like little gifts."

"I think they are gifts from her. And from Jesus." Ruth smiled.

"You know the counseling we do here is faith-based, so I'm not going to hold back on what I think. Is that okay?"

"Yes, of course."

"I see your mama in heaven at Jesus's feet, and I think she's finally free of all the burdens she struggled with here on earth. And like you said, I think she's happy now. And beautiful again. And even though she died when your kids were young, she's been with you all along. And with them. And she's a part of your life even now. Because you think of her every day."

"I do. I really do. Sometimes I'll hear a song and I'll remember… or Petey will say something playful. His lively, spirited personality is so much like Sunny's."

"That's a blessing. And I believe your dreams are her way of letting you know she's fine now, and wants you to be happy."

"Do you think so?" I wanted to believe this so badly.

"I do." She nodded emphatically. "And you know what else, Desi? I think you should forgive yourself for what happened with Tom."

I breathed. "How'd you know?"

"Because people who're abused often feel like they're to blame. And you need to know, that no matter what—"

"But you don't understand. We had this thing—Mama used to call it oodling. It makes me sick to even say it now, but I knew I could get what I wanted if I did it. I got my dog, Winston, that way, and a lot of other things. Oodling was—"

"It doesn't matter what it was. He was a grown man. What he did was wrong."

I ignored her, pushing on. "It was sitting on his lap, talking to him really sweet. Kind of begging," I choked out. Dropped my head into my hands, reeling with shame.

"Desi." Ruth touched my hand. "You were a child. You're not to blame. What happened was not your fault."

I couldn't raise my head to look her in the eye.

"This shame you've carried for so long is unwarranted. Jesus loves you. He bore your shame on the cross. He removed it, and

He restored you to honor. Holding on to it like this, it's robbing you of the good life Jesus wants for you."

I nodded, full of misery. And yet an inkling of redemption twinkled along the edges.

"Have you told anyone else about what happened?"

"Lenny, my husband. Although I spared him the details. He loves me anyway." I smiled at Ruth.

She hugged me. "What about your friend Robin?"

"Well, that's a little more complicated."

"I think you should talk to her," Ruth suggested. "When the time is right. I know she has a lot on her plate now. But I think you'd be surprised how sharing this would deepen your friendship."

"Maybe you're right," I agreed. "When the time is right."

Now that I'd met Timothy and Ruth and some of the other North Lake staff, I enjoyed going to Sunday services. Although Robin was always dressed to the nines, she assured me my moo-moo dresses were fine. "You look nice, Desi. And you've seen how casually everyone dresses. Shorts, flip-flops."

Lenny bounded down the stairs in jeans and a casual polo shirt. "What?" He looked at me, and then at his feet. "No flip-flops." He winked at Sterling, who hovered next to his dad's wheelchair.

Dean had insisted Sterling and Violet continue with their school semesters as usual, but that didn't stop them from driving home on weekends and attending church as a family. It was heartbreaking to see how happy Robin was on these days, especially as Dean's decline was evident. His deterioration showed in his jaundice color and his dwindling energy. He also went through oxygen tanks twice as fast lately. Thanks to Billy, his pain was under control. Billy had a gift for predicting Dean's peaks and valleys and dosing him accordingly.

Lenny and Sterling helped load Dean and his wheelchair into the church van, while Robin, Violet, and I followed in the car.

Flashing lights could be seen a mile away from North Lake as police directed traffic at every entrance.

The parking lot was packed, and people of every size, color, and age received a chipper "Good morning" or "How are ya?" from the crossing guards.

As we walked in, I put my arm around Violet and pulled her close. "How're you holding up, honey?" Although she was taller than me by almost a foot, her demeanor suggested she'd rather shrink into herself and go unnoticed.

"I'm mad. It's not fair."

Who could argue with that? As I tried to imagine Micah in this situation, my heart broke for Violet and Robin. For all of them.

We kept an eye on Dean and Robin as we followed the congregation into the auditorium. I was touched by the overflow of warm greetings. Hugs for Robin, and handshakes and encouragement for Dean. Reassuring nods for Sterling and Violet. Someone handed them a bag of fresh produce from their garden. Someone else asked about a good time to drop off a homemade dinner. There were lots of prayers, of course, and I even overheard one woman whisper to another, "We meet at ten in the morning at the edge of their driveway to pray. Wanna join?"

"Definitely," replied the new recruit. No intrusion, no boasting about what they were doing, just taking time out of their day to send up prayers at a respectful distance.

As we entered the auditorium, red T-shirted staff handed out neon bracelets. "Hey, Robin! Dean!" said a dark-haired woman. "We're having fun today. Put these on."

"Thanks, Veronica." Dean beamed. "I love jewelry."

Robin laughed, her face aglow with... something. Contentment? Happiness? Peace? I'd never seen her look more beautiful.

When Billy and his nephew arrived, Billy endured some ragging from Lenny and Dean over his "spiffy" street clothes. Naturally, we all teased Dean for being the only person who still used the word *spiffy*.

Robin was fastening Dean's neon bracelet, when a camera-wielding guy wearing a red T-shirt waved. "Hey, Dean, how's it going? Why don't we get your family and friends in a picture? Everybody say *Deano!*"

"Deano!" We grinned as we gathered around Dean's wheelchair. Our bracelets glowed against the lights in the auditorium.

"Isn't this the best?" Dean said. "Wow!"

"Yes," Robin told him. "It's the best."

As the guys moved ahead with Dean to help him get settled, Robin held back and gave me a tight hug. "I'm so glad y'all are here. He's so happy." She blinked back tears. "And you know what? I am too." After a beat she added, "Isn't that sad?"

I couldn't admit that it was, so I just put my arm around her and walked up the auditorium steps to join the family.

Timothy's onstage presence was as genuine and enthusiastic as it was offstage, and his willingness to present himself as flawed and vulnerable heightened the sermon. The theme was fear and shame, which seemed especially germane to me.

"Think about the worse mistakes you've ever made. Or the most shameful things you've ever done." He paused, as if to give us a moment to recall our errors. "Now," he said, "were they driven by fear?"

He let that sink in and continued with examples. "Maybe you were fearful of failing so you took a short cut that you knew wasn't morally right. Like cheating on a test or using performance-enhancing drugs for a sporting event. Or maybe you were fearful of being criticized or ridiculed, so you participated in something you knew in your heart was wrong. Or maybe you were afraid of telling the truth, of opening up and being honest with someone, so you told another lie. And then another. Folks, when you think about it, so many of our greatest sins and mistakes are driven by fear.

"Maybe you've been badly hurt by someone you love, and now

you feel betrayed. No matter how hard you try, you just can't get past it. I know I've felt that way. Have you?"

"Amen," someone said.

"We're scared and we're ashamed," Timothy went on. "Our pain haunts us, damages us, and we start to believe the devil's lies. We're not worthy, we think. God doesn't love us, we think. How could he love me? The way I am?"

Timothy paced. Swiveled his head across the congregation. "Friends, the devil is a liar. Fear and shame are liars."

"Amen!" agreed the crowd.

"Jesus told us exactly what we should do to fight off the devil's lies. He gave us the answer. Instead of being destructive, we can be constructive. And one of the best ways to be constructive is to forgive. Forgiveness is tricky though, because contrary to popular belief, it's not a feeling. It's a choice. And it's hard. We must keep working at it, and some days are harder than others. Some days it's a struggle to temper those hurt, wronged feelings. You know another way we can be constructive?"

Timothy held up his Bible. "God tells us. Right here. Every day we choose what we set our minds on, what thoughts we let consume us. Philippians 4, verse 8, says, 'Whatever is true, whatever is noble, whatever is right, whatever is pure, whatever is lovely, whatever is admirable, if anything is praiseworthy, think about such things.'"

As Timothy bowed his head in the closing prayer, Lenny reached for my hand. He raised it toward his cheek and rested it there, tenderly caressing it with the soft whiskers along his chin. Before lowering my hand to his lap, he gently kissed it, then whispered in my ear, "I love you, Desi. And I forgive you."

I looked across the row and saw Robin, the kids, and Dean clasping one another's hands. As we reached out to one another, our little row became linked in sorrow, grief, and forgiveness.

A few nights later, Lenny and I were whispering softly to

each other in the dark, my head resting lightly on his chest, his fingers brushing along my shoulder. "I've been talking to the other pastor at church," he said. "His name is Bob. Big, tall guy. More quiet and reserved than Timothy."

"Tattoos?"

"Not that I can see." He guffawed. "But he's helped me a lot. He's shown me ways I can be more supportive, more mindful about the things you've gone through."

"Lenny, you're the best man I've ever known. I don't deserve you—"

A loud crash echoed through the house. Lenny was up in a flash, tugging on his shorts and running down the hall. I grabbed my robe and followed, fearing the worst.

"Robin? Dean?" When Lenny pushed on their bedroom door, we found Dean on the floor and Robin in tears, desperately trying to help him up. It was obvious from the smell and the mess he'd had an accident.

"It's okay. I've got it," Robin said, trying to preserve Dean's dignity. Lenny wasn't having it and quickly moved to help Dean up, carefully steering him into the bathroom.

Robin tried to pull herself up, teetering. "Billy will be here in the morning. He showed me what to do—" Her eyes fluttered, and her body crumpled to the floor.

"Robin!" I got to her just before her head hit the edge of the end table. "Are you okay?" I patted her face until her eyes found focus. "Tell me you're okay."

"Yes," she breathed. "I'm just so…" Tears flowed without sound.

"Robin? Are you okay?" Dean hollered from the bathroom in a panic. "What happened? Bring me back in there."

"She's fine. Everything is fine," I said loud enough to reassure him. I heard the shower turn on as Lenny encouraged Dean in soothing tones.

"Desi?" Lenny finally popped his head out of the bathroom. "I've got him tonight."

"No," Robin argued. "I can take care of him!"

"See if you can get her to sleep," Lenny said. "She needs some rest."

I turned to Robin, easing her up, "Come on, Robin. I've got you."

"No," she cried in a weak, defeated voice. "I need to take care of my husband."

"Lenny said he's fine." I led her out of the room. "Tonight you need to rest. Come on with me."

I'd finally got Robin cleaned up, fed, and settled in bed next to me. The room was dark, only the light of the moon shining through the huge shuttered window.

"I never knew a glass of cold milk could taste so good," she mumbled drowsily.

"I know, right?" I rested on my side and studied Robin's worn, tired face. "And the chocolate chip cookie. What is it about church-lady cookies? They're always the best."

"I must admit, it was delicious." Her expression turned sad. "Even Mabel would've been impressed." She closed her eyes, "I'd give anything to have my mama right now. I need her so much," she said through tears.

"I know." I brushed her tears away. "I'm so sorry, Robin. I'm right here. I'm not going anywhere." I didn't know what else to say, so I just continued to hold her close.

After a while she asked, "Do you like our church?"

"Yes, very much. It's helping Lenny and me. We've grown closer, stronger since we've been here. I think... no, I know we're going to be okay now."

"Good. Sunny was right, you know? You and Lenny are meant to be together. It's God's plan. No man can tear it apart. Not even Adam Freaking Straight."

I laughed out loud, relieved to see the color returning to her face. "You know, coming here, and visiting your church has made me realize I've just been going through the motions in Shady Gully. There's so much strife—"

Robin's breathing had deepened, and her face had softened. She was sound asleep. I turned off the lamp, and held her close in the dark. I prayed that my friend would find some peace in her slumber tonight.

It was a beautiful morning in Kentucky. The kind you see on TV around derby time, where the mist rises off the vivid green blankets of bluegrass and the black horse fences frame frisky equines in the pastures.

There was a crispness in the air that hinted at a new season. The horses sensed it, and so did we. Billy had rolled Dean's wheelchair out to the fence line, and Lenny had carried lawn chairs for the rest of us. Robin and I had cut up carrots and apples, and she had tossed a bag of peppermints into the bucket. "They love them." She smiled. Happy today. Rested. Looking almost peaceful. "Especially the little teenager, Kuzco."

As I helped Lenny unfold the lawn chairs, he whispered, "What were you and Dean talking about earlier?" He was referring to a moment when Robin was in the shower and he had gone to help Billy unload oxygen tanks.

"Robin," I answered, my expression tight.

Lenny nodded in understanding.

Everyone sipped coffee as we settled in the soothing sun. Except for Dean, who drank his liquid meal in a bottle, and Billy, who guzzled a Red Bull.

"You warm enough, Dean?" Billy asked.

Robin pulled a sweater around Dean's shoulders and carefully tucked a blanket over his legs. "How's that?"

"Perfect." Dean smiled up at her.

A connection bounced between them, and for a moment it was so palpable it unsettled me. I glanced at Lenny, and I knew he'd felt it too. We all watched quietly as she kissed Dean on the lips, held his face in her hands.

"Here they come," Billy said. We watched as Sam and Ellie's

horses sashayed over to the fence. Two beautiful mares, a white one with chocolate eyes and a noble brown one with a rich, shiny coat. They huffed around the bucket Lenny held in his hand. "If you ask me," Billy quipped, "they're a little entitled. Always expecting something in that bucket."

"And there always is, isn't there?" Robin laughed as she cleaned Dean's glasses and set them back on his ears.

"There's Kuzco," Dean said in an enthusiastic but undeniably weak voice. "Wow!" The youngster trotted over, kicking his legs up in the back, clearly delighted by the crispness in the air.

His mama, the dark-colored mare, whinnied at him to mind his manners. Kuzco tucked his head then and joined the others at the fence. As Lenny and I fed them treats, Robin said, "He knows the sound of the peppermint paper being opened."

And he did. Kuzco impatiently stomped his hoof when Lenny wasn't fast enough getting the peppermint out of the wrapper.

"Uh-huh," Billy nodded. "I told y'all."

We all laughed, lost in the beauty and the playfulness of the horses. Delighted as Kuzco swished his tale and happily chomped the peppermint. "There you go. Now you have minty-fresh breath," Lenny told the colt.

Filled with immense joy, I turned to Robin, as you do when you are eager to recognize a moment of such profound grace from God. But when I saw her face, I knew.

Dean was gone. I didn't have to look at his head slumped at an awkward angle. Nor at his glasses, which had fallen to the tip of his nose. I only had to look at my friend's face.

With the sounds of Kuzco chomping on his peppermint, and the fall breeze whipping up the grass, it was at this moment we all crossed into a new season. I'd always remember that Robin and Dean were still holding hands, and the last word he said was…

Wow!

Chapter Twenty-Five

Enough
Robin (93 Pounds)

T he North Lake Church wasted no time putting together a lovely memorial service for Dean. It was beautiful, according to Desi. While it was mostly a blur to me, the one thing I knew for sure was that I'd never been more grateful for my friend. Despite the occasional bouts of jealousy, sprinkled with mistrust, frustration, and even disappointment, Desi had risen to the occasion when it mattered the most.

She and Lenny. Loving me and loving my kids. Wrapping us up in their strength and support, holding us up when we couldn't stand. Especially me, because I couldn't seem to eat, and it was a challenge simply to rise and carry myself through the day. One step at a time turned into one day at a time, but beyond that, I couldn't imagine a life without Dean.

I now gazed at the cherrywood coffin, custom made in extra tall, which held my greatest love. I wanted to crawl inside with him. The memorial service in Lexington had been one thing, but this, this funeral in Shady Gully, when they actually lowered him into the ground…

"Mama, watch your step." Sterling tightened his grip around my waist as we traipsed through the damp grass in the cemetery. My little man. Practically grown but still too young to lose his daddy. I glanced behind me and saw Micah and Violet holding hands, trailing behind.

"This way, Aunt Robin," said Petey, who bookended me between Sterling. "We're gonna sit you down right next to the casket." They did, and I felt relieved that I could rest for a moment.

Luke, Desi's handsome firstborn, brought me a glass of water. "Mama said to give you this, and I'm not supposed to leave until you drink it." His face was so earnest, so much like Dean's at that age.

I drank half the water and looked at him in surrender.

"Okay," he whispered, pouring the rest in the grass. "I'll tell her you enjoyed it."

Max and Ernie were there, along with their wives and kids. I couldn't help but feel pained that their kids showed no interest in mine. I watched a number of times as both Violet and Sterling made attempts to connect with their cousins, but the exchanges were awkward and strained. *I'm so sorry, Mama.* I sent up a prayer of regret. *I've failed you and Daddy and haven't been able to hold our family together.*

Desi had pulled some strings, and Brother Wyatt said a few words over Dean. Once again, I was grateful. The notion of either Jesse or James carrying on like they knew Dean was sickening. Brother Wyatt, at least, had a history with my parents, and because of that, he spoke sincerely.

The big news, of course, was the return of Dolly. I didn't dwell on the fact that there was more talk about her than of Dean. I was too weary to work up much outrage. Claire also had made an appearance, but I felt sure she would avoid me, as she was only here to gather intel.

After the service, I was allowed to sit as people strolled by and offered their condolences. Most were genuine, like Coach Cal, who I barely recognized. And Mrs. Shanna May, who was now retired and enjoying her grandkids. Denise had come along with her partner, who was polite and soft spoken. Ricky, Shady

Gully's newly elected sheriff, was there in his uniform. Bubba and Daryl passed by, looking out of place wearing their best dress clothes. Both sported impressive beer bellies and reeked of salt-of-the-earth integrity.

I was surprised when Brad Wolfheart showed up. "I'm sorry Dean got sick," he said with sincerity. He was pencil thin, his blue-black hair mostly gray now, and his eyes were cloudy and bloodshot. "He's probably the only millionaire I ever met," Brad said, clearly uncomfortable as he endured disdainful smirks from most of the other well-wishers. "But I know for sure the thing he was most proud of was you and the twins."

I thanked him, touched by his insight into my husband, the brilliant executive who in the end found joy in simple things like neon bracelets and colts eating candy. As I watched the town's outcast drive away in the same beat-up black truck he'd driven years ago, I realized there was a whole lot of good in this small town… although it wasn't always found in the pristine, shiny places you'd expect.

Desi and Lenny navigated the receiving line with the skill of the Secret Service. It wasn't until the line dwindled that I saw the prodigal daughter herself. "Well hello, Dolly," I said. She looked much the same, just older like the rest of us.

"Hey, Robin. Shoot, you're so skinny, I almost didn't recognize you."

"Yep, I'm the one next to the casket. The one with the dead husband."

Desi sidled over then, guarding me like a hawk. "Hey, Dolly," she said. "How've you been?"

Dolly sat down, which disappointed me, because it meant she was going to stay awhile.

"Well, I guess y'all know I got a divorce and I've decided to move back home. It's been so hard." She glanced at both Desi and me beneath heavily mascaraed eyes, "I guess y'all heard about all that, huh?"

"I'm really sorry," Desi said. "About what happened with Mitch and the suffering that caused you."

"Yeah. Mitch put me through some rough years. I should have left him. I don't know why it took me so long to do it, but I guess it's never too late to start over, right?" Dolly looked over my head, obviously making eye contact with someone more interesting. Ashley. "Well, it was really good seeing y'all." She gave me a bouncy little hug and was off.

Desi fumed with indignation. "What the heck? She didn't even offer condolences."

"And she didn't even apologize for the way she left your house," I offered wearily.

"I guess with Dolly, the only relevant transgressions are the ones committed against her," Desi said. "It's like we're all just peripheral characters in the movie of her life."

Lenny sat heavily in the seat Dolly had just vacated. "And that's not a movie you'd want to see."

After a terribly long day, I was glad to shed my church clothes and put on a pair of shorts. It was still humid and hot in Louisiana, and Lenny had drug out the barbecue pit. Desi had set out some watermelon on a picnic table in the backyard, and Sterling and Luke unfolded lawn chairs. "Here ya go, Aunt Robin," Luke said, patting the one in the shade.

"Thank you, honey." Luke's deferential demeanor was so like Dean's, it hurt to look at him. "How's school going?"

"Really well," he said. "I don't know if Uncle Dean told you, but he kept in touch with me, gave me a lot of good suggestions about classes. Thanks to his advice, I'm going to get my business degree in a little over a year."

"He'd be so proud of you." I squeezed his arm.

"Just like his mama," Desi said as she sat in the chair next to me. Luke shrugged off his mama's flattery. "What?" Desi asked, "What'd I say?"

We all turned as Petey arrived with his girlfriend, Tammy Jo. He handed Lenny a beer before tucking the rest of the six-pack in the ice chest. The pretty girl smiled as she approached me with a gift bag and a soft word of sympathy.

Micah walked outside carrying a glass of white wine, as Violet followed behind with a tray of chicken. Lenny took the chicken and gave Micah the eye. "I know that's not for you."

"It's for Aunt Robin," she insisted. When she handed it to me, I couldn't help but notice a smidge of lip gloss that bore a striking resemblance to the ruby tone on her lips. "Here you go. Petey said you have to drink it. He paid a whole four dollars for it."

"What?" Petey exclaimed. "Only the best for Aunt Robin. It was six dollars, and the dude at the liquor store said it was the best bang for my buck."

"Thank you, Petey," I said after a sip. "It's quite good."

"See," Petey boasted. "I got class. Ain't that right, Violet?" He nudged Violet, who blushed.

When my sullen, sad girl giggled, it lifted my spirits. While Sterling hovered over me constantly, I couldn't get through to her. She was angry, at me in particular, and it seemed that everything I said was wrong.

I wasn't Dean, and even if I tried, I couldn't replicate the bond she'd had with her daddy. They were so similar, not only in their tall, towering physiques but in their logical, pragmatic makeup. I was encouraged, however, that she seemed to be finding solace in her friendship with Micah.

I forced myself to sip the wine and eat some of Lenny's barbecue, although my heart wasn't in it. After dinner Lenny offered me an apple fritter that someone had brought from church. To my surprise it tasted a lot like mama's.

"I'd give it a nine out of ten," Lenny declared as he handed Desi the last bite of his fritter. "'Cause nobody can make them as good as Mrs. Mabel."

Desi agreed as she wiped her hands on a napkin. The three of us sat comfortably together as the sun went down and the cicadas starting singing. We enjoyed watching the kids toss tiny beanbags into a board with a hole positioned twenty feet away.

Violet laughed out loud when Petey's turn came, and he threw his bag behind his back, horribly missing the mark.

Desi rubbed my hand. "Hear that, Mama? That's actual laughter."

I nodded, hopeful. "Thank you for this. It's the most peaceful I've felt in a long time."

"Why don't you stay with us for a while?" Desi asked.

"I can't. I've got to get back and try to get my kids settled. At least before the next semester starts. And… I have no idea how to do the things Dean did. Paying bills, handling the finances. I find it all daunting."

"Seems Bob told me there was a guy on staff at North Lake who actually coached people on that kind of thing," Lenny said. "I have no doubt they'd get you squared away."

When Lenny stood and began to clean up around the grill, Desi said in a low voice, "I wish you'd stay. I worry about your health."

"Gosh, you and Dean. He used to always say that."

"You're not taking those pills anymore, are you?" She held my gaze, not letting it go. "Don't even try to lie to me. I'll know it."

"I'm not," I said honestly. "I threw them all away the day I found out Dean had cancer. I swear." I held her hand. "I regret ever starting those things."

"Yeah, well, we have Sunny to thank for that."

"It wasn't her fault. I would have found my way to them eventually. The thing is, after a while, they altered my personality. Made me paranoid and distrustful. More than I already was. Poor Dean." I felt the tears coming. Just when I thought I had no more. "I was so happy at the end. Isn't that strange? Whether it was getting off the pills or finally letting go of all my suspicions or just giving my whole self to Dean. It felt like a blessed time."

"It was." Desi agreed as Lenny came over with another apple fritter. "And it's going to get better. Eventually."

Lenny handed me the fritter on a napkin. I took a bite, and the pastry set well on my stomach. I took another bite.

"Now that's what I like to see," Lenny said. "Once you get the kids settled, Desi will fly up to see you. Whenever you're ready."

"Really?" Desi lit up. "You'd be okay with that?"

"Absolutely," Lenny said. "But if y'all start having too much fun, I'll have to join you."

"I like that idea." I grinned as I devoured the rest of my fritter, which pleased Lenny immensely.

"Flight Attendants," the pilot said, "prepare the cabin for takeoff."

I tightened my seat buckle and stared out the window as the early morning sun broke over Lexington. I had a vague sense of adventure as the plane took off, like I was a young girl leaving in the early morning hours of a field trip.

Although it felt strange without Dean or the kids, I was looking forward to going to Santa Fe with Desi. I'd had several weeks to channel the Dean in me, and I swear I could feel him coaching me as to what bills needed to be paid when. I was also sure he had a hand in my setting up an appointment with our financial planner (which I'd always blown off before), and I was positive he'd be happy with the trust funds I set up for the kids.

Even in death he was finding new ways to amaze me. He'd set up a life insurance policy on himself many years ago, so I was flabbergasted when the company contacted me to inquire where they should wire the funds.

While these sorts of tasks kept my mind engaged and distracted, writing the thank-you notes for the memorial and the funeral were another story altogether. It took sheer will and an abundance of courage to sit down with pen in hand. It was heart wrenching, and when I couldn't bear it another minute, I'd get up and have a cookie.

Between the checklist of tasks and keeping a close watch on Sterling and Violet, I'd dug up Mama's old cookbooks. I discovered I had a knack for baking. Who knew? Not only did I enjoy packing extra boxes of baked goods to send with the kids back to North Carolina, but I felt sure Desi would approve of the five extra pounds I'd gained.

She was going to meet me at DFW airport in Dallas, and after a little layover we were off to New Mexico. Considering the reason for our sudden trip, I hoped I'd find her in good spirits. Apparently, Connie had called last week and told her Harry had passed away. Just like that. A phone call. Desi had been frantically checking flights to come for the funeral, when Connie told her that it was already done. "We had a quiet life, just the two of us," she'd explained. "And that's the way he wanted it."

I didn't think Desi believed that for a minute. Nevertheless, it gave us time to plan the trip to Harry, and afterwards she was coming home with me. Lenny would probably follow when he rested his back or got bored.

As the plane descended, I freshened my lipstick, and when it landed, I turned on my phone. Right away there was a text from her. *I'm here! Terminal A. Can't wait to see you!*

I saw her as soon as I entered the terminal and was taken aback at how beautiful she looked. She had one of her signature comfy dresses on, but she'd lost weight and apparently had just freshened her lipstick as well.

"Well look at us," I said as I hugged her tight. When she bent her forehead to mine, I added, "I've missed you. I'm so sorry about Harry."

"I know. I'm okay. I mean, I knew he was sick. I could tell the last few times I talked to him. And I'm trying to work through my anger toward Connie."

"Maybe some lunch will help." We found a semi-quiet place in the airport to sit down and have a bite, and since it was Sunday, we were able to catch the tail end of North Lake's sermon online. We shared an earbud and put the iPad between us.

"People probably think we're nuts." Desi laughed.

I was sure she was right. But it made me happy that she'd found hope at North Lake. "He even has a presence online, doesn't he?" Desi said of Timothy. "Lenny and I have been watching every Sunday, and now Micah is campaigning to forego church in Shady Gully altogether."

The message today was on imperfect love. Timothy said that as much as our friends and family love us, the reality is people make mistakes. They have bad days. They're even selfish at times. Even a parent's love is imperfect. The only true and absolute love is from Jesus because he's never selfish—his agenda is always noble, and he never has a bad day. If we only look to our loved ones for approval, and for validation, we're going to be disappointed. They're going to let us down. Only Jesus, Timothy concluded, can give us perfect love.

"Flight 3370 boarding in fifteen minutes to Santa Fe, New Mexico," echoed the airport intercom.

"Oh, that's us," Desi said as we headed to the terminal. "Did you get a hotel? I don't think Connie would welcome us."

"I sure did. A fancy one too." I grinned. There were other passengers like us on the flight. Middle-aged ladies jaunting off to the City Different for a few days. Native Santa Feans, at home in their turquoise jewelry and straw hats.

While my sense of adventure increased, I detected a sudden melancholy in Desi. I assumed it was because of Harry.

"Sunny told me that once, what Timothy was saying." She sighed as the plane took off. "But I didn't understand."

"What did she tell you?"

"The day I was baptized, Sunny told me that she was glad I'd found God, because I would never be alone. I would always be loved. She told me that he loved me more than she did." Desi sipped from her water bottle and gazed out the window. "At the time I took it as a rejection. It hurt me."

"But Sunny was right," I told her. "Looking back, she was right about a lot of things. About men of substance being better than those with flowery words."

"Yeah," Desi agreed. "But she was wrong about a lot of things too."

"But she loved us. She just had a hard time loving herself."

Desi cocked her head. "Sounds familiar, huh?"

"Yes," I breathed. "I've wasted so much of my life needing other people's approval, their praise. When I didn't get it, I felt inadequate. Like I wasn't enough. Every day I'd get on the scales, looking for validation."

"Every day?" Desi was stunned. "Good gracious."

"Every day. And most of the time, I didn't get it. And if I'm honest, even when I did get a magical number, I still doubted myself." I rubbed my temples, suddenly weary. "My insecurities and fears robbed me of a good, true life with Dean. I could have been a better wife. I'm so ashamed I wasted his love."

The flight was well on its way when the flight attendant brought us orange juice. As she rolled her cart down the aisle, Desi said, "You know what I regret?"

I looked at her, unsure why I felt a flutter in my chest. "What?"

"That I was so consumed with my own anger and hurt that I couldn't see how much trouble Sunny was in…"

"Are you ever going to tell me what you were so angry about? What happened between you two?"

Desi looked out the window so long I thought she was ignoring me. But finally, she said, "You're kind of a captive audience right now. Are you sure you're up for it?"

"Always."

After a deep breath, she said, "It had to do with what Tom did to me…"

I was still reeling from the horrible, grotesque revelation about Tom as we drove the rental car to the cemetery in Santa Fe. It struck me then how unjust it was that both my parents, and now both of Desi's, were gone. And yet Tom still walked around Shady Gully happily living out his golden years.

Poor Desi. I now understood so many things. Her need to be baptized after being molested by Tom. How she felt dirty, soiled, and in her mind needed to be cleansed. And then, feeling victimized all over again when Sunny was too weak and paralyzed to make a stand against him. And finally, the ultimate shame… being attracted to the very kind of man her mother had warned her about, the exact same kind of man as Tom.

"Why didn't you ever tell me?" I said impulsively as we found Harry's grave. "I could have helped you. I could have shared your burden."

Desi knelt, running her fingers along her father's name on the tombstone. I handed her the flowers we'd picked up in town. She sniffed them briefly before placing them on his grave. "I don't know. I guess that's the thing about regret. It really sucks."

We spent the next few hours watching the sunset over Harry, embracing the beauty of the bright orange and red hues as they shimmered to life over the Jemez Mountains.

"Harry was the best," I said after a long moment. "I always liked him."

"He was the opposite of Tom. Nothing flowery, but steady. A man of substance. Just like Lenny."

"Yeah," I agreed. "Thankfully, you know that now, and you have plenty of time to love your man of substance."

She put her arm around me, and bent her forehead to mine, understanding the implication that it was too late for me.

The next day we drove through the mountains like tourists, stopping to snap pictures at the scenic spots. After a shower in the hotel, we took to the plaza, admiring the homemade jewelry the Native Americans sold on the square. I bought turquoise and melanite earrings for Micah, Violet, and Desi.

We ate tacos and drank a margarita and strolled the city as if we were carefree middle-aged ladies on vacation, just like the ones on the plane. There were moments we almost forgot the grief and turmoil of the last several months.

"Let's go into that art gallery," I suggested. "I like the look of that painting in the window." Desi followed me in, and we quietly admired the artwork and paintings. "This one kind of looks like something Sunny would paint."

"Kind of," Desi said, turning to look at a striking painting of a feisty fox hiding in a log. "I like this one."

"You should think about featuring some of Sunny's paintings in a place like this—"

"No, I don't want to do that." Desi turned and walked out. When I joined her on the sidewalk, she said, "I don't have them anymore. I had to sell them because we needed the money."

"Desi—"

"I don't want to talk about it, Robin." When her phone chimed, she looked at the caller ID, held her finger up. "It's Lenny. I better take it. Or he'll think we've been kidnapped."

I watched her as she held the phone to her ear, strolling absently down the sidewalk. I turned back to the museum with the lovely paintings. Suddenly struck with the clarity I'd lacked for so many years, I walked back inside and presented my questions to the curator.

Even though it was barely four o'clock in the afternoon in Lexington, Desi and I were so jetlagged from the trip we stayed in and ordered pizza.

Desi yawned as she padded down the stairs wearing her jammies. "It's good to be home."

"I know." I smiled. "And I'm so glad you're here. It gets too quiet when the kids are gone."

"That's what Lenny and I were afraid of." She watched, baffled, as I opened a bottle of champagne. "What are you doing?"

"I have a surprise for you," I popped the cork and poured us both a glass of bubbly. "Follow me." I led her down to the basement, which was fully finished with a pool table and a huge flat-screen TV. Sterling loved the space, especially to host parties. Violet thought it was creepy.

"I didn't even know this was down here," Desi said. "It's got a kitchen and everything. I'm glad you went with the granite."

"And it also has this room. I think you're going to love it." I clinked her glass with mine, and opened the door to the spare room, following her into another place and time.

Perched on an easel was Sunny's ill-fated ship in tumultuous waters. Leaning against the window was another of my favorites, a toy car in a fruit bowl. On the opposite side of the window, I'd framed a rustic, red shed on a riverbend. Next to it was Sunny's painting of the Battle of Waterloo.

"Oh… my." Desi's voice was thick with emotion as she was drawn to the painting on the center wall. It was the showpiece. Sunny, Desi, and Harry, in Santa Fe at Christmastime. Happy, with Farolitos glowing behind them. "Oh my," Desi sobbed. "I thought they were all gone. I thought I'd never see them again."

In a state of shock, she revisited each of the paintings one by one, pausing next to them, as if greeting a long-lost friend.

"They're all here," I told her, struggling to hold my own composure. "The ones I haven't framed yet are in the closet. There is one I couldn't find though."

Desi looked astonished. "The bonfire? Of us?" She grabbed me in a heartfelt hug. "I have that one. I could never part with it."

"Oh, thank goodness."

"And I have one of Winston too. I never even knew Mama painted it. Lenny took the boys to Tom's, and they found it." Desi's eyes swept the room, moved by the sheer number of paintings. "I thought I'd lost them forever. Oh, Robin, I don't know what to say."

I took a sip of champagne. "Say you'll listen to my idea."

The remnants of the pizza had been swept to one side of the table, and the champagne had barely been touched. I underlined the numbers on the notepad in front of me.

"And you would never have to sell any of Sunny's original paintings. Buyers could only purchase giclee prints. They're like digital prints made with a jet ink printer on canvas. Look at how much some of the high-end ones go for—" I tapped the figure again.

"That's crazy. Lenny is going to flip."

"Isn't this a great idea? I knew you'd love it. And I've got the money to rent a great space to display Sunny's paintings. We could do it in Santa Fe, or even here in Lexington. I have connections, media folks, local bloggers, chamber of commerce types. We could create a buzz. It could be the trendiest place downtown!"

"What would we call it? How about Sunny's Place?"

"I love it."

"I think she always fantasized about being a famous artist. She never was, but this way the world, or whoever comes to the gallery, can see her work. I'm so excited."

"This will be good for all of us." I picked up my glass. "We'll travel, visit galleries, figure out how we want ours to be."

"I can't wait," Desi said. "Can Lenny come?"

"Of course!" I laughed. "We'll need a chaperone!"

The next morning UPS left a package at my door. Desi had gone for a walk around the neighborhood and brought it in with the mail. "It feels like a painting." She handed it to me. "But it says it's from North Lake."

I gripped the frame and tugged at the brown paper until the picture came into focus. "Oh my," I exclaimed. "They framed the photograph from church that day." I wasn't aware that I was crying, until Desi embraced me. "There's Dean. So happy with his neon bracelet."

"Look at the kids," she said. "And Billy."

But as I zeroed in on my own image, I felt the snarl of an unwelcome and all-too-familiar emotion. As hard as I tried to fight it, it coiled and twisted inside me.

"What?" Desi asked. "What's wrong?"

I put the picture down and wandered to the coffeepot. Prayed that I was strong enough to resist. But I wasn't. "It's good of everyone, but honestly, Desi, could my face be any fatter?"

"Stop! Stop it now, Robin! Don't do this." She steered me to the barstool, sat me down, and glared at me. "Do you remember that day?"

"Of course."

"Do you remember what you said to me right after that picture was taken? You were filled with joy. When that picture was snapped you were glorious."

I said nothing.

"I know in my heart how delighted God was with you in that moment." She tapped the picture of my face. "Who are you to disagree with God?"

I shook my head. "I know. You're right. And shame on me for getting tripped up so easily. After all I've been through and the way my faith has grown."

Desi looked thoughtful. And then decisive. "Let's see if we can get some time with Timothy before church Sunday. He told me once that everyone needs spiritual checkups now and then."

Timothy greeted us with affection, pushing aside the Post-its and yellow pads full of notes for today's sermon. We could hear the muffled sounds of the band rehearsing their opening number, and Millie's strong, melodic voice promising something enchanting for the congregation.

"I hope we aren't bothering you," I told him. And then, shooting Desi a peeved look, added, "Desi insisted."

"Not at all," Timothy said. "You've been heavy on my heart lately. This is the hardest time. The months after the funeral, when everybody goes back to their lives but yours is, well, forever changed. How've the two of you been?"

"Good," Desi said. "The counseling helped Lenny and me. And I'm slowly working through some things." She swallowed. "And trying to do some forgiving of my own."

"And how does that make you feel?" Timothy asked.

"Lighter. More hopeful." Desi seemed momentarily lost in her thoughts. Then she looked at me. "But the reason we're here today is because of Robin."

"No," I insisted. "I'm okay."

As Timothy waited me out, I grew uncomfortable. Eventually I submitted, "I thought I was stronger. After all I've been through and the way my faith has grown..." I trailed off. "How is it so easy for the devil to provoke me into falling into my old pattern of self-condemnation?"

Timothy leaned back in his chair and bobbed his head. "I get it. What does the Bible say? 'The devil prowls around like a roaring lion looking for someone to devour.'" He leaned forward, resting his elbows on his desk. "Let's get to the root of this. Tell me, what do you fear the most?"

Desi glanced at me, thinking she was off the hook, when Timothy said, "Both of you. Think about it. What scares you? What do you fear?"

Desi cleared her throat. "I guess for me it's... feeling tainted. Dirty. Sometimes the shame comes over me so hard, I feel like I'm going to smother."

My heart hurt for her, my beautiful friend who'd been crippled by a horrible thing a horrible person did to her. And then she turned to me and prompted, "Robin?" and I could have clobbered her myself.

Timothy studied me, waiting for an answer, which for me boiled down to one thing. "Not being enough."

He looked between the two of us for a moment. "Fears aren't reality. And you," he said to Desi, "are not dirty. And you"—Timothy looked at me with his dark-blue eyes—"are enough. In fact, God knows you both by name, and He delights in you. We must always be aware, be vigilant, because Satan knows just where to strike us so it hurts. But," he said as he rose from his desk, "I have an idea."

During the service Desi and I sat in the same chairs Dean and I always sat, and we held hands and sang and worshiped with the highest of hopes. Beautiful Millie crooned a song that moved us to tears, as the lyrics were so poignant on this day.

I squeezed Desi's hand, and as we sang the chorus, we raised our joined hands up especially high, so moved by the musical selection.

After the service, along with more music, we took communion. And finally, tall, quiet Bob walked out, and invited everyone to have a seat and celebrate a few special baptisms.

Desi and I were now in the shallow end of the baptismal pool. We each wore shorts and sported our new red T-shirts that the North Lake staff had made for us during Timothy's sermon.

I looked at Desi in the water next to me. Her shirt read, *Cleansed.* "I should have done this with you years ago when you asked me," I told her.

"Better late than never," she said, eyeing my shirt, which read *Enough.*

We bent our foreheads together, just as Timothy joined us in the water.

He placed his hand gently on my shoulder, and I followed him. Our legs and feet were bare, and there was an intimacy in that I hadn't expected. It was an unfamiliar emotion, and it made me feel suddenly unsure. Vulnerable.

"Just breathe," he said.

I obeyed. Shivered as I let myself go deeper in the water. Soon my calves were submerged, and seconds later the water was up to my waist. He was so tall that the water hadn't yet reached his upper thighs.

His presence, so large and looming, reassured me. It reminded me I wasn't alone. However unsteady my body was, and it was, his capable hands guided me deeper and deeper into the water.

He was speaking softly to me now.

Distracted by the comforting embrace of the warm water, I had trouble focusing. Felt my knees buckle again.

I looked at his mouth, the sincerity in his eyes, and finally, I smiled. Nodded with conviction.

No more anxiety, no more fear. Just excited now.

I said words back to him. Repeated what he said.

The tone coming out of my mouth was confident. It sounded strange to me. I'd never been confident a day in my life. But on this day my words were full of something akin to… peace.

Finality.

Why had it taken me so long to get here? So many wasted years. Such a wasted life. Tears slipped from my eyes as I thought of the insecure girl, the anxious wife, the unrewarded mother. The failures, the losses, the disappointments.

But I didn't regret that. Those were simply things I experienced. What I regretted now, in this moment of clarity and grace, was that I let all that anguish define me. Shame me into hiding. I let the brokenness rob my life away from me.

I was a slave to my fears. My insecurities.

But not anymore. Not after this.

Timothy placed his hand gently along the middle of my back. "Death, burial…"

Just before the water washed over me, I wondered fleetingly about the years I'd lost… enslaved and broken.

But when I emerged from the water, the thought had vanished. "Resurrection!" Timothy said joyfully.

Freedom was stronger than regret. And I was a slave no longer.

I turned then to Desi, my lifelong friend, and smiled as she bent her forehead to mine.

Shame Is A Robber
Desi, a Year Later

Now that money wasn't an issue, Lenny had gone back to school and was enjoying a few business classes. He couldn't decide which was more fun—learning how to better assist Robin and me with the gallery, or embarrassing Luke during classes. We visited Robin monthly, often for over a week. She had rough days, to be sure, but between running the day-to-day operations at Sunny's Place, keeping tabs on the twins, and spoiling her new cat, Buford, she was finding her way. She also volunteered regularly at North Lake, and hadn't missed a Sunday service since Dean died.

Micah, Sterling, and Violet had all graduated from high school, and were considering colleges everywhere from the University of Kentucky to LSU.

Petey and Tammy Jo were still an item, so perhaps I'd be planning a wedding soon. It might be fun, especially since I'd been feeling good lately. I'd lost some weight, and Robin had found some of it, so together we were... just enough, as Robin liked to say.

I addressed her card and slipped Dean's note inside, just as he'd asked me to the day he died. Had he known he was going to die only hours later? I chose to think he'd sensed it, because of the peaceful, serene expression on his face when he'd made the request. Of course, I'd read his note, as he'd known I would.

My sweet Robin,

I guess if you're reading this, I've been gone a year. I hope you're taking care of yourself. I asked Desi to make sure of that, along with sending you this note around the anniversary of my death.

Honestly, I'm tired and ready to go. I only resist because I worry about you. I beg you, Robin, have FUN with the rest of your life. Please, don't waste any more time chasing things that don't matter.

If you could only see yourself the way I do, and the way the Dynamic Duo does... and Desi and Lenny as well... you wouldn't waste another day feeling not good enough. I will see you again someday. But until then, thank you for loving me. Thank you for giving me a beautiful family. I can't wait until we're all reunited.

Yours in Christ,

Dean

PS: I apologize for the errors and incorrect structure in this missive. Even though I'm a bit under the weather, it really bugs me.

I believed Robin would see Dean again, just as I would see Harry and Sunny. And while the devil still prowls around, spitting and snarling, pushing my buttons and causing me to stumble, Jesus remains patient with me. He knows that I am part sinner and part saint, and he uses my failures for his glory. Meanwhile, I'll wait with confidence for that trumpet to sound... and the glorious reunion that will follow!

A Message
From the Author

Thank you for spending time with me in Shady Gully. I hope you enjoyed Desi and Robin's journey and found it inspiring. They'll be back in Book Two, along with some of your favorite heroes and villains.

If you loved *Paint Me Fearless*, and look forward to Book Two, can I ask you for a big favor? Please take a few minutes to leave a review on your favorite social media site, or wherever you purchased this book. And maybe tell a friend. I would love for as many readers as possible to discover this story, and your voice can help do that. Leave a review and tell a friend! Word-of-mouth is the best way to introduce this story to other readers.

Finally, check out my website, www.hallielee.com, for all things Shady Gully, including Book Club Questions, contests, giveaways, recipes, newsletters, and more!

I'll see y'all back at the Cozy Corner in Book Two! Until then ...blessings to you and yours.

and now a sneak peek at

Book 2 of The Shady Gully Series
Healing on the Creek

T he good folks of Shady Gully wouldn't be surprised by my actions. Not on a night when the moon drooped hazily over the swamp, and the air dripped with pre-storm humidity. As usual, the folks of Shady Gully would assume I was up to no good.

And they'd be right.

As the irony caused me to stumble, I stilled my body, and slowed my breathing. Within seconds I became one with the animals who guarded the night. The snakes that slithered along the cypress trees. The owls that hunted for prey. The cicadas oblivious and intoxicated by the sound of their own symphony.

On this night, I felt a kinship with the shadows that wandered in the suffocating heat. Like ghosts, they seemed to cry out, desperate to be remembered. I tipped my head in recognition of them all, even as blood stained my own hands.

I shifted the lifeless body in my arms, carefully lowering it to the ground. I stood slowly, my back aching with the strain. It took me a while to find the shovel, as my legs were awkward with arthritis. Regrettably, I was no longer young.

The shovel was in the usual place. Always four clicks behind the cypress tree festooned with umbrella shaped moss.

Not everybody could find the shovel. Only my people. The

Creek People. Or who some in Shady Gully referred to as… the Creek Freaks.

My gaze swept over the sticks, rocks, and feathers strewn amid the dirt. I understood the purpose in their placement, appreciated the memories and reverence in each trinket. I shook off the unwelcome emotion as it rose within me, focusing instead on the dig.

Within minutes my brow grew moist with sweat, and the gore on my shirt dampened the skin on my stomach with blood. Probably where I'd tucked the body close against mine on the hike to the sacred land.

When a sudden flicker of lightning created a floodlight across the ground, I realized the hole I'd dug was big enough. Too big, in fact.

"Stop putting it off," I hissed loud enough to wake a snake from its slumber. The water moccasin slipped into the marsh, deciding I wasn't worth the effort.

I picked up the body, gently placing it into the grave. *Why gently,* I wondered? Gentleness had never been a word used to describe him. And God knew he hadn't been gentle tonight.

I shoveled dirt atop the grave at an emotional, feverish pace. Anything to temper the memories that threatened. The emotions that came uninvited.

Fury.

When the hole was nearly covered, I knelt next to the grave. Mumbled a prayer.

Regret.

I pulled a ragged blue wolf from the pocket of my jeans, and cradled the worn, scruffy material against my forehead. The stuffed animal's eyes seemed to skewer me with disappointment. I mumbled another prayer.

Grief.

I carefully placed the blue wolf into the grave. *The hell with the consequences,* I thought. At least now the torment was over.

I allowed myself one more glance, one more memory.

A flash of jagged light lit up the southern sky, and thunder pounded the ground. I watched as the storm descended on Shady Gully, Louisiana.

Because it had come to rage.

Acknowledgements & Thanks

This book is fiction. That means I made it all up. For real.

I'm grateful to Mike Parker and Wordcrafts Press for your expertise, your guidance, and especially, your patience.

As always, a shout out to my mentor and favorite producer, Ronnie Clemmer. You have the rarest of gifts, and that is to nurture and inspire growth, without destroying the student.

A huge thank you to the A Team—Jeff, Steve, and Bill, who took the time to lead this technically challenged introvert through scary, unfamiliar territory...aka Marketing.

Kudos to Jennifer Adams, my smart and capable friend, who not only provided a lot of hand holding, but organized my wonderful Launch Team. Thank you, Best Team Ever! Thank you also to Ms. Lerlene, for your support, and to my friend, Gwen, for the best memories.

Thanks also to Rachel Buettner, for her technical brilliance and generous spirit. And to my friend, gifted writer Charly Cox, thank you for paving the way, and allowing me to follow and take notes.

Tammy Lynne, my sister-friend and forever-first reader, your heart filled notes on every page of every screenplay and every manuscript kept me hopeful during this journey. While I didn't always believe it would happen, I knew I'd always have someone to write for...

Aunt Lindy, your unwavering belief in me reminds me of someone beautiful we both once knew, and I'm grateful that you so willingly picked up where she left off.

And finally, to the two people I love most in this world, my husband and daughter. Writing is a lonely calling, chocked full of self-doubt, disappointment, and rarely anything tangible to present to your loved ones. But you've been there, from the inklings of aspiration, to the realization of my dream, and I'm grateful to share this win with you. To Bruce, my superstar husband, thank you for steadying me when there was no ground beneath my feet. And to my strong, smart, and beautiful daughter, Bree, YOU are my Very Best Thing. I love you both.

About the Author

Born and raised in Louisiana, Hallie Lee's screenplays and books are inspired by the southern landscape, which she says is "rich with cantankerous, salt of the earth folks destined to be on the page."

Paint Me Fearless is the first volume in *The Shady Gully Series* which promises thought-provoking, relatable journeys and a cast of characters who tend to be ornery but loveable, dramatic but kind, and quirky—but smarter than they appear.

She and her family, furry kids included, now live in the hills of Kentucky, near Lexington.

At the moment, she's gathering research as she prepares for her daughter's wedding. Yes, readers! You will be invited to a Big Shady Gully wedding in the very near future.

Connect with Hallie online at:
www.HallieLee.com

also available from

WordCrafts Press

Angela's Treasures
 by Marian Rizzo

Maggie's Song
 by Marcia Ware

The Pruning
 by Jan Cline

Kiss Me Once Again
 by Gail Kittleson

Pipe Dream
 by KL Collins

www.wordcrafts.net

Made in the USA
Coppell, TX
15 January 2021